AN ENGLISHMAN LOOKS AT THE WORLD

Herbert George Wells

An Englishman Looks at The World

Being a Series of Unrestrained Remarks
upon Contemporary Matters

BIBLIOBAZAAR

AN ENGLISHMAN LOOKS AT THE WORLD

CONTENTS

THE COMING OF BLÉRIOT

(July, 1909.)

The telephone bell rings with the petulant persistence that marks a trunk call, and I go in from some ineffectual gymnastics on the lawn to deal with the irruption. There is the usual trouble in connecting up, minute voices in Folkestone and Dover and London call to one another and are submerged by buzzings and throbbings. Then in elfin tones the real message comes through: "Blériot has crossed the Channel . . . An article . . . about what it means."

I make a hasty promise and go out and tell my friends.

From my garden I look straight upon the Channel, and there are white caps upon the water, and the iris and tamarisk are all asway with the south-west wind that was also blowing yesterday. M. Blériot has done very well, and Mr. Latham, his rival, had jolly bad luck. That is what it means to us first of all. It also, I reflect privately, means that I have under-estimated the possible stability of aeroplanes. I did not expect anything of the sort so soon. This is a good five years before my reckoning of the year before last.

We all, I think, regret that being so near we were not among the fortunate ones who saw that little flat shape skim landward out of the blue; surely they have an enviable memory; and then we fell talking and disputing about what that swift arrival may signify. It starts a swarm of questions.

First one remarks that here is a thing done, and done with an astonishing effect of ease, that was incredible not simply to ignorant people but to men well informed in these matters. It cannot be fifteen years ago since Sir Hiram Maxim made the first machine that could lift its weight from the ground, and I well remember how the clumsy quality of that success confirmed the universal doubt that men could ever in any effectual manner fly.

Since then a conspiracy of accidents has changed the whole problem; the bicycle and its vibrations developed the pneumatic tyre, the pneumatic tyre rendered a comfortable mechanically driven road vehicle possible, the motor-car set an enormous premium on the development of very light, very efficient engines, and at last the engineer was able to offer the experimentalists in gliding one strong enough and light enough for the new purpose. And here we are! Or, rather, M. Blériot is!

What does it mean for us?

One meaning, I think, stands out plainly enough, unpalatable enough to our national pride. This thing from first to last was made abroad. Of all that made it possible we can only claim so much as is due to the improvement of the bicycle. Gliding began abroad while our young men of muscle and courage were braving the dangers of the cricket field. The motor-car and its engine was being worked out "over there," while in this country the mechanically propelled road vehicle, lest it should frighten the carriage horses of the gentry, was going meticulously at four miles an hour behind a man with a red flag. Over there, where the prosperous classes have some regard for education and some freedom of imaginative play, where people discuss all sorts of things fearlessly, and have a respect for science, this has been achieved.

And now our insularity is breached by the foreigner who has got ahead with flying.

It means, I take it, first and foremost for us, that the world cannot wait for the English.

It is not the first warning we have had. It has been raining warnings upon us; never was a slacking, dull people so liberally served with warnings of what was in store for them. But this event—this foreigner-invented, foreigner-built, foreigner-steered thing, taking our silver streak as a bird soars across a rivulet—puts the case dramatically. We have fallen behind in the quality of our manhood. In the men of means and leisure in this island there was neither enterprise enough, imagination enough, knowledge nor skill enough to lead in this matter. I do not see how one can go into the history of this development and arrive at any other conclusion. The French and Americans can laugh at our aeroplanes, the Germans are ten years ahead of our poor navigables. We are displayed a soft, rather backward people. Either we are a people essentially and incurably inferior, or there is something wrong in our training, something benumbing in our atmosphere and circumstances. That is the first and gravest intimation in M. Blériot's feat.

The second is that, in spite of our fleet, this is no longer, from the military point of view, an inaccessible island.

So long as one had to consider the navigable balloon the aerial side of warfare remained unimportant. A Zeppelin is little good for any purpose but scouting and espionage. It can carry very little weight in proportion to its vast size, and, what is more important, it cannot drop things without sending itself up like a bubble in soda water. An armada of navigables sent against this island would end in a dispersed, deflated state, chiefly in the seas between Orkney and Norway—though I say it who should not. But these aeroplanes can fly all round the fastest navigable that ever drove before the wind; they can drop weights, take up weights, and do all sorts of able, inconvenient things. They are birds. As for the birds, so for aeroplanes; there is an upward limit of size. They are not going to be very big, but they are going to be very able and active. Within a year we shall have—or rather *they* will have—aeroplanes capable of starting from Calais, let us say, circling over London, dropping a hundredweight or so of explosive upon the printing machines of *The Times*, and returning securely to Calais for another similar parcel. They are things neither difficult nor costly to make. For the price of a Dreadnought one might have hundreds. They will be extremely hard to hit with any sort of missile. I do not think a large army of under-educated, under-trained, extremely unwilling conscripts is going to be any good against this sort of thing.

I do not think that the arrival of M. Blériot means a panic resort to conscription. It is extremely desirable that people should realise that these foreign machines are not a temporary and incidental advantage that we can make good by fussing and demanding eight, and saying we won't wait, and so on, and then subsiding into indolence again. They are just the first-fruits of a steady, enduring lead that the foreigner has won. The foreigner is ahead of us in education, and this is especially true of the middle and upper classes, from which invention and enterprise come—or, in our own case, do not come. He makes a better class of man than we do. His science is better than ours. His training is better than ours. His imagination is livelier. His mind is more active. His requirements in a novel, for example, are not kindly, sedative pap; his uncensored plays deal with reality. His schools are places for vigorous education instead of genteel athleticism, and his home has books in it, and thought and conversation. Our homes and schools are relatively dull and uninspiring; there is no intellectual guide or stir in them; and to that we owe this new generation of nicely behaved, unenterprising sons, who play golf and dominate the tailoring of the world, while Brazilians, Frenchmen, Americans and Germans fly.

That we are hopelessly behindhand in aeronautics is not a fact by itself. It is merely an indication that we are behindhand in our mechanical knowledge and invention M. Blériot's aeroplane points also to the fleet.

The struggle for naval supremacy is not merely a struggle in shipbuilding and expenditure. Much more is it a struggle in knowledge and invention. It is not the Power that has the most ships or the biggest ships that is going to win in a naval conflict. It is the Power that thinks quickest of what to do, is most resourceful and inventive. Eighty Dreadnoughts manned by dull men are only eighty targets for a quicker adversary. Well, is there any reason to suppose that our Navy is going to keep above the general national level in these things? Is the Navy *bright*?

The arrival of M. Blériot suggests most horribly to me how far behind we must be in all matters of ingenuity, device, and mechanical contrivance. I am reminded again of the days during the Boer war, when one realised that it had never occurred to our happy-go-lucky Army that it was possible to make a military use of barbed wire or construct a trench to defy shrapnel. Suppose in the North Sea we got a surprise like that, and fished out a parboiled, half-drowned admiral explaining what a confoundedly slim, unexpected, almost ungentlemanly thing the enemy had done to him.

Very probably the Navy is the exception to the British system; its officers are rescued from the dull homes and dull schools of their class while still of tender years, and shaped after a fashion of their own. But M. Blériot reminds us that we may no longer shelter and degenerate behind these blue backs. And the keenest men at sea are none the worse for having keen men on land behind them.

Are we an awakening people?

It is the vital riddle of our time. I look out upon the windy Channel and think of all those millions just over there, who seem to get busier and keener every hour. I could imagine the day of reckoning coming like a swarm of birds.

Here the air is full of the clamour of rich and prosperous people invited to pay taxes, and beyond measure bitter. They are going to live abroad, cut their charities, dismiss old servants, and do all sorts of silly, vindictive things. We seem to be doing feeble next-to-nothings in the endowment of research. Not one in twenty of the boys of the middle and upper classes learns German or gets more than a misleading smattering of physical science. Most of them never learn to speak French. Heaven alone knows what they do with their brains! The British reading and thinking public probably does not number fifty thousand people all told. It is difficult to see whence the necessary impetus for a national renascence is to come . . . The universities are poor and spiritless, with no ambition to lead the country. I met a Boy Scout recently. He was hopeful in his way, but a little inadequate, I thought, as a basis for confidence in the future of the Empire.

We have still our Derby Day, of course . . .

Apart from these patriotic solicitudes, M. Blériot has set quite another train of thought going in my mind. The age of natural democracy is surely at an end through these machines. There comes a time when men will be sorted out into those who will have the knowledge, nerve, and courage to do these splendid, dangerous things, and those who will prefer the humbler level. I do not think numbers are going to matter so much in the warfare of the future, and that when organised intelligence differs from the majority, the majority will have no adequate power of retort. The common man with a pike, being only sufficiently indignant and abundant, could chase the eighteenth century gentleman as he chose, but I fail to see what he can do in the way of mischief to an elusive chevalier with wings. But that opens too wide a discussion for me to enter upon now.

MY FIRST FLIGHT

(EASTBOURNE, *August 5, 1912—*
three years later.)

Hitherto my only flights have been flights of imagination but this morning I flew. I spent about ten or fifteen minutes in the air; we went out to sea, soared up, came back over the land, circled higher, planed steeply down to the water, and I landed with the conviction that I had had only the foretaste of a great store of hitherto unsuspected pleasures. At the first chance I will go up again, and I will go higher and further.

This experience has restored all the keenness of my ancient interest in flying, which had become a little fagged and flat by too much hearing and reading about the thing and not enough participation. Sixteen years ago, in the days of Langley and Lilienthal, I was one of the few journalists who believed and wrote that flying was possible; it affected my reputation unfavourably, and produced in the few discouraged pioneers of those days a quite touching gratitude. Over my mantel as I write hangs a very blurred and bad but interesting photograph that Professor Langley sent me sixteen years ago. It shows the flight of the first piece of human machinery heavier than air that ever kept itself up for any length of time. It was a model, a little affair that would not have lifted a cat; it went up in a spiral and came down unsmashed, bringing back, like Noah's dove, the promise of tremendous things.

That was only sixteen years ago, and it is amusing to recall how cautiously even we out-and-out believers did our prophesying. I was quite a desperate fellow; I said outright that in my lifetime we should see men flying. But I qualified that by repeating that for many years to come it would be an enterprise only for quite fantastic daring and skill. We conjured up stupendous difficulties and risks. I was deeply impressed and greatly discouraged by a paper a distinguished Cambridge mathematician produced to show that a flying machine was bound to pitch fearfully, that as it flew on its pitching *must* increase until up went its nose, down went its tail, and it fell like a knife. We exaggerated every possibility of instability. We imagined that when the aeroplane wasn't "kicking up ahind and afore" it would be heeling over to the lightest side wind. A sneeze might upset it. We contrasted our poor human equipment with the instinctive balance of a bird, which has had ten million years of evolution by way of a start . . .

The waterplane in which I soared over Eastbourne this morning with Mr. Grahame-White was as steady as a motor-car running on asphalt.

Then we went on from those anticipations of swaying insecurity to speculations about the psychological and physiological effects of flying. Most people who look down from the top of a cliff or high tower feel some slight qualms of dread, many feel a quite sickening dread. Even if men struggled high into the air, we asked, wouldn't they be smitten up there by such a lonely and reeling dismay as to lose all self-control? And, above all, wouldn't the pitching and tossing make them quite horribly sea-sick?

I have always been a little haunted by that last dread. It gave a little undertow of funk to the mood of lively curiosity with which I got aboard the waterplane this morning—that sort of faint, thin funk that so readily invades one on the verge of any new experience; when one tries one's first dive, for example, or pushes off for the first time down an ice run. I thought I should very probably be sea-sick—or, to be more precise, air-sick; I thought also that I might be very giddy, and that I might get thoroughly cold and uncomfortable None of those things happened.

I am still in a state of amazement at the smooth steadfastness of the motion. There is nothing on earth to compare with that, unless—and that I can't judge—it is an ice yacht travelling on perfect ice. The finest motor-car in the world on the best road would be a joggling, quivering thing beside it.

To begin with, we went out to sea before the wind, and the plane would not readily rise. We went with an undulating movement, leaping with a light splashing pat upon the water, from wave to wave. Then we came about into the wind and rose, and looking over I saw that there were no longer those periodic flashes of white foam. I was flying. And it was as still and steady as dreaming. I watched the widening distance between our floats and the waves. It wasn't by any means a windless day; there was a brisk, fluctuating breeze blowing out of the north over the downs. It seemed hardly to affect our flight at all.

And as for the giddiness of looking down, one does not feel it at all. It is difficult to explain why this should be so, but it is so. I suppose in such matters I am neither exceptionally steady-headed nor is my head exceptionally given to swimming. I can stand on the edge of cliffs of a thousand feet or so and look down, but I can never bring myself right up to the edge nor crane over to look to the very bottom. I should want to lie down to do that. And the other day I was on that Belvedere place at the top of the Rotterdam sky-scraper, a rather high wind was blowing, and one looks down through the chinks between the boards one stands on upon the heads of the people in the streets below; I didn't like it. But this morning I looked directly down on a little fleet of fishing boats over which we passed, and on the crowds assembling on the beach, and on the bathers who stared up at us from the breaking surf, with an entirely agreeable exaltation. And Eastbourne, in the early morning sunshine, had all the brightly detailed littleness of a town viewed from high up on the side of a great mountain.

When Mr. Grahame-White told me we were going to plane down I will confess I tightened my hold on the sides of the car and prepared for something like the down-going sensation of a switchback railway on a larger scale. Just for a moment there was that familiar feeling of something pressing one's heart up towards one's shoulders, and one's lower jaw up into its socket and of grinding one's lower teeth against the upper, and then it passed. The nose of the car and all the machine was slanting downwards, we were gliding quickly down, and yet there was no feeling that one rushed, not even as one rushes in coasting a hill on a bicycle. It wasn't a tithe of the thrill of those three descents one gets on the great mountain railway in the White City. There one gets a disagreeable quiver up one's backbone from the wheels, and a real sense of falling.

It is quite peculiar to flying that one is incredulous of any collision. Some time ago I was in a motor-car that ran over and killed a small dog, and this wretched little incident has left an open wound upon my nerves. I am never quite happy in a car now; I can't help keeping an apprehensive eye ahead. But you fly with an exhilarating assurance that you cannot possibly run over anything or run into anything—except the land or the sea, and even those large essentials seem a beautifully safe distance away.

I had heard a great deal of talk about the deafening uproar of the engine. I counted a headache among my chances. There again reason reinforced conjecture. When in the early morning Mr. Travers came from Brighton in this Farman in which I flew I could hear the hum of the great insect when it still seemed abreast of Beachy Head, and a good two miles away. If one can hear a thing at two miles, how much the more will one not hear it at a distance of two yards? But at the risk of seeming too contented for anything I will assert I heard that noise no more than one hears the drone of an electric ventilator upon one's table. It was only when I came to speak to Mr. Grahame-White, or he to me, that I discovered that our voices had become almost infinitesimally small.

And so it was I went up into the air at Eastbourne with the impression that flying was still an uncomfortable experimental, and slightly heroic thing to do, and came down to the cheerful gathering crowd upon the sands again with the knowledge that it is a thing achieved for everyone. It will get much cheaper, no doubt, and much swifter, and be improved in a dozen ways—we *must* get self-starting engines, for example, for both our aeroplanes and motor-cars—but it is available to-day for anyone who can reach it. An invalid lady of seventy could have enjoyed all that I did if only one could have got her into the passenger's seat. Getting there was a little difficult, it is true; the waterplane was out in the surf, and I was carried to it on a boatman's back, and then had to clamber carefully through the wires, but that is a matter of detail. This flying is indeed so certain to become a general experience that I am sure that this description will in a few years seem almost as quaint as if I had set myself to record the fears and sensations of my First Ride in a Wheeled Vehicle. And I suspect that learning to control a Farman waterplane now is probably not much more difficult than, let us say, twice the difficulty in learning the control and management of a motor-bicycle. I cannot understand the sort of young man who won't learn how to do it if he gets half a chance.

The development of these waterplanes is an important step towards the huge and swarming popularisation of flying which is now certainly imminent. We ancient survivors of those who believed in and wrote about flying before there was any flying used to make a great fuss about the dangers and difficulties of landing and getting up. We wrote with vast gravity about "starting rails" and "landing stages," and it is still true that landing an aeroplane, except upon a well-known and quite level expanse, is a risky and uncomfortable business. But getting up and landing upon fairly smooth water is easier than getting into bed. This alone is likely to determine the aeroplane routes along the line of the world's coastlines and lake groups and waterways. The airmen will go to and fro over water as the midges do. Wherever there is a square mile of water the waterplanes will come and go like hornets at the mouth of their nest. But there are much stronger reasons than this convenience for keeping over water. Over water the air, it seems, lies in great level expanses; even when there are gales it moves in uniform masses like the swift, still rush of a deep river. The airman, in Mr. Grahame-White's phrase, can go to sleep on it. But over the land, and for thousands of feet up into the sky, the air is more irregular than a torrent among rocks; it is—if only we could see it—a waving, whirling, eddying, flamboyant confusion. A slight hill, a ploughed field, the streets of a town, create riotous, rolling, invisible streams and cataracts of air that catch the airman unawares, make him drop disconcertingly, try his nerves. With a powerful enough engine he climbs at once again, but these sudden downfalls are the least pleasant and most dangerous experience in aviation. They exact a tiring vigilance.

Over lake or sea, in sunshine, within sight of land, this is the perfect way of the flying tourist. Gladly would I have set out for France this morning instead of returning to Eastbourne. And then coasted round to Spain and into the Mediterranean. And so by leisurely stages to India. And the East Indies . . .

I find my study unattractive to-day.

OFF THE CHAIN

(December, 1910)

I was ill in bed, reading Samuel Warren's "Ten Thousand a Year," and noting how much the world can change in seventy years.

I had just got to the journey of Titmouse from London to Yorkshire in that ex-sheriff's coach he bought in Long Acre— where now the motor-cars are sold—when there came a telegram to bid me note how a certain Mr. Holt was upon the ocean, coming back to England from a little excursion. He had left London last Saturday week at midday; he hoped to be back by Thursday; and he had talked to the President in Washington, visited Philadelphia, and had a comparatively loitering afternoon in New York. What had I to say about it?

Firstly, that I wish this article could be written by Samuel Warren. And failing that, I wish that Charles Dickens, who wrote in his "American Notes" with such passionate disgust and hostility about the first Cunarder, retailing all the discomfort and misery of crossing the Atlantic by steamship, could have shared Mr. Holt's experience.

Because I am chiefly impressed by the fact not that Mr. Holt has taken days where weeks were needed fifty years ago, but that he has done it very comfortably, without undue physical exertion, and at no greater expense, I suppose, than it cost Dickens, whom the journey nearly killed.

If Mr. Holt's expenses were higher, it was for the special trains and the sake of the record. Anyone taking ordinary trains and ordinary passages may do what he has done in eighteen or twenty days.

When I was a boy, "Around the World in Eighty Days" was still a brilliant piece of imaginative fiction. Now that is almost an invalid's pace. It will not be very long before a man will be able to go round the world if he wishes to do so ten times in a year. And it is perhaps forgivable if those who, like Jules Verne, saw all these increments in speed, motor-cars, and airships aeroplanes, and submarines, wireless telegraphy and what not, as plain and necessary deductions from the promises of physical science, should turn upon a world that read and doubted and jeered with "I told you so. *Now* will you respect a prophet?"

It was not that the prophets professed any mystical and inexplicable illumination at which a sceptic might reasonably mock; they were prepared with ample reasons for the things they foretold. Now, quite as confidently, they point on to a new series of consequences, high probabilities that follow on all this tremendous development of swift, secure, and cheapened locomotion, just as they followed almost necessarily upon the mechanical developments of the last century.

Briefly, the ties that bind men to place are being severed; we are in the beginning of a new phase in human experience.

For endless ages man led the hunting life, migrating after his food, camping, homeless, as to this day are many of the Indians and Esquimaux in the Hudson Bay Territory. Then began agriculture, and for the sake of securer food man tethered himself to a place. The history of man's progress from savagery to civilisation is essentially a story of settling down. It begins in caves and shelters; it culminates in a wide spectacle of farms and peasant villages, and little towns among the farms. There were wars, crusades, barbarous invasions, set-backs, but to that state all Asia, Europe, North Africa worked its way with an indomitable pertinacity. The enormous majority of human beings stayed at home at last; from the cradle to the grave they lived, married, died in the same district, usually in the same village; and to that condition, law, custom, habits, morals, have adapted themselves. The whole plan and conception of human society is based on the rustic home and the needs and characteristics of the agricultural family. There have been gipsies, wanderers, knaves, knights-errant and adventurers, no doubt, but the settled permanent rustic home and the tenure of land about it, and the hens and the cow, have constituted the fundamental reality of the whole scene. Now, the really wonderful thing in this astonishing development of cheap, abundant, swift locomotion we have seen in the last seventy years—in the development of which Mauretanias, aeroplanes, mile-a-minute expresses, tubes, motor-buses and motor cars are just the bright, remarkable points—is this: that it dissolves almost all the reason and necessity why men should go on living permanently in any one place or rigidly disciplined to one set of conditions. The former attachment to the soil ceases to be an advantage. The human spirit has never quite subdued itself to the laborious and established life; it achieves its best with variety and occasional vigorous exertion under the stimulus of novelty rather than by constant toil, and this revolution in human locomotion that brings nearly all the globe within a few days of any man is the most striking aspect of the unfettering again of the old restless, wandering, adventurous tendencies in man's composition.

Already one can note remarkable developments of migration. There is, for example, that flow to and fro across the Atlantic of labourers from the Mediterranean. Italian workmen by the hundred thousand go to the United States in the spring and return in the autumn. Again, there is a stream of thousands of prosperous Americans to summer in Europe. Compared with any European country, the whole population of the United States is fluid. Equally notable is the enormous proportion of the British prosperous which winters either in the high Alps or along the Riviera. England is rapidly developing the former Irish grievance of an absentee propertied class. It is only now by the most strenuous artificial banking back that migrations on a far huger scale from India into Africa, and from China and Japan into Australia and America are prevented.

All the indications point to a time when it will be an altogether exceptional thing for a man to follow one occupation in one place all his life, and still rarer for a son to follow in his father's footsteps or die in his father's house.

The thing is as simple as the rule of three. We are off the chain of locality for good and all. It was necessary heretofore for a man to live in immediate contact with his occupation, because the only way for him to reach it was to have it at his door, and the cost and delay of transport were relatively too enormous for him to shift once he was settled. *Now* he may live twenty or thirty miles away from his occupation; and it often pays him to spend the small amount of time and money needed to move—it may be half-way round the world—to healthier conditions or more profitable employment.

And with every diminution in the cost and duration of transport it becomes more and more possible, and more and more likely, to be profitable to move great multitudes of workers seasonally between regions where work is needed in this season and regions where work is needed in that. They can go out to the agricultural lands at one time and come back into towns for artistic work and organised work in factories at another. They can move from rain and darkness into sunshine, and from heat into the coolness of mountain forests. Children can be sent for education to sea beaches and healthy mountains.

Men will harvest in Saskatchewan and come down in great liners to spend the winter working in the forests of Yucatan.

People have hardly begun to speculate about the consequences of the return of humanity from a closely tethered to a migratory existence. It is here that the prophet finds his chief opportunity. Obviously, these great forces of transport are already straining against the limits of existing political areas. Every country contains now an increasing ingredient of unenfranchised Uitlanders. Every country finds a growing section of its home-born people either living largely abroad, drawing the bulk of their income from the exterior, and having their essential interests wholly or partially across the frontier.

In every locality of a Western European country countless people are found delocalised, uninterested in the affairs of that particular locality, and capable of moving themselves with a minimum of loss and a maximum of facility into any other region that proves more attractive. In America political life, especially State life as distinguished from national political life, is degraded because of the natural and inevitable apathy of a large portion of the population whose interests go beyond the State.

Politicians and statesmen, being the last people in the world to notice what is going on in it, are making no attempt whatever to re-adapt this hugely growing floating population of delocalised people to the public service. As Mr. Marriott puts it in his novel, *"Now,"* they "drop out" from politics as we understand politics at present. Local administration falls almost entirely—and the decision of Imperial affairs tends more and more to fall—into the hands of that dwindling and adventurous moiety which sits tight in one place from the cradle to the grave. No one has yet invented any method for the political expression and collective direction of a migratory population, and nobody is attempting to do so. It is a new problem . . .

Here, then, is a curious prospect, the prospect of a new kind of people, a floating population going about the world, uprooted, delocalised, and even, it may be, denationalised, with wide interests and wide views, developing no doubt, customs and habits of its own, a morality of its own, a philosophy of its own, and yet from the point of view of current politics and legislation unorganised and ineffective.

Most of the forces of international finance and international business enterprise will be with it. It will develop its own characteristic standards of art and literature and conduct in accordance with its new necessities. It is, I believe, the mankind of the future. And the last thing it will be able to do will be to legislate. The history of the immediate future will, I am convinced, be very largely the history of the conflict of the needs of this new population with the institutions, the boundaries the laws, prejudices, and deep-rooted traditions established during the home-keeping, localised era of mankind's career.

This conflict follows as inevitably upon these new gigantic facilities of locomotion as the *Mauretania* followed from the discoveries of steam and steel.

OF THE NEW REIGN

(June, 1911.)

The bunting and the crimson vanish from the streets. Already the vast army of improvised carpenters that the Coronation has created set themselves to the work of demolition, and soon every road that converges upon Central London will be choked again with great loads of timber—but this time going outward—as our capital emerges from this unprecedented inundation of loyalty. The most elaborately conceived, the most stately of all recorded British Coronations is past.

What new phase in the life of our nation and our Empire does this tremendous ceremony inaugurate? The question is inevitable. There is nothing in all the social existence of men so full of challenge as the crowning of a king. It is the end of the overture; the curtain rises. This is a new beginning-place for histories.

To us, the great mass of common Englishmen, who have no place in the hierarchy of our land, who do not attend Courts nor encounter uniforms, whose function is at most spectacular, who stand in the street and watch the dignitaries and the liveries pass by, this sense of critical expectation is perhaps greater than it is for those more immediately concerned in the spectacle. They have had their parts to play, their symbolic acts to perform, they have sat in their privileged places, and we have waited at the barriers until their comfort and dignity was assured. I can conceive many of them, a little fatigued, preparing now for social dispersal, relaxing comfortably into gossip, discussing the detail of these events with an air of things accomplished. They will decide whether the Coronation has been a success and whether everything has or has not passed off very well. For us in the great crowd nothing has as yet succeeded or passed off well or ill. We are intent upon a King newly anointed and crowned, a King of whom we know as yet very little, but who has, nevertheless, roused such expectation as no King before him has done since Tudor times, in the presence of gigantic opportunities.

There is a conviction widespread among us—his own words, perhaps, have done most to create it—that King George is inspired, as no recent predecessor has been inspired, by the conception of kingship, that his is to be no rôle of almost indifferent abstinence from the broad processes of our national and imperial development. That greater public life which is above party and above creed and sect has, we are told, taken hold of his imagination; he is to be no crowned image of unity and correlation, a layer of foundation-stones and a signature to documents, but an actor in our drama, a living Prince.

Time will test these hopes, but certainly we, the innumerable democracy of individually unimportant men, have felt the need for such a Prince. Our consciousness of defects, of fields of effort untilled, of vast possibilities neglected and slipping away from us for ever, has never really slumbered again since the chastening experiences of the Boer War. Since then the national spirit, hampered though it is by the traditions of party government and a legacy of intellectual and social heaviness, has been in uneasy and ineffectual revolt against deadness, against stupidity and slackness, against waste and hypocrisy in every department of life. We have come to see more and more clearly how little we can hope for from politicians, societies and organised movements in these essential things. It is this that has invested the energy and manhood, the untried possibilities of the new King with so radiant a light of hope for us.

Think what it may mean for us all—I write as one of that great ill-informed multitude, sincerely and gravely patriotic, outside the echoes of Court gossip and the easy knowledge of exalted society—if our King does indeed care for these wider and profounder things! Suppose we have a King at last who cares for the advancement of science, who is willing to do the hundred things that are so easy in his position to increase research, to honour and to share in scientific thought. Suppose we have a King whose head rises above the level of the Court artist, and who not only can but will appeal to the latent and discouraged power of artistic creation in our race. Suppose we have a King who understands the need for incessant, acute criticism to keep our collective activities intelligent and efficient, and for a flow of bold, unhampered thought through every department of the national life, a King liberal without laxity and patriotic without pettiness or vulgarity. Such, it seems to us who wait at present almost inexpressively outside the immediate clamours of a mere artificial loyalty, are the splendid possibilities of the time.

For England is no exhausted or decaying country. It is rich with an unmeasured capacity for generous responses. It is a country burthened indeed, but not overwhelmed, by the gigantic responsibilities of Empire, a little relaxed by wealth, and hampered rather than enslaved by a certain shyness of temperament, a certain habitual timidity, slovenliness and insincerity of mind. It is a little distrustful of intellectual power and enterprise, a little awkward and ungracious to brave and beautiful things, a little too tolerant of dull, well-meaning and industrious men and arrogant old women. It suffers hypocrites gladly, because its criticism is poor, and it is wastefully harsh to frank unorthodoxy. But its heart is sound if its judgments fall short of acuteness and if its standards of achievement are low. It needs but a quickening spirit upon the throne, always the traditional centre of its respect, to rise from even the appearance of decadence. There is a new quality seeking expression in England like the rising of sap in the spring, a new generation asking only for such leadership and such emancipation from restricted scope and ungenerous hostility as a King alone can give it . . .

When in its turn this latest reign comes at last to its reckoning, what will the sum of its achievement be? What will it leave of things visible? Will it leave a London preserved and beautified, or will it but add abundantly to the lumps of dishonest statuary, the scars and masses of ill-conceived rebuilding which testify to the aesthetic degradation of the Victorian period? Will a great constellation of artists redeem the ambitious sentimentalities and genteel skilfulness that find their fitting mausoleum in the Tate Gallery? Will our literature escape at last from pretentiousness and timidity, our philosophy from the foolish cerebrations of university "characters" and eminent politicians at leisure, and our starved science find scope and resources adequate to its gigantic needs? Will our universities, our teaching, our national training, our public services, gain a new health from the reviving vigour of the national brain? Or is all this a mere wild hope, and shall we, after perhaps some small flutterings of effort, the foundation of some ridiculous little academy of literary busybodies and hangers-on, the public recognition of this or that sociological pretender or financial "scientist," and a little polite jobbery with picture-buying, relapse into lassitude and a contented acquiescence in the rivalry of Germany and the United States for the moral, intellectual and material leadership of the world?

The deaths and accessions of Kings, the changing of names and coins and symbols and persons, a little force our minds in the marking off of epochs. We are brought to weigh one generation against another, to reckon up our position and note the characteristics of a new phase. What lies before us in the next decades? Is England going on to fresh achievements, to a renewed and increased predominance, or is she falling into a secondary position among the peoples of the world?

The answer to that depends upon ourselves. Have we pride enough to attempt still to lead mankind, and if we have, have we the wisdom and the quality? Or are we just the children of Good Luck, who are being found out?

Some years ago our present King exhorted this island to "wake up" in one of the most remarkable of British royal utterances, and Mr. Owen Seaman assures him in verse of an altogether laureate quality that we are now

"Free of the snare of slumber's silken bands,"

though I have not myself observed it. It is interesting to ask, Is England really waking up? and if she is, what sort of awakening is she likely to have?

It is possible, of course, to wake up in various different ways. There is the clear and beautiful dawn of new and balanced effort, easy, unresting, planned, assured, and there is also the blundering-up of a still half-somnolent man, irascible, clumsy, quarrelsome, who stubs his toe in his first walk across the room, smashes his too persistent alarum clock in a fit of nerves, and cuts his throat while shaving. All patriotic vehemence does not serve one's country.

Exertion is a more critical and dangerous thing than inaction, and the essence of success is in the ability to develop those qualities which make action effective, and without which strenuousness is merely a clumsy and noisy protest against inevitable defeat. These necessary qualities, without which no community may hope for pre-eminence to-day, are a passion for fine and brilliant achievement, relentless veracity of thought and method, and richly imaginative fearlessness of enterprise. Have we English those qualities, and are we doing our utmost to select and develop them?

I doubt very much if we are. Let me give some of the impressions that qualify my assurance in the future of our race.

I have watched a great deal of patriotic effort during the last decade, I have seen enormous expenditures of will, emotion and material for the sake of our future, and I am deeply impressed, not indeed by any effect of lethargy, but by the second-rate quality and the shortness and weakness of aim in very much that has been done. I miss continually that sharply critical imaginativeness which distinguishes all excellent work, which shines out supremely in Cromwell's creation of the New Model, or Nelson's plan of action at Trafalgar, as brightly as it does in Newton's investigation of gravitation, Turner's rendering of landscape, or Shakespeare's choice of words, but which cannot be absent altogether if any achievement is to endure. We seem to have busy, energetic people, no doubt, in abundance, patient and industrious administrators and legislators; but have we any adequate supply of really creative ability?

Let me apply this question to one matter upon which England has certainly been profoundly in earnest during the last decade. We have been almost frantically resolved to keep the empire of the sea. But have we really done all that could have been done? I ask it with all diffidence, but has our naval preparation been free from a sort of noisy violence, a certain massive dullness of conception? Have we really made anything like a sane use of our resources? I do not mean of our resources in money or stuff. It is manifest that the next naval war will be beyond all precedent a war of mechanisms, giving such scope for invention and scientifically equipped wit and courage as the world has never had before. Now, have we really developed any considerable proportion of the potential human quality available to meet the demand for wits? What are we doing to discover, encourage and develop those supreme qualities of personal genius that become more and more decisive with every new weapon and every new complication and unsuspected possibility it introduces? Suppose, for example, there was among us to-day a one-eyed, one-armed adulterer, rather fragile, prone to sea-sickness, and with just that one supreme quality of imaginative courage which made Nelson our starry admiral. Would he be given the ghost of a chance now of putting that gift at his country's disposal? I do not think he would, and I do not think he would because we underrate gifts and exceptional qualities, because there is no quickening appreciation for the exceptional best in a man, and because we overvalue the good behaviour, the sound physique, the commonplace virtues of mediocrity.

I have but the knowledge of the man in the street in these things, though once or twice I have chanced on prophecy, and I am uneasily apprehensive of the quality of all our naval preparations. We go on launching these lumping great Dreadnoughts, and I cannot bring myself to believe in them. They seem vulnerable from the air above and the deep below, vulnerable in a shallow channel and in a fog (and the North Sea is both foggy and shallow), and immensely costly. If I were Lord High Admiral of England at war I would not fight the things. I would as soon put to sea in St. Paul's Cathedral. If I were fighting Germany, I would stow half of them away in the Clyde and half in the Bristol Channel, and take the good men out of them and fight with mines and torpedoes and destroyers and airships and submarines.

And when I come to military matters my persuasion that things are not all right, that our current hostility to imaginative activity and our dull acceptance of established methods and traditions is leading us towards grave dangers, intensifies. In South Africa the Boers taught us in blood and bitterness the obvious fact that barbed wire had its military uses, and over the high passes on the way to Lhassa (though, luckily, it led to no disaster) there was not a rifle in condition to use because we had not thought to take glycerine. The perpetual novelty of modern conditions demands an imaginative alertness we eliminate. I do not believe that the Army Council or anyone in authority has worked out a tithe of the essential problems of contemporary war. If they have, then it does not show. Our military imagination is half-way back to bows and arrows. The other day I saw a detachment of the Legion of Frontiersmen disporting itself at Totteridge. I presume these young heroes consider they are preparing for a possible conflict in England or Western Europe, and I presume the authorities are satisfied with them. It is at any rate the only serious war of which there is any manifest probability. Western Europe is now a network of railways, tramways, high roads, wires of all sorts; its chief beasts of burthen are the railway train and the motor car and the bicycle; towns and hypertrophied villages are often practically continuous over large areas; there is abundant water and food, and the commonest form of cover is the house. But the Legion of Frontiersmen is equipped for war, oh!—in Arizona in 1890, and so far as I am able to judge the most modern sections of the army extant are organised for a colonial war in (say) 1899 or 1900. There is, of course, a considerable amount of vague energy demanding conscription and urging our youth towards a familiarity with arms and the backwoodsman's life, but of any thought-out purpose in our arming widely understood, of any realisation of what would have to be done and where it would have to be done, and of any attempts to create an instrument for that novel unprecedented undertaking, I discover no trace.

In my capacity of devil's advocate pleading against national over-confidence, I might go on to the quality of our social and political movements. One hears nowadays a vast amount of chatter about efficiency—that magic word—and social organisation, and there is no doubt a huge expenditure of energy upon these things and a widespread desire to rush about and make showy and startling changes. But it does not follow that this involves progress if the enterprise itself is dully conceived and most of it does seem to me to be dully conceived. In the absence of penetrating criticism, any impudent industrious person may set up as an "expert," organise and direct the confused good intentions at large, and muddle disastrously with the problem in hand. The "expert" quack and the bureaucratic intriguer increase and multiply in a dull-minded, uncritical, strenuous period as disease germs multiply in darkness and heat.

I find the same doubts of our quality assail me when I turn to the supreme business of education. It is true we all seem alive nowadays to the need of education, are all prepared for more expenditure upon it and more, but it does not follow necessarily in a period of stagnating imagination that we shall get what we pay for. The other day I discovered my little boy doing a subtraction sum, and I found he was doing it in a slower, clumsier, less businesslike way than the one I was taught in an old-fashioned "Commercial Academy" thirty odd years ago. The educational "expert," it seems, has been at work substituting a bad method for a good one in our schools because it is easier of exposition. The educational "expert," in the lack of a lively public intelligence, develops all the vices of the second-rate energetic, and he is, I am only too disposed to believe, making a terrible mess of a great deal of our science teaching and of the teaching of mathematics and English . . .

I have written enough to make clear the quality of my doubts. I think the English mind cuts at life with a dulled edge, and that its energy may be worse than its somnolence. I think it undervalues gifts and fine achievement, and overvalues the commonplace virtues of mediocre men. One of the greatest Liberal statesmen in the time of Queen Victoria never held office because he was associated with a divorce case a quarter of a century ago. For him to have taken office would have been regarded as a scandal. But it is not regarded as a scandal that our Government includes men of no more ability than any average assistant behind a grocer's counter. These are your gods, O England!—and with every desire to be optimistic I find it hard under the circumstances to anticipate that the New Epoch is likely to be a blindingly brilliant time for our Empire and our race.

WILL THE EMPIRE LIVE?

What will hold such an Empire as the British together, this great, laxly scattered, sea-linked association of ancient states and new-formed countries, Oriental nations, and continental colonies? What will enable it to resist the endless internal strains, the inevitable external pressures and attacks to which it must be subjected This is the primary question for British Imperialism; everything else is secondary or subordinated to that.

There is a multitude of answers. But I suppose most of them will prove under examination either to be, or to lead to, or to imply very distinctly this generalisation that if most of the intelligent and active people in the Empire want it to continue it will, and that if a large proportion of such active and intelligent people are discontented and estranged, nothing can save it from disintegration. I do not suppose that a navy ten times larger than ours, or conscription of the most irksome thoroughness, could oblige Canada to remain in the Empire if the general will and feeling of Canada were against it, or coerce India into a sustained submission if India presented a united and resistant front. Our Empire, for all its roll of battles, was not created by force; colonisation and diplomacy have played a far larger share in its growth than conquest; and there is no such strength in its sovereignty as the rule of pride and pressure demand. It is to the free consent and participation of its constituent peoples that we must look for its continuance.

A large and influential body of politicians considers that in preferential trading between the parts of the Empire, and in the erection of a tariff wall against exterior peoples, lies the secret of that deepened emotional understanding we all desire. I have never belonged to that school. I am no impassioned Free Trader—the sacred principle of Free Trade has always impressed me as a piece of party claptrap; but I have never been able to understand how an attempt to draw together dominions so scattered and various as ours by a network of fiscal manipulation could end in anything but mutual inconvenience mutual irritation, and disruption.

In an open drawer in my bureau there lies before me now a crumpled card on which are the notes I made of a former discussion of this very issue, a discussion between a number of prominent politicians in the days before Mr. Chamberlain's return from South Africa and the adoption of Tariff Reform by the Unionist Party; and I decipher again the same considerations, unanswered and unanswerable, that leave me sceptical to-day.

Take a map of the world and consider the extreme differences in position and condition between our scattered states. Here is Canada, lying along the United States, looking eastward to Japan and China, westward to all Europe. See the great slashes of lake, bay, and mountain chain that cut it meridianally. Obviously its main routes and trades and relations lie naturally north and south; obviously its full development can only be attained with those ways free, open, and active. Conceivably, you may build a fiscal wall across the continent; conceivably, you may shut off the east and half the west by impossible tariffs, and narrow its trade to one artificial duct to England, but only at the price of a hampered development It will be like nourishing the growing body of a man with the heart and arteries of a mouse.

Then here, again, are New Zealand and Australia, facing South America and the teeming countries of Eastern Asia; surely it is in relation to these vast proximities that their economic future lies. Is it possible to believe that shipping mutton to London is anything but the mere beginning of their commercial development Look at India, again, and South Africa. Is it not manifest that from the economic and business points of view each of these is an entirely separate entity, a system apart, under distinct necessities, needing entire freedom to make its own bargains and control its trade in its own way in order to achieve its fullest material possibilities?

Nor can I believe that financial entanglements greatly strengthen the bonds of an empire in any case. We lost the American colonies because we interfered with their fiscal arrangements, and it was Napoleon's attempt to strangle the Continental trade with Great Britain that began his downfall.

I do not find in the ordinary relations of life that business relations necessarily sustain intercourse. The relations of buyer and seller are ticklish relations, very liable to strains and conflicts. I do not find people grow fond of their butchers and plumbers, and I doubt whether if one were obliged by some special taxation to deal only with one butcher or one plumber, it would greatly endear the relationship. Forced buying is irritated buying, and it is the forbidden shop that contains the coveted goods. Nor do I find, to take another instance, among the hotel staffs of Switzerland and the Riviera—who live almost entirely upon British gold—those impassioned British imperialist views the economic link theory would lead me to expect.

And another link, too, upon which much stress is laid but about which I have very grave doubts, is the possibility of a unified organisation of the Empire for military defence. We are to have, it is suggested, an imperial Army and an imperial Navy, and so far, no doubt, as the guaranteeing of a general peace goes, we may develop a sense of participation in that way. But it is well in these islands to remember that our extraordinary Empire has no common enemy to weld it together from without.

It is too usual to regard Germany as the common enemy. We in Great Britain are now intensely jealous of Germany. We are intensely jealous of Germany not only because the Germans outnumber us, and have a much larger and more diversified country than ours, and lie in the very heart and body of Europe, but because in the last hundred years, while we have fed on platitudes and vanity, they have had the energy and humility to develop a splendid system of national education, to toil at science and art and literature, to develop social organisation, to master and better our methods of business and industry, and to clamber above us in the scale of civilisation. This has humiliated and irritated rather than chastened us, and our irritation has been greatly exacerbated by the swaggering bad manners, the talk of "Blood and Iron" and Mailed Fists, the Welt-Politik rubbish that inaugurated the new German phase.

The British middle-class, therefore, is full of an angry, vague disposition to thwart that expansion which Germans regard very reasonably as their natural destiny; there are all the possibilities of a huge conflict in that disposition, and it is perhaps well to remember how insular—or, at least, how European—the essentials of this quarrel are. We have lost our tempers, but Canada has not. There is nothing in Germany to make Canada envious and ashamed of wasted years. Canada has no natural quarrel with Germany, nor has India, nor South Africa, nor Australasia. They have no reason to share our insular exasperation. On the other hand, all these states have other special preoccupations. New Zealand, for example, having spent half a century and more in sheep-farming, land legislation, suppressing its drink traffic, lowering its birth-rate, and, in short, the achievement of an ideal preventive materialism, is chiefly consumed by hate and fear of Japan, which in the same interval has made a stride from the thirteenth to the twentieth century, and which teems with art and life and enterprise and offspring. Now Japan in Welt-Politik is our ally.

You see, the British Empire has no common economic interests and no natural common enemy. It is not adapted to any form of Zollverein or any form of united aggression. Visibly, on the map of the world it has a likeness to open hands, while the German Empire—except for a few ill-advised and imitative colonies—is clenched into a central European unity.

Physically, our Empire is incurably scattered, various, and divided, and it is to quite other links and forces, it seems to me, than fiscal or military unification that we who desire its continuance must look to hold it together. There never was anything like it before. Essentially it is an adventure of the British spirit, sanguine, discursive, and beyond comparison insubordinate, adaptable, and originating. It has been made by odd and irregular means by trading companies, pioneers, explorers, unauthorised seamen, adventurers like Clive, eccentrics like Gordon, invalids like Rhodes. It has been made, in spite of authority and officialdom, as no other empire was ever made. The nominal rulers of Britain never planned it. It happened almost in spite of them. Their chief contribution to its history has been the loss of the United States. It is a living thing that has arisen, not a dead thing put together. Beneath the thin legal and administrative ties that hold it together lies the far more vital bond of a traditional free spontaneous activity. It has a common medium of expression in the English tongue, a unity of liberal and tolerant purpose amidst its enormous variety of localised life and colour. And it is in the development and strengthening, the enrichment the rendering more conscious and more purposeful, of that broad creative spirit of the British that the true cement and continuance of our Empire is to be found.

The Empire must live by the forces that begot it. It cannot hope to give any such exclusive prosperity as a Zollverein might afford; it can hold out no hopes of collective conquests and triumphs—its utmost military rôle must be the guaranteeing of a common inaggressive security; but it can, if it is to survive, it must, give all its constituent parts such a civilisation as none of them could achieve alone, a civilisation, a wealth and fullness of life increasing and developing with the years. Through that, and that alone, can it be made worth having and worth serving.

And in the first place the whole Empire must use the English language. I do not mean that any language must be stamped out, that a thousand languages may not flourish by board and cradle and in folk-songs and village gossip—Erse, the Taal, a hundred Indian and other Eastern tongues, Canadian French—but I mean that also English must be available, that everywhere there must be English teaching. And everyone who wants to read science or history or philosophy, to come out of the village life into wider thoughts and broader horizons, to gain appreciation in art, must find ready to hand, easily attainable in English, all there is to know and all that has been said thereon. It is worth a hundred Dreadnoughts and a million soldiers to the Empire, that wherever the imperial posts reach, wherever there is a curious or receptive mind, there in English and by the imperial connection the full thought of the race should come. To the lonely youth upon the New Zealand sheep farm, to the young Hindu, to the trapper under a Labrador tilt, to the half-breed assistant at a Burmese oil-well, to the self-educating Scottish miner or the Egyptian clerk, the Empire and the English language should exist, visibly and certainly, as the media by which his spirit escapes from his immediate surroundings and all the urgencies of every day, into a limitless fellowship of thought and beauty.

Now I am not writing this in any vague rhetorical way; I mean specifically that our Empire has to become the medium of knowledge and thought to every intelligent person in it, or that it is bound to go to pieces. It has no economic, no military, no racial, no religious unity. Its only conceivable unity is a unity of language and purpose and outlook. If it is not held together by thought and spirit, it cannot be held together. No other cement exists that can hold it together indefinitely.

Not only English literature, but all other literatures well translated into English, and all science and all philosophy, have to be brought within the reach of everyone capable of availing himself of such reading. And this must be done, not by private enterprise or for gain, but as an Imperial function. Wherever the Empire extends there its presence must signify all that breadth of thought and outlook no localised life can supply.

Only so is it possible to establish and maintain the wide understandings, the common sympathy necessary to our continued association. The Empire, mediately or immediately, must become the universal educator, news-agent, book-distributor, civiliser-general, and vehicle of imaginative inspiration for its peoples, or else it must submit to the gravitation of its various parts to new and more invigorating associations.

No empire, it may be urged, has ever attempted anything of this sort, but no empire like the British has ever yet existed. Its conditions and needs are unprecedented, its consolidation is a new problem, to be solved, if it is solved at all, by untried means. And in the English language as a vehicle of thought and civilisation alone is that means to be found.

Now it is idle to pretend that at the present time the British Empire is giving its constituent peoples any such high and rewarding civilisation as I am here suggesting. It gives them a certain immunity from warfare, a penny post, an occasional spectacular coronation, a few knighthoods and peerages, and the services of an honest, unsympathetic, narrow-minded, and unattractive officialism. No adequate effort is being made to render the English language universal throughout its limits, none at all to use it as a medium of thought and enlightenment. Half the good things of the human mind are outside English altogether, and there is not sufficient intelligence among us to desire to bring them in. If one would read honest and able criticism, one must learn French; if one would be abreast of scientific knowledge and philosophical thought, or see many good plays or understand the contemporary European mind, German.

And yet it would cost amazingly little to get every good foreign thing done into English as it appeared. It needs only a little understanding and a little organisation to ensure the immediate translation of every significant article, every scientific paper of the slightest value. The effort and arrangement needed to make books, facilities for research, and all forms of art accessible throughout the Empire, would be altogether trivial in proportion to the consolidation it would effect.

But English people do not understand these things. Their Empire is an accident. It was made for them by their exceptional and outcast men, and in the end it will be lost, I fear, by the intellectual inertness of their commonplace and dull-minded leaders. Empire has happened to them and civilisation has happened to them as fresh lettuces come to tame rabbits. They do not understand how they got, and they will not understand how to keep. Art, thought, literature, all indeed that raises men above locality and habit, all that can justify and consolidate the Empire, is nothing to them. They are provincials mocked by a world-wide opportunity, the stupid legatees of a great generation of exiles. They go out of town for the "shootin'," and come back for the fooleries of Parliament, and to see what the Censor has left of our playwrights and Sir Jesse Boot of our writers, and to dine in restaurants and wear clothes.

Mostly they call themselves Imperialists, which is just their harmless way of expressing their satisfaction with things as they are. In practice their Imperialism resolves itself into a vigorous resistance to taxation and an ill-concealed hostility to education. It matters nothing to them that the whole next generation of Canadians has drawn its ideas mainly from American publications, that India and Egypt, in despite of sounder mental nourishment, have developed their own vernacular Press, that Australia and New Zealand even now gravitate to America for books and thought. It matters nothing to them that the poverty and insularity of our intellectual life has turned American art to France and Italy, and the American universities towards Germany. The slow starvation and decline of our philosophy and science, the decadence of British invention and enterprise, troubles them not at all, because they fail to connect these things with the tangible facts of empire. "The world cannot wait for the English." . . . And the sands of our Imperial opportunity twirl through the neck of the hour-glass.

THE LABOUR UNREST

(May, 1912.)

Sec. 1

Our country is, I think, in a dangerous state of social disturbance. The discontent of the labouring mass of the community is deep and increasing. It may be that we are in the opening phase of a real and irreparable class war.

Since the Coronation we have moved very rapidly indeed from an assurance of extreme social stability towards the recognition of a spreading disorganisation. It is idle to pretend any longer that these Labour troubles are the mere give and take of economic adjustment. No adjustment is in progress. New and strange urgencies are at work in our midst, forces for which the word "revolutionary" is only too faithfully appropriate. Nothing is being done to allay these forces; everything conspires to exasperate them.

Whither are these forces taking us? What can still be done and what has to be done to avoid the phase of social destruction to which we seem to be drifting?

Hitherto, in Great Britain at any rate, the working man has shown himself a being of the most limited and practical outlook. His narrowness of imagination, his lack of general ideas, has been the despair of the Socialist and of every sort of revolutionary theorist. He may have struck before, but only for definite increments of wages or definite limitations of toil; his acceptance of the industrial system and its methods has been as complete and unquestioning as his acceptance of earth and sky. Now, with an effect of suddenness, this ceases to be the case. A new generation of workers is seen replacing the old, workers of a quality unfamiliar to the middle-aged and elderly men who still manage our great businesses and political affairs. The worker is beginning now to strike for unprecedented ends—against the system, against the fundamental conditions of labour, to strike for no defined ends at all, perplexingly and disconcertingly. The old-fashioned strike was a method of bargaining, clumsy and violent perhaps, but bargaining still; the new-fashioned strike is far less of a haggle, far more of a display of temper. The first thing that has to be realised if the Labour question is to be understood at all is this, that the temper of Labour has changed altogether in the last twenty or thirty years. Essentially that is a change due to intelligence not merely increased but greatly stimulated, to the work, that is, of the board schools and of the cheap Press. The outlook of the workman has passed beyond the works and his beer and his dog. He has become—or, rather, he has been replaced by—a being of eyes, however imperfect, and of criticism, however hasty and unjust. The working man of to-day reads, talks, has general ideas and a sense of the round world; he is far nearer to the ruler of to-day in knowledge and intellectual range than he is to the working man of fifty years ago. The politician or business magnate of to-day is no better educated and very little better informed than his equals were fifty years ago. The chief difference is golf. The working man questions a thousand things his father accepted as in the very nature of the world, and among others he begins to ask with the utmost alertness and persistence why it is that he in particular is expected to toil. The answer, the only justifiable answer, should be that that is the work for which he is fitted by his inferior capacity and culture, that these others are a special and select sort, very specially trained and prepared for their responsibilities, and that at once brings this new fact of a working-class criticism of social values into play. The old workman might and did quarrel very vigorously with his specific employer, but he never set out to arraign all employers; he took the law and the Church and Statecraft and politics for the higher and noble things they claimed to be. He wanted an extra shilling or he wanted an hour of leisure, and that was as much as he wanted. The young workman, on the other hand, has put the whole social system upon its trial, and seems quite disposed to give an adverse verdict. He looks far beyond the older conflict of interests between employer and employed. He criticises the good intentions of the whole system of governing and influential people, and not only their good intentions, but their ability. These are the new conditions, and the middle-aged and elderly gentlemen who are dealing with the crisis on the supposition that their vast experience of Labour questions in the 'seventies and 'eighties furnishes valuable guidance in this present issue are merely bringing the gunpowder of misapprehension to the revolutionary fort.

The workman of the new generation is full of distrust the most demoralising of social influences. He is like a sailor who believes no longer either in the good faith or seamanship of his captain, and, between desperation and contempt, contemplates vaguely but persistently the assumption of control by a collective forecastle. He is like a private soldier obsessed with the idea that nothing can save the situation but the death of an incompetent officer. His distrust is so profound that he ceases not only to believe in the employer, but he ceases to believe in the law, ceases to believe in Parliament, as a means to that tolerable life he desires; and he falls back steadily upon his last resource of a strike, and—if by repressive tactics we make it so—a criminal strike. The central fact of all this present trouble is that distrust. There is only one way in which our present drift towards revolution or revolutionary disorder can be arrested, and that is by restoring the confidence of these alienated millions, who visibly now are changing from loyalty to the Crown, from a simple patriotism, from habitual industry, to the more and more effective expression of a deepening resentment.

This is a psychological question, a matter of mental states. Feats of legal subtlety are inopportune, arithmetical exploits still more so. To emerge with the sum of 4s. 6-1/2d. as a minimum, by calculating on the basis of the mine's present earnings, from a conference which the miners and everybody else imagined was to give a minimum of 5s., may be clever, but it is certainly not politic in the present stage of Labour feeling. To stamp violently upon obscure newspapers nobody had heard of before and send a printer to prison, and to give thereby a flaming advertisement to the possible use of soldiers in civil conflicts and set every barrack-room talking, may be permissible, but it is certainly very ill-advised. The distrust deepens.

The real task before a governing class that means to go on governing is not just at present to get the better of an argument or the best of a bargain, but to lay hold of the imaginations of this drifting, sullen and suspicious multitude, which is the working body of the country. What we prosperous people, who have nearly all the good things of life and most of the opportunity, have to do now is to justify ourselves. We have to show that we are indeed responsible and serviceable, willing to give ourselves, and to give ourselves generously for what we have and what we have had. We have to meet the challenge of this distrust.

The slack days for rulers and owners are over. If there are still to be rulers and owners and managing and governing people, then in the face of the new masses, sensitive, intelligent, critical, irritable, as no common people have ever been before, these rulers and owners must be prepared to make themselves and display themselves wise, capable and heroic—beyond any aristocratic precedent. The alternative, if it is an alternative, is resignation—to the Social Democracy.

And it is just because we are all beginning to realise the immense need for this heroic quality in those who rule and are rich and powerful, as the response and corrective to these distrusts and jealousies that are threatening to disintegrate our social order, that we have all followed the details of this great catastrophe in the Atlantic with such intense solicitude. It was one of those accidents that happen with a precision of time and circumstance that outdoes art; not an incident in it all that was not supremely typical. It was the penetrating comment of chance upon our entire social situation. Beneath a surface of magnificent efficiency was—slap-dash. The third-class passengers had placed themselves on board with an infinite confidence in the care that was to be taken of them, and they went down, and most of their women and children went down with the cry of those who find themselves cheated out of life.

In the unfolding record of behaviour it is the stewardesses and bandsmen and engineers—persons of the trade-union class—who shine as brightly as any. And by the supreme artistry of Chance it fell to the lot of that tragic and unhappy gentleman, Mr. Bruce Ismay, to be aboard and to be caught by the urgent vacancy in the boat and the snare of the moment. No untried man dare say that he would have behaved better in his place. He escaped.

He thought it natural to escape. His class thinks it was right and proper that he did escape. It is not the man I would criticise, but the manifest absence of any such sense of the supreme dignity of his position as would have sustained him in that crisis. He was a rich man and a ruling man, but in the test he was not a proud man. In the common man's realisation that such is indeed the case with most of those who dominate our world, lies the true cause and danger of our social indiscipline. And the remedy in the first place lies not in social legislation and so forth, but in the consciences of the wealthy. Heroism and a generous devotion to the common good are the only effective answer to distrust. If such dominating people cannot produce these qualities there will have to be an end to them, and the world must turn to some entirely different method of direction.

Sec. 2

The essential trouble in our growing Labour disorder is the profound distrust which has grown up in the minds of the new generation of workers of either the ability or the good faith of the property owning, ruling and directing class. I do not attempt to judge the justice or not of this distrust; I merely point to its existence as one of the striking and essential factors in the contemporary Labour situation.

This distrust is not, perhaps, the proximate cause of the strikes that now follow each other so disconcertingly, but it embitters their spirit, it prevents their settlement, and leads to their renewal. I have tried to suggest that, whatever immediate devices for pacification might be employed, the only way to a better understanding and co-operation, the only escape from a social slide towards the unknown possibilities of Social Democracy, lies in an exaltation of the standard of achievement and of the sense of responsibility in the possessing and governing classes. It is not so much "Wake up, England!" that I would say as "Wake up, gentlemen!"—for the new generation of the workers is beyond all question quite alarmingly awake and critical and angry. And they have not merely to wake up, they have to wake up visibly and ostentatiously if those old class reliances on which our system is based are to be preserved and restored.

We need before anything else a restoration of class confidence. It is a time when class should speak with class very frankly.

There is too much facile misrepresentation, too ready a disposition on either side to accept caricatures as portraits and charges as facts. However tacit our understandings were in the past, with this new kind of Labour, this young, restive Labour of the twentieth century, which can read, discuss and combine, we need something in the nature of a social contract. And it is when one comes to consider by what possible means these suspicious third-class passengers in our leaking and imperilled social liner can be brought into generous co-operation with the second and the first that one discovers just how lamentably out of date and out of order our political institutions, which should supply the means for just this inter-class discussion, have become. Between the busy and preoccupied owning and employing class on the one hand, and the distressed, uneasy masses on the other, intervenes the professional politician, not as a mediator, but as an obstacle, who must be propitiated before any dealings are possible. Our national politics no longer express the realities of the national life; they are a mere impediment in the speech of the community. With our whole social order in danger, our Legislature is busy over the trivial little affairs of the Welsh Established Church, whose endowment probably is not equal to the fortune of any one of half a dozen *Titanic* passengers or a tithe of the probable loss of another strike among the miners. We have a Legislature almost antiquarian, compiling a museum of Gladstonian legacies rather than governing our world to-day.

Law is the basis of civilisation, but the lawyer is the law's consequence, and, with us at least, the legal profession is the political profession. It delights in false issues and merely technical politics. Steadily with the ascendancy of the House of Commons the barristers have ousted other types of men from political power. The decline of the House of Lords has been the last triumph of the House of Lawyers, and we are governed now to a large extent not so much by the people for the people as by the barristers for the barristers. They set the tone of political life. And since they are the most specialised, the most specifically trained of all the professions, since their training is absolutely antagonistic to the creative impulses of the constructive artist and the controlled experiments of the scientific man, since the business is with evidence and advantages and the skilful use of evidence and advantages, and not with understanding, they are the least statesmanlike of all educated men, and they give our public life a tone as hopelessly discordant with our very great and urgent social needs as one could well imagine. They do not want to deal at all with great and urgent social needs. They play a game, a long and interesting game, with parties as sides, a game that rewards the industrious player with prominence, place, power and great rewards, and the less that game involves the passionate interests of other men, the less it draws them into participation and angry interference, the better for the steady development of the politician's career. A distinguished and active fruitlessness, leaving the world at last as he found it, is the political barrister's ideal career. To achieve that, he must maintain legal and political monopolies, and prevent the invasion of political life by living interests. And so far as he has any views about Labour beyond the margin of his brief, the barrister politician seems to regard getting men back to work on any terms and as soon as possible as the highest good.

And it is with such men that our insurgent modern Labour, with its vaguely apprehended wants, its large occasions and its rapid emotional reactions, comes into contact directly it attempts to adjust itself in the social body. It is one of the main factors in the progressive embitterment of the Labour situation that whatever business is afoot—arbitration, conciliation, inquiry—our contemporary system presents itself to Labour almost invariably in a legal guise. The natural infirmities of humanity rebel against an unimaginative legality of attitude, and the common workaday man has no more love for this great and necessary profession to-day than he had in the time of Jack Cade. Little reasonable things from the lawyers' point of view—the rejection, for example, of certain evidence in the *Titanic* inquiry because it might amount to a charge of manslaughter, the constant interruption and checking of a Labour representative at the same tribunal upon trivial points— irritate quite disproportionately.

Lawyer and working man are antipathetic types, and it is a very grave national misfortune that at this time, when our situation calls aloud for statecraft and a certain greatness of treatment, our public life should be dominated as it has never been dominated before by this most able and illiberal profession.

Now for that great multitude of prosperous people who find themselves at once deeply concerned in our present social and economic crisis, and either helplessly entangled in party organisation or helplessly outside politics, the elimination and cure of this disease of statecraft, the professional politician, has become a very urgent matter. To destroy him, to get him back to his law courts and keep him there, it is necessary to destroy the machinery of the party system that sustains him, and to adopt some electoral method that will no longer put the independent representative man at a hopeless disadvantage against the party nominee. Such a method is to be found in proportional representation with large constituencies, and to that we must look for our ultimate liberation from our present masters, these politician barristers. But the Labour situation cannot wait for this millennial release, and for the current issue it seems to me patent that every reasonable prosperous man will, even at the cost to himself of some trouble and hard thinking, do his best to keep as much of this great and acute controversy as he possibly can out of the lawyer's and mere politician's hands and in his own. Leave Labour to the lawyers, and we shall go very deeply into trouble indeed before this business is over. They will score their points, they will achieve remarkable agreements full of the possibility of subsequent surprises, they will make reputations, and do everything Heaven and their professional training have made them to do, and they will exasperate and exasperate!

Lawyers made the first French Revolution, and now, on a different side, they may yet bring about an English one. These men below there are still, as a class, wonderfully patient and reasonable, quite prepared to take orders and recognise superior knowledge, wisdom and nobility. They make the most reasonable claims for a tolerable life, for certain assurances and certain latitudes. Implicit rather than expressed is their demand for wisdom and right direction from those to whom the great surplus and freedom of civilisation are given. It is an entirely reasonable demand if man is indeed a social animal. But we have got to treat them fairly and openly. This patience and reasonableness and willingness for leadership is not limitless. It is no good scoring our mean little points, for example, and accusing them of breach of contract and all sorts of theoretical wrongs because they won't abide by agreements to accept a certain scale of wages when the purchasing power of money has declined. When they made that agreement they did not think of that possibility. When they said a pound they thought of what was then a poundsworth of living. The Mint has since been increasing its annual output of gold coins to two or three times the former amount, and we have, as it were, debased the coinage with extraordinary quantities of gold. But we who know and own did nothing to adjust that; we did not tell the working man of that; we have let him find it out slowly and indirectly at the grocer's shop. That may be permissible from the lawyer's point of view, but it certainly isn't from the gentleman's, and it is only by the plea that its inequalities give society a gentleman that our present social system can claim to endure.

I would like to accentuate that, because if we are to emerge again from these acute social dissensions a reunited and powerful people, there has to be a change of tone, a new generosity on the part of those who deal with Labour speeches, Labour literature, Labour representatives, and Labour claims. Labour is necessarily at an enormous disadvantage in discussion; in spite of a tremendous inferiority in training and education it is trying to tell the community its conception of its needs and purposes. It is not only young as a participator in the discussion of affairs; it is actually young. The average working man is not half the age of the ripe politicians and judges and lawyers and wealthy organisers who trip him up legally, accuse him of bad faith, mark his every inconsistency. It isn't becoming so to use our forensic advantages. It isn't—if that has no appeal to you—wise.

The thing our society has most to fear from Labour is not organised resistance, not victorious strikes and raised conditions, but the black resentment that follows defeat. Meet Labour half-way, and you will find a new co-operation in government; stick to your legal rights, draw the net of repressive legislation tighter, then you will presently have to deal with Labour enraged. If the anger burns free, that means revolution; if you crush out the hope of that, then sabotage and a sullen general sympathy for anarchistic crime.

Sec. 3

In the preceding pages I have discussed certain aspects of the present Labour situation. I have tried to show the profound significance in this discussion of the distrust which has grown up in the minds of the workers, and how this distrust is being exacerbated by our entirely too forensic method of treating their claims. I want now to point out a still more powerful set of influences which is steadily turning our Labour struggles from mere attempts to adjust hours and wages into movements that are gravely and deliberately revolutionary.

This is the obvious devotion of a large and growing proportion of the time and energy of the owning and ruling classes to pleasure and excitement, and the way in which this spectacle of amusement and adventure is now being brought before the eyes and into the imagination of the working man.

The intimate psychology of work is a thing altogether too little considered and discussed. One asks: "What keeps a workman working properly at his work?" and it seems a sufficient answer to say that it is the need of getting a living. But that is not the complete answer. Work must to some extent interest; if it bores, no power on earth will keep a man doing it properly. And the tendency of modern industrialism has been to subdivide processes and make work more boring and irksome. Also the workman must be satisfied with the living he is getting, and the tendency of newspaper, theatre, cinematograph show and so forth is to fill his mind with ideas of ways of living infinitely more agreeable and interesting than his own. Habit also counts very largely in the regular return of the man to his job, and the fluctuations of employment, the failure of the employing class to provide any alternative to idleness during slack time, break that habit of industry. And then, last but not least, there is self-respect. Men and women are capable of wonders of self-discipline and effort if they feel that theirs is a meritorious service, if they imagine the thing they are doing is the thing they ought to do. A miner will cut coal in a different spirit and with a fading zest if he knows his day's output is to be burnt to waste secretly by a lunatic. Man is a social animal; few men are naturally social rebels, and most will toil very cheerfully in subordination if they feel that the collective end is a fine thing and a great thing.

Now, this force of self-respect is much more acutely present in the mind of the modern worker than it was in the thought of his fathers. He is intellectually more active than his predecessors, his imagination is relatively stimulated, he asks wide questions. The worker of a former generation took himself for granted; it is a new phase when the toilers begin to ask, not one man here or there, but in masses, in battalions, in trades: "Why, then, are *we* toilers, and for what is it that we toil?"

What answer do we give them?

I ask the reader to put himself in the place of a good workman, a young, capable miner, let us say, in search of an answer to that question. He is, we will suppose, temporarily unemployed through the production of a glut of coal, and he goes about the world trying to see the fine and noble collective achievements that justify the devotion of his whole life to humble toil. I ask the reader: What have we got to show that man? What are we doing up in the light and air that justifies our demand that he should go on hewing in narrow seams and cramped corners until he can hew no more? Where is he to be taken to see these crowning fruits of our release from toil? Shall we take him to the House of Commons to note which of the barristers is making most headway over Welsh Disestablishment, or shall we take him to the *Titanic* inquiry to hear the latest about those fifty-five third-class children (out of eighty-three) who were drowned? Shall we give him an hour or so among the portraits at the Royal Academy, or shall we make an enthusiastic tour of London sculpture and architecture and saturate his soul with the beauty he makes possible? The new Automobile Club, for example. "Without you and your subordination we could not have had that." Or suppose we took him the round of the West-End clubs and restaurants and made him estimate how many dinners London can produce at a pinch at the price of his local daily minimum, say, and upward; or borrow an aeroplane at Hendon and soar about counting all the golfers in the Home Counties on any week-day afternoon. "You suffer at the roots of things, far below there, but see all this nobility and splendour, these sweet, bright flowers to which your rootlet life contributes." Or we might spend a pleasant morning trying to get a passable woman's hat for the price of his average weekly wages in some West-End shop . . .

But indeed this thing is actually happening. The older type of miner was illiterate, incurious; he read nothing, lived his own life, and if he had any intellectual and spiritual urgencies in him beyond eating and drinking and dog-fighting, the local little Bethel shunted them away from any effective social criticism. The new generation of miners is on an altogether different basis. It is at once less brutal and less spiritual; it is alert, informed, sceptical, and the Press, with photographic illustrations, the cinema, and a score of collateral forces, are giving it precisely that spectacular view of luxury, amusement, aimlessness and excitement, taunting it with just that suggestion that it is for that, and that alone, that the worker's back aches and his muscles strain. Whatever gravity and spaciousness of aim there may be in our prosperous social life does not appear to him. He sees, and he sees all the more brightly because he is looking at it out of toil and darkness, the glitter, the delight for delight's sake, the show and the pride and the folly. Cannot you understand how it is that these young men down there in the hot and dangerous and toilsome and inglorious places of life are beginning to cry out, "We are being made fools of," and to fling down their tools, and cannot you see how futile it is to dream that Mr. Asquith or some other politician by some trick of a Conciliation Act or some claptrap of Compulsory Arbitration, or that any belated suppression of discussion and strike organisations by the law, will avert this gathering storm? The Spectacle of Pleasure, the parade of clothes, estates, motor-cars, luxury and vanity in the sight of the workers is the culminating irritant of Labour. So long as that goes on, this sombre resolve to which we are all awakening, this sombre resolve rather to wreck the whole fabric than to continue patiently at work, will gather strength. It does not matter that such a resolve is hopeless and unseasonable; we are dealing here with the profounder impulses that underlie reason. Crush this resentment; it will recur with accumulated strength.

It does not matter that there is no plan in existence for any kind of social order that could be set up in the place of our present system; no plan, that is, that will endure half an hour's practical criticism. The cardinal fact before us is that the workers do not intend to stand things as they are, and that no clever arguments, no expert handling of legal points, no ingenious appearances of concession, will stay that progressive embitterment.

But I think I have said enough to express and perhaps convey my conviction that our present Labour troubles are unprecedented, and that they mean the end of an epoch. The supply of good-tempered, cheap labour—upon which the fabric of our contemporary ease and comfort is erected—is giving out.

The spread of information and the means of presentation in every class and the increase of luxury and self-indulgence in the prosperous classes are the chief cause of that. In the place of that old convenient labour comes a new sort of labour, reluctant, resentful, critical, and suspicious. The replacement has already gone so far that I am certain that attempts to baffle and coerce the workers back to their old conditions must inevitably lead to a series of increasingly destructive outbreaks, to stresses and disorder culminating in revolution. It is useless to dream of going on now for much longer upon the old lines; our civilisation, if it is not to enter upon a phase of conflict and decay, must begin to adapt itself to the new conditions of which the first and foremost is that the wages-earning labouring class as a distinctive class, consenting to a distinctive treatment and accepting life at a disadvantage is going to disappear. Whether we do it soon as the result of our reflections upon the present situation, or whether we do it presently through the impoverishment that must necessarily result from a lengthening period of industrial unrest, there can be little doubt that we are going to curtail very considerably the current extravagance of the spending and directing classes upon food, clothing, display, and all the luxuries of life. The phase of affluence is over. And unless we are to be the mere passive spectators of an unprecedented reduction of our lives, all of us who have leisure and opportunity have to set ourselves very strenuously to the problem not of reconciling ourselves to the wage-earners, for that possibility is over, but of establishing a new method of co-operation with those who seem to be definitely decided not to remain wage-earners for very much longer. We have, as sensible people, to realise that the old arrangement which has given us of the fortunate minority so much leisure, luxury, and abundance, advantages we have as a class put to so vulgar and unprofitable a use, is breaking down, and that we have to discover a new, more equable way of getting the world's work done.

Certain things stand out pretty obviously. It is clear that in the times ahead of us there must be more economy in giving trouble and causing work, a greater willingness to do work for ourselves, a great economy of labour through machinery and skilful management. So much is unavoidable if we are to meet these enlarged requirements upon which the insurgent worker insists. If we, who have at least some experience of affairs, who own property, manage businesses, and discuss and influence public organisation, if we are not prepared to undertake this work of discipline and adaptation for ourselves, then a time is not far distant when insurrectionary leaders, calling themselves Socialists or Syndicalists, or what not, men with none of our experience, little of our knowledge, and far less hope of success, will take that task out of our hands.[1]

We have, in fact, to "pull ourselves together," as the phrase goes, and make an end to all this slack, extravagant living, this spectacle of pleasure, that has been spreading and intensifying in every civilised community for the last three or four decades. What is happening to Labour is indeed, from one point of view, little else than the correlative of what has been happening to the more prosperous classes in the community. They have lost their self-discipline, their gravity, their sense of high aims, they have become the victims of their advantages and Labour, grown observant and intelligent, has discovered itself and declares itself no longer subordinate. Just what powers of recovery and reconstruction our system may have under these circumstances the decades immediately before us will show.

Sec. 4

Let us try to anticipate some of the social developments that are likely to spring out of the present Labour situation.

It is quite conceivable, of course, that what lies before us is not development but disorder. Given sufficient suspicion on one side and sufficient obstinacy and trickery on the other, it may be impossible to restore social peace in any form, and industrialism may degenerate into a wasteful and incurable conflict. But that distressful possibility is the worst and perhaps the least probable of many. It is much more acceptable to suppose that our social order will be able to adjust itself to the new outlook and temper and quality of the labour stratum that elementary education, a Press very cheap and free, and a period of great general affluence have brought about.

---

1   Larkinism comes to endorse me since this was written.

One almost inevitable feature of any such adaptation will be a changed spirit in the general body of society. We have come to a serious condition of our affairs, and we shall not get them into order again without a thorough bracing-up of ourselves in the process. There can be no doubt that for a large portion of our comfortable classes existence has been altogether too easy for the last lifetime or so. The great bulk of the world's work has been done out of their sight and knowledge; it has seemed unnecessary to trouble much about the general conduct of things, unnecessary, as they say, to "take life too seriously." This has not made them so much vicious as slack, lazy, and over-confident; there has been an elaboration of trivial things and a neglect of troublesome and important things. The one grave shock of the Boer War has long been explained and sentimentalised away. But it will not be so easy to explain away a dislocated train service and an empty coal cellar as it was to get a favourable interpretation upon some demonstration of national incompetence half the world away.

It is indeed no disaster, but a matter for sincere congratulation that the British prosperous and the British successful, to whom warning after warning has rained in vain from the days of Ruskin, Carlyle, Matthew Arnold, should be called to account at last in their own household. They will grumble, they will be very angry, but in the end, I believe, they will rise to the opportunities of their inconvenience. They will shake off their intellectual lassitude, take over again the public and private affairs they have come to leave so largely in the hands of the political barrister and the family solicitor, become keen and critical and constructive, bring themselves up to date again.

That is not, of course, inevitable, but I am taking now the more hopeful view.

And then? What sort of working arrangements are our renascent owning and directing classes likely to make with the new labouring class? How is the work going to be done in the harder, cleaner, more equalised, and better managed State that, in one's hopeful mood, one sees ahead of us?

Now after the experiences of the past twelve months it is obvious that the days when most of the directed and inferior work of the community will be done by intermittently employed and impecunious wage-earners is drawing to an end. A large part of the task of reconstruction ahead of us will consist in the working out of schemes for a more permanent type of employment and for a direct participation of the worker in the pride, profits, and direction of the work. Such schemes admit of wide variations between a mere bonus system, a periodic tipping of the employees to prevent their striking and a real and honest co-partnery.

In the latter case a great enterprise, forced to consider its "hands" as being also in their degree "heads," would include a department of technical and business instruction for its own people. From such ideas one passes very readily to the conception of guild-managed businesses in which the factor of capital would no longer stand out as an element distinct from and contrasted with the proprietorship of the workers. One sees the worker as an active and intelligent helper during the great portion of his participation, and as an annuitant and perhaps, if he has devised economies and improvements, a receiver of royalties during his declining years.

And concurrently with the systematic reconstruction of a large portion of our industries upon these lines there will have to be a vigorous development of the attempts that are already being made, in garden cities, garden suburbs, and the like, to re-house the mass of our population in a more civilised and more agreeable manner. Probably that is not going to pay from the point of view of the money-making business man, but we prosperous people have to understand that there are things more important and more profitable than money-making, and we have to tax ourselves not merely in money, but in time, care, and effort in the matter. Half the money that goes out of England to Switzerland and the Riviera ought to go to the extremely amusing business of clearing up ugly corners and building jolly and convenient workmen's cottages— even if we do it at a loss. It is part of our discharge for the leisure and advantages the system has given us, part of that just give and take, over and above the solicitor's and bargain-hunter's and money-lender's conception of justice, upon which social order ultimately rests. We have to do it not in a mood of patronage, but in a mood of attentive solicitude. If not on high grounds, then on low grounds our class has to set to work and make those other classes more interested and comfortable and contented. It is what we are for. It is quite impossible for workmen and poor people generally to plan estates and arrange their own homes; they are entirely at the mercy of the wealthy in this matter. There is not a slum, not a hovel, not an eyesore upon the English landscape for which some well-off owner is not ultimately to be blamed or excused, and the less we leave of such things about the better for us in that day of reckoning between class and class which now draws so near.

It is as plain now as the way from Calais to Paris that if the owning class does not attend to these amenities the mass of the people, doing its best to manage the thing through the politicians, presently will. They may make a frightful mess of it, but that will never bring back things again into the hands that hold them and neglect them. Their time will have passed for ever.

But these are the mere opening requirements of this hope of mine of a quickened social consciousness among the more fortunate and leisurely section of the community I believe that much profounder changes in the conditions of labour are possible than those I have suggested I am beginning to suspect that scarcely any of our preconceptions about the way work must be done, about the hours of work and the habits of work, will stand an exhaustive scientific analysis. It is at least conceivable that we could get much of the work that has to be done to keep our community going in far more toil-saving and life-saving ways than we follow at the present time. So far scientific men have done scarcely anything to estimate under what conditions a man works best, does most work, works more happily. Suppose it turns out to be the case that a man always following one occupation throughout his lifetime, working regularly day after day for so many hours, as most wage-earners do at the present time, does not do nearly so much or nearly so well as he would do if he followed first one occupation and then another, or if he worked as hard as he possibly could for a definite period and then took holiday? I suspect very strongly, indeed I am convinced, that in certain occupations, teaching, for example, or surgery, a man begins by working clumsily and awkwardly, that his interest and skill rise rapidly, that if he is really well suited in his profession he may presently become intensely interested and capable of enormous quantities of his very best work, and that then his interest and vigour rapidly decline I am disposed to believe that this is true of most occupations, of coal-mining or engineering, or brick-laying or cotton-spinning. The thing has never been properly thought about. Our civilisation has grown up in a haphazard kind of way, and it has been convenient to specialise workers and employ them piecemeal. But if it is true that in respect of any occupation a man has his period of maximum efficiency, then we open up a whole world of new social possibilities. What we really want from a man for our social welfare in that case is not regular continuing work, but a few strenuous years of high-pressure service. We can as a community afford to keep him longer at education and training before he begins, and we can release him with a pension while he is still full of life and the capacity for enjoying freedom. But obviously this is impossible upon any basis of weekly wages and intermittent employment; we must be handling affairs in some much more comprehensive way than that before we can take and deal with the working life of a man as one complete whole.

That is one possibility that is frequently in my thoughts about the present labour crisis. There is another, and that is the great desirability of every class in the community having a practical knowledge of what labour means. There is a vast amount of work which either is now or is likely to be in the future within the domain of the public administration—road-making, mining, railway work, post-office and telephone work, medical work, nursing, a considerable amount of building for example. Why should we employ people to do the bulk of these things at all? Why should we not as a community do them ourselves? Why, in other words, should we not have a labour conscription and take a year or so of service from everyone in the community, high or low? I believe this would be of enormous moral benefit to our strained and relaxed community. I believe that in making labour a part of everyone's life and the whole of nobody's life lies the ultimate solution of these industrial difficulties.

Sec. 5

It is almost a national boast that we "muddle through" our troubles, and I suppose it is true and to our credit that by virtue of a certain kindliness of temper, a humorous willingness to make the best of things, and an entirely amiable forgetfulness, we do come out of pressures and extremities that would smash a harder, more brittle people only a little chipped and damaged. And it is quite conceivable that our country will, in a measure, survive the enormous stresses of labour adjustment that are now upon us, even if it never rises to any heroic struggle against these difficulties. But it may survive as a lesser country, as an impoverished and second-rate country. It will certainly do no more than that, if in any part of the world there is to be found a people capable of taking up this gigantic question in a greater spirit. Perhaps there is no such people, and the conflicts and muddles before us will be world-wide. Or suppose that it falls to our country in some strange way to develop a new courage and enterprise, and to be the first to go forward into this new phase of civilisation I foresee, from which a distinctive labouring class, a class that is of expropriated wage-earners, will have almost completely disappeared.

Now hitherto the utmost that any State, overtaken by social and economic stresses, has ever achieved in the way of adapting itself to them has been no more than patching.

Individuals and groups and trades have found themselves in imperfectly apprehended and difficult times, and have reluctantly altered their ways and ideas piecemeal under pressure. Sometimes they have succeeded in rubbing along upon the new lines, and sometimes the struggle has submerged them, but no community has ever yet had the will and the imagination to recast and radically alter its social methods as a whole. The idea of such a reconstruction has never been absent from human thought since the days of Plato, and it has been enormously reinforced by the spreading material successes of modern science, successes due always to the substitution of analysis and reasoned planning for trial and the rule of thumb. But it has never yet been so believed in and understood as to render any real endeavour to reconstruct possible. The experiment has always been altogether too gigantic for the available faith behind it, and there have been against it the fear of presumption, the interests of all advantaged people, and the natural sloth of humanity. We do but emerge now from a period of deliberate happy-go-lucky and the influence of Herbert Spencer, who came near raising public shiftlessness to the dignity of a national philosophy. Everything would adjust itself—if only it was left alone.

Yet some things there are that cannot be done by small adjustments, such as leaping chasms or killing an ox or escaping from the roof of a burning house. You have to decide upon a certain course on such occasions and maintain a continuous movement. If you wait on the burning house until you scorch and then turn round a bit or move away a yard or so, or if on the verge of a chasm you move a little in the way in which you wish to go, disaster will punish your moderation. And it seems to me that the establishment of the world's work upon a new basis—and that and no less is what this Labour Unrest demands for its pacification—is just one of those large alterations which will never be made by the collectively unconscious activities of men, by competitions and survival and the higgling of the market. Humanity is rebelling against the continuing existence of a labour class as such, and I can see no way by which our present method of weekly wages employment can change by imperceptible increments into a method of salary and pension—for it is quite evident that only by reaching that shall we reach the end of these present discontents. The change has to be made on a comprehensive scale or not at all. We need nothing less than a national plan of social development if the thing is to be achieved.

Now that, I admit, is, as the Americans say, a large proposition. But we are living in a time of more and more comprehensive plans, and the mere fact that no scheme so extensive has ever been tried before is no reason at all why we should not consider one. We think nowadays quite serenely of schemes for the treatment of the nation's health as one whole, where our fathers considered illness as a blend of accident with special providences; we have systematised the community's water supply, education, and all sorts of once chaotic services, and Germany and our own infinite higgledy-piggledy discomfort and ugliness have brought home to us at last even the possibility of planning the extension of our towns and cities. It is only another step upward in scale to plan out new, more tolerable conditions of employment for every sort of worker and to organise the transition from our present disorder.

The essential difficulty between the employer and the statesman in the consideration of this problem is the difference in the scope of their view. The employer's concern with the man who does his work is day-long or week-long; the statesman's is life-long. The conditions of private enterprise and modern competition oblige the employer to think only of the worker as a hand, who appears and does his work and draws his wages and vanishes again. Only such strikes as we have had during the past year will rouse him from that attitude of mind. The statesman at the other extremity has to consider the worker as a being with a beginning, a middle, an end—and offspring. He can consider all these possibilities of deferring employment and making the toil of one period of life provide for the leisure and freedom of another, which are necessarily entirely out of the purview of an employer pure and simple. And I find it hard to see how we can reconcile the intermittency of competitive employment with the unremitting demands of a civilised life except by the intervention of the State or of some public organisation capable of taking very wide views between the business organiser on the one hand and the subordinate worker on the other. On the one hand we need some broader handling of business than is possible in the private adventure of the solitary proprietor or the single company, and on the other some more completely organised development of the collective bargain. We have to bring the directive intelligence of a concern into an organic relation with the conception of the national output as a whole, and either through a trade union or a guild, or some expansion of a trade union, we have to arrange a secure, continuous income for the worker, to be received not directly as wages from an employer but intermediately through the organisation. We need a census of our national production, a more exhaustive estimate of our resources, and an entirely more scientific knowledge of the conditions of maximum labour efficiency. One turns to the State . . . And it is at this point that the heart of the patriotic Englishman sinks, because it is our national misfortune that all the accidents of public life have conspired to retard the development of just that body of knowledge, just that scientific breadth of imagination which is becoming a vital necessity for the welfare of a modern civilised community.

We are caught short of scientific men just as in the event of a war with Germany we shall almost certainly be caught short of scientific sailors and soldiers. You cannot make that sort of thing to order in a crisis. Scientific education—and more particularly the scientific education of our owning and responsible classes—has been crippled by the bitter jealousy of the classical teachers who dominate our universities, by the fear and hatred of the Established Church, which still so largely controls our upper-class schools, and by the entire lack of understanding and support on the part of those able barristers and financiers who rule our political life. Science has been left more and more to men of modest origin and narrow outlook, and now we are beginning to pay in internal dissensions, and presently we may have to pay in national humiliation for this almost organised rejection of stimulus and power.

But however thwarted and crippled our public imagination may be, we have still got to do the best we can with this situation; we have to take as comprehensive views as we can, and to attempt as comprehensive a method of handling as our party-ridden State permits. In theory I am a Socialist, and were I theorising about some nation in the air I would say that all the great productive activities and all the means of communication should be national concerns and be run as national services. But our State is peculiarly incapable of such functions; at the present time it cannot even produce a postage stamp that will stick; and the type of official it would probably evolve for industrial organisation, slowly but unsurely, would be a maddening combination of the district visitor and the boy clerk. It is to the independent people of some leisure and resource in the community that one has at last to appeal for such large efforts and understandings as our present situation demands. In the default of our public services, there opens an immense opportunity for voluntary effort. Deference to our official leaders is absurd; it is a time when men must, as the phrase goes, "come forward."

We want a National Plan for our social and economic development which everyone may understand and which will serve as a unifying basis for all our social and political activities. Such a plan is not to be flung out hastily by an irresponsible writer. It can only come into existence as the outcome of a wide movement of inquiry and discussion. My business in these pages has been not prescription but diagnosis. I hold it to be the clear duty of every intelligent person in the country to do his utmost to learn about these questions of economic and social organisation and to work them out to conclusions and a purpose. We have come to a phase in our affairs when the only alternative to a great, deliberate renascence of will and understanding is national disorder and decay.

I have attempted a diagnosis of this aspect of our national situation. I have pointed out that nearly all the social forces of our time seem to be in conspiracy to bring about the disappearance of a labour class as such and the rearrangement of our work and industry upon a new basis. That rearrangement demands an unprecedented national effort and the production of an adequate National Plan. Failing that, we seem doomed to a period of chronic social conflict and possibly even of frankly revolutionary outbreaks that may destroy us altogether or leave us only a dwarfed and enfeebled nation . . .

And before we can develop that National Plan and the effective realisation of such a plan that is needed to save us from that fate, two things stand immediately before us to be done, unavoidable preliminaries to that more comprehensive work. The first of these is the restoration of representative government, and the second a renascence of our public thought about political and social things.

As I have already suggested, a main factor in our present national inability to deal with this profound and increasing social disturbance is the entirely unrepresentative and unbusinesslike nature of our parliamentary government.

It is to a quite extraordinary extent a thing apart from our national life. It becomes more and more so. To go into the House of Commons is to go aside out of the general stream of the community's vitality into a corner where little is learnt and much is concocted, into a specialised Assembly which is at once inattentive to and monstrously influential in our affairs. There was a period when the debates in the House of Commons were an integral, almost a dominant, part of our national thought, when its speeches were read over in tens of thousands of homes, and a large and sympathetic public followed the details of every contested issue. Now a newspaper that dared to fill its columns mainly with parliamentary debates, with a full report of the trivialities the academic points, the little familiar jokes, and entirely insincere pleadings which occupy that gathering would court bankruptcy.

This diminishing actuality of our political life is a matter of almost universal comment to-day. But it is extraordinary how much of that comment is made in a tone of hopeless dissatisfaction, how rarely it is associated with any will to change a state of affairs that so largely stultifies our national purpose. And yet the causes of our present political ineptitude are fairly manifest, and a radical and effective reconstruction is well within the wit of man.

All causes and all effects in our complex modern State are complex, but in this particular matter there can be little doubt that the key to the difficulty lies in the crudity and simplicity of our method of election, a method which reduces our apparent free choice of rulers to a ridiculous selection between undesirable alternatives, and hands our whole public life over to the specialised manipulator. Our House of Commons could scarcely misrepresent us more if it was appointed haphazard by the Lord Chamberlain or selected by lot from among the inhabitants of Netting Hill. Election of representatives in one-member local constituencies by a single vote gives a citizen practically no choice beyond the candidates appointed by the two great party organisations in the State. It is an electoral system that forbids absolutely any vote splitting or any indication of shades of opinion. The presence of more than two candidates introduces an altogether unmanageable complication, and the voter is at once reduced to voting not to secure the return of the perhaps less hopeful candidate he likes, but to ensure the rejection of the candidate he most dislikes. So the nimble wire-puller slips in. In Great Britain we do not have Elections any more; we have Rejections. What really happens at a general election is that the party organisations—obscure and secretive conclaves with entirely mysterious funds—appoint about 1,200 men to be our rulers, and all that we, we so-called self-governing people, are permitted to do is, in a muddled, angry way, to strike off the names of about half of these selected gentlemen.

Take almost any member of the present Government and consider his case. You may credit him with a lifelong industrious intention to get there, but ask yourself what is this man's distinction, and for what great thing in our national life does he stand? By the complaisance of our party machinery he was able to present himself to a perplexed constituency as the only possible alternative to Conservatism and Tariff Reform, and so we have him. And so we have most of his colleagues.

Now such a system of representation is surely a system to be destroyed at any cost, because it stifles our national discussion and thwarts our national will. And we can leave no possible method of alteration untried. It is not rational that a great people should be baffled by the mere mechanical degeneration of an electoral method too crudely conceived. There exist alternatives, and to these alternatives we must resort. Since John Stuart Mill first called attention to the importance of the matter there has been a systematic study of the possible working of electoral methods, and it is now fairly proved that in proportional representation, with large constituencies returning each many members, there is to be found a way of escape from this disastrous embarrassment of our public business by the party wire-puller and the party nominee.

I will not dwell upon the particulars of the proportional representation system here. There exists an active society which has organised the education of the public in the details of the proposal. Suffice it that it does give a method by which a voter may vote with confidence for the particular man he prefers, with no fear whatever that his vote will be wasted in the event of that man's chance being hopeless. There is a method by which the order of the voter's subsequent preference is effectively indicated. That is all, but see how completely it modifies the nature of an election. Instead of a hampered choice between two, you have a free choice between many. Such a change means a complete alteration in the quality of public life.

The present immense advantage of the party nominee—which is the root cause, which is almost the sole cause of all our present political ineptitude—would disappear. He would be quite unable to oust any well-known and representative independent candidate who chose to stand against him. There would be an immediate alteration in type in the House of Commons. In the place of these specialists in political getting-on there would be few men who had not already gained some intellectual and moral hold upon the community; they would already be outstanding and distinguished men before they came to the work of government. Great sections of our national life, science, art, literature, education, engineering, manufacture would cease to be under-represented, or misrepresented by the energetic barrister and political specialist, and our Legislature would begin to serve, as we have now such urgent need of its serving, as the means and instrument of that national conference upon the social outlook of which we stand in need.

And it is to the need and nature of that Conference that I would devote myself. I do not mean by the word Conference any gathering of dull and formal and inattentive people in this dusty hall or that, with a jaded audience and intermittently active reporters, such as this word may conjure up to some imaginations. I mean an earnest direction of attention in all parts of the country to this necessity for a studied and elaborated project of conciliation and social co-operation We cannot afford to leave such things to specialised politicians and self-appointed, self-seeking "experts" any longer. A modern community has to think out its problems as a whole and co-operate as a whole in their solution. We have to bring all our national life into this discussion of the National Plan before us, and not simply newspapers and periodicals and books, but pulpit and college and school have to bear their part in it. And in that particular I would appeal to the schools, because there more than anywhere else is the permanent quickening of our national imagination to be achieved.

We want to have our young people filled with a new realisation that History is not over, that nothing is settled, and that the supreme dramatic phase in the story of England has still to come. It was not in the Norman Conquest, not in the flight of King James II, nor the overthrow of Napoleon; it is here and now. It falls to them to be actors not in a reminiscent pageant but a living conflict, and the sooner they are prepared to take their part in that the better our Empire will acquit itself. How absurd is the preoccupation of our schools and colleges with the little provincialisms of our past history before A.D. 1800! "No current politics," whispers the schoolmaster, "no religion—except the coldest formalities *Some parent might object.*" And he pours into our country every year a fresh supply of gentlemanly cricketing youths, gapingly unprepared— unless they have picked up a broad generalisation or so from some surreptitious Socialist pamphlet—for the immense issues they must control, and that are altogether uncontrollable if they fail to control them. The universities do scarcely more for our young men. All this has to be altered, and altered vigorously and soon, if our country is to accomplish its destinies. Our schools and colleges exist for no other purpose than to give our youths a vision of the world and of their duties and possibilities in the world. We can no longer afford to have them the last preserves of an elderly orthodoxy and the last repository of a decaying gift of superseded tongues. They are needed too urgently to make our leaders leader-like and to sustain the active understandings of the race.

And from the labour class itself we are also justified in demanding a far more effectual contribution to the National Conference than it is making at the present time. Mere eloquent apologies for distrust, mere denunciations of Capitalism and appeals for a Socialism as featureless as smoke, are unsatisfactory when one regards them as the entire contribution of the ascendant worker to the discussion of the national future. The labour thinker has to become definite in his demands and clearer upon the give and take that will be necessary before they can be satisfied. He has to realise rather more generously than he has done so far the enormous moral difficulty there is in bringing people who have been prosperous and at an advantage all their lives to the pitch of even contemplating a social reorganisation that may minimise or destroy their precedence. We have all to think, to think hard and think generously, and there is not a man in England to-day, even though his hands are busy at work, whose brain may not be helping in this great task of social rearrangement which lies before us all.

SOCIAL PANACEAS

(June, 1912.)

To have followed the frequent discussions of the Labour Unrest in the Press is to have learnt quite a lot about the methods of popular thought. And among other things I see now much better than I did why patent medicines are so popular. It is clear that as a community we are far too impatient of detail and complexity, we want overmuch to simplify, we clamour for panaceas, we are a collective invitation to quacks.

Our situation is an intricate one, it does not admit of a solution neatly done up in a word or a phrase. Yet so powerful is this wish to simplify that it is difficult to make it clear that one is not oneself a panacea-monger. One writes and people read a little inattentively and more than a little impatiently, until one makes a positive proposal Then they jump. "So *that's* your Remedy!" they say. "How absurdly inadequate!" I was privileged to take part in one such discussion in 1912, and among other things in my diagnosis of the situation I pointed out the extreme mischief done to our public life by the futility of our electoral methods. They make our whole public life forensic and ineffectual, and I pointed out that this evil effect, which vitiates our whole national life, could be largely remedied by an infinitely better voting system known as Proportional Representation. Thereupon the *Westminster Gazette* declared in tones of pity and contempt that it was no Remedy— and dismissed me. It would be as intelligent to charge a doctor who pushed back the crowd about a broken-legged man in the street with wanting to heal the limb by giving the sufferer air.

The task before our community, the task of reorganising labour on a basis broader than that of employment for daily or weekly wages, is one of huge complexity, and it is as entirely reasonable as it is entirely preliminary to clean and modernise to the utmost our representative and legislative machinery.

It is remarkable how dominant is this disposition to get a phrase, a word, a simple recipe, for an undertaking so vast in reality that for all the rest of our lives a large part of the activities of us, forty million people, will be devoted to its partial accomplishment. In the presence of very great issues people become impatient and irritated, as they would not allow themselves to be irritated by far more limited problems. Nobody in his senses expects a panacea for the comparatively simple and trivial business of playing chess. Nobody wants to be told to "rely wholly upon your pawns," or "never, never move your rook"; nobody clamours "give me a third knight and all will be well"; but that is exactly what everybody seems to be doing in our present discussion And as another aspect of the same impatience, I note the disposition to clamour against all sorts of necessary processes in the development of a civilisation. For example, I read over and over again of the failure of representative government, and in nine cases out of ten I find that this amounts to a cry against any sort of representative government. It is perfectly true that our representative institutions do not work well and need a vigorous overhauling, but while I find scarcely any support for such a revision, the air is full of vague dangerous demands for aristocracy, for oligarchy, for autocracy. It is like a man who jumps out of his automobile because he has burst a tyre, refuses a proffered Stepney, and bawls passionately for anything—for a four-wheeler, or a donkey, as long as he can be free from that exploded mechanism. There are evidently quite a considerable number of people in this country who would welcome a tyrant at the present time, a strong, silent, cruel, imprisoning, executing, melodramatic sort of person, who would somehow manage everything while they went on—being silly. I find that form of impatience cropping up everywhere. I hear echoes of Mr. Blatchford's "Wanted, a Man," and we may yet see a General Boulanger prancing in our streets. There never was a more foolish cry. It is not a man we want, but just exactly as many million men as there are in Great Britain at the present time, and it is you, the reader, and I, and the rest of us who must together go on with the perennial task of saving the country by *firstly*, doing our own jobs just as well as ever we can, and *secondly*—and this is really just as important as firstly—doing our utmost to grasp our national purpose, doing our utmost, that is, to develop and carry out our National Plan. It is Everyman who must be the saviour of the State in a modern community; we cannot shift our share in the burthen; and here again, I think, is something that may well be underlined and emphasised. At present our "secondly" is unduly subordinated to our "firstly"; our game is better individually than collectively; we are like a football team that passes badly, and our need is not nearly so much to change the players as to broaden their style. And this brings me, in a spirit entirely antagonistic, up against Mr. Galsworthy's suggestion of an autocratic revolution in the methods of our public schools.

But before I go on to that, let me first notice a still more comprehensive cry that has been heard again and again in this discussion, and that is the alleged failure of education generally. There is never any remedial suggestion made with this particular outcry; it is merely a gust of abuse and insult for schools, and more particularly board schools, carrying with it a half-hearted implication that they should be closed, and then the contribution concludes. Now there is no outcry at the present time more unjust or—except for the "Wanted, a Man" clamour—more foolish. No doubt our educational resources, like most other things, fall far short of perfection, but of all this imperfection the elementary schools are least imperfect; and I would almost go so far as to say that, considering the badness of their material, the huge, clumsy classes they have to deal with, the poorness of their directive administration, their bad pay and uncertain outlook, the elementary teachers of this country are amazingly efficient. And it is not simply that they are good under their existing conditions, but that this service has been made out of nothing whatever in the course of scarcely forty years. An educational system to cover an Empire is not a thing that can be got for the asking, it is not even to be got for the paying; it has to be grown; and in the beginning it is bound to be thin, ragged, forced, crammy, text-bookish, superficial, and all the rest of it. As reasonable to complain that the children born last year were immature. A little army of teachers does not flash into being at the passing of an Education Act. Not even an organisation for training those teachers comes to anything like satisfactory working order for many years, without considering the delays and obstructions that have been caused by the bickerings and bitterness of the various Christian Churches. So that it is not the failure of elementary education we have really to consider, but the continuance and extension of its already almost miraculous results.

And when it comes to the education of the ruling and directing classes, there is kindred, if lesser reason, for tempering zeal with patience. This upper portion of our educational organisation needs urgently to be bettered, but it is not to be bettered by trying to find an archangel who will better it dictatorially. For the good of our souls there are no such beings to relieve us of our collective responsibility. It is clear that appointments in this field need not only far more care and far more insistence upon creative power than has been shown in the past, but for the rest we have to do with the men we have and the schools we have. We cannot have an educational purge, if only because we have not the new men waiting. Here again the need is not impatience, not revolution, but a sustained and penetrating criticism, a steadfast, continuous urgency towards effort and well-planned reconstruction and efficiency.

And as a last example of the present hysterical disposition to scrap things before they have been fairly tried is the outcry against examinations, which has done so much to take the keenness off the edge of school work in the last few years. Because a great number of examiners chosen haphazard turned out to be negligent and incompetent as examiners, because their incapacity created a cynical trade in cramming, a great number of people have come to the conclusion, just as examinations are being improved into efficiency, that all examinations are bad. In particular that excellent method of bringing new blood and new energy into the public services and breaking up official gangs and cliques, the competitive examination system, has been discredited, and the wire-puller and the influential person are back again tampering with a steadily increasing proportion of appointments . . .

But I have written enough of this impatience, which is, as it were, merely the passion for reconstruction losing its head and defeating its own ends. There is no hope for us outside ourselves. No violent changes, no Napoleonic saviours can carry on the task of building the Great State, the civilised State that rises out of our disorders That is for us to do, all of us and each one of us. We have to think clearly, and study and consider and reconsider our ideas about public things to the very utmost of our possibilities. We have to clarify our views and express them and do all we can to stir up thinking and effort in those about us.

I know it would be more agreeable for all of us if we could have some small pill-like remedy for all the troubles of the State, and take it and go on just as we are going now. But, indeed, to say a word for that idea would be a treason. We are the State, and there is no other way to make it better than to give it the service of our lives. Just in the measure of the aggregate of our devotions and the elaborated and criticised sanity of our public proceedings will the world mend.

I gather from a valuable publication called "Secret Remedies," which analyses many popular cures, that this hasty passion for simplicity, for just one thing that will settle the whole trouble, can carry people to a level beyond an undivided trust in something warranted in a bottle. They are ready to put their faith in what amounts to practically nothing in a bottle. And just at present, while a number of excellent people of the middle class think that only a "man" is wanted and all will be well with us, there is a considerable wave of hopefulness among the working class in favour of a weak solution of nothing, which is offered under the attractive label of Syndicalism. So far I have been able to discuss the present labour situation without any use of this empty word, but when one finds it cropping up in every other article on the subject, it becomes advisable to point out what Syndicalism is not. And incidentally it may enable me to make clear what Socialism in the broader sense, constructive Socialism, that is to say, is.

SYNDICALISM OR CITIZENSHIP

"Is a railway porter a railway porter first and a man afterwards, or is he a man first and incidentally a railway porter?"

That is the issue between this tawdrification of trade unionism which is called Syndicalism, and the ideals of that Great State, that great commonweal, towards which the constructive forces in our civilisation tend. Are we to drift on to a disastrous intensification of our present specialisation of labour as labour, or are we to set to work steadfastly upon a vast social reconstruction which will close this widening breach and rescue our community from its present dependence upon the reluctant and presently insurgent toil of a wages-earning proletariat? Regarded as a project of social development, Syndicalism is ridiculous; regarded as an illuminating and unintentionally ironical complement to the implicit theories of our present social order, it is worthy of close attention. The dream of the Syndicalist is an impossible social fragmentation. The transport service is to be a democratic republic, the mines are to be a democratic republic, every great industry is to be a democratic republic within the State; our community is to become a conflict of inter-woven governments of workers, incapable of progressive changes of method or of extension or transmutation of function, the whole being of a man is to lie within his industrial specialisation, and, upon lines of causation not made clear, wages are to go on rising and hours of work are to go on falling . . . There the mind halts, blinded by the too dazzling vistas of an unimaginative millennium And the way to this, one gathers, is by striking—persistent, destructive striking—until it comes about.

Such is Syndicalism, the cheap Labour Panacea, to which the more passionate and less intelligent portion of the younger workers, impatient of the large constructive developments of modern Socialism, drifts steadily. It is the direct and logical reaction to our present economic system, which has counted our workers neither as souls nor as heads, but as hands They are beginning to accept the suggestions of that method. It is the culmination in aggression of that, at first, entirely protective trade unionism which the individual selfishness and collective short-sightedness and State blindness of our owning and directing and ruling classes forced upon the working man. At first trade unionism was essentially defensive; it was the only possible defence of the workers, who were being steadily pressed over the margin of subsistence. It was a nearly involuntary resistance to class debasement. Mr. Vernon Hartshorn has expressed it as that in a recent article. But his paper, if one read it from beginning to end, displayed, compactly and completely, the unavoidable psychological development of the specialised labour case. He began in the mildest tones with those now respectable words, a "guaranteed minimum" of wages, housing, and so forth, and ended with a very clear intimation of an all-labour community.

If anything is certain in this world, it is that the mass of the community will not rest satisfied with these guaranteed minima. All those possible legislative increments in the general standard of living are not going to diminish the labour unrest; they are going to increase it. A starving man may think he wants nothing in the world but bread, but when he has eaten you will find he wants all sorts of things beyond. Mr. Hartshorn assures us that the worker is "not out for a theory." So much the worse for the worker and all of us when, like the mere hand we have made him, he shows himself unable to define or even forecast his ultimate intentions. He will in that case merely clutch. And the obvious immediate next objective of that clutch directly its imagination passes beyond the "guaranteed minima" phase is the industry as a whole.

I do not see how anyone who desires the continuing development of civilisation can regard a trade union as anything but a necessary evil, a pressure-relieving contrivance an arresting and delaying organisation begotten by just that class separation of labour which in the commonweal of the Great State will be altogether destroyed. It leads nowhither; it is a shelter hut on the road. The wider movement of modern civilisation is against class organisation and caste feeling. These are forces antagonistic to progress, continually springing up and endeavouring to stereotype the transitory organisation, and continually being defeated.

Of all the solemn imbecilities one hears, surely the most foolish is this, that we are in "an age of specialisation." The comparative fruitfulness and hopefulness of our social order, in comparison with any other social system, lies in its flat contradiction of that absurdity. Our medical and surgical advances, for example, are almost entirely due to the invasion of medical research by the chemist; our naval development to the supersession of the sailor by the engineer; we sweep away the coachman with the railway, beat the suburban line with the electric tramway, and attack that again with the petrol omnibus, oust brick and stonework in substantial fabrics by steel frames, replace the skilled maker of woodcuts by a photographer, and so on through the whole range of our activities. Change of function, arrest of specialisation by innovations in method and appliance, progress by the infringement of professional boundaries and the defiance of rule: these are the commonplaces of our time. The trained man, the specialised man, is the most unfortunate of men; the world leaves him behind, and he has lost his power of overtaking it. Versatility, alert adaptability, these are our urgent needs. In peace and war alike the unimaginative, uninventive man is a burthen and a retardation, as he never was before in the world's history. The modern community, therefore, that succeeds most rapidly and most completely in converting both its labourers and its leisure class into a population of active, able, unhurried, educated, and physically well-developed people will be inevitably the dominant community in the world. That lies on the face of things about us; a man who cannot see that must be blind to the traffic in our streets.

Syndicalism is not a plan of social development. It is a spirit of conflict. That conflict lies ahead of us, the open war of strikes, or—if the forces of law and order crush that down—then sabotage and that black revolt of the human spirit into crime which we speak of nowadays as anarchism, unless we can discover a broad and promising way from the present condition of things to nothing less than the complete abolition of the labour class.

That, I know, sounds a vast proposal, but this is a gigantic business altogether, and we can do nothing with it unless we are prepared to deal with large ideas. If St. Paul's begins to totter it is no good propping it up with half a dozen walking-sticks, and small palliatives have no legitimate place at all in this discussion. Our generation has to take up this tremendous necessity of a social reconstruction in a great way; its broad lines have to be thought out by thousands of minds, and it is for that reason that I have put the stress upon our need of discussion, of a wide intellectual and moral stimulation of a stirring up in our schools and pulpits, and upon the modernisation and clarification of what should be the deliberative assembly of the nation.

It would be presumptuous to anticipate the National Plan that must emerge from so vast a debate, but certain conclusions I feel in my bones will stand the test of an exhaustive criticism. The first is that a distinction will be drawn between what I would call "interesting work" and what I would call "mere labour." The two things, I admit, pass by insensible gradations into one another, but while on the one hand such work as being a master gardener and growing roses, or a master cabinet maker and making fine pieces, or an artist of almost any sort, or a story writer, or a consulting physician, or a scientific investigator, or a keeper of wild animals, or a forester, or a librarian, or a good printer, or many sorts of engineer, is work that will always find men of a certain temperament enthusiastically glad to do it, if they can only do it for comfortable pay—for such work is in itself *living*—there is, on the other hand, work so irksome and toilsome, such as coal mining, or being a private soldier during a peace, or attending upon lunatics, or stoking, or doing over and over again, almost mechanically, little bits of a modern industrial process, or being a cash desk clerk in a busy shop, that few people would undertake if they could avoid it.

And the whole strength of our collective intelligence will be directed first to reducing the amount of such irksome work by labour-saving machinery, by ingenuity of management, and by the systematic avoidance of giving trouble as a duty, and then to so distributing the residuum of it that it will become the whole life of no class whatever in our population. I have already quoted the idea of Professor William James of a universal conscription for such irksome labour, and while he would have instituted that mainly for its immense moral effect upon the community, I would point out that, combined with a nationalisation of transport, mining, and so forth, it is also a way to a partial solution of this difficulty of "mere toil."

And the mention of a compulsory period of labour service for everyone—a year or so with the pickaxe as well as with the rifle—leads me to another idea that I believe will stand the test of unlimited criticism, and that is a total condemnation of all these eight-hour-a-day, early-closing, guaranteed-weekly-half-holiday notions that are now so prevalent in Liberal circles. Under existing conditions, in our system of private enterprise and competition, these restrictions are no doubt necessary to save a large portion of our population from lives of continuous toil, but, like trade unionism, they are a necessity of our present conditions, and not a way to a better social state. If we rescue ourselves as a community from poverty and discomfort, we must take care not to fling ourselves into something far more infuriating to a normal human being—and that is boredom. The prospect of a carefully inspected sanitary life, tethered to some light, little, uninteresting daily job, six or eight hours of it, seems to me—and I am sure I write here for most normal, healthy, active people—more awful than hunger and death. It is far more in the quality of the human spirit, and still more what we all in our hearts want the human spirit to be, to fling itself with its utmost power at a job and do it with passion.

For my own part, if I was sentenced to hew a thousand tons of coal, I should want to get at it at once and work furiously at it, with the shortest intervals for rest and refreshment and an occasional night holiday, until I hewed my way out, and if some interfering person with a benevolent air wanted to restrict me to hewing five hundredweight, and no more and no less, each day and every day, I should be strongly disposed to go for that benevolent person with my pick. That is surely what every natural man would want to do, and it is only the clumsy imperfection of our social organisation that will not enable a man to do his stint of labour in a few vigorous years and then come up into the sunlight for good and all.

It is along that line that I feel a large part of our labour reorganisation, over and beyond that conscription, must ultimately go. The community as a whole would, I believe, get far more out of a man if he had such a comparatively brief passion of toil than if he worked, with occasional lapses into unemployment, drearily all his life. But at present, with our existing system of employment, one cannot arrange so comprehensive a treatment of a man's life. There is needed some State or quasi-public organisation which shall stand between the man and the employer, act as his banker and guarantor, and exact his proper price. Then, with his toil over, he would have an adequate pension and be free to do nothing or anything else as he chose. In a Socialistic order of society, where the State would also be largely the employer, such a method would be, of course, far more easily contrived.

The more modern statements of Socialism do not contemplate making the State the sole employer; it is chiefly in transport, mining, fisheries, forestry, the cultivation of the food staples, and the manufacture of a few such articles as bricks and steel, and possibly in housing in what one might call the standardisable industries, that the State is imagined as the direct owner and employer and it is just in these departments that the bulk of the irksome toil is to be found. There remain large regions of more specialised and individualised production that many Socialists nowadays are quite prepared to leave to the freer initiatives of private enterprise. Most of these are occupations involving a greater element of interest, less direction and more co-operation, and it is just here that the success of co-partnery and a sustained life participation becomes possible . . .

This complete civilised system without a specialised, property-less labour class is not simply a possibility, it is necessary; the whole social movement of the time, the stars in their courses, war against the permanence of the present state of affairs. The alternative to this gigantic effort to rearrange our world is not a continuation of muddling along, but social war. The Syndicalist and his folly will be the avenger of lost opportunities. Not a Labour State do we want, nor a Servile State, but a powerful Leisure State of free men.

THE GREAT STATE

For many years now I have taken a part in the discussion of Socialism. During that time Socialism has become a more and more ambiguous term. It has seemed to me desirable to clear up my own ideas of social progress and the public side of my life by restating them, and this I have attempted in this essay.

In order to do so it has been convenient to coin two expressions, and to employ them with a certain defined intention. They are firstly: The Normal Social Life, and secondly: The Great State. Throughout this essay these expressions will be used in accordance with the definitions presently to be given, and the fact that they are so used will be emphasised by the employment of capitals. It will be possible for anyone to argue that what is here defined as the Normal Social Life is not the normal social life, and that the Great State is indeed no state at all. That will be an argument outside the range delimited by these definitions.

Now what is intended by the Normal Social Life here is a type of human association and employment, of extreme prevalence and antiquity, which appears to have been the lot of the enormous majority of human beings as far back as history or tradition or the vestiges of material that supply our conceptions of the neolithic period can carry us. It has never been the lot of all humanity at any time, to-day it is perhaps less predominant than it has ever been, yet even to-day it is probably the lot of the greater moiety of mankind.

Essentially this type of association presents a localised community, a community of which the greater proportion of the individuals are engaged more or less directly in the cultivation of the land. With this there is also associated the grazing or herding over wider or more restricted areas, belonging either collectively or discretely to the community, of sheep, cattle, goats, or swine, and almost always the domestic fowl is commensal with man in this life. The cultivated land at least is usually assigned, temporarily or inalienably, as property to specific individuals, and the individuals are grouped in generally monogamic families of which the father is the head. Essentially the social unit is the Family, and even where, as in Mohammedan countries, there is no legal or customary restriction upon polygamy, monogamy still prevails as the ordinary way of living. Unmarried women are not esteemed, and children are desired. According to the dangers or securities of the region, the nature of the cultivation and the temperament of the people, this community is scattered either widely in separate steadings or drawn together into villages. At one extreme, over large areas of thin pasture this agricultural community may verge on the nomadic; at another, in proximity to consuming markets, it may present the concentration of intensive culture. There may be an adjacent Wild supplying wood, and perhaps controlled by a simple forestry. The law that holds this community together is largely traditional and customary and almost always as its primordial bond there is some sort of temple and some sort of priest. Typically, the temple is devoted to a local god or a localised saint, and its position indicates the central point of the locality, its assembly place and its market. Associated with the agriculture there are usually a few imperfectly specialised tradesmen, a smith, a garment-maker perhaps, a basket-maker or potter, who group about the church or temple. The community may maintain itself in a state of complete isolation, but more usually there are tracks or roads to the centres of adjacent communities, and a certain drift of travel, a certain trade in non-essential things. In the fundamentals of life this normal community is independent and self-subsisting, and where it is not beginning to be modified by the novel forces of the new times it produces its own food and drink, its own clothing, and largely intermarries within its limits.

This in general terms is what is here intended by the phrase the Normal Social Life. It is still the substantial part of the rural life of all Europe and most Asia and Africa, and it has been the life of the great majority of human beings for immemorial years.

It is the root life. It rests upon the soil, and from that soil below and its reaction to the seasons and the moods of the sky overhead have grown most of the traditions, institutions, sentiments, beliefs, superstitions, and fundamental songs and stories of mankind.

But since the very dawn of history at least this Normal Social Life has never been the whole complete life of mankind. Quite apart from the marginal life of the savage hunter, there have been a number of forces and influences within men and women and without, that have produced abnormal and surplus ways of living, supplemental, additional, and even antagonistic to this normal scheme.

And first as to the forces within men and women. Long as it has lasted, almost universal as it has been, the human being has never yet achieved a perfect adaptation to the needs of the Normal Social Life. He has attained nothing of that frictionless fitting to the needs of association one finds in the bee or the ant. Curiosity, deep stirrings to wander, the still more ancient inheritance of the hunter, a recurrent distaste for labour, and resentment against the necessary subjugations of family life have always been a straining force within the agricultural community. The increase of population during periods of prosperity has led at the touch of bad seasons and adversity to the desperate reliefs of war and the invasion of alien localities. And the nomadic and adventurous spirit of man found reliefs and opportunities more particularly along the shores of great rivers and inland seas. Trade and travel began, at first only a trade in adventitious things, in metals and rare objects and luxuries and slaves. With trade came writing and money; the inventions of debt and rent, usury and tribute. History finds already in its beginnings a thin network of trading and slaving flung over the world of the Normal Social Life, a network whose strands are the early roads, whose knots are the first towns and the first courts.

Indeed, all recorded history is in a sense the history of these surplus and supplemental activities of mankind. The Normal Social Life flowed on in its immemorial fashion, using no letters, needing no records, leaving no history. Then, a little minority, bulking disproportionately in the record, come the trader, the sailor, the slave, the landlord and the tax-compeller, the townsman and the king.

All written history is the story of a minority and their peculiar and abnormal affairs. Save in so far as it notes great natural catastrophes and tells of the spreading or retrocession of human life through changes of climate and physical conditions it resolves itself into an account of a series of attacks and modifications and supplements made by excessive and superfluous forces engendered within the community upon the Normal Social Life. The very invention of writing is a part of those modifying developments. The Normal Social Life is essentially illiterate and traditional. The Normal Social Life is as mute as the standing crops; it is as seasonal and cyclic as nature herself, and reaches towards the future only an intimation of continual repetitions.

Now this human over-life may take either beneficent or maleficent or neutral aspects towards the general life of humanity. It may present itself as law and pacification, as a positive addition and superstructure to the Normal Social Life, as roads and markets and cities, as courts and unifying monarchies, as helpful and directing religious organisations, as literature and art and science and philosophy, reflecting back upon the individual in the Normal Social Life from which it arose, a gilding and refreshment of new and wider interests and added pleasures and resources. One may define certain phases in the history of various countries when this was the state of affairs, when a countryside of prosperous communities with a healthy family life and a wide distribution of property, animated by roads and towns and unified by a generally intelligible religious belief, lived in a transitory but satisfactory harmony under a sympathetic government. I take it that this is the condition to which the minds of such original and vigorous reactionary thinkers as Mr. G.K. Chesterton and Mr. Hilaire Belloc for example turn, as being the most desirable state of mankind.

But the general effect of history is to present these phases as phases of exceptional good luck, and to show the surplus forces of humanity as on the whole antagonistic to any such equilibrium with the Normal Social Life. To open the book of history haphazard is, most commonly, to open it at a page where the surplus forces appear to be in more or less destructive conflict with the Normal Social Life. One opens at the depopulation of Italy by the aggressive great estates of the Roman Empire, at the impoverishment of the French peasantry by a too centralised monarchy before the revolution, or at the huge degenerative growth of the great industrial towns of western Europe in the nineteenth century. Or again one opens at destructive wars. One sees these surplus forces over and above the Normal Social Life working towards unstable concentrations of population, to centralisation of government, to migrations and conflicts upon a large scale; one discovers the process developing into a phase of social fragmentation and destruction and then, unless the whole country has been wasted down to its very soil, the Normal Social Life returns as the heath and furze and grass return after the burning of a common. But it never returns in precisely its old form. The surplus forces have always produced some traceable change; the rhythm is a little altered. As between the Gallic peasant before the Roman conquest, the peasant of the Gallic province, the Carlovingian peasant, the French peasant of the thirteenth, the seventeenth, and the twentieth centuries, there is, in spite of a general uniformity of life, of a common atmosphere of cows, hens, dung, toil, ploughing, economy, and domestic intimacy, an effect of accumulating generalising influences and of wider relevancies. And the oscillations of empires and kingdoms, religious movements, wars, invasions, settlements leave upon the mind an impression that the surplus life of mankind, the less-localised life of mankind, that life of mankind which is not directly connected with the soil but which has become more or less detached from and independent of it, is becoming proportionately more important in relation to the Normal Social Life. It is as if a different way of living was emerging from the Normal Social Life and freeing itself from its traditions and limitations.

And this is more particularly the effect upon the mind of a review of the history of the past two hundred years. The little speculative activities of the alchemist and natural philosopher, the little economic experiments of the acquisitive and enterprising landed proprietor, favoured by unprecedented periods of security and freedom, have passed into a new phase of extraordinary productivity. They had added preposterously and continue to add on a gigantic scale and without any evident limits to the continuation of their additions, to the resources of humanity. To the strength of horses and men and slaves has been added the power of machines and the possibility of economies that were once incredible The Normal Social Life has been overshadowed as it has never been overshadowed before by the concentrations and achievements of the surplus life. Vast new possibilities open to the race; the traditional life of mankind, its traditional systems of association, are challenged and threatened; and all the social thought, all the political activity of our time turns in reality upon the conflict of this ancient system whose essentials we have here defined and termed the Normal Social Life with the still vague and formless impulses that seem destined either to involve it and the race in a final destruction or to replace it by some new and probably more elaborate method of human association.

Because there is the following difference between the action of the surplus forces as we see them to-day and as they appeared before the outbreak of physical science and mechanism. Then it seemed clearly necessary that whatever social and political organisation developed, it must needs; rest ultimately on the tiller of the soil, the agricultural holding, and the Normal Social Life. But now even in agriculture huge wholesale methods have appeared. They are declared to be destructive; but it is quite conceivable that they may be made ultimately as recuperative as that small agriculture which has hitherto been the inevitable social basis. If that is so, then the new ways of living may not simply impose themselves in a growing proportion upon the Normal Social Life, but they may even oust it and replace it altogether. Or they may oust it and fail to replace it. In the newer countries the Normal Social Life does not appear to establish itself at all rapidly. No real peasantry appears in either America or Australia; and in the older countries, unless there is the most elaborate legislative and fiscal protection, the peasant population wanes before the large farm, the estate, and overseas production.

Now most of the political and social discussion of the last hundred years may be regarded and rephrased as an attempt to apprehend this defensive struggle of the Normal Social Life against waxing novelty and innovation and to give a direction and guidance to all of us who participate. And it is very largely a matter of temperament and free choice still, just where we shall decide to place ourselves. Let us consider some of the key words of contemporary thought, such as Liberalism, Individualism, Socialism, in the light of this broad generalisation we have made; and then we shall find it easier to explain our intention in employing as a second technicality the phrase of The Great State as an opposite to the Normal Social Life, which we have already defined.

Sec. 2

The Normal Social Life has been defined as one based on agriculture, traditional and essentially unchanging. It has needed no toleration and displayed no toleration for novelty and strangeness. Its beliefs have been on such a nature as to justify and sustain itself, and it has had an intrinsic hostility to any other beliefs. The God of its community has been a jealous god even when he was only a tribal and local god. Only very occasionally in history until the coming of the modern period do we find any human community relaxing from this ancient and more normal state of entire intolerance towards ideas or practices other than its own. When toleration and a receptive attitude towards alien ideas was manifested in the Old World, it was at some trading centre or political centre; new ideas and new religions came by water along the trade routes. And such toleration as there was rarely extended to active teaching and propaganda. Even in liberal Athens the hemlock was in the last resort at the service of the ancient gods and the ancient morals against the sceptical critic.

But with the steady development of innovating forces in human affairs there has actually grown up a cult of receptivity, a readiness for new ideas, a faith in the probable truth of novelties. Liberalism—I do not, of course, refer in any way to the political party which makes this profession—is essentially anti-traditionalism; its tendency is to commit for trial any institution or belief that is brought before it. It is the accuser and antagonist of all the fixed and ancient values and imperatives and prohibitions of the Normal Social Life. And growing up in relation to Liberalism and sustained by it is the great body of scientific knowledge, which professes at least to be absolutely undogmatic and perpetually on its trial and under assay and re-examination.

Now a very large part of the advanced thought of the past century is no more than the confused negation of the broad beliefs and institutions which have been the heritage and social basis of humanity for immemorial years. This is as true of the extremest Individualism as of the extremest Socialism. The former denies that element of legal and customary control which has always subdued the individual to the needs of the Normal Social Life, and the latter that qualified independence of distributed property which is the basis of family autonomy. Both are movements against the ancient life, and nothing is more absurd than the misrepresentation which presents either as a conservative force. They are two divergent schools with a common disposition to reject the old and turn towards the new. The Individualist professes a faith for which he has no rational evidence, that the mere abandonment of traditions and controls must ultimately produce a new and beautiful social order; while the Socialist, with an equal liberalism, regards the outlook with a kind of hopeful dread, and insists upon an elaborate readjustment, a new and untried scheme of social organisation to replace the shattered and weakening Normal Social Life.

Both these movements, and, indeed, all movements that are not movements for the subjugation of innovation and the restoration of tradition, are vague in the prospect they contemplate. They produce no definite forecasts of the quality of the future towards which they so confidently indicate the way. But this is less true of modern socialism than of its antithesis, and it becomes less and less true as socialism, under an enormous torrent of criticism, slowly washes itself clean from the mass of partial statement, hasty misstatement, sheer error and presumption that obscured its first emergence.

But it is well to be very clear upon one point at this stage, and that is, that this present time is not a battle-ground between individualism and socialism; it is a battle-ground between the Normal Social Life on the one hand and a complex of forces on the other which seek a form of replacement and seem partially to find it in these and other doctrines.

Nearly all contemporary thinkers who are not too muddled to be assignable fall into one of three classes, of which the third we shall distinguish is the largest and most various and divergent. It will be convenient to say a little of each of these classes before proceeding to a more particular account of the third. Our analysis will cut across many accepted classifications, but there will be ample justification for this rearrangement. All of them may be dealt with quite justly as accepting the general account of the historical process which is here given.

Then first we must distinguish a series of writers and thinkers which one may call—the word conservative being already politically assigned—the Conservators.

These are people who really do consider the Normal Social Life as the only proper and desirable life for the great mass of humanity, and they are fully prepared to subordinate all exceptional and surplus lives to the moral standards and limitations that arise naturally out of the Normal Social Life. They desire a state in which property is widely distributed, a community of independent families protected by law and an intelligent democratic statecraft from the economic aggressions of large accumulations and linked by a common religion. Their attitude to the forces of change is necessarily a hostile attitude. They are disposed to regard innovations in transit and machinery as undesirable, and even mischievous disturbances of a wholesome equilibrium. They are at least unfriendly to any organisation of scientific research, and scornful of the pretensions of science. Criticisms of the methods of logic, scepticism of the more widely diffused human beliefs, they would classify as insanity. Two able English writers, Mr. G.K. Chesterton and Mr. Belloc, have given the clearest expression to this system of ideals, and stated an admirable case for it. They present a conception of vinous, loudly singing, earthy, toiling, custom-ruled, wholesome, and insanitary men; they are pagan in the sense that their hearts are with the villagers and not with the townsmen, Christian in the spirit of the parish priest. There are no other Conservators so clear-headed and consistent. But their teaching is merely the logical expression of an enormous amount of conservative feeling. Vast multitudes of less lucid minds share their hostility to novelty and research; hate, dread, and are eager to despise science, and glow responsive to the warm, familiar expressions of primordial feelings and immemorial prejudices The rural conservative, the liberal of the allotments and small-holdings type, Mr. Roosevelt—in his Western-farmer, philoprogenitive phase as distinguished from the phase of his more imperialist moments—all present themselves as essentially Conservators as seekers after and preservers of the Normal Social Life.

So, too, do Socialists of the William Morris type. The mind of William Morris was profoundly reactionary He hated the whole trend of later nineteenth-century modernism with the hatred natural to a man of considerable scholarship and intense aesthetic sensibilities. His mind turned, exactly as Mr. Belloc's turns, to the finished and clinched Normal Social Life of western Europe in the middle ages, but, unlike Mr. Belloc, he believed that, given private ownership of land and the ordinary materials of life, there must necessarily be an aggregatory process, usury, expropriation, the development of an exploiting wealthy class. He believed profit was the devil. His "News from Nowhere" pictures a communism that amounted in fact to little more than a system of private ownership of farms and trades without money or any buying and selling, in an atmosphere of geniality, generosity, and mutual helpfulness. Mr. Belloc, with a harder grip upon the realities of life, would have the widest distribution of proprietorship, with an alert democratic government continually legislating against the protean reappearances of usury and accumulation and attacking, breaking up, and redistributing any large unanticipated bodies of wealth that appeared. But both men are equally set towards the Normal Social Life, and equally enemies of the New. The so-called "socialist" land legislation of New Zealand again is a tentative towards the realisation of the same school of ideas: great estates are to be automatically broken up, property is to be kept disseminated; a vast amount of political speaking and writing in America and throughout the world enforces one's impression of the widespread influence of Conservator ideals.

Of course, it is inevitable that phases of prosperity for the Normal Social Life will lead to phases of over-population and scarcity, there will be occasional famines and occasional pestilences and plethoras of vitality leading to the blood-letting of war. I suppose Mr. Chesterton and Mr. Belloc at least have the courage of their opinions, and are prepared to say that such things always have been and always must be; they are part of the jolly rhythms of the human lot under the sun, and are to be taken with the harvest home and love-making and the peaceful ending of honoured lives as an integral part of the unending drama of mankind.

Sec. 3

Now opposed to the Conservators are all those who do not regard contemporary humanity as a final thing nor the Normal

Social Life as the inevitable basis of human continuity. They believe in secular change, in Progress, in a future for our species differing continually more from its past. On the whole, they are prepared for the gradual disentanglement of men from the Normal Social Life altogether, and they look for new ways of living and new methods of human association with a certain adventurous hopefulness.

Now, this second large class does not so much admit of subdivision into two as present a great variety of intermediaries between two extremes. I propose to give distinctive names to these extremes, with the very clear proviso that they are not antagonised, and that the great multitude of this second, anti-conservator class, this liberal, more novel class modern conditions have produced falls between them, and is neither the one nor the other, but partaking in various degrees of both. On the one hand, then, we have that type of mind which is irritated by and distrustful of all collective proceedings which is profoundly distrustful of churches and states, which is expressed essentially by Individualism. The Individualist appears to regard the extensive disintegrations of the Normal Social Life that are going on to-day with an extreme hopefulness. Whatever is ugly or harsh in modern industrialism or in the novel social development of our time he seems to consider as a necessary aspect of a process of selection and survival, whose tendencies are on the whole inevitably satisfactory. The future welfare of man he believes in effect may be trusted to the spontaneous and planless activities of people of goodwill, and nothing but state intervention can effectively impede its attainment. And curiously close to this extreme optimistic school in its moral quality and logical consequences, though contrasting widely in the sinister gloom of its spirit, is the socialism of Karl Marx. He declared the contemporary world to be a great process of financial aggrandisement and general expropriation, of increasing power for the few and of increasing hardship and misery for the many, a process that would go on until at last a crisis of unendurable tension would be reached and the social revolution ensue. The world had, in fact, to be worse before it could hope to be better. He contemplated a continually exacerbated Class War, with a millennium of extraordinary vagueness beyond as the reward of the victorious workers. His common quality with the Individualist lies in his repudiation of and antagonism to plans and arrangements, in his belief in the overriding power of

Law. Their common influence is the discouragement of collective understandings upon the basis of the existing state. Both converge in practice upon *laissez faire*. I would therefore lump them together under the term of Planless Progressives, and I would contrast with them those types which believe supremely in systematised purpose.

The purposeful and systematic types, in common with the Individualist and Marxist, regard the Normal Social Life, for all the many thousands of years behind it, as a phase, and as a phase which is now passing, in human experience; and they are prepared for a future society that may be ultimately different right down to its essential relationships from the human past. But they also believe that the forces that have been assailing and disintegrating the Normal Social Life, which have been, on the one hand, producing great accumulations of wealth, private freedom, and ill-defined, irresponsible and socially dangerous power, and, on the other, labour hordes, for the most part urban, without any property or outlook except continuous toil and anxiety, which in England have substituted a dischargeable agricultural labourer for the independent peasant almost completely, and in America seem to be arresting any general development of the Normal Social Life at all, are forces of wide and indefinite possibility that need to be controlled by a collective effort implying a collective design, deflected from merely injurious consequences and organised for a new human welfare upon new lines. They agree with that class of thinking I have distinguished as the Conservators in their recognition of vast contemporary disorders and their denial of the essential beneficence of change. But while the former seem to regard all novelty and innovation as a mere inundation to be met, banked back, defeated and survived, these more hopeful and adventurous minds would rather regard contemporary change as amounting on the whole to the tumultuous and almost catastrophic opening-up of possible new channels, the violent opportunity of vast, deep, new ways to great unprecedented human ends, ends that are neither feared nor evaded.

Now while the Conservators are continually talking of the "eternal facts" of human life and human nature and falling back upon a conception of permanence that is continually less true as our perspectives extend, these others are full of the conception of adaptation, of deliberate change in relationship and institution to meet changing needs. I would suggest for them, therefore, as opposed to the Conservators and contrasted with the Planless Progressives, the name of Constructors. They are the extreme right, as it were, while the Planless Progressives are the extreme left of Anti-Conservator thought.

I believe that these distinctions I have made cover practically every clear form of contemporary thinking, and are a better and more helpful classification than any now current. But, of course, nearly every individual nowadays is at least a little confused, and will be found to wobble in the course even of a brief discussion between one attitude and the other. This is a separation of opinions rather than of persons. And particularly that word Socialism has become so vague and incoherent that for a man to call himself a socialist nowadays is to give no indication whatever whether he is a Conservator like William Morris, a non-Constructor like Karl Marx, or a Constructor of any of half a dozen different schools. On the whole, however, modern socialism tends to fall towards the Constructor wing. So, too, do those various movements in England and Germany and France called variously nationalist and imperialist, and so do the American civic and social reformers. Under the same heading must come such attempts to give the vague impulses of Syndicalism a concrete definition as the "Guild Socialism" of Mr. Orage. All these movements are agreed that the world is progressive towards a novel and unprecedented social order, not necessarily and fatally better, and that it needs organised and even institutional guidance thither, however much they differ as to the form that order should assume.

For the greater portion of a century socialism has been before the world, and it is not perhaps premature to attempt a word or so of analysis of that great movement in the new terms we are here employing. The origins of the socialist idea were complex and multifarious never at any time has it succeeded in separating out a statement of itself that was at once simple, complete and acceptable to any large proportion of those who call themselves socialists. But always it has pointed to two or three definite things. The first of these is that unlimited freedoms of private property, with increasing facilities of exchange, combination, and aggrandisement, become more and more dangerous to human liberty by the expropriation and reduction to private wages slavery of larger and larger proportions of the population. Every school of socialism states this in some more or less complete form, however divergent the remedial methods suggested by the different schools. And, next, every school of socialism accepts the concentration of management and property as necessary, and declines to contemplate what is the typical Conservator remedy, its re-fragmentation. Accordingly it sets up not only against the large private owner, but against owners generally, the idea of a public proprietor, the State, which shall hold in the collective interest. But where the earlier socialisms stopped short, and where to this day socialism is vague, divided, and unprepared, is upon the psychological problems involved in that new and largely unprecedented form of proprietorship, and upon the still more subtle problems of its attainment. These are vast, and profoundly, widely, and multitudinously difficult problems, and it was natural and inevitable that the earlier socialists in the first enthusiasm of their idea should minimise these difficulties, pretend in the fullness of their faith that partial answers to objections were complete answers, and display the common weaknesses of honest propaganda the whole world over. Socialism is now old enough to know better. Few modern socialists present their faith as a complete panacea, and most are now setting to work in earnest upon these long-shirked preliminary problems of human interaction through which the vital problem of a collective head and brain can alone be approached.

A considerable proportion of the socialist movement remains, as it has been from the first, vaguely democratic. It points to collective ownership with no indication of the administrative scheme it contemplates to realise that intention. Necessarily it remains a formless claim without hands to take hold of the thing it desires. Indeed in a large number of cases it is scarcely more than a resentful consciousness in the expropriated masses of social disintegration. It spends its force very largely in mere revenges upon property as such, attacks simply destructive by reason of the absence of any definite ulterior scheme. It is an ill-equipped and planless belligerent who must destroy whatever he captures because he can neither use nor take away. A council of democratic socialists in possession of London would be as capable of an orderly and sustained administration as the Anabaptists in Munster. But the discomforts and disorders of our present planless system do tend steadily to the development of this crude socialistic spirit in the mass of the proletariat; merely vindictive attacks upon property, sabotage, and the general strike are the logical and inevitable consequences of an uncontrolled concentration of property in a few hands, and such things must and will go on, the deep undertow in the deliquescence of the Normal Social Life, until a new justice, a new scheme of compensations and satisfactions is attained, or the Normal Social Life re-emerges.

Fabian socialism was the first systematic attempt to meet the fatal absence of administrative schemes in the earlier socialisms. It can scarcely be regarded now as anything but an interesting failure, but a failure that has all the educational value of a first reconnaissance into unexplored territory. Starting from that attack on aggregating property, which is the common starting-point of all socialist projects, the Fabians, appalled at the obvious difficulties of honest confiscation and an open transfer from private to public hands, conceived the extraordinary idea of *filching* property for the state. A small body of people of extreme astuteness were to bring about the municipalisation and nationalisation first of this great system of property and then of that, in a manner so artful that the millionaires were to wake up one morning at last, and behold, they would find themselves poor men! For a decade or more Mr. Pease, Mr. Bernard Shaw, Mr. and Mrs. Sidney Webb, Mrs. Besant, Dr. Lawson Dodd, and their associates of the London Fabian Society, did pit their wits and ability, or at any rate the wits and ability of their leisure moments, against the embattled capitalists of England and the world, in this complicated and delicate enterprise, without any apparent diminution of the larger accumulations of wealth. But in addition they developed another side of Fabianism, still more subtle, which professed to be a kind of restoration in kind of property to the proletariat and in this direction they were more successful. A dexterous use, they decided, was to be made of the Poor Law, the public health authority, the education authority, and building regulations and so forth, to create, so to speak, a communism of the lower levels. The mass of people whom the forces of change had expropriated were to be given a certain minimum of food, shelter, education, and sanitation, and this, the socialists were assured, could be used as the thin end of the wedge towards a complete communism. The minimum, once established, could obviously be raised continually until either everybody had what they needed, or the resources of society gave out and set a limit to the process.

This second method of attack brought the Fabian movement into co-operation with a large amount of benevolent and constructive influence outside the socialist ranks altogether. Few wealthy people really grudge the poor a share of the necessities of life, and most are quite willing to assist in projects for such a distribution. But while these schemes naturally involved a very great amount of regulation and regimentation of the affairs of the poor, the Fabian Society fell away more and more from its associated proposals for the socialisation of the rich. The Fabian project changed steadily in character until at last it ceased to be in any sense antagonistic to wealth as such. If the lion did not exactly lie down with the lamb, at any rate the man with the gun and the alleged social mad dog returned very peaceably together. The Fabian hunt was up.

Great financiers contributed generously to a School of Economics that had been founded with moneys left to the Fabian Society by earlier enthusiasts for socialist propaganda and education. It remained for Mr. Belloc to point the moral of the whole development with a phrase, to note that Fabianism no longer aimed at the socialisation of the whole community, but only at the socialisation of the poor. The first really complete project for a new social order to replace the Normal Social Life was before the world, and this project was the compulsory regimentation of the workers and the complete state control of labour under a new plutocracy. Our present chaos was to be organised into a Servile State.

Sec. 4

Now to many of us who found the general spirit of the socialist movement at least hopeful and attractive and sympathetic, this would be an almost tragic conclusion, did we believe that Fabianism was anything more than the first experiment in planning—and one almost inevitably shallow and presumptuous—of the long series that may be necessary before a clear light breaks upon the road humanity must follow. But we decline to be forced by this one intellectual fiasco towards the *laissez faire* of the Individualist and the

Marxist, or to accept the Normal Social Life with its atmosphere of hens and cows and dung, its incessant toil, its servitude of women, and its endless repetitions as the only tolerable life conceivable for the bulk of mankind—as the ultimate life, that is, of mankind. With less arrogance and confidence, but it may be with a firmer faith, we declare that we believe a more spacious social order than any that exists or ever has existed, a Peace of the World in which there is an almost universal freedom, health, happiness, and well-being and which contains the seeds of a still greater future, is possible to mankind. We propose to begin again with the recognition of those same difficulties the Fabians first realised. But we do not propose to organise a society, form a group for the control of the two chief political parties, bring about "socialism" in twenty-five years, or do anything beyond contributing in our place and measure to that constructive discussion whose real magnitude we now begin to realise.

We have faith in a possible future, but it is a faith that makes the quality of that future entirely dependent upon the strength and clearness of purpose that this present time can produce. We do not believe the greater social state is inevitable.

Yet there is, we hold, a certain qualified inevitability about this greater social state because we believe any social state not affording a general contentment, a general freedom, and a general and increasing fullness of life, must sooner or later collapse and disintegrate again, and revert more or less completely to the Normal Social Life, and because we believe the Normal Social Life is itself thick-sown with the seeds of fresh beginnings. The Normal Social Life has never at any time been absolutely permanent, always it has carried within itself the germs of enterprise and adventure and exchanges that finally attack its stability. The superimposed social order of to-day, such as it is, with its huge development of expropriated labour, and the schemes of the later Fabians to fix this state of affairs in an organised form and render it plausibly tolerable, seem also doomed to accumulate catastrophic tensions. Bureaucratic schemes for establishing the regular lifelong subordination of a labouring class, enlivened though they may be by frequent inspection, disciplinary treatment during seasons of unemployment, compulsory temperance, free medical attendance, and a cheap and shallow elementary education fail to satisfy the restless cravings in the heart of man. They are cravings that even the baffling methods of the most ingeniously worked Conciliation Boards cannot permanently restrain. The drift of any Servile State must be towards a class revolt, paralysing sabotage and a general strike. The more rigid and complete the Servile State becomes, the more thorough will be its ultimate failure. Its fate is decay or explosion. From its débris we shall either revert to the Normal Social Life and begin again the long struggle towards that ampler, happier, juster arrangement of human affairs which we of this book, at any rate, believe to be possible, or we shall pass into the twilight of mankind.

This greater social life we put, then, as the only real alternative to the Normal Social Life from which man is continually escaping. For it we do not propose to use the expressions the "socialist state" or "socialism," because we believe those terms have now by constant confused use become so battered and bent and discoloured by irrelevant associations as to be rather misleading than expressive. We propose to use the term The Great State to express this ideal of a social system no longer localised, no longer immediately tied to and conditioned by the cultivation of the land, world-wide in its interests and outlook and catholic in its tolerance and sympathy, a system of great individual freedom with a universal understanding among its citizens of a collective thought and purpose.

Now, the difficulties that lie in the way of humanity in its complex and toilsome journey through the coming centuries towards this Great State are fundamentally difficulties of adaptation and adjustment. To no conceivable social state is man inherently fitted: he is a creature of jealousy and suspicion, unstable, restless, acquisitive, aggressive, intractable, and of a most subtle and nimble dishonesty. Moreover, he is imaginative, adventurous, and inventive. His nature and instincts are as much in conflict with the necessary restrictions and subjugation of the Normal Social Life as they are likely to be with any other social net that necessity may weave about him. But the Normal Social Life has this advantage that it has a vast accumulated moral tradition and a minutely worked-out material method. All the fundamental institutions have arisen in relation to it and are adapted to its conditions. To revert to it after any phase of social chaos and distress is and will continue for many years to be the path of least resistance for perplexed humanity.

This conception of the Great State, on the other hand, is still altogether unsubstantial. It is a project as dream-like to-day as electric lighting, electric traction, or aviation would have been in the year 1850. In 1850 a man reasonably conversant with the physical science of his time could have declared with a very considerable confidence that, given a certain measure of persistence and social security, these things were more likely to be attained than not in the course of the next century. But such a prophecy was conditional on the preliminary accumulation of a considerable amount of knowledge, on many experiments and failures. Had the world of 1850, by some wave of impulse, placed all its resources in the hands of the ablest scientific man alive, and asked him to produce a practicable paying electric vehicle before 1852, at best he would have produced some clumsy, curious toy, more probably he would have failed altogether; and, similarly, if the whole population of the world came to the present writer and promised meekly to do whatever it was told, we should find ourselves still very largely at a loss in our project for a millennium. Yet just as nearly every man at work upon Voltaic electricity in 1850 knew that he was preparing for electric traction, so do I know quite certainly, in spite of a whole row of unsolved problems before me, that I am working towards the Great State.

Let me briefly recapitulate the main problems which have to be attacked in the attempt to realise the outline of the Great State. At the base of the whole order there must be some method of agricultural production, and if the agricultural labourer and cottager and the ancient life of the small householder on the holding, a life laborious, prolific, illiterate, limited, and in immediate contact with the land used, is to recede and disappear it must recede and disappear before methods upon a much larger scale, employing wholesale machinery and involving great economies. It is alleged by modern writers that the permanent residence of the cultivator in close relation to his ground is a legacy from the days of cumbrous and expensive transit, that the great proportion of farm work is seasonal, and that a migration to and fro between rural and urban conditions would be entirely practicable in a largely planned community. The agricultural population could move out of town into an open-air life as the spring approached, and return for spending, pleasure, and education as the days shortened. Already something of this sort occurs under extremely unfavourable conditions in the movement of the fruit and hop pickers from the east end of London into Kent, but that is a mere hint of the extended picnic which a broadly planned cultivation might afford. A fully developed civilisation, employing machines in the hands of highly skilled men, will minimise toil to the very utmost, no man will shove where a machine can shove, or carry where a machine can carry; but there will remain, more particularly in the summer, a vast amount of hand operations, invigorating and even attractive to the urban population Given short hours, good pay, and all the jolly amusement in the evening camp that a free, happy, and intelligent people will develop for themselves, and there will be little difficulty about this particular class of work to differentiate it from any other sort of necessary labour.

One passes, therefore, with no definite transition from the root problem of agricultural production in the Great State to the wider problem of labour in general.

A glance at the countryside conjures up a picture of extensive tracts being cultivated on a wholesale scale, of skilled men directing great ploughing, sowing, and reaping plants, steering cattle and sheep about carefully designed enclosures, constructing channels and guiding sewage towards its proper destination on the fields, and then of added crowds of genial people coming out to spray trees and plants, pick and sort and pack fruits. But who are these people? Why are they in particular doing this for the community? Is our Great State still to have a majority of people glad to do commonplace work for mediocre wages, and will there be other individuals who will ride by on the roads, sympathetically, no doubt, but with a secret sense of superiority? So one opens the general problem of the organisation for labour.

I am careful here to write "for labour" and not "of Labour," because it is entirely against the spirit of the Great State that any section of the people should be set aside as a class to do most of the monotonous, laborious, and uneventful things for the community. That is practically the present arrangement, and that, with a quickened sense of the need of breaking people in to such a life, is the ideal of the bureaucratic Servile State to which, in common with the Conservators, we are bitterly opposed. And here I know I am at my most difficult, most speculative, and most revolutionary point. We who look to the Great State as the present aim of human progress believe a state may solve its economic problem without any section whatever of the community being condemned to lifelong labour. And contemporary events, the phenomena of recent strikes, the phenomena of sabotage, carry out the suggestion that in a community where nearly everyone reads extensively travels about, sees the charm and variety in the lives of prosperous and leisurely people, no class is going to submit permanently to modern labour conditions without extreme resistance, even after the most elaborate Labour Conciliation schemes and social minima are established Things are altogether too stimulating to the imagination nowadays. Of all impossible social dreams that belief in tranquillised and submissive and virtuous Labour is the wildest of all. No sort of modern men will stand it. They will as a class do any vivid and disastrous thing rather than stand it. Even the illiterate peasant will only endure lifelong toil under the stimulus of private ownership and with the consolations of religion; and the typical modern worker has neither the one nor the other. For a time, indeed, for a generation or so even, a labour mass may be fooled or coerced, but in the end it will break out against its subjection, even if it breaks out to a general social catastrophe.

We have, in fact, to invent for the Great State, if we are to suppose any Great State at all, an economic method without any specific labour class. If we cannot do so, we had better throw ourselves in with the Conservators forthwith, for they are right and we are absurd. Adhesion to the conception of the Great State involves adhesion to the belief that the amount of regular labour, skilled and unskilled, required to produce everything necessary for everyone living in its highly elaborate civilisation may, under modern conditions, with the help of scientific economy and power-producing machinery, be reduced to so small a number of working hours per head in proportion to the average life of the citizen, as to be met as regards the greater moiety of it by the payment of wages over and above the gratuitous share of each individual in the general output; and as regards the residue, a residue of rough, disagreeable, and monotonous operations, by some form of conscription, which will demand a year or so, let us say, of each person's life for the public service. If we reflect that in the contemporary state there is already food, shelter, and clothing of a sort for everyone, in spite of the fact that enormous numbers of people do no productive work at all because they are too well off, that great numbers are out of work, great numbers by bad nutrition and training incapable of work, and that an enormous amount of the work actually done is the overlapping production of competitive trade and work upon such politically necessary but socially useless things as Dreadnoughts, it becomes clear that the absolutely unavoidable labour in a modern community and its ratio to the available vitality must be of very small account indeed. But all this has still to be worked out even in the most general terms. An intelligent science of economics should afford standards and technicalities and systematised facts upon which to base an estimate. The point was raised a quarter of a century ago by Morris in his "News from Nowhere," and indeed it was already discussed by More in his "Utopia." Our contemporary economics is, however, still a foolish, pretentious pseudo-science, a festering mass of assumptions about buying and selling and wages-paying, and one would as soon consult Bradshaw or the works of Dumas as our orthodox professors of economics for any light upon this fundamental matter.

Moreover, we believe that there is a real disposition to work in human beings, and that in a well-equipped community, in which no one was under an unavoidable urgency to work, the greater proportion of productive operations could be made sufficiently attractive to make them desirable occupations. As for the irreducible residue of undesirable toil, I owe to my friend the late Professor William James this suggestion of a general conscription and a period of public service for everyone, a suggestion which greatly occupied his thoughts during the last years of his life. He was profoundly convinced of the high educational and disciplinary value of universal compulsory military service, and of the need of something more than a sentimental ideal of duty in public life. He would have had the whole population taught in the schools and prepared for this year (or whatever period it had to be) of patient and heroic labour, the men for the mines, the fisheries, the sanitary services, railway routine, the women for hospital, and perhaps educational work, and so forth. He believed such a service would permeate the whole state with a sense of civic obligation . . .

But behind all these conceivable triumphs of scientific adjustment and direction lies the infinitely greater difficulty on our way to the Great State, the difficulty of direction. What sort of people are going to distribute the work of the community, decide what is or is not to be done, determine wages, initiate enterprises; and under what sort of criticism, checks, and controls are they going to do this delicate and extensive work? With this we open the whole problem of government, administration and officialdom.

The Marxist and the democratic socialist generally shirk this riddle altogether; the Fabian conception of a bureaucracy, official to the extent of being a distinct class and cult, exists only as a starting-point for healthy repudiations. Whatever else may be worked out in the subtler answers our later time prepares, nothing can be clearer than that the necessary machinery of government must be elaborately organised to prevent the development of a managing caste in permanent conspiracy, tacit or expressed, against the normal man. Quite apart from the danger of unsympathetic and fatally irritating government there can be little or no doubt that the method of making men officials for life is quite the worst way of getting official duties done. Officialdom is a species of incompetence. This rather priggish, teachable, and well-behaved sort of boy, who is attracted by the prospect of assured income and a pension to win his way into the Civil Service, and who then by varied assiduities rises to a sort of timidly vindictive importance, is the last person to whom we would willingly entrust the vital interests of a nation. We want people who know about life at large, who will come to the public service seasoned by experience, not people who have specialised and acquired that sort of knowledge which is called, in much the same spirit of qualification as one speaks of German Silver, Expert Knowledge. It is clear our public servants and officials must be so only for their periods of service. They must be taught by life, and not "trained" by pedagogues. In every continuing job there is a time when one is crude and blundering, a time, the best time, when one is full of the freshness and happiness of doing well, and a time when routine has largely replaced the stimulus of novelty. The Great State will, I feel convinced, regard changes in occupation as a proper circumstance in the life of every citizen; it will value a certain amateurishness in its service, and prefer it to the trite omniscience of the stale official. On that score of the necessity or versatility, if on no other score, I am flatly antagonistic to the conceptions of "Guild Socialism" which have arisen recently out of the impact of Mr. Penty and Syndicalism upon the uneasy intelligence of Mr. Orage.

And since the Fabian socialists have created a widespread belief that in their projected state every man will be necessarily a public servant or a public pupil because the state will be the only employer and the only educator, it is necessary to point out that the Great State presupposes neither the one nor the other. It is a form of liberty and not a form of enslavement. We agree with the older forms of socialism in supposing an initial proprietary independence in every citizen. The citizen is a shareholder in the state. Above that and after that, he works if he chooses. But if he likes to live on his minimum and do nothing—though such a type of character is scarcely conceivable—he can. His earning is his own surplus. Above the basal economics of the Great State we assume with confidence there will be a huge surplus of free spending upon extra-collective ends. Public organisations, for example, may distribute impartially and possibly even print and make ink and paper for the newspapers in the Great State, but they will certainly not own them. Only doctrine-driven men have ever ventured to think they would. Nor will the state control writers and artists, for example, nor the stage—though it may build and own theatres—the tailor, the dressmaker, the restaurant cook, an enormous multitude of other busy workers-for-preferences. In the Great State of the future, as in the life of the more prosperous classes of to-day, the greater proportion of occupations and activities will be private and free.

I would like to underline in the most emphatic way that it is possible to have this Great State, essentially socialistic, owning and running the land and all the great public services, sustaining everybody in absolute freedom at a certain minimum of comfort and well-being, and still leaving most of the interests, amusements, and adornments of the individual life, and all sorts of collective concerns, social and political discussion, religious worship, philosophy, and the like to the free personal initiatives of entirely unofficial people.

This still leaves the problem of systematic knowledge and research, and all the associated problems of aesthetic, moral, and intellectual initiative to be worked out in detail; but at least it dispels the nightmare of a collective mind organised as a branch of the civil service, with authors, critics, artists, scientific investigators appointed in a phrensy of wire-pulling—as nowadays the British state appoints its bishops for the care of its collective soul.

Let me now indicate how these general views affect the problem of family organisation and the problem of women's freedom. In the Normal Social Life the position of women is easily defined. They are subordinated but important. The citizenship rests with the man, and the woman's relation to the community as a whole is through a man. But within that limitation her functions as mother, wife, and home-maker are cardinal. It is one of the entirely unforeseen consequences that have arisen from the decay of the Normal Social Life and its autonomous home that great numbers of women while still subordinate have become profoundly unimportant They have ceased to a very large extent to bear children, they have dropped most of their home-making arts, they no longer nurse nor educate such children as they have, and they have taken on no new functions that compensate for these dwindling activities of the domestic interior. That subjugation which is a vital condition to the Normal Social Life does not seem to be necessary to the Great State. It may or it may not be necessary. And here we enter upon the most difficult of all our problems. The whole spirit of the Great State is against any avoidable subjugation; but the whole spirit of that science which will animate the Great State forbids us to ignore woman's functional and temperamental differences. A new status has still to be invented for women, a Feminine Citizenship differing in certain respects from the normal masculine citizenship. Its conditions remain to be worked out. We have indeed to work out an entire new system of relations between men and women, that will be free from servitude, aggression, provocation, or parasitism. The public Endowment of Motherhood as such may perhaps be the first broad suggestion of the quality of this new status. A new type of family, a mutual alliance in the place of a subjugation, is perhaps the most startling of all the conceptions which confront us directly we turn ourselves definitely towards the Great State.

And as our conception of the Great State grows, so we shall begin to realise the nature of the problem of transition, the problem of what we may best do in the confusion of the present time to elucidate and render practicable this new phase of human organisation. Of one thing there can be no doubt, that whatever increases thought and knowledge moves towards our goal; and equally certain is it that nothing leads thither that tampers with the freedom of spirit, the independence of soul in common men and women. In many directions, therefore, the believer in the Great State will display a jealous watchfulness of contemporary developments rather than a premature constructiveness. We must watch wealth; but quite as necessary it is to watch the legislator, who mistakes propaganda for progress and class exasperation to satisfy class vindictiveness for construction. Supremely important is it to keep discussion open, to tolerate no limitation on the freedom of speech, writing, art and book distribution, and to sustain the utmost liberty of criticism upon all contemporary institutions and processes.

This briefly is the programme of problems and effort to which my idea of the Great State, as the goal of contemporary progress, leads me.

The diagram on p. 131 shows compactly the gist of the preceding discussion; it gives the view of social development upon which I base all my political conceptions.

THE NORMAL SOCIAL LIFE

produces an increasing surplus of energy and opportunity, more particularly under modern conditions of scientific organisation and power production; and this through the operation of rent and of usury tends to

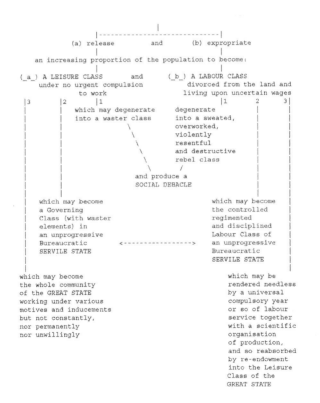

```
                          |
             |---------------------------------|
             (a) release       and       (b) expropriate
             |                                 |
         an increasing proportion of the population to become:
             |                                 |
(_a_) A LEISURE CLASS     and     (_b_) A LABOUR CLASS
     under no urgent compulsion        divorced from the land and
            to work                    living upon uncertain wages
  |3      |2      |1                         |1      2      3|
  |       |       which may degenerate    degenerate  |      |
  |       |       into a waster class     into a sweated,    |
  |       |                 \             overworked,   |    |
  |       |                  \            violently     |    |
  |       |                   \           resentful     |    |
  |       |                    \          and destructive|   |
  |       |                     \         rebel class    |   |
  |       |                      \          /            |   |
  |       |                    and produce a             |   |
  |       |                    SOCIAL DEBACLE            |   |
  |       |                                              |   |
  |     which may become                    which may become |
  |     a Governing                         the controlled   |
  |     Class (with waster                  regimented       |
  |     elements) in                        and disciplined  |
  |     an unprogressive                    Labour Class of  |
  |     Bureaucratic      <----------------->  an unprogressive|
  |     SERVILE STATE                        Bureaucratic    |
  |                                          SERVILE STATE   |
  |                                                          |
  which may become                          which may be
  the whole community                       rendered needless
  of the GREAT STATE                        by a universal
  working under various                     compulsory year
  motives and inducements                   or so of labour
  but not constantly,                       service together
  nor permanently                           with a scientific
  nor unwillingly                           organisation
                                            of production,
                                            and so reabsorbed
                                            by re-endowment
                                            into the Leisure
                                            Class of the
                                            GREAT STATE
```

THE COMMON SENSE OF WARFARE

Sec. 1

CONSCRIPTION

I want to say as compactly as possible why I do not believe that conscription would increase the military efficiency of this country, and why I think it might be a disastrous step for this country to take.

By conscription I mean the compulsory enlistment for a term of service in the Army of the whole manhood of the country. And I am writing now from the point of view merely of military effectiveness. The educational value of a universal national service, the idea which as a Socialist I support very heartily, of making every citizen give a year or so of his life to our public needs, are matters quite outside my present discussion. What I am writing about now is this idea that the country can be strengthened for war by making every man in it a bit of a soldier.

And I want the reader to be perfectly clear about the position I assume with regard to war preparations generally. I am not pleading for peace when there is no peace; this country has been constantly threatened during the past decade, and is threatened now by gigantic hostile preparations; it is our common interest to be and to keep at the maximum of military efficiency possible to us. My case is not merely that conscription will not contribute to that, but that it would be a monstrous diversion of our energy and emotion and material resources from the things that need urgently to be done. It would be like a boxer filling his arms with empty boxing-gloves and then rushing—his face protruding over the armful—into the fray.

Let me make my attack on this prevalent and increasing superstition of the British need for conscription in two lines, one following the other. For, firstly, it is true that Britain at the present time is no more capable of creating such a conscript army as France or Germany possesses in the next ten years than she is of covering her soil with a tropical forest, and, secondly, it is equally true that if she had such an army it would not be of the slightest use to her. For the conscript armies in which Europe still so largely believes are only of use against conscript armies and adversaries who will consent to play the rules of the German war game; they are, if we chose to determine they shall be, if we chose to deal with them as they should be dealt with, as out of date as a Roman legion or a Zulu impi.

Now, first, as to the impossibility of getting our great army into existence. All those people who write and talk so glibly in favour of conscription seem to forget that to take a common man, and more particularly a townsman, clap him into a uniform and put a rifle in his hand does not make a soldier. He has to be taught not only the use of his weapons, but the methods of a strange and unfamiliar life out of doors; he has to be not simply drilled, but accustomed to the difficult modern necessities of open order fighting, of taking cover, of entrenchment, and he has to have created within him, so that it will stand the shock of seeing men killed round about him, confidence in himself, in his officers, and the methods and weapons of his side. Body, mind, and imagination have all to be trained— and they need trainers. The conversion of a thousand citizens into anything better than a sheep-like militia demands the enthusiastic services of scores of able and experienced instructors who know what war is; the creation of a universal army demands the services of many scores of thousands of not simply "old soldiers," but keen, expert, modern-minded *officers*.

Without these officers our citizen army would be a hydra without heads. And we haven't these officers. We haven't a tithe of them.

We haven't these officers, and we can't make them in a hurry. It takes at least five years to make an officer who knows his trade. It needs a special gift, in addition to that knowledge, to make a man able to impart it. And our Empire is at a peculiar disadvantage in the matter, because India and our other vast areas of service and opportunity overseas drain away a large proportion of just those able and educated men who would in other countries gravitate towards the army. Such small wealth of officers as we have—and I am quite prepared to believe that the officers we have are among the very best in the world—are scarcely enough to go round our present supply of private soldiers. And the best and most brilliant among this scanty supply are being drawn upon more and more for aerial work, and for all that increasing quantity of highly specialised services which are manifestly destined to be the real fighting forces of the future. We cannot spare the best of our officers for training conscripts; we shall get the dismallest results from the worst of them; and so even if it were a vital necessity for our country to have an army of all its manhood now, we could not have it, and it would be a mere last convulsion to attempt to make it with the means at our disposal.

But that brings me to my second contention, which is that we do not want such an army. I believe that the vast masses of men in uniform maintained by the Continental Powers at the present time are enormously overrated as fighting machines. I see Germany in the likeness of a boxer with a mailed fist as big as and rather heavier than its body, and I am convinced that when the moment comes for that mailed fist to be lifted, the whole disproportionate system will topple over. The military ascendancy of the future lies with the country that dares to experiment most, that experiments best, and meanwhile keeps its actual fighting force fit and admirable and small and flexible. The experience of war during the last fifteen years has been to show repeatedly the enormous defensive power of small, scientifically handled bodies of men. These huge conscript armies are made up not of masses of military muscle, but of a huge proportion of military fat. Their one way of fighting will be to fall upon an antagonist with all their available weight, and if he is mobile and dexterous enough to decline that issue of adiposity they will become a mere embarrassment to their own people. Modern weapons and modern contrivance are continually decreasing the number of men who can be employed efficiently upon a length of front. I doubt if there is any use for more than 400,000 men upon the whole Franco-Belgian frontier at the present time. Such an army, properly supplied, could—so far as terrestrial forces are concerned—hold that frontier against any number of assailants. The bigger the forces brought against it the sooner the exhaustion of the attacking power. Now, it is for employment upon that frontier, and for no other conceivable purpose in the world, that Great Britain is asked to create a gigantic conscript army.

And if too big an army is likely to be a mere encumbrance in war, it is perhaps even a still graver blunder to maintain one during that conflict of preparation which is at present the European substitute for actual hostilities. It consumes. It produces nothing. It not only eats and drinks and wears out its clothes and withdraws men from industry, but under the stress of invention it needs constantly to be re-armed and freshly equipped at an expenditure proportionate to its size. So long as the conflict of preparation goes on, then the bigger the army your adversary maintains under arms the bigger is his expenditure and the less his earning power. The less the force you employ to keep your adversary over-armed, and the longer you remain at peace with him while he is over-armed, the greater is your advantage. There is only one profitable use for any army, and that is victorious conflict. Every army that is not engaged in victorious conflict is an organ of national expenditure, an exhausting growth in the national body. And for Great Britain an attempt to create a conscript army would involve the very maximum of moral and material exhaustion with the minimum of military efficiency. It would be a disastrous waste of resources that we need most urgently for other things.

Sec. 2

In the popular imagination the Dreadnought is still the one instrument of naval war. We count our strength in Dreadnoughts and Super-Dreadnoughts, and so long as we are spending our national resources upon them faster than any other country, if we sink at least £160 for every £100 sunk in these obsolescent monsters by Germany, we have a reassuring sense of keeping ahead and being thoroughly safe. This confidence in big, very expensive battleships is, I believe and hope, shared by the German Government and by Europe generally, but it is, nevertheless, a very unreasonable confidence, and it may easily lead us into the most tragic of national disillusionments.

We of the general public are led to suppose that the next naval war—if ever we engage in another naval war—will begin with a decisive fleet action. The plan of action is presented with an alluring simplicity. Our adversary will come out to us, in a ratio of 10 to 16, or in some ratio still more advantageous to us, according as our adversary happens to be this Power or that Power, there will be some tremendous business with guns and torpedoes, and our admirals will return victorious to discuss the discipline and details of the battle and each other's little weaknesses in the monthly magazines. This is a desirable but improbable anticipation. No hostile Power is in the least likely to send out any battleships at all against our invincible Dreadnoughts. They will promenade the seas, always in the ratio of 16 or more to 10, looking for fleets securely tucked away out of reach. They will not, of course, go too near the enemy's coast, on account of mines, and, meanwhile, our cruisers will hunt the enemy's commerce into port.

Then other things will happen.

The enemy we shall discover using unsportsmanlike devices against our capital ships. Unless he is a lunatic, he will prove to be much stronger in reality than he is on paper in the matter of submarines, torpedo-boats, waterplanes and aeroplanes. These are things cheap to make and easy to conceal. He will be richly stocked with ingenious devices for getting explosives up to these two million pound triumphs of our naval engineering. On the cloudy and foggy nights so frequent about these islands he will have extraordinary chances, and sooner or later, unless we beat him thoroughly in the air above and in the waters beneath, for neither of which proceedings we are prepared, some of these chances will come off, and we shall lose a Dreadnought.

It will be a poor consolation if an ill-advised and stranded Zeppelin or so enlivens the quiet of the English countryside by coming down and capitulating. It will be a trifling countershock to wing an aeroplane or so, or blow a torpedo-boat out of the water. Our Dreadnoughts will cease to be a source of unmitigated confidence A second battleship disaster will excite the Press extremely. A third will probably lead to a retirement of the battle fleet to some east coast harbour, a refuge liable to aeroplanes, or to the west coast of Ireland—and the real naval war, which, as I have argued in an earlier chapter, will be a war of destroyers, submarines and hydroplanes, will begin. Incidentally a commerce destroyer may take advantage of the retirement of our fleet to raid our trade routes.

We shall then realise that the actual naval weapons are these smaller weapons, and especially the destroyer, the submarine, and the waterplane—the waterplane most of all, because of its possibilities of a comparative bigness—in the hands of competent and daring men. And I find myself, as a patriotic Englishman, more and more troubled by doubts whether we are as certainly superior to any possible adversary in these essential things as we are in the matter of Dreadnoughts. I find myself awake at nights, after a day much agitated by a belligerent Press, wondering whether the real Empire of the Sea may not even now have slipped out of our hands while our attention has been fixed on our stately procession of giant warships, while our country has been in a dream, hypnotised by the Dreadnought idea.

For some years there seems to have been a complete arrest of the British imagination in naval and military matters. That declining faculty, never a very active or well-exercised one, staggered up to the conception of a Dreadnought, and seems now to have sat down for good. Its reply to every demand upon it has been "more Dreadnoughts." The future, as we British seem to see it, is an avenue of Dreadnoughts and Super-Dreadnoughts and Super-Super-Dreadnoughts, getting bigger and bigger in a kind of inverted perspective. But the ascendancy of fleets of great battleships in naval warfare, like the phase of huge conscript armies upon land, draws to its close. The progress of invention makes both the big ship and the army crowd more and more vulnerable and less and less effective. A new phase of warfare opens beyond the vista of our current programmes. Smaller, more numerous and various and mobile weapons and craft and contrivances, manned by daring and highly skilled men, must ultimately take the place of those massivenesses. We are entering upon a period in which the invention of methods and material for war is likely to be more rapid and diversified than it has ever been before, and the question of what we have been doing behind the splendid line of our Dreadnoughts to meet the demands of this new phase is one of supreme importance. Knowing, as I do, the imaginative indolence of my countrymen, it is a question I face with something very near to dismay.

But it is one that has to be faced. The question that should occupy our directing minds now is no longer "How can we get more Dreadnoughts?" but "What have we to follow the Dreadnought?"

To the Power that has most nearly guessed the answer to that riddle belongs the future Empire of the Seas. It is interesting to guess for oneself and to speculate upon the possibility of a kind of armoured mother-ship for waterplanes and submarines and torpedo craft, but necessarily that would be a mere journalistic and amateurish guessing. I am not guessing, but asking urgent questions. What force, what council, how many imaginative and inventive men has the country got at the present time employed not casually but professionally in anticipating the new strategy, the new tactics, the new material, the new training that invention is so rapidly rendering necessary? I have the gravest doubts whether we are doing anything systematic at all in this way.

Now, it is the tremendous seriousness of this deficiency to which I want to call attention. Great Britain has in her armour a gap more dangerous and vital than any mere numerical insufficiency of men or ships. She is short of minds. Behind its strength of current armaments to-day, a strength that begins to evaporate and grow obsolete from the very moment it comes into being, a country needs more and more this profounder strength of intellectual and creative activity.

This country most of all, which was left so far behind in the production of submarines, airships and aeroplanes, must be made to realise the folly of its trust in established things. Each new thing we take up more belatedly and reluctantly than its predecessor. The time is not far distant when we shall be "caught" lagging unless we change all this.

We need a new arm to our service; we need it urgently, and we shall need it more and more, and that arm is Research. We need to place inquiry and experiment upon a new footing altogether, to enlist for them and organise them, to secure the pick of our young chemists and physicists and engineers, and to get them to work systematically upon the anticipation and preparation of our future war equipment. We need a service of invention to recover our lost lead in these matters.

And it is because I feel so keenly the want of such a service, and the want of great sums of money for it, that I deplore the disposition to waste millions upon the hasty creation of a universal service army and upon excessive Dreadnoughting. I am convinced that we are spending upon the things of yesterday the money that is sorely needed for the things of to-morrow.

With our eyes averted obstinately from the future we are backing towards disaster.

Sec. 3

In the present armament competition there are certain considerations that appear to be almost universally overlooked, and which tend to modify our views profoundly of what should be done. Ultimately they will affect our entire expenditure upon war preparation.

Expenditure upon preparation for war falls, roughly, into two classes: there is expenditure upon things that have a diminishing value, things that grow old-fashioned and wear out, such as fortifications, ships, guns, and ammunition, and expenditure upon things that have a permanent and even growing value, such as organised technical research, military and naval experiment, and the education and increase of a highly trained class of war experts.

I want to suggest that we are spending too much money in the former and not enough in the latter direction We are buying enormous quantities of stuff that will be old iron in twenty years' time, and we are starving ourselves of that which cannot be bought or made in a hurry, and upon which the strength of nations ultimately rests altogether; we are failing to get and maintain a sufficiency of highly educated and developed men inspired by a tradition of service and efficiency.

No doubt we must be armed to-day, but every penny we divert from men-making and knowledge-making to armament beyond the margin of bare safety is a sacrifice of the future to the present. Every penny we divert from national wealth-making to national weapons means so much less in resources, so much more strain in the years ahead. But a great system of laboratories and experimental stations, a systematic, industrious increase of men of the officer-aviator type, of the research student type, of the engineer type, of the naval-officer type, of the skilled sergeant-instructor type, a methodical development of a common sentiment and a common zeal among such a body of men, is an added strength that grows greater from the moment you call it into being. In our schools and military and naval colleges lies the proper field for expenditure upon preparation for our ultimate triumph in war. All other war preparation is temporary but that.

This would be obvious in any case, but what makes insistence upon it peculiarly urgent is the manifestly temporary nature of the present European situation and the fact that within quite a small number of years our war front will be turned in a direction quite other than that to which it faces now.

For a decade and more all Western Europe has been threatened by German truculence; the German, inflamed by the victories of 1870 and 1871, has poured out his energy in preparation for war by sea and land, and it has been the difficult task of France and England to keep the peace with him. The German has been the provocator and leader of all modern armaments. But that is not going on. It is already more than half over. If we can avert war with Germany for twenty years, we shall never have to fight Germany. In twenty years' time we shall be talking no more of sending troops to fight side by side on the frontier of France; we shall be talking of sending troops to fight side by side with French and Germans on the frontiers of Poland.

And the justification of that prophecy is a perfectly plain one. The German has filled up his country, his birth-rate falls, and the very vigour of his military and naval preparations, by raising the cost of living, hurries it down. His birth-rate falls as ours and the Frenchman's falls, because he is nearing his maximum of population It is an inevitable consequence of his geographical conditions. But eastward of him, from his eastern boundaries to the Pacific, is a country already too populous to conquer, but with possibilities of further expansion that are gigantic. The Slav will be free to increase and multiply for another hundred years. Eastward and southward bristle the Slavs, and behind the Slavs are the colossal possibilities of Asia.

Even German vanity, even the preposterous ambitions that spring from that brief triumph of Sedan, must awaken at last to these manifest facts, and on the day when Germany is fully awake we may count the Western European Armageddon as "off" and turn our eyes to the greater needs that will arise beyond Germany. The old game will be over and a quite different new game will begin in international relations.

During these last few years of worry and bluster across the North Sea we have a little forgotten India in our calculations. As Germany faces round eastward again, as she must do before very long, we shall find India resuming its former central position in our ideas of international politics. With India we may pursue one of two policies: we may keep her divided and inefficient for war, as she is at present, and hold her and own her and defend her as a prize, or we may arm her and assist her development into a group of quasi-independent English-speaking States—in which case she will become our partner and possibly at last even our senior partner. But that is by the way. What I am pointing out now is that whether we fight Germany or not, a time is drawing near when Germany will cease to be our war objective and we shall cease to be Germany's war objective, and when there will have to be a complete revision of our military and naval equipment in relation to those remoter, vaster Asiatic possibilities.

Now that possible campaign away there, whatever its particular nature may be, which will be shaping our military and naval policy in the year 1933 or thereabouts, will certainly be quite different in its conditions from the possible campaign in Europe and the narrow seas which determines all our preparations now. We cannot contemplate throwing an army of a million British conscripts on to the North-West Frontier of India, and a fleet of Super-Dreadnoughts will be ineffective either in Thibet or the Baltic shallows. All our present stuff, indeed, will be on the scrap-heap then. What will not be on the scrap-heap will be such enterprise and special science and inventive power as we have got together. That is versatile. That is good to have now and that will be good to have then.

Everyone nowadays seems demanding increased expenditure upon war preparation. I will follow the fashion. I will suggest that we have the courage to restrain and even to curtail our monstrous outlay upon war material and that we begin to spend lavishly upon military and naval education and training, upon laboratories and experimental stations, upon chemical and physical research and all that makes knowledge and leading, and that we increase our expenditure upon these things as fast as we can up to ten or twelve millions a year. At present we spend about eighteen and a half millions a year upon education out of our national funds, but fourteen and a half of this, supplemented by about as much again from local sources, is consumed in merely elementary teaching. So that we spend only about four millions a year of public money on every sort of research and education above the simple democratic level. Nearly thirty millions for the foundations and only a seventh for the edifice of will and science! Is it any marvel that we are a badly organised nation, a nation of very widely diffused intelligence and very second-rate guidance and achievement? Is it any marvel that directly we are tested by such a new development as that of aeroplanes or airships we show ourselves in comparison with the more braced-up nations of the Continent backward, unorganised unimaginative, unenterprising?

Our supreme want to-day, if we are to continue a belligerent people, is a greater supply of able educated men, versatile men capable of engines, of aviation, of invention, of leading and initiative. We need more laboratories, more scholarships out of the general mass of elementary scholars, a quasi-military discipline in our colleges and a great array of new colleges, a much readier access to instruction in aviation and military and naval practice. And if we are to have national service let us begin with it where it is needed most and where it is least likely to disorganise our social and economic life; let us begin at the top. Let us begin with the educated and propertied classes and exact a couple of years' service in a destroyer or a waterplane, or an airship, or a, research laboratory, or a training camp, from the sons of everybody who, let us say, pays income tax without deductions. Let us mix with these a big proportion—a proportion we may increase steadily—of keen scholarship men from the elementary schools. Such a braced-up class as we should create in this way would give us the realities of military power, which are enterprise, knowledge, and invention; and at the same time it would add to and not subtract from the economic wealth of the community Make men; that is the only sane, permanent preparation for war. So we should develop a strength and create a tradition that would not rust nor grow old-fashioned in all the years to come.

THE CONTEMPORARY NOVEL

Circumstances have made me think a good deal at different times about the business of writing novels, and what it means, and is, and may be; and I was a professional critic of novels long before I wrote them. I have been writing novels, or writing about novels, for the last twenty years. It seems only yesterday that I wrote a review—the first long and appreciative review he had—of Mr. Joseph Conrad's "Almayer's Folly" in the *Saturday Review*. When a man has focussed so much of his life upon the novel, it is not reasonable to expect him to take too modest or apologetic a view of it. I consider the novel an important and necessary thing indeed in that complicated system of uneasy adjustments and readjustments which is modern civilisation I make very high and wide claims for it. In many directions I do not think we can get along without it.

Now this, I know, is not the usually received opinion. There is, I am aware, the theory that the novel is wholly and solely a means of relaxation. In spite of manifest facts, that was the dominant view of the great period that we now in our retrospective way speak of as the Victorian, and it still survives to this day. It is the man's theory of the novel rather than the woman's. One may call it the Weary Giant theory. The reader is represented as a man, burthened, toiling, worn. He has been in his office from ten to four, with perhaps only two hours' interval at his club for lunch; or he has been playing golf; or he has been waiting about and voting in the House; or he has been fishing; or he has been disputing a point of law; or writing a sermon; or doing one of a thousand other of the grave important things which constitute the substance of a prosperous man's life. Now at last comes the little precious interval of leisure, and the Weary Giant takes up a book. Perhaps he is vexed: he may have been bunkered, his line may have been entangled in the trees, his favourite investment may have slumped,

115

or the judge have had indigestion and been extremely rude to him. He wants to forget the troublesome realities of life He wants to be taken out of himself, to be cheered, consoled, amused—above all, amused. He doesn't want ideas, he doesn't want facts; above all, he doesn't want—*Problems*. He wants to dream of the bright, thin, gay excitements of a phantom world—in which he can be hero— of horses ridden and lace worn and princesses rescued and won. He wants pictures of funny slums, and entertaining paupers, and laughable longshoremen, and kindly impulses making life sweet. He wants romance without its defiance, and humour without its sting; and the business of the novelist, he holds, is to supply this cooling refreshment. That is the Weary Giant theory of the novel. It ruled British criticism up to the period of the Boer war—and then something happened to quite a lot of us, and it has never completely recovered its old predominance. Perhaps it will; perhaps something else may happen to prevent its ever doing so.

Both fiction and criticism to-day are in revolt against that tired giant, the prosperous Englishman. I cannot think of a single writer of any distinction to-day, unless it is Mr. W.W. Jacobs, who is content merely to serve the purpose of those slippered hours. So far from the weary reader being a decently tired giant, we realise that he is only an inexpressibly lax, slovenly and under-trained giant, and we are all out with one accord resolved to exercise his higher ganglia in every possible way. And so I will say no more of the idea that the novel is merely a harmless opiate for the vacant hours of prosperous men. As a matter of fact, it never has been, and by its nature I doubt if it ever can be.

I do not think that women have ever quite succumbed to the tired giant attitude in their reading. Women are more serious, not only about life, but about books. No type or kind of woman is capable of that lounging, defensive stupidity which is the basis of the tired giant attitude, and all through the early 'nineties, during which the respectable frivolity of Great Britain left its most enduring marks upon our literature, there was a rebel undertow of earnest and aggressive writing and reading, supported chiefly by women and supplied very largely by women, which gave the lie to the prevailing trivial estimate of fiction. Among readers, women and girls and young men at least will insist upon having their novels significant and real, and it is to these perpetually renewed elements in the public that the novelist must look for his continuing emancipation from the wearier and more massive influences at work in contemporary British life.

And if the novel is to be recognised as something more than a relaxation, it has also, I think, to be kept free from the restrictions imposed upon it by the fierce pedantries of those who would define a general form for it. Every art nowadays must steer its way between the rocks of trivial and degrading standards and the whirlpool of arbitrary and irrational criticism. Whenever criticism of any art becomes specialised and professional whenever a class of adjudicators is brought into existence, those adjudicators are apt to become as a class distrustful of their immediate impressions, and anxious for methods of comparison between work and work, they begin to emulate the classifications and exact measurements of a science, and to set up ideals and rules as data for such classification and measurements. They develop an alleged sense of technique, which is too often no more than the attempt to exact a laboriousness of method, or to insist upon peculiarities of method which impress the professional critic not so much as being merits as being meritorious. This sort of thing has gone very far with the critical discussion both of the novel and the play. You have all heard that impressive dictum that some particular theatrical display, although moving, interesting, and continually entertaining from start to finish, was for occult technical reasons "not a play," and in the same way you are continually having your appreciation of fiction dashed by the mysterious parallel condemnation, that the story you like "isn't a novel." The novel has been treated as though its form was as well-defined as the sonnet. Some year or so ago, for example, there was a quite serious discussion, which began, I believe, in a weekly paper devoted to the interests of various nonconformist religious organisations, about the proper length for a novel. The critic was to begin his painful duties with a yard measure. The matter was taken up with profound gravity by the *Westminster Gazette*, and a considerable number of literary men and women were circularised and asked to state, in the face of "Tom Jones," "The Vicar of Wakefield," "The Shabby-Genteel Story," and "Bleak House," just exactly how long the novel ought to be. Our replies varied according to the civility of our natures, but the mere attempt to raise the question shows, I think, how widespread among the editorial, paragraph-writing, opinion-making sort of people is this notion of prescribing a definite length and a definite form for the novel. In the newspaper correspondence that followed, our friend the weary giant made a transitory appearance again. We were told the novel ought to be long enough for him to take up after dinner and finish before his whisky at eleven.

That was obviously a half-forgotten echo of Edgar Allan Poe's discussion of the short story. Edgar Allan Poe was very definite upon the point that the short story should be finished at a sitting. But the novel and short story are two entirely different things, and the train of reasoning that made the American master limit the short story to about an hour of reading as a maximum, does not apply to the longer work. A short story is, or should be, a simple thing; it aims at producing one single, vivid effect; it has to seize the attention at the outset, and never relaxing, gather it together more and more until the climax is reached. The limits of the human capacity to attend closely therefore set a limit to it; it must explode and finish before interruption occurs or fatigue sets in. But the novel I hold to be a discursive thing; it is not a single interest, but a woven tapestry of interests; one is drawn on first by this affection and curiosity, and then by that; it is something to return to, and I do not see that we can possibly set any limit to its extent. The distinctive value of the novel among written works of art is in characterisation, and the charm of a well-conceived character lies, not in knowing its destiny, but in watching its proceedings. For my own part, I will confess that I find all the novels of Dickens, long as they are, too short for me. I am sorry they do not flow into one another more than they do. I wish Micawber and Dick Swiveller and Sairey Gamp turned up again in other novels than their own, just as Shakespeare ran the glorious glow of Falstaff through a group of plays. But Dickens tried this once when he carried on the Pickwick Club into "Master Humphrey's Clock." That experiment was unsatisfactory, and he did not attempt anything of the sort again. Following on the days of Dickens, the novel began to contract, to subordinate characterisation to story and description to drama; considerations of a sordid nature, I am told, had to do with that; something about a guinea and a half and six shillings with which we will not concern ourselves—but I rejoice to see many signs to-day that that phase of narrowing and restriction is over, and that there is every encouragement for a return towards a laxer, more spacious form of novel-writing. The movement is partly of English origin, a revolt against those more exacting and cramping conceptions of artistic perfection to which I will recur in a moment, and a return to the lax freedom of form, the rambling discursiveness, the right to roam, of the earlier English novel, of "Tristram Shandy" and of "Tom Jones"; and partly it comes from abroad, and derives a stimulus from such bold and original enterprises as that of Monsieur Rolland in his "Jean Christophe." Its double origin involves a double nature; for while the English spirit is towards discursiveness and variety, the new French movement is rather towards exhaustiveness. Mr. Arnold Bennett has experimented in both forms of amplitude. His superb "Old Wives' Tale," wandering from person to person and from scene to scene, is by far the finest "long novel" that has been written in English in the English fashion in this generation, and now in "Clayhanger" and its promised collaterals, he undertakes that complete, minute, abundant presentation of the growth and modification of one or two individual minds, which is the essential characteristic of the Continental movement towards the novel of amplitude. While the "Old Wives' Tale" is discursive, "Clayhanger" is exhaustive; he gives us both types of the new movement in perfection.

I name "Jean Christophe" as a sort of archetype in this connection, because it is just at present very much in our thoughts by reason of the admirable translation Mr. Cannan is giving us; but there is a greater predecessor to this comprehensive and spectacular treatment of a single mind and its impressions and ideas, or of one or two associated minds, that comes to us now *via* Mr. Bennett and Mr. Cannan from France. The great original of all this work is that colossal last unfinished book of Flaubert, "Bouvard et Pécuchet." Flaubert, the bulk of whose life was spent upon the most austere and restrained fiction—Turgenev was not more austere and restrained—broke out at last into this gay, sad miracle of intellectual abundance. It is not extensively read in this country; it is not yet, I believe, translated into English; but there it is—and if it is new to the reader I make him this present of the secret of a book that is a precious wilderness of wonderful reading. But if Flaubert is really the Continental emancipator of the novel from the restrictions of form, the master to whom we of the English persuasion, we of the discursive school, must for ever recur is he, whom I will maintain against all comers to be the subtlest and greatest *artist*—I lay stress upon that word *artist*—that Great Britain has ever produced in all that is essentially the novel, Laurence Sterne . . .

The confusion between the standards of a short story and the standards of the novel which leads at last to these—what shall I call them?—*Westminster Gazettisms?*—about the correct length to which the novelist should aspire, leads also to all kinds of absurd condemnations and exactions upon matters of method and style. The underlying fallacy is always this: the assumption that the novel, like the story, aims at a single, concentrated impression. From that comes a fertile growth of error. Constantly one finds in the reviews of works of fiction the complaint that this, that or the other thing in a novel is irrelevant. Now it is the easiest thing, and most fatal thing, to become irrelevant in a short story. A short story should go to its point as a man flies from a pursuing tiger: he pauses not for the daisies in his path, or to note the pretty moss on the tree he climbs for safety. But the novel by comparison is like breakfasting in the open air on a summer morning; nothing is irrelevant if the waiter's mood is happy, and the tapping of the thrush upon the garden path, or the petal of apple-blossom that floats down into my coffee, is as relevant as the egg I open or the bread and butter I bite. And all sorts of things that inevitably mar the tense illusion which is the aim of the short story—the introduction, for example, of the author's personality—any comment that seems to admit that, after all, fiction is fiction, a change in manner between part and part, burlesque, parody, invective, all such thing's are not necessarily wrong in the novel. Of course, all these things may fail in their effect; they may jar, hinder, irritate, and all are difficult to do well; but it is no artistic merit to evade a difficulty any more than it is a merit in a hunter to refuse even the highest of fences. Nearly all the novels that have, by the lapse of time, reached an assured position of recognised greatness, are not only saturated in the personality of the author, but have in addition quite unaffected personal outbreaks. The least successful instance the one that is made the text against all such first-personal interventions, is, of course, Thackeray. But I think the trouble with Thackeray is not that he makes first-personal interventions, but that he does so with a curious touch of dishonesty. I agree with the late Mrs. Craigie that there was something profoundly vulgar about Thackeray. It was a sham thoughtful, sham man-of-the-world pose he assumed; it is an aggressive, conscious, challenging person astride before a fire, and a little distended by dinner and a sense of social and literary precedences, who uses the first person in Thackeray's novels. It isn't the real Thackeray; it isn't a frank man who looks you in the eyes and bares his soul and demands your sympathy. That is a criticism of Thackeray, but it isn't a condemnation of intervention.

I admit that for a novelist to come in person in this way before his readers involves grave risks; but when it is done without affectations, starkly as a man comes in out of the darkness to tell of perplexing things without—as, for instance, Mr. Joseph Conrad does for all practical purposes in his "Lord Jim"—then it gives a sort of depth, a sort of subjective reality, that no such cold, almost affectedly ironical detachment as that which distinguishes the work of Mr. John Galsworthy, for example, can ever attain. And in some cases the whole art and delight of a novel may lie in the author's personal interventions; let such novels as "Elizabeth and her German Garden," and the same writer's "Elizabeth in Rügen," bear witness.

Now, all this time I have been hacking away at certain hampering and limiting beliefs about the novel, letting it loose, as it were, in form and purpose; I have still to say just what I think the novel is, and where, if anywhere, its boundary-line ought to be drawn. It is by no means an easy task to define the novel. It is not a thing premeditated. It is a thing that has grown up into modern life, and taken upon itself uses and produced results that could not have been foreseen by its originators. Few of the important things in the collective life of man started out to be what they are. Consider, for example, all the unexpected aesthetic values, the inspiration and variety of emotional result which arises out of the cross-shaped plan of the Gothic cathedral, and the undesigned delight and wonder of white marble that has ensued, as I have been told, through the ageing and whitening of the realistically coloured statuary of the Greeks and Romans. Much of the charm of the old furniture and needlework, again, upon which the present time sets so much store, lies in acquired and unpremeditated qualities. And no doubt the novel grew up out of simple story-telling, and the universal desire of children, old and young alike, for a story. It is only slowly that we have developed the distinction of the novel from the romance, as being a story of human beings, absolutely credible and conceivable as distinguished from human beings frankly endowed with the glamour, the wonder, the brightness, of a less exacting and more vividly eventful world. The novel is a story that demands, or professes to demand, no make-believe. The novelist undertakes to present you people and things as real as any that you can meet in an omnibus. And I suppose it is conceivable that a novel might exist which was just purely a story of that kind and nothing more. It might amuse you as one is amused by looking out of a window into a street, or listening to a piece of agreeable music, and that might be the limit of its effect. But almost always the novel is something more than that, and produces more effect than that. The novel has inseparable moral consequences. It leaves impressions, not simply of things seen, but of acts judged and made attractive or unattractive. They may prove very slight moral consequences, and very shallow moral impressions in the long run, but there they are, none the less, its inevitable accompaniments. It is unavoidable that this should be so. Even if the novelist attempts or affects to be impartial, he still cannot prevent his characters setting examples; he still cannot avoid, as people say, putting ideas into his readers' heads. The greater his skill, the more convincing his treatment the more vivid his power of suggestion. And it is equally impossible for him not to betray his sense that the proceedings of this person are rather jolly and admirable, and of that, rather ugly and detestable. I suppose Mr. Bennett, for example, would say that he should not do so; but it is as manifest to any disinterested observer that he greatly loves and admires his Card, as that Richardson admired his Sir Charles Grandison, or that Mrs. Humphry Ward considers her Marcella a very fine and estimable young woman. And I think it is just in this, that the novel is not simply a fictitious record of conduct, but also a study and judgment of conduct, and through that of the ideas that lead to conduct, that the real and increasing value—or perhaps to avoid controversy I had better say the real and increasing importance—of the novel and of the novelist in modern life comes in.

It is no new discovery that the novel, like the drama, is a powerful instrument of moral suggestion. This has been understood in England ever since there has been such a thing as a novel in England. This has been recognised equally by novelists, novel-readers, and the people who wouldn't read novels under any condition whatever. Richardson wrote deliberately for edification, and "Tom Jones" is a powerful and effective appeal for a charitable, and even indulgent, attitude towards loose-living men. But excepting Fielding and one or two other of those partial exceptions that always occur in the case of critical generalisations, there is a definable difference between the novel of the past and what I may call the modern novel. It is a difference that is reflected upon the novel from a difference in the general way of thinking. It lies in the fact that formerly there was a feeling of certitude about moral values and standards of conduct that is altogether absent to-day. It wasn't so much that men were agreed upon these things—about these things there have always been enormous divergences of opinion—as that men were emphatic, cocksure, and unteachable about whatever they did happen to believe to a degree that no longer obtains. This is the Balfourian age, and even religion seeks to establish itself on doubt. There were, perhaps, just as many differences in the past as there are now, but the outlines were harder—they were, indeed, so hard as to be almost, to our sense, savage. You might be a Roman Catholic, and in that case you did not want to hear about Protestants, Turks, Infidels, except in tones of horror and hatred. You knew exactly what was good and what was evil. Your priest informed you upon these points, and all you needed in any novel you read was a confirmation, implicit or explicit, of these vivid, rather than charming, prejudices. If you were a Protestant you were equally clear and unshakable. Your sect, whichever sect you belonged to, knew the whole of truth and included all the nice people. It had nothing to learn in the world, and it wanted to learn nothing outside its sectarian convictions. The unbelievers you know, were just as bad, and said their creeds with an equal fury—merely interpolating *nots*. People of every sort—Catholic, Protestant, Infidel, or what not—were equally clear that good was good and bad was bad, that the world was made up of good characters whom you had to love, help and admire, and of bad characters to whom one might, in the interests of goodness, even lie, and whom one had to foil, defeat and triumph over shamelessly at every opportunity. That was the quality of the times. The novel reflected this quality of assurance, and its utmost charity was to unmask an apparent villain and show that he or she was really profoundly and correctly good, or to unmask an apparent saint and show the hypocrite. There was no such penetrating and pervading element of doubt and curiosity—and charity, about the rightfulness and beauty of conduct, such as one meets on every hand to-day.

The novel-reader of the past, therefore, like the novel-reader of the more provincial parts of England to-day, judged a novel by the convictions that had been built up in him by his training and his priest or his pastor. If it agreed with these convictions he approved; if it did not agree he disapproved—often with great energy. The novel, where it was not unconditionally banned altogether as a thing disturbing and unnecessary, was regarded as a thing subordinated to the teaching of the priest or pastor, or whatever director and dogma was followed. Its modest moral confirmations began when authority had completed its direction. The novel was good—if it seemed to harmonise with the graver exercises conducted by Mr. Chadband—and it was bad and outcast if Mr. Chadband said so. And it is over the bodies of discredited and disgruntled Chadbands that the novel escapes from its servitude and inferiority.

Now the conflict of authority against criticism is one of the eternal conflicts of humanity. It is the conflict of organisation against initiative, of discipline against freedom. It was the conflict of the priest against the prophet in ancient Judaea, of the Pharisee against the Nazarene, of the Realist against the Nominalist, of the Church against the Franciscan and the Lollard, of the Respectable Person against the Artist, of the hedge-clippers of mankind against the shooting buds. And to-day, while we live in a period of tightening and extending social organisation, we live also in a period of adventurous and insurgent thought, in an intellectual spring unprecedented in the world's history. There is an enormous criticism going on of the faiths upon which men's lives and associations are based, and of every standard and rule of conduct. And it is inevitable that the novel, just in the measure of its sincerity and ability, should reflect and co-operate in the atmosphere and uncertainties and changing variety of this seething and creative time.

And I do not mean merely that the novel is unavoidably charged with the representation of this wide and wonderful conflict. It is a necessary part of the conflict. The essential characteristic of this great intellectual revolution amidst which we are living to-day, that revolution of which the revival and restatement of nominalism under the name of pragmatism is the philosophical aspect, consists in the reassertion of the importance of the individual instance as against the generalisation. All our social, political, moral problems are being approached in a new spirit, in an inquiring and experimental spirit, which has small respect for abstract principles and deductive rules. We perceive more and more clearly, for example, that the study of social organisation is an empty and unprofitable study until we approach it as a study of the association and inter-reaction of individualised human beings inspired by diversified motives, ruled by traditions, and swayed by the suggestions of a complex intellectual atmosphere. And all our conceptions of the relationships between man and man, and of justice and rightfulness and social desirableness, remain something misfitting and inappropriate, something uncomfortable and potentially injurious, as if we were trying to wear sharp-edged clothes made for a giant out of tin, until we bring them to the test and measure of realised individualities.

And this is where the value and opportunity of the modern novel comes in. So far as I can see, it is the only medium through which we can discuss the great majority of the problems which are being raised in such bristling multitude by our contemporary social development Nearly every one of those problems has at its core a psychological problem, and not merely a psychological problem, but one in which the idea of individuality is an essential factor. Dealing with most of these questions by a rule or a generalisation is like putting a cordon round a jungle full of the most diversified sort of game. The hunting only begins when you leave the cordon behind you and push into the thickets.

Take, for example, the immense cluster of difficulties that arises out of the increasing complexity of our state. On every hand we are creating officials, and compared with only a few years ago the private life in a dozen fresh directions comes into contact with officialdom. But we still do practically nothing to work out the interesting changes that occur in this sort of man and that, when you withdraw him as it were from the common crowd of humanity, put his mind if not his body into uniform and endow him with powers and functions and rules. It is manifestly a study of the profoundest public and personal importance. It is manifestly a study of increasing importance. The process of social and political organisation that has been going on for the last quarter of a century is pretty clearly going on now if anything with increasing vigour— and for the most part the entire dependence of the consequences of the whole problem upon the reaction between the office on the one hand and the weak, uncertain, various human beings who take office on the other, doesn't seem even to be suspected by the energetic, virtuous and more or less amiable people whose activities in politics and upon the backstairs of politics bring about these developments. They assume that the sort of official they need, a combination of god-like virtue and intelligence with unfailing mechanical obedience, can be made out of just any young nephew. And I know of no means of persuading people that this is a rather unjustifiable assumption, and of creating an intelligent controlling criticism of officials and of assisting conscientious officials to an effective self-examination, and generally of keeping the atmosphere of official life sweet and healthy, except the novel. Yet so far the novel has scarcely begun its attack upon this particular field of human life, and all the attractive varied play of motive it contains.

Of course we have one supreme and devastating study of the illiterate minor official in Bumble. That one figure lit up and still lights the whole problem of Poor Law administration for the English reading community. It was a translation of well-meant regulations and pseudo-scientific conceptions of social order into blundering, arrogant, ill-bred flesh and blood. It was worth a hundred Royal Commissions. You may make your regulations as you please, said Dickens in effect; this is one sample of the stuff that will carry them out. But Bumble stands almost alone. Instead of realising that he is only one aspect of officialdom, we are all too apt to make him the type of all officials, and not an urban district council can get into a dispute about its electric light without being denounced as a Bumbledom by some whirling enemy or other. The burthen upon Bumble's shoulders is too heavy to be borne, and we want the contemporary novel to give us a score of other figures to put beside him, other aspects and reflections upon this great problem of officialism made flesh. Bumble is a magnificent figure of the follies and cruelties of ignorance in office—I would have every candidate for the post of workhouse master pass a severe examination upon "Oliver Twist"—but it is not only caricature and satire I demand. We must have not only the fullest treatment of the temptations, vanities, abuses, and absurdities of office, but all its dreams, its sense of constructive order, its consolations, its sense of service, and its nobler satisfactions. You may say that is demanding more insight and power in our novels and novelists than we can possibly hope to find in them. So much the worse for us. I stick to my thesis that the complicated social organisation of to-day cannot get along without the amount of mutual understanding and mutual explanation such a range of characterisation in our novels implies. The success of civilisation amounts ultimately to a success of sympathy and understanding. If people cannot be brought to an interest in one another greater than they feel to-day, to curiosities and criticisms far keener, and co-operations far subtler, than we have now; if class cannot be brought to measure itself against, and interchange experience and sympathy with class, and temperament with temperament then we shall never struggle very far beyond the confused discomforts and uneasiness of to-day, and the changes and complications of human life will remain as they are now, very like the crumplings and separations and complications of an immense avalanche that is sliding down a hill. And in this tremendous work of human reconciliation and elucidation, it seems to me it is the novel that must attempt most and achieve most.

You may feel disposed to say to all this: We grant the major premises, but why look to the work of prose fiction as the main instrument in this necessary process of, so to speak, sympathising humanity together? Cannot this be done far more effectively through biography and autobiography, for example? Isn't there the lyric; and, above all, isn't there the play? Well, so far as the stage goes, I think it is a very charming and exciting form of human activity, a display of actions and surprises of the most moving and impressive sort; but beyond the opportunity it affords for saying startling and thought-provoking things—opportunities Mr. Shaw, for example, has worked to the utmost limit—I do not see that the drama does much to enlarge our sympathies and add to our stock of motive ideas. And regarded as a medium for startling and thought-provoking things, the stage seems to me an extremely clumsy and costly affair. One might just as well go about with a pencil writing up the thought-provoking phrase, whatever it is, on walls. The drama excites our sympathies intensely, but it seems to me it is far too objective a medium to widen them appreciably, and it is that widening, that increase in the range of understanding, at which I think civilisation is aiming. The case for biography, and more particularly autobiography, as against the novel, is, I admit, at the first blush stronger. You may say: Why give us these creatures of a novelist's imagination, these phantom and fantastic thinkings and doings, when we may have the stories of real lives, really lived—the intimate record of actual men and women? To which one answers: "Ah, if one could!" But it is just because biography does deal with actual lives, actual facts, because it radiates out to touch continuing interests and sensitive survivors, that it is so unsatisfactory, so untruthful. Its inseparable falsehood is the worst of all kinds of falsehood—the falsehood of omission. Think what an abounding, astonishing, perplexing person Gladstone must have been in life, and consider Lord Morley's "Life of Gladstone," cold, dignified—not a life at all, indeed, so much as embalmed remains; the fire gone, the passions gone, the bowels carefully removed. All biography has something of that post-mortem coldness and respect, and as for autobiography—a man may show his soul in a thousand half-conscious ways, but to turn upon oneself and explain oneself is given to no one. It is the natural liars and braggarts, your Cellinis and Casanovas, men with a habit of regarding themselves with a kind of objective admiration, who do best in autobiography. And, on the other hand, the novel has neither the intense self-consciousness of autobiography nor the paralysing responsibilities of the biographer. It is by comparison irresponsible and free. Because its characters are figments and phantoms, they can be made entirely transparent. Because they are fictions, and you know they are fictions, so that they cannot hold you for an instant so soon as they cease to be true, they have a power of veracity quite beyond that of actual records. Every novel carries its own justification and its own condemnation in its success or failure to convince you that *the thing was so.* Now history, biography, blue-book and so forth, can hardly ever get beyond the statement that the superficial fact was so.

You see now the scope of the claim I am making for the novel; it is to be the social mediator, the vehicle of understanding, the instrument of self-examination, the parade of morals and the exchange of manners, the factory of customs, the criticism of laws and institutions and of social dogmas and ideas. It is to be the home confessional, the initiator of knowledge, the seed of fruitful self-questioning. Let me be very clear here. I do not mean for a moment that the novelist is going to set up as a teacher, as a sort of priest with a pen, who will make men and women believe and do this and that. The novel is not a new sort of pulpit; humanity is passing out of the phase when men *sit under* preachers and dogmatic influences. But the novelist is going to be the most potent of artists, because he is going to present conduct, devise beautiful conduct, discuss conduct analyse conduct, suggest conduct, illuminate it through and through. He will not teach, but discuss, point out, plead, and display. And this being my view you will be prepared for the demand I am now about to make for an absolutely free hand for the novelist in his choice of topic and incident and in his method of treatment; or rather, if I may presume to speak for other novelists, I would say it is not so much a demand we make as an intention we proclaim. We are going to write, subject only to our limitations, about the whole of human life. We are going to deal with political questions and religious questions and social questions. We cannot present people unless we have this free hand, this unrestricted field. What is the good of telling stories about people's lives if one may not deal freely with the religious beliefs and organisations that have controlled or failed to control them? What is the good of pretending to write about love, and the loyalties and treacheries and quarrels of men and women, if one must not glance at those varieties of physical temperament and organic quality, those deeply passionate needs and distresses from which half the storms of human life are brewed? We mean to deal with all these things, and it will need very much more than the disapproval of provincial librarians, the hostility of a few influential people in London, the scurrility of one paper, and the deep and obstinate silences of another, to stop the incoming tide of aggressive novel-writing. We are going to write about it all. We are going to write about business and finance and politics and precedence and pretentiousness and decorum and indecorum, until a thousand pretences and ten thousand impostures shrivel in the cold, clear air of our elucidations. We are going to write of wasted opportunities and latent beauties until a thousand new ways of living open to men and women. We are going to appeal to the young and the hopeful and the curious, against the established, the dignified, and defensive. Before we have done, we will have all life within the scope of the novel.

THE PHILOSOPHER'S PUBLIC LIBRARY

Suppose a philosopher had a great deal of money to spend—though this is not in accordance with experience, it is not inherently impossible—and suppose he thought, as any philosopher does think, that the British public ought to read much more and better books than they do, and that founding public libraries was the way to induce them to do so, what sort of public libraries would he found? That, I submit, is a suitable topic for a disinterested speculator.

He would, I suppose, being a philosopher, begin by asking himself what a library essentially was, and he would probably come to the eccentric conclusion that it was essentially a collection of books. He would, in his unworldliness, entirely overlook the fact that it might be a job for a municipally influential builder, a costly but conspicuous monument to opulent generosity, a news-room, an employment bureau, or a meeting-place for the glowing young; he would never think for a moment of a library as a thing one might build, it would present itself to him with astonishing simplicity as a thing one would collect. Bricks ceased to be literature after Babylon.

His first proceeding would be, I suppose, to make a list of that collection. What books, he would say, have all my libraries to possess anyhow? And he would begin to jot down—with the assistance of a few friends, perhaps—this essential list.

He would, being a philosopher, insist on good editions, and he would also take great pains with the selection. It would not be a limited or an exclusive list—when in doubt he would include. He would disregard modern fiction very largely, because any book that has any success can always be bought for sixpence, and modern poetry, because, with an exception or so, it does not signify at all. He would set almost all the Greek and Roman literature in well-printed translations and with luminous introductions—and if there were no good translations he would give some good man £500 or so to make one—translations of all that is good in modern European literatures, and, last but largest portion of his list, editions of all that is worthy of our own. He would make a very careful list of thoroughly modern encyclopaedias, atlases, and volumes of information, and a particularly complete catalogue of all literature that is still copyright; and then—with perhaps a secretary or so—he would revise all his lists and mark against every book whether he would have two, five or ten or twenty copies, or whatever number of copies of it he thought proper in each library.

Then next, being a philosopher, he would decide that if he was going to buy a great number of libraries in this way, he was going to make an absolutely new sort of demand for these books, and that he was entitled to a special sort of supply.

He would not expect the machinery of retail book-selling to meet the needs of wholesale buying. So he would go either to wholesale booksellers, or directly to the various publishers of the books and editions he had chosen, and ask for reasonable special prices for the two thousand or seven thousand or fifty thousand of each book he required. And the publishers would, of course, give him very special prices, more especially in the case of the out-of-copyright books. He would probably find it best to buy whole editions in sheets and bind them himself in strong bindings. And he would emerge from these negotiations in possession of a number of complete libraries each of—how many books? Less than twenty thousand ought to do it, I think, though that is a matter for separate discussion, and that should cost him, buying in this wholesale way, under rather than over £2,000 a library.

And next he would bethink himself of the readers of these books. "These people," he would say, "do not know very much about books, which, indeed, is why I am giving them this library."

Accordingly, he would get a number of able and learned people to write him guides to his twenty thousand books, and, in fact, to the whole world of reading, a guide, for example, to the books on history in general, a special guide to books on English history, or French or German history, a guide to the books on geology, a guide to poetry and poetical criticisms, and so forth.

Some such books our philosopher would find already done—the "Bibliography of American History," of the American Libraries'

Association, for example, and Mr. Nield's "Guide to Historical Fiction"—and what are not done he would commission good men to do for him. Suppose he had to commission forty such guides altogether and that they cost him on the average £500 each, for he would take care not to sweat their makers, then that would add another £20,000 to his expenditure. But if he was going to found 400 libraries, let us say, that would only be £50 a library—a very trivial addition to his expenditure.

The rarer books mentioned in these various guides would remind him, however, of the many even his ample limit of twenty thousand forced him to exclude, and he would, perhaps, consider the need of having two or three libraries each for the storage of a hundred thousand books or so not kept at the local libraries, but which could be sent to them at a day's notice at the request of any reader. And then, and only then, would he give his attention to the housing and staffing that this reality of books would demand.

Being a philosopher and no fool, he would draw a very clear, hard distinction between the reckless endowment of the building trade and the dissemination of books. He would distinguish, too, between a library and a news-room, and would find no great attraction in the prospect of supplying the national youth with free but thumby copies of the sixpenny magazines. He would consider that all that was needed for his library was, first, easily accessible fireproof shelving for his collection, with ample space for his additions, an efficient distributing office, a cloak-room, and so forth, and eight or nine not too large, well lit, well carpeted, well warmed and well ventilated rooms radiating from that office, in which the guides and so forth could be consulted, and where those who had no convenient, quiet room at home could read.

He would find that, by avoiding architectural vulgarities, a simple, well proportioned building satisfying all these requirements and containing housing for the librarian, assistant, custodian and staff could be built for between £4,000 and £5,000, excluding the cost of site, and his sites, which he would not choose for their conspicuousness, might average something under another £1,000.

He would try to make a bargain with the local people for their co-operation in his enterprise, though he would, as a philosopher, understand that where a public library is least wanted it is generally most needed. But in most cases he would succeed in stipulating for a certain standard of maintenance by the local authority. Since moderately prosperous illiterate men undervalue education and most town councillors are moderately illiterate men, he would do his best to keep the salary and appointment of the librarian out of such hands. He would stipulate for a salary of at least £400, in addition to housing, light and heat, and he would probably find it advisable to appoint a little committee of visitors who would have the power to examine qualifications, endorse the appointment, and recommend the dismissal of all his four hundred librarians. He would probably try to make the assistantship at £100 a year or thereabout a sort of local scholarship to be won by competition, and only the cleaner and caretaker's place would be left to the local politician. And, of course, our philosopher would stipulate that, apart from all other expenditure, a sum of at least £200 a year should be set aside for buying new books.

So our rich philosopher would secure at the minimum cost a number of efficiently equipped libraries throughout the country. Eight thousand pounds down and £900 a year is about as cheap as a public library can be. Below that level, it would be cheaper to have no public library. Above that level, a public library that is not efficient is either dishonestly or incapably organised or managed, or it is serving too large a district and needs duplication, or it is trying to do too much.

ABOUT CHESTERTON AND BELLOC

It has been one of the less possible dreams of my life to be a painted Pagan God and live upon a ceiling. I crown myself becomingly in stars or tendrils or with electric coruscations (as the mood takes me), and wear an easy costume free from complications and appropriate to the climate of those agreeable spaces. The company about me on the clouds varies greatly with the mood of the vision, but always it is in some way, if not always a very obvious way, beautiful. One frequent presence is G.K. Chesterton, a joyous whirl of brush work, appropriately garmented and crowned. When he is there, I remark, the whole ceiling is by a sort of radiation convivial. We drink limitless old October from handsome flagons, and we argue mightily about Pride (his weak point) and the nature of Deity. A hygienic, attentive, and essentially anaesthetic Eagle checks, in the absence of exercise, any undue enlargement of our Promethean livers . . . Chesterton often—but never by any chance Belloc. Belloc I admire beyond measure, but there is a sort of partisan viciousness about Belloc that bars him from my celestial dreams. He never figures, no, not even in the remotest corner, on my ceiling. And yet the divine artist, by some strange skill that my ignorance of his technique saves me from the presumption of explaining, does indicate exactly where Belloc is. A little quiver of the paint, a faint aura, about the spectacular masses of Chesterton? I am not certain. But no intelligent beholder can look up and miss the remarkable fact that Belloc exists—and that he is away, safely away, away in his heaven, which is, of course, the Park Lane Imperialist's hell. There he presides . . .

But in this life I do not meet Chesterton exalted upon clouds, and there is but the mockery of that endless leisure for abstract discussion afforded by my painted entertainments. I live in an urgent and incessant world, which is at its best a wildly beautiful confusion of impressions and at its worst a dingy uproar. It crowds upon us and jostles us, we get our little interludes for thinking and talking between much rough scuffling and laying about us with our fists. And I cannot afford to be continually bickering with Chesterton and Belloc about forms of expression. There are others for whom I want to save my knuckles. One may be wasteful in peace and leisure, but economies are the soul of conflict.

In many ways we three are closely akin; we diverge not by necessity but accident, because we speak in different dialects and have divergent metaphysics. All that I can I shall persuade to my way of thinking about thought and to the use of words in my loose, expressive manner, but Belloc and Chesterton and I are too grown and set to change our languages now and learn new ones; we are on different roads, and so we must needs shout to one another across intervening abysses. These two say Socialism is a thing they do not want for men, and I say Socialism is above all what I want for men. We shall go on saying that now to the end of our days. But what we do all three want is something very alike. Our different roads are parallel. I aim at a growing collective life, a perpetually enhanced inheritance for our race, through the fullest, freest development of the individual life. What they aim at ultimately I do not understand, but it is manifest that its immediate form is the fullest and freest development of the individual life. We all three hate equally and sympathetically the spectacle of human beings blown up with windy wealth and irresponsible power as cruelly and absurdly as boys blow up frogs; we all three detest the complex causes that dwarf and cripple lives from the moment of birth and starve and debase great masses of mankind. We want as universally as possible the jolly life, men and women warm-blooded and well-aired, acting freely and joyously, gathering life as children gather corn-cockles in corn. We all three want people to have property of a real and personal sort, to have the son, as Chesterton put it, bringing up the port his father laid down, and pride in the pears one has grown in one's own garden. And I agree with Chesterton that giving—giving oneself out of love and fellowship—is the salt of life.

But there I diverge from him, less in spirit, I think, than in the manner of his expression. There is a base because impersonal way of giving. "Standing drink," which he praises as noble, is just the thing I cannot stand, the ultimate mockery and vulgarisation of that fine act of bringing out the cherished thing saved for the heaven-sent guest. It is a mere commercial transaction, essentially of the evil of our time. Think of it! Two temporarily homeless beings agree to drink together, and they turn in and face the public supply of drink (a little vitiated by private commercial necessities) in the public-house. (It is horrible that life should be so wholesale and heartless.) And Jones, with a sudden effusion of manner, thrusts twopence or ninepence (got God knows how) into the economic mysteries and personal delicacy of Brown. I'd as soon a man slipped sixpence down my neck. If Jones has used love and sympathy to detect a certain real thirst and need in Brown and knowledge and power in its assuaging by some specially appropriate fluid, then we have an altogether different matter; but the common business of "standing treat" and giving presents and entertainments is as proud and unspiritual as cock-crowing, as foolish and inhuman as that sorry compendium of mercantile vices, the game of poker, and I am amazed to find Chesterton commend it.

But that is a criticism by the way. Chesterton and Belloc agree with the Socialist that the present world does not give at all what they want. They agree that it fails to do so through a wild derangement of our property relations. They are in agreement with the common contemporary man (whose creed is stated, I think, not unfairly, but with the omission of certain important articles by Chesterton), that the derangements of our property relations are to be remedied by concerted action and in part by altered laws. The land and all sorts of great common interests must be, if not owned, then at least controlled, managed, checked, redistributed by the State. Our real difference is only about a little more or a little less owning. I do not see how Belloc and Chesterton can stand for anything but a strong State as against those wild monsters of property, the strong, big private owners. The State must be complex and powerful enough to prevent them. State or plutocrat there is really no other practical alternative before the world at the present time. Either we have to let the big financial adventurers, the aggregating capitalist and his Press, in a loose, informal combination, rule the earth, either we have got to stand aside from preventive legislation and leave things to work out on their present lines, or we have to construct a collective organisation sufficiently strong for the protection of the liberties of the some-day-to-be-jolly common man. So far we go in common. If Belloc and Chesterton are not Socialists, they are at any rate not anti Socialists. If they say they want an organised Christian State (which involves practically seven-tenths of the Socialist desire), then, in the face of our big common enemies, of adventurous capital, of alien Imperialism, base ambition, base intelligence, and common prejudice and ignorance, I do not mean to quarrel with them politically, so long as they force no quarrel on me. Their organised Christian State is nearer the organised State I want than our present plutocracy. Our ideals will fight some day, and it will be, I know, a first-rate fight, but to fight now is to let the enemy in. When we have got all we want in common, then and only then can we afford to differ. I have never believed that a Socialist Party could hope to form a Government in this country in my lifetime; I believe it less now than ever I did. I don't know if any of my Fabian colleagues entertain so remarkable a hope. But if they do not, then unless their political aim is pure cantankerousness, they must contemplate a working political combination between the Socialist members in Parliament and just that non-capitalist section of the Liberal Party for which Chesterton and Belloc speak. Perpetual opposition is a dishonourable aim in politics; and a man who mingles in political development with no intention of taking on responsible tasks unless he gets all his particular formulae accepted is a pervert, a victim of Irish bad example, and unfit far decent democratic institutions . . .

I digress again, I see, but my drift I hope is clear. Differ as we may, Belloc and Chesterton are with all Socialists in being on the same side of the great political and social cleavage that opens at the present time. We and they are with the interests of the mass of common men as against that growing organisation of great owners who have common interests directly antagonistic to those of the community and State. We Socialists are only secondarily politicians. Our primary business is not to impose upon, but to ram right into the substance of that object of Chesterton's solicitude, the circle of ideas of the common man, the idea of the State as his own, as a thing he serves and is served by. We want to add to his sense of property rather than offend it. If I had my way I would do that at the street corners and on the trams, I would take down that alien-looking and detestable inscription "L.C.C.," and put up, "This Tram, this Street, belongs to the People of London." Would Chesterton or Belloc quarrel with that? Suppose that Chesterton is right, and that there are incurable things in the mind of the common man flatly hostile to our ideals; so much of our ideals will fail. But we are doing our best by our lights, and all we can. What are Chesterton and Belloc doing? If our ideal is partly right and partly wrong, are they trying to build up a better ideal? Will they state a Utopia and how they propose it shall be managed? If they lend their weight only to such fine old propositions as that a man wants freedom, that he has a right to do as he likes with his own, and so on, they won't help the common man much. All that fine talk, without some further exposition, goes to sustain Mr. Rockefeller's simple human love of property, and the woman and child sweating manufacturer in his fight for the inspector-free home industry. I bought on a bookstall the other day a pamphlet full of misrepresentation and bad argument against Socialism by an Australian Jew, published by the Single-Tax people apparently in a disinterested attempt to free the land from the landowner by the simple expedient of abusing anyone else who wanted to do as much but did not hold Henry George to be God and Lord; and I know Socialists who will protest with tears in their eyes against association with any human being who sings any song but the "Red Flag" and doubts whether Marx had much experience of affairs. Well, there is no reason why Chesterton and Belloc should at their level do the same sort of thing. When we talk on a ceiling or at a dinner-party with any touch of the celestial in its composition, Chesterton and I, Belloc and I, are antagonists with an undying feud, but in the fight against human selfishness and narrowness and for a finer, juster law, we are brothers—at the remotest, half-brothers.

Chesterton isn't a Socialist—agreed! But now, as between us and the Master of Elibank or Sir Hugh Bell or any other Free Trade Liberal capitalist or landlord, which side is he on? You cannot have more than one fight going on in the political arena at the same time, because only one party or group of parties can win.

And going back for a moment to that point about a Utopia, I want one from Chesterton. Purely unhelpful criticism isn't enough from a man of his size. It isn't justifiable for him to go about sitting on other people's Utopias. I appeal to his sense of fair play. I have done my best to reconcile the conception of a free and generous style of personal living with a social organisation that will save the world from the harsh predominance of dull, persistent, energetic, unscrupulous grabbers tempered only by the vulgar extravagance of their wives and sons. It isn't an adequate reply to say that nobody stood treat there, and that the simple, generous people like to beat their own wives and children on occasion in a loving and intimate manner, and that they won't endure the spirit of Mr. Sidney Webb.

ABOUT SIR THOMAS MORE

There are some writers who are chiefly interesting in themselves, and some whom chance and the agreement of men have picked out as symbols and convenient indications of some particular group or temperament of opinions. To the latter it is that Sir Thomas More belongs. An age and a type of mind have found in him and his Utopia a figurehead and a token; and pleasant and honourable as his personality and household present themselves to the modern reader, it is doubtful if they would by this time have retained any peculiar distinction among the many other contemporaries of whom we have chance glimpses in letters and suchlike documents, were it not that he happened to be the first man of affairs in England to imitate the "Republic" of Plato. By that chance it fell to him to give the world a noun and an adjective of abuse, "Utopian," and to record how under the stimulus of Plato's releasing influence the opening problems of our modern world presented themselves to the English mind of his time. For the most part the problems that exercised him are the problems that exercise us to-day, some of them, it may be, have grown up and intermarried, new ones have joined their company, but few, if any, have disappeared, and it is alike in his resemblances to and differences from the modern speculative mind that his essential interest lies.

The portrait presented by contemporary mention and his own intentional and unintentional admissions, is of an active-minded and agreeable-mannered man, a hard worker, very markedly prone to quips and whimsical sayings and plays upon words, and aware of a double reputation as a man of erudition and a wit. This latter quality it was that won him advancement at court, and it may have been his too clearly confessed reluctance to play the part of an informal table jester to his king that laid the grounds of that deepening royal resentment that ended only with his execution. But he was also valued by the king for more solid merits, he was needed by the king, and it was more than a table scorned or a clash of opinion upon the validity of divorce; it was a more general estrangement and avoidance of service that caused that fit of regal petulance by which he died.

It would seem that he began and ended his career in the orthodox religion and a general acquiescence in the ideas and customs of his time, and he played an honourable and acceptable part in that time; but his permanent interest lies not in his general conformity but in his incidental scepticism, in the fact that underlying the observances and recognised rules and limitations that give the texture of his life were the profoundest doubts, and that, stirred and disturbed by Plato, he saw fit to write them down. One may question if such scepticism is in itself unusual, whether any large proportion of great statesmen, great ecclesiastics and administrators have escaped phases of destructive self-criticism of destructive criticism of the principles upon which their general careers were framed. But few have made so public an admission as Sir Thomas More. A good Catholic undoubtedly he was, and yet we find him capable of conceiving a non-Christian community excelling all Christendom in wisdom and virtue; in practice his sense of conformity and orthodoxy was manifest enough, but in his "Utopia" he ventures to contemplate, and that not merely wistfully, but with some confidence, the possibility of an absolute religious toleration.

The "Utopia" is none the less interesting because it is one of the most inconsistent of books. Never were the forms of Socialism and Communism animated by so entirely an Individualist soul. The hands are the hands of Plato, the wide-thinking Greek, but the voice is the voice of a humane, public-spirited, but limited and very practical English gentleman who takes the inferiority of his inferiors for granted, dislikes friars and tramps and loafers and all undisciplined and unproductive people, and is ruler in his own household. He abounds in sound practical ideas, for the migration of harvesters, for the universality of gardens and the artificial incubation of eggs, and he sweeps aside all Plato's suggestion of the citizen woman as though it had never entered his mind. He had indeed the Whig temperament, and it manifested itself down even to the practice of reading aloud in company, which still prevails among the more representative survivors of the Whig tradition. He argues ably against private property, but no thought of any such radicalism as the admission of those poor peons of his, with head half-shaved and glaring uniform against escape, to participation in ownership appears in his proposals. His communism is all for the convenience of his Syphogrants and Tranibores, those gentlemen of gravity and experience, lest one should swell up above the others. So too is the essential Whiggery of the limitation of the Prince's revenues. It is the very spirit of eighteenth century Constitutionalism. And his Whiggery bears Utilitarianism instead of the vanity of a flower. Among his cities, all of a size, so that "he that knoweth one knoweth all," the Benthamite would have revised his sceptical theology and admitted the possibility of heaven.

Like any Whig, More exalted reason above the imagination at every point, and so he fails to understand the magic prestige of gold, making that beautiful metal into vessels of dishonour to urge his case against it, nor had he any perception of the charm of extravagance, for example, or the desirability of various clothing. The Utopians went all in coarse linen and undyed wool—why should the world be coloured?—and all the economy of labour and shortening of the working day was to no other end than to prolong the years of study and the joys of reading aloud, the simple satisfactions of the good boy at his lessons, to the very end of life. "In the institution of that weal publique this end is only and chiefly pretended and minded, that what time may possibly be spared from the necessary occupations and affairs of the commonwealth, all that the citizens should withdraw from the bodily service to the free liberty of the mind and garnishing of the same. For herein they suppose the felicity of this life to consist."

Indeed, it is no paradox to say that "Utopia," which has by a conspiracy of accidents become a proverb for undisciplined fancifulness in social and political matters, is in reality a very unimaginative work. In that, next to the accident of its priority, lies the secret of its continuing interest. In some respects it is like one of those precious and delightful scrapbooks people disinter in old country houses; its very poverty of synthetic power leaves its ingredients, the cuttings from and imitations of Plato, the recipe for the hatching of eggs, the stern resolutions against scoundrels and rough fellows, all the sharper and brighter. There will always be found people to read in it, over and above the countless multitudes who will continue ignorantly to use its name for everything most alien to More's essential quality.

TRAFFIC AND REBUILDING

The London traffic problem is just one of those questions that appeal very strongly to the more prevalent and less charitable types of English mind. It has a practical and constructive air, it deals with impressively enormous amounts of tangible property, it rests with a comforting effect of solidity upon assumptions that are at once doubtful and desirable. It seems free from metaphysical considerations, and it has none of those disconcerting personal applications, those penetrations towards intimate qualities, that makes eugenics, for example, faintly but persistently uncomfortable. It is indeed an ideal problem for a healthy, hopeful, and progressive middle-aged public man. And, as I say, it deals with enormous amounts of tangible property.

Like all really serious and respectable British problems it has to be handled gently to prevent its coming to pieces in the gift. It is safest in charge of the expert, that wonderful last gift of time. He will talk rapidly about congestion, long-felt wants, low efficiency, economy, and get you into his building and rebuilding schemes with the minimum of doubt and head-swimming. He is like a good Hendon pilot. Unspecialised writers have the destructive analytical touch. They pull the wrong levers. So far as one can gather from the specialists on the question, there is very considerable congestion in many of the London thoroughfares, delays that seem to be avoidable occur in the delivery of goods, multitudes of empty vans cumber the streets, we have hundreds of acres of idle trucks—there are more acres of railway sidings than of public parks in Greater London—and our Overseas cousins find it ticklish work crossing Regent Street and Piccadilly. Regarding life simply as an affair of getting people and things from where they are to where they appear to be wanted, this seems all very muddled and wanton. So far it is quite easy to agree with the expert. And some of the various and entirely incompatible schemes experts are giving us by way of a remedy, appeal very strongly to the imagination. For example, there is the railway clearing house, which, it is suggested, should cover I do not know how many acres of what is now slumland in Shoreditch. The position is particularly convenient for an underground connection with every main line into London. Upon the underground level of this great building every goods train into London will run. Its trucks and vans will be unloaded, the goods passed into lifts, which will take every parcel, large and small, at once to a huge, ingeniously contrived sorting-floor above. There in a manner at once simple, ingenious and effective, they will be sorted and returned, either into delivery vans at the street level or to the trains emptied and now reloading on the train level. Above and below these three floors will be extensive warehouse accommodation. Such a scheme would not only release almost all the vast area of London now under railway yards for parks and housing, but it would give nearly every delivery van an effective load, and probably reduce the number of standing and empty vans or half-empty vans on the streets of London to a quarter or an eighth of the present number. Mostly these are heavy horse vans, and their disappearance would greatly facilitate the conversion of the road surfaces to the hard and even texture needed for horseless traffic.

But that is a scheme too comprehensive and rational for the ordinary student of the London traffic problem, whose mind runs for the most part on costly and devastating rearrangements of the existing roadways. Moreover, it would probably secure a maximum of effect with a minimum of property manipulation; always an undesirable consideration in practical politics. And it would commit London and England to goods transit by railway for another century. Far more attractive to the expert advisers of our various municipal authorities are such projects as a new Thames bridge scheme, which will (with incalculable results) inject a new stream of traffic into Saint Paul's Churchyard; and the removal of Charing Cross Station to the south side of the river. Then, again, we have the systematic widening of various thoroughfares, the shunting of tramways into traffic streams, and many amusing, expensive, and interesting tunnellings and clearances. Taken together, these huge reconstructions of London are incoherent and conflicting; each is based on its own assumptions and separate "expert" advice, and the resulting new opening plays its part in the general circulation as duct or aspirator, often with the most surprising results. The discussion of the London traffic problem as we practise it in our clubs is essentially the sage turning over and over again of such fragmentary schemes, headshakings over the vacant sites about Aldwych and the Strand, brilliant petty suggestions and—dispersal. Meanwhile the experts intrigue; one partial plan after another gets itself accepted, this and that ancient landmark perish, builders grow rich, and architects infamous, and some Tower Bridge horror, some vulgarity of the Automobile Club type, some Buckingham Palace atrocity, some Regent Street stupidity, some such cramped and thwarted thing as that new arch which gives upon Charing Cross is added to the confusion. I do not see any reason to suppose that this continuous muddle of partial destruction and partial rebuilding is not to constitute the future history of London.

Let us, however, drop the expert methods and handle this question rather more rudely. Do we want London rebuilt? If we do, is there, after all, any reason why we should rebuild it on its present site? London is where it is for reasons that have long ceased to be valid; it grew there, it has accumulated associations, an immense tradition, that this constant mucking about of builders and architects is destroying almost as effectually as removal to a new site. The old sort of rebuilding was a natural and picturesque process, house by house, and street by street, a thing as pleasing and almost as natural in effect as the spreading and interlacing of trees; as this new building, this clearance of areas, the piercing of avenues, becomes more comprehensive, it becomes less reasonable. If we can do such big things we may surely attempt bigger things, so that whether we want to plan a new capital or preserve the old, it comes at last to the same thing, that it is unreasonable to be constantly pulling down the London we have and putting it up again. Let us drain away our heavy traffic into tunnels, set up that clearing-house plan, and control the growth at the periphery, which is still so witless and ugly, and, save for the manifest tidying and preserving that is needed, begin to leave the central parts of London, which are extremely interesting even where they are not quite beautiful, in peace.

THE SO-CALLED
SCIENCE OF SOCIOLOGY

It has long been generally recognised that there are two quite divergent ways of attacking sociological and economic questions, one that is called scientific and one that is not, and I claim no particular virtue in the recognition of that; but I do claim a certain freshness in my analysis of this difference, and it is to that analysis that your attention is now called. When I claim freshness I do not make, you understand, any claim to original discovery. What I have to say, and have been saying for some time, is also more or less, and with certain differences to be found in the thought of Professor Bosanquet, for example, in Alfred Sidgwick's "Use of Words in Reasoning," in Sigwart's "Logic," in contemporary American metaphysical speculation. I am only one incidental voice speaking in a general movement of thought. My trend of thought leads me to deny that sociology is a science, or only a science in the same loose sense that modern history is a science, and to throw doubt upon the value of sociology that follows too closely what is called the scientific method.

The drift of my argument is to dispute not only that sociology is a science, but also to deny that Herbert Spencer and Comte are to be exalted as the founders of a new and fruitful system of human inquiry. I find myself forced to depreciate these modern idols, and to reinstate the Greek social philosophers in their vacant niches, to ask you rather to go to Plato for the proper method, the proper way of thinking sociologically.

We certainly owe the word Sociology to Comte, a man of exceptionally methodical quality. I hold he developed the word logically from an arbitrary assumption that the whole universe of being was reducible to measurable and commeasurable and exact and consistent expressions.

In a very obvious way, sociology seemed to Comte to crown the edifice of the sciences; it was to be to the statesman what pathology and physiology were to the doctor; and one gathers that, for the most part, he regarded it as an intellectual procedure in no way differing from physics. His classification of the sciences shows pretty clearly that he thought of them all as exact logical systematisations of fact arising out of each other in a synthetic order, each lower one containing the elements of a lucid explanation of those above it—physics explaining chemistry; chemistry, physiology; physiology, sociology; and so forth. His actual method was altogether unscientific; but through all his work runs the assumption that in contrast with his predecessors he is really being as exact and universally valid as mathematics. To Herbert Spencer—very appropriately since his mental characteristics make him the English parallel to Comte—we owe the naturalisation of the word in English. His mind being of greater calibre than Comte's, the subject acquired in his hands a far more progressive character. Herbert Spencer was less unfamiliar with natural history than with any other branch of practical scientific work; and it was natural he should turn to it for precedents in sociological research. His mind was invaded by the idea of classification, by memories of specimens and museums; and he initiated that accumulation of desiccated anthropological anecdotes that still figures importantly in current sociological work. On the lines he initiated sociological investigation, what there is of it, still tends to go.

From these two sources mainly the work of contemporary sociologists derives. But there persists about it a curious discursiveness that reflects upon the power and value of the initial impetus. Mr. V.V. Branford, the able secretary of the Sociological Society, recently attempted a useful work in a classification of the methods of what he calls "approach," a word that seems to me eminently judicious and expressive. A review of the first volume the Sociological Society has produced brings home the aptness of this image of exploratory operations, of experiments in "taking a line." The names of Dr. Beattie Crozier and Mr. Benjamin Kidd recall works that impress one as large-scale sketches of a proposed science rather than concrete beginnings and achievements. The search for an arrangement, a "method," continues as though they were not. The desperate resort to the analogical method of Comincius is confessed by Dr. Steinmetz, who talks of social morphology, physiology, pathology, and so forth. There is also a less initiative disposition in the Vicomte Combes de Lestrade and in the work of Professor Giddings. In other directions sociological work is apt to lose its general reference altogether, to lapse towards some department of activity not primarily sociological at all. Examples of this are the works of Mr. and Mrs. Sidney Webb, M. Ostrogorski and M. Gustave le Bon. From a contemplation of all this diversity Professor Durkheim emerges, demanding a "synthetic science," "certain synthetic conceptions"—and Professor Karl Pearson endorses the demand—to fuse all these various activities into something that will live and grow. What is it that tangles this question so curiously that there is not only a failure to arrive at a conclusion, but a failure to join issue?

Well, there is a certain not too clearly recognised order in the sciences to which I wish to call your attention, and which forms the gist of my case against this scientific pretension. There is a gradation in the importance of the instance as one passes from mechanics and physics and chemistry through the biological sciences to economics and sociology, a gradation whose correlatives and implications have not yet received adequate recognition, and which do profoundly affect the method of study and research in each science.

Let me begin by pointing out that, in the more modern conceptions of logic, it is recognised that there are no identically similar objective experiences; the disposition is to conceive all real objective being as individual and unique. This is not a singular eccentric idea of mine; it is one for which ample support is to be found in the writings of absolutely respectable contemporaries, who are quite untainted by association with fiction. It is now understood that conceivably only in the subjective world, and in theory and the imagination, do we deal with identically similar units, and with absolutely commensurable quantities. In the real world it is reasonable to suppose we deal at most with *practically* similar units and *practically* commensurable quantities. But there is a strong bias, a sort of labour-saving bias in the normal human mind to ignore this, and not only to speak but to think of a thousand bricks or a thousand sheep or a thousand sociologists as though they were all absolutely true to sample. If it is brought before a thinker for a moment that in any special case this is not so, he slips back to the old attitude as soon as his attention is withdrawn. This source of error has, for instance, caught nearly the whole race of chemists, with one or two distinguished exceptions, and *atoms* and *ions* and so forth of the same species are tacitly assumed to be similar one to another. Be it noted that, so far as the practical results of chemistry and physics go, it scarcely matters which assumption we adopt. For purposes of inquiry and discussion the incorrect one is infinitely more convenient.

But this ceases to be true directly we emerge from the region of chemistry and physics. In the biological sciences of the eighteenth century, commonsense struggled hard to ignore individuality in shells and plants and animals. There was an attempt to eliminate the more conspicuous departures as abnormalities, as sports, nature's weak moments, and it was only with the establishment of Darwin's great generalisation that the hard and fast classificatory system broke down, and individuality came to its own. Yet there had always been a clearly felt difference between the conclusions of the biological sciences and those dealing with lifeless substance, in the relative vagueness, the insubordinate looseness and inaccuracy of the former. The naturalist accumulated facts and multiplied names, but he did not go triumphantly from generalisation to generalisation after the fashion of the chemist or physicist. It is easy to see, therefore, how it came about that the inorganic sciences were regarded as the true scientific bed-rock. It was scarcely suspected that the biological sciences might perhaps, after all, be *truer* than the experimental, in spite of the difference in practical value in favour of the latter. It was, and is by the great majority of people to this day, supposed to be the latter that are invincibly true; and the former are regarded as a more complex set of problems merely, with obliquities and refractions that presently will be explained away. Comte and Herbert Spencer certainly seem to me to have taken that much for granted. Herbert Spencer no doubt talked of the unknown and the unknowable, but not in this sense, as an element of inexactness running through all things. He thought of the unknown as the indefinable beyond to an immediate world that might be quite clearly and exactly known.

Well, there is a growing body of people who are beginning to hold the converse view—that counting, classification, measurement, the whole fabric of mathematics, is subjective and deceitful, and that the uniqueness of individuals is the objective truth. As the number of units taken diminishes, the amount of variety and inexactness of generalisation increases, because individuality tells more and more. Could you take men by the thousand billion, you could generalise about them as you do about atoms; could you take atoms singly, it may be you would find them as individual as your aunts and cousins. That concisely is the minority belief, and it is the belief on which this present paper is based.

Now, what is called the scientific method is the method of ignoring individualities; and, like many mathematical conventions, its great practical convenience is no proof whatever of its final truth. Let me admit the enormous value, the wonder of its results in mechanics, in all the physical sciences, in chemistry, even in physiology—but what is its value beyond that? Is the scientific method of value in biology? The great advances made by Darwin and his school in biology were not made, it must be remembered, by the scientific method, as it is generally conceived, at all. He conducted a research into pre-documentary history. He collected information along the lines indicated by certain interrogations; and the bulk of his work was the digesting and critical analysis of that. For documents and monuments he had fossils and anatomical structures and germinating eggs too innocent to lie, and so far he was nearer simplicity. But, on the other hand, he had to correspond with breeders and travellers of various sorts, classes entirely analogous, from the point of view of evidence, to the writers of history and memoirs. I question profoundly whether the word "science," in current usage anyhow, ever means such patient disentanglement as Darwin pursued. It means the attainment of something positive and emphatic in the way of a conclusion, based on amply repeated experiments capable of infinite repetition, "proved," as they say, "up to the hilt."

It would be, of course, possible to dispute whether the word "science" should convey this quality of certitude; but to most people it certainly does at the present time. So far as the movements of comets and electric trams go, there is, no doubt, practically cocksure science; and indisputably Comte and Herbert Spencer believed that cocksure could be extended to every conceivable finite thing. The fact that Herbert Spencer called a certain doctrine Individualism reflects nothing on the non-individualising quality of his primary assumptions and of his mental texture. He believed that individuality (heterogeneity) was and is an evolutionary product from an original homogeneity. It seems to me that the general usage is entirely for the limitation of the use of the word "science" to knowledge and the search after knowledge of a high degree of precision. And not simply the general usage: "Science is measurement," Science is "organised common sense," proud, in fact, of its essential error, scornful of any metaphysical analysis of its terms.

If we quite boldly face the fact that hard positive methods are less and less successful just in proportion as our "ologies" deal with larger and less numerous individuals; if we admit that we become less "scientific" as we ascend the scale of the sciences, and that we do and must change our method, then, it is humbly submitted we shall be in a much better position to consider the question of "approaching" sociology. We shall realise that all this talk of the organisation of sociology, as though presently the sociologist would be going about the world with the authority of a sanitary engineer, is and will remain nonsense.

In one respect we shall still be in accordance with the Positivist map of the field of human knowledge; with us as with that, sociology stands at the extreme end of the scale from the molecular sciences. In these latter there is an infinitude of units; in sociology, as Comte perceived, there is only one unit. It is true that Herbert Spencer, in order to get classification somehow, did, as Professor Durkheim has pointed out, separate human society into societies, and made believe they competed one with another and died and reproduced just like animals, and that economists, following List, have for the purposes of fiscal controversy discovered economic types; but this is a transparent device, and one is surprised to find thoughtful and reputable writers off their guard against such bad analogy. But, indeed, it is impossible to isolate complete communities of men, or to trace any but rude general resemblances between group and group. These alleged units have as much individuality as pieces of cloud; they come, they go, they fuse and separate. And we are forced to conclude that not only is the method of observation, experiment, and verification left far away down the scale, but that the method of classification under types, which has served so useful a purpose in the middle group of subjects, the subjects involving numerous but a finite number of units, has also to be abandoned here. We cannot put Humanity into a museum, or dry it for examination; our one single still living specimen is all history, all anthropology, and the fluctuating world of men. There is no satisfactory means of dividing it, and nothing else in the real world with which to compare it. We have only the remotest ideas of its "life-cycle" and a few relics of its origin and dreams of its destiny . . .

Sociology, it is evident, is, upon any hypothesis, no less than the attempt to bring that vast, complex, unique Being, its subject, into clear, true relations with the individual intelligence. Now, since individual intelligences are individual, and each is a little differently placed in regard to the subject under consideration, since the personal angle of vision is much wider towards humanity than towards the circumambient horizon of matter, it should be manifest that no sociology of universal compulsion, of anything approaching the general validity of the physical sciences, is ever to be hoped for—at least upon the metaphysical assumptions of this paper. With that conceded, we may go on to consider the more hopeful ways in which that great Being may be presented in a comprehensible manner. Essentially this presentation must involve an element of self-expression must partake quite as much of the nature of art as of science. One finds in the first conference of the Sociological Society, Professor Stein, speaking, indeed a very different philosophical dialect from mine, but coming to the same practical conclusion in the matter, and Mr. Osman Newland counting "evolving ideals for the future" as part of the sociologist's work. Mr. Alfred Fouillée also moves very interestingly in the region of this same idea; he concedes an essential difference between sociology and all other sciences in the fact of a "certain kind of liberty belonging to society in the exercise of its higher functions." He says further: "If this view be correct, it will not do for us to follow in the steps of Comte and Spencer, and transfer, bodily and ready-made, the conceptions and the methods of the natural sciences into the science of society. For here the fact of *consciousness* entails a reaction of the whole assemblage of social phenomena upon themselves, such as the natural sciences have no example of."

And he concludes: "Sociology ought, therefore, to guard carefully against the tendency to crystallise that which is essentially fluid and moving, the tendency to consider as given fact or dead data that which creates itself and gives itself into the world of phenomena continually by force of its own ideal conception." These opinions do, in their various keys, sound a similar *motif* to mine. If, indeed, the tendency of these remarks is justifiable, then unavoidably the subjective element, which is beauty, must coalesce with the objective, which is truth; and sociology mast be neither art simply, nor science in the narrow meaning of the word at all, but knowledge rendered imaginatively, and with an element of personality that is to say, in the highest sense of the term, literature.

If this contention is sound, if therefore we boldly set aside Comte and Spencer altogether, as pseudo-scientific interlopers rather than the authoritative parents of sociology, we shall have to substitute for the classifications of the social sciences an inquiry into the chief literary forms that subserve sociological purposes. Of these there are two, one invariably recognised as valuable and one which, I think, under the matter-of-fact scientific obsession, is altogether underrated and neglected The first, which is the social side of history, makes up the bulk of valid sociological work at the present time. Of history there is the purely descriptive part, the detailed account of past or contemporary social conditions, or of the sequence of such conditions; and, in addition, there is the sort of historical literature that seeks to elucidate and impose general interpretations upon the complex of occurrences and institutions, to establish broad historical generalisations, to eliminate the mass of irrelevant incident, to present some great period of history, or all history, in the light of one dramatic sequence, or as one process. This Dr. Beattie Crozier, for example, attempts in his "History of Intellectual Development." Equally comprehensive is Buckle's "History of Civilisation." Lecky's "History of European Morals," during the onset of Christianity again, is essentially sociology. Numerous works—Atkinson's "Primal Law," and Andrew Lang's "Social Origins," for example—may be considered, as it were, to be fragments to the same purport. In the great design of Gibbon's "Decline and Fall of the Roman Empire," or Carlyle's "French Revolution," you have a greater insistence upon the dramatic and picturesque elements in history, but in other respects an altogether kindred endeavour to impose upon the vast confusions of the past a scheme of interpretation, valuable just to the extent of its literary value, of the success with which the discrepant masses have been fused and cast into the shape the insight of the writer has determined. The writing of great history is entirely analogous to fine portraiture, in which fact is indeed material, but material entirely subordinate to vision.

One main branch of the work of a Sociological Society therefore should surely be to accept and render acceptable, to provide understanding, criticism, and stimulus for such literary activities as restore the dead bones of the past to a living participation in our lives.

But it is in the second and at present neglected direction that I believe the predominant attack upon the problem implied by the word "sociology" must lie; the attack that must be finally driven home. There is no such thing in sociology as dispassionately considering what *is*, without considering what is *intended to be*. In sociology, beyond any possibility of evasion, ideas are facts. The history of civilisation is really the history of the appearance and reappearance, the tentatives and hesitations and alterations, the manifestations and reflections in this mind and that, of a very complex, imperfect elusive idea, the Social Idea. It is that idea struggling to exist and realise itself in a world of egotisms, animalisms, and brute matter. Now, I submit it is not only a legitimate form of approach, but altogether the most promising and hopeful form of approach, to endeavour to disentangle and express one's personal version of that idea, and to measure realities from the stand-point of that idealisation. I think, in fact, that the creation of Utopias—and their exhaustive criticism—is the proper and distinctive method of sociology.

Suppose now the Sociological Society, or some considerable proportion of it, were to adopt this view, that sociology is the description of the Ideal Society and its relation to existing societies, would not this give the synthetic framework Professor Durkheim, for example, has said to be needed?

Almost all the sociological literature beyond the province of history that has stood the test of time and established itself in the esteem of men is frankly Utopian. Plato, when his mind turned to schemes of social reconstruction thrust his habitual form of dialogue into a corner; both the "Republic" and the "Laws" are practically Utopias in monologue; and Aristotle found the criticism of the Utopian suggestions of his predecessors richly profitable. Directly the mind of the world emerged again at the Renascence from intellectual barbarism in the brief breathing time before Sturm and the schoolmasters caught it and birched it into scholarship and a new period of sterility, it went on from Plato to the making of fresh Utopias. Not without profit did More discuss pauperism in this form and Bacon the organisation of research; and the yeast of the French Revolution was Utopias. Even Comte, all the while that he is professing science, fact, precision, is adding detail after detail to the intensely personal Utopia of a Western Republic that constitutes his one meritorious gift to the world. Sociologists cannot help making Utopias; though they avoid the word, though they deny the idea with passion, their very silences shape a Utopia. Why should they not follow the precedent of Aristotle, and accept Utopias as material?

There used to be in my student days, and probably still flourishes, a most valuable summary of fact and theory in comparative anatomy, called Rolleston's "Forms of Animal Life." I figure to myself a similar book, a sort of dream book of huge dimensions, in reality perhaps dispersed in many volumes by many hands, upon the Ideal Society. This book, this picture of the perfect state, would be the backbone of sociology. It would have great sections devoted to such questions as the extent of the Ideal Society, its relation to racial differences, the relations of the sexes in it, its economic organisations, its organisation for thought and education, its "Bible"—as Dr. Beattie Crozier would say— its housing and social atmosphere, and so forth. Almost all the divaricating work at present roughly classed together as sociological could be brought into relation in the simplest manner, either as new suggestions, as new discussion or criticism, as newly ascertained facts bearing upon such discussions and sustaining or eliminating suggestions. The institutions of existing states would come into comparison with the institutions of the Ideal State, their failures and defects would be criticised most effectually in that relation, and the whole science of collective psychology, the psychology of human association, would be brought to bear upon the question of the practicability of this proposed ideal.

This method would give not only a boundary shape to all sociological activities, but a scheme of arrangement for text books and lectures, and points of direction and reference for the graduation and post graduate work of sociological students.

Only one group of inquiries commonly classed as sociological would have to be left out of direct relationship with this Ideal State; and that is inquiries concerning the rough expedients to meet the failure of imperfect institutions. Social emergency work of all sorts comes under this head. What to do with the pariah dogs of Constantinople, what to do with the tramps who sleep in the London parks, how to organise a soup kitchen or a Bible coffee van, how to prevent ignorant people, who have nothing else to do, getting drunk in beer-houses, are no doubt serious questions for the practical administrator, questions of primary importance to the politician; but they have no more to do with sociology than the erection of a temporary hospital after the collision of two trains has to do with railway engineering.

So much for my second and most central and essential portion of sociological work. It should be evident that the former part, the historical part, which conceivably will be much the bulkier and more abundant of the two, will in effect amount to a history of the suggestions in circumstance and experience of that Idea of Society of which the second will consist, and of the instructive failures in attempting its incomplete realisation.

DIVORCE

The time is fast approaching when it will be necessary for the general citizen to form definite opinions upon proposals for probably quite extensive alterations of our present divorce laws, arising out of the recommendations of the recent Royal Commission on the subject. It may not be out of place, therefore, to run through some of the chief points that are likely to be raised, and to set out the main considerations affecting these issues.

Divorce is not one of those things that stand alone, and neither divorce law nor the general principles of divorce are to be discussed without a reference to antecedent arrangements. Divorce is a sequel to marriage, and a change in the divorce law is essentially a change in the marriage law. There was a time in this country when our marriage was a practically divorceless bond, soluble only under extraordinary circumstances by people in situations of exceptional advantage for doing so. Now it is a bond under conditions, and in the event of the adultery of the wife, or of the adultery plus cruelty or plus desertion of the husband, and of one or two other rarer and more dreadful offences, it can be broken at the instance of the aggrieved party. A change in the divorce law is a change in the dissolution clauses, so to speak, of the contract for the marriage partnership. It is a change in the marriage law.

A great number of people object to divorce under any circumstances whatever. This is the case with the orthodox Catholic and with the orthodox Positivist. And many religious and orthodox people carry their assertion of the indissolubility of marriage to the grave; they demand that the widow or widower shall remain unmarried, faithful to the vows made at the altar until death comes to the release of the lonely survivor also. Re-marriage is regarded by such people as a posthumous bigamy. There is certainly a very strong and logical case to be made out for a marriage bond that is indissoluble even by death. It banishes step-parents from the world. It confers a dignity of tragic inevitability upon the association of husband and wife, and makes a love approach the gravest, most momentous thing in life. It banishes for ever any dream of escape from the presence and service of either party, or of any separation from the children of the union. It affords no alternative to "making the best of it" for either husband or wife; they have taken a step as irrevocable as suicide. And some logical minds would even go further, and have no law as between the members of a family, no rights, no private property within that limit. The family would be the social unit and the father its public representative, and though the law might intervene if he murdered or ill-used wife or children, or they him, it would do so in just the same spirit that it might prevent him from self-mutilation or attempted suicide, for the good of the State simply, and not to defend any supposed independence of the injured member. There is much, I assert, to be said for such a complete shutting up of the family from the interference of the law, and not the least among these reasons is the entire harmony of such a view with the passionate instincts of the natural man and woman in these matters. All unsophisticated human beings appear disposed to a fierce proprietorship in their children and their sexual partners, and in no respect is the ordinary mortal so easily induced to vehemence and violence.

For my own part, I do not think the maintenance of a marriage that is indissoluble, that precludes the survivor from re-marriage, that gives neither party an external refuge from the misbehaviour of the other, and makes the children the absolute property of their parents until they grow up, would cause any very general unhappiness Most people are reasonable enough, good-tempered enough, and adaptable enough to shake down even in a grip so rigid, and I would even go further and say that its very rigidity, the entire absence of any way out at all, would oblige innumerable people to accommodate themselves to its conditions and make a working success of unions that, under laxer conditions, would be almost certainly dissolved. We should have more people of what I may call the "broken-in" type than an easier release would create, but to many thinkers the spectacle of a human being thoroughly "broken-in" is in itself extremely satisfactory. A few more crimes of desperation perhaps might occur, to balance against an almost universal effort to achieve contentment and reconciliation. We should hear more of the "natural law" permitting murder by the jealous husband or by the jealous wife, and the traffic in poisons would need a sedulous attention—but even there the impossibility of re-marriage would operate to restrain the impatient. On the whole, I can imagine the world rubbing along very well with marriage as unaccommodating as a perfected steel trap. Exceptional people might suffer or sin wildly—to the general amusement or indignation.

But when once we part from the idea of such a rigid and eternal marriage bond—and the law of every civilised country and the general thought and sentiment everywhere have long since done so—then the whole question changes. If marriage is not so absolutely sacred a bond, if it is not an eternal bond, but a bond we may break on this account or that, then at once we put the question on a different footing. If we may terminate it for adultery or cruelty, or any cause whatever, if we may suspend the intimacy of husband and wife by separation orders and the like, if we recognise their separate property and interfere between them and their children to ensure the health and education of the latter, then we open at once the whole question of a terminating agreement. Marriage ceases to be an unlimited union and becomes a definite contract. We raise the whole question of "What are the limits in marriage, and how and when may a marriage terminate?"

Now, many answers are being given to that question at the present time. We may take as the extremest opposite to the eternal marriage idea the proposal of Mr. Bernard Shaw, that marriage should be terminable at the instance of either party. You would give due and public notice that your marriage was at an end, and it would be at an end. This is marriage at its minimum, as the eternal indissoluble marriage is marriage at its maximum, and the only conceivable next step would be to have a marriage makeable by the oral declaration of both parties and terminable by the oral declaration of either, which would be, indeed, no marriage at all, but an encounter. You might marry a dozen times in that way in a day . . . Somewhere between these extremes lies the marriage law of a civilised state. Let us, rather than working down from the eternal marriage of the religious idealists, work up from Mr. Shaw. The former course is, perhaps, inevitable for the legislator, but the latter is much more convenient for our discussion.

Now, the idea of a divorce so easy and wilful as Mr. Shaw proposes arises naturally out of an exclusive consideration of what I may call the amorous sentimentalities of marriage. If you regard marriage as merely the union of two people in love, then, clearly, it is intolerable, an outrage upon human dignity, that they should remain intimately united when either ceases to love. And in that world of Mr. Shaw's dreams, in which everybody is to have an equal income and nobody is to have children, in that culminating conversazione of humanity, his marriage law will, no doubt, work with the most admirable results. But if we make a step towards reality and consider a world in which incomes are unequal, and economic difficulties abound—for the present we will ignore the complication of offspring—we at once find it necessary to modify the first fine simplicity of divorce at either partner's request. Marriage is almost always a serious economic disturbance for both man and woman: work has to be given up and rearranged, resources have to be pooled; only in the rarest cases does it escape becoming an indefinite business partnership. Accordingly, the withdrawal of one partner raises at once all sorts of questions of financial adjustment, compensation for physical, mental, and moral damage, division of furniture and effects and so forth. No doubt a very large part of this could be met if there existed some sort of marriage settlement providing for the dissolution of the partnership. Otherwise the petitioner for a Shaw-esque divorce must be prepared for the most exhaustive and penetrating examination before, say, a court of three assessors—representing severally the husband, the wife, and justice—to determine the distribution of the separation. This point, however, leads me to note in passing the need that does exist even to-day for a more precise business supplement to marriage as we know it in England and America. I think there ought to be a very definite and elaborate treaty of partnership drawn up by an impartial private tribunal for every couple that marries, providing for most of the eventualities of life, taking cognizance of the earning power, the property and prospects of either party, insisting upon due insurances, ensuring private incomes for each partner, securing the welfare of the children, and laying down equitable conditions in the event of a divorce or separation. Such a treaty ought to be a necessary prelude to the issue of a licence to marry. And given such a basis to go upon, then I see no reason why, in the case of couples who remain childless for five or six years, let us say, and seem likely to remain childless, the Shaw-esque divorce at the instance of either party, without reason assigned, should not be a very excellent thing indeed.

And I take up this position because I believe in the family as the justification of marriage. Marriage to me is no mystical and eternal union, but a practical affair, to be judged as all practical things are judged—by its returns in happiness and human welfare. And directly we pass from the mists and glamours of amorous passion to the warm realities of the nursery, we pass into a new system of considerations altogether. We are no longer considering A. in relation to Mrs. A., but A. and Mrs. A. in relation to an indefinite number of little A.'s, who are the very life of the State in which they live. Into the case of Mr. A. *v.* Mrs. A. come Master A. and Miss A. intervening. They have the strongest claim against both their parents for love, shelter and upbringing, and the legislator and statesman, concerned as he is chiefly with the future of the community, has the strongest reasons for seeing that they get these things, even at the price of considerable vexation, boredom or indignity to Mr. and Mrs. A. And here it is that there arises the rational case against free and frequent divorce and the general unsettlement and fluctuation of homes that would ensue.

At this point we come to the verge of a jungle of questions that would demand a whole book for anything like a complete answer. Let us try as swiftly and simply as possible to form a general idea at least of the way through. Remember that we are working upward from Mr. Shaw's question of "Why not separate at the choice of either party?" We have got thus far, that no two people who do not love each other should be compelled to live together, except where the welfare of their children comes in to override their desire to separate, and now we have to consider what may or may not be for the welfare of the children. Mr. Shaw, following the late Samuel Butler, meets this difficulty by the most extravagant abuse of parents. He would have us believe that the worst enemies a child can have are its mother and father, and that the only civilised path to citizenship is by the incubator, the crèche, and the mixed school and college. In these matters he is not only ignorant, but unfeeling and unsympathetic, extraordinarily so in view of his great capacity for pity and sweetness in other directions and of his indignant hatred of cruelty and unfairness, and it is not necessary to waste time in discussing what the common experience confutes Neither is it necessary to fly to the other extreme, and indulge in preposterous sentimentalities about the magic of fatherhood and a mother's love. These are not magic and unlimited things, but touchingly qualified and human things. The temperate truth of the matter is that in most parents there are great stores of pride, interest, natural sympathy, passionate love and devotion which can be tapped in the interests of the children and the social future, and that it is the mere commonsense of statecraft to use their resources to the utmost. It does not follow that every parent contains these reservoirs, and that a continual close association with the parents is always beneficial to children. If it did, we should have to prosecute everyone who employed a governess or sent away a little boy to a preparatory school. And our real task is to establish a test that will gauge the desirability and benefit of a parent's continued parentage. There are certainly parents and homes from which the children might be taken with infinite benefit to themselves and to society, and whose union it is ridiculous to save from the divorce court shears.

Suppose, now, we made the willingness of a parent to give up his or her children the measure of his beneficialness to them. There is no reason why we should restrict divorce only to the relation of husband and wife. Let us broaden the word and make it conceivable for a husband or wife to divorce not only the partner, but the children. Then it might be possible to meet the demands of the Shaw-esque extremist up to the point of permitting a married parent, who desired freedom, to petition for a divorce, not from his or her partner simply, but from his or her family, and even for a widow or widower to divorce a family. Then would come the task of the assessors. They would make arrangements for the dissolution of the relationship, erring from justice rather in the direction of liberality towards the divorced group, they would determine contributions, exact securities appoint trustees and guardians . . . On the whole, I do not see why such a system should not work very well. It would break up many loveless homes, quarrelling and bickering homes, and give a safety-valve for that hate which is the sinister shadow of love. I do not think it would separate one child from one parent who was really worthy of its possession.

So far I have discussed only the possibility of divorce without offences, the sort of divorce that arises out of estrangement and incompatibilities. But divorce, as it is known in most Christian countries, has a punitive element, and is obtained through the failure of one of the parties to observe the conditions of the bond and the determination of the other to exact suffering. Divorce as it exists at present is not a readjustment but a revenge. It is the nasty exposure of a private wrong. In England a husband may divorce his wife for a single act of infidelity, and there can be little doubt that we are on the eve of an equalisation of the law in this respect. I will confess I consider this an extreme concession to the passion of jealousy, and one likely to tear off the roof from many a family of innocent children. Only infidelity leading to supposititious children in the case of the wife, or infidelity obstinately and offensively persisted in or endangering health in the case of the husband, really injure the home sufficiently to justify a divorce on the assumptions of our present argument. If we are going to make the welfare of the children our criterion in these matters, then our divorce law does in this direction already go too far. A husband or wife may do far more injury to the home by constantly neglecting it for the companionship of some outside person with whom no "matrimonial offence" is ever committed. Of course, if our divorce law exists mainly for the gratification of the fiercer sexual resentments, well and good, but if that is so, let us abandon our pretence that marriage is an institution for the establishment and protection of homes. And while on the one hand existing divorce laws appear to be obsessed by sexual offences, other things of far more evil effect upon the home go without a remedy. There are, for example, desertion, domestic neglect, cruelty to the children drunkenness or harmful drug-taking, indecency of living and uncontrollable extravagance. I cannot conceive how any logical mind, having once admitted the principle of divorce, can hesitate at making these entirely home-wrecking things the basis of effective pleas. But in another direction, some strain of sentimentality in my nature makes me hesitate to go with the great majority of divorce law reformers. I cannot bring myself to agree that either a long term of imprisonment or the misfortune of insanity should in itself justify a divorce. I admit the social convenience, but I wince at the thought of those tragic returns of the dispossessed. So far as insanity goes, I perceive that the cruelty of the law would but endorse the cruelty of nature. But I do not like men to endorse the cruelty of nature.

And, of course, there is no decent-minded person nowadays but wants to put an end to that ugly blot upon our civilisation, the publication of whatever is most spicy and painful in divorce court proceedings. It is an outrage which falls even more heavily on the innocent than on the guilty, and which has deterred hundreds of shy and delicate-minded people from seeking legal remedies for nearly intolerable wrongs. The sort of person who goes willingly to the divorce court to-day is the sort of person who would love a screaming quarrel in a crowded street. The emotional breach of the marriage bond is as private an affair as its consummation, and it would be nearly as righteous to subject young couples about to marry to a blustering cross-examination by some underbred bully of a barrister upon their motives, and then to publish whatever chance phrases in their answers appeared to be amusing in the press, as it is to publish contemporary divorce proceedings. The thing is a nastiness, a stream of social contagion and an extreme cruelty, and there can be no doubt that whatever other result this British Royal Commission may have, there at least will be many sweeping alterations.

THE SCHOOLMASTER AND THE EMPIRE

Sec. 1

"If Youth but Knew" is the title of a book published some years ago, but still with a quite living interest, by "Kappa"; it is the bitter complaint of a distressed senior against our educational system. He is hugely disappointed in the public-school boy, and more particularly in one typical specimen. He is—if one might hazard a guess—an uncle bereft of great expectations. He finds an echo in thousands of other distressed uncles and parents. They use the most divergent and inadequate forms of expression for this vague sense that the result has not come out good enough; they put it contradictorily and often wrongly, but the sense is widespread and real and justifiable and we owe a great debt to "Kappa" for an accurate diagnosis of what in the aggregate amounts to a grave national and social evil.

The trouble with "Kappa's" particular public-school boy is his unlit imagination, the apathetic commonness of his attitude to life at large. He is almost stupidly not interested in the mysteries of material fact, nor in the riddles and great dramatic movements of history, indifferent to any form of beauty, and pedantically devoted to the pettiness of games and clothing and social conduct. It is, in fact, chiefly by his style in these latter things, his extensive unilluminated knowledge of Greek and Latin, and his greater costliness, that he differs from a young carpenter or clerk. A young carpenter or clerk of the same temperament would have no narrower prejudices nor outlook, no less capacity for the discussion of broad questions and for imaginative thinking. And it has come to the mind of "Kappa" as a discovery, as an exceedingly remarkable and moving thing, a thing to cry aloud about, that this should be so, that this is all that the best possible modern education has achieved. He makes it more than a personal issue. He has come to the conclusion that this is not an exceptional case at all, but a fair sample of what our upper-class education does for the imagination of those who must presently take the lead among us. He declares plainly that we are raising a generation of rulers and of those with whom the duty of initiative should chiefly reside, who have minds atrophied by dull studies and deadening suggestions, and he thinks that this is a matter of the gravest concern for the future of this land and Empire. It is difficult to avoid agreeing with him either in his observation or in his conclusion. Anyone who has seen much of undergraduates, or medical students, or Army candidates, and also of their social subordinates, must be disposed to agree that the difference between the two classes is mainly in unimportant things—in polish, in manner, in superficialities of accent and vocabulary and social habit—and that their minds, in range and power, are very much on a level. With an invincibly aristocratic tradition we are failing altogether to produce a leader class adequate to modern needs. The State is light-headed.

But while one agrees with "Kappa" and shares his alarm, one must confess the remedies he considers indicated do not seem quite so satisfactory as his diagnosis of the disease. He attacks the curriculum and tells us we must reduce or revolutionise instruction and exercise in the dead languages, introduce a broader handling of history, a more inspiring arrangement of scientific courses, and so forth. I wish, indeed, it were possible to believe that substituting biology for Greek prose composition or history with models and photographs and diagrams for Latin versification, would make any considerable difference in this matter. For so one might discuss this question and still give no offence to a most amiable and influential class of men. But the roots of the evil, the ultimate cause of that typical young man's deadness, lie not at all in that direction. To indicate the direction in which it does lie is quite unavoidably to give offence to an indiscriminatingly sensitive class. Yet there is need to speak plainly. This deadening of soul comes not from the omission or inclusion of this specific subject or that; it is the effect of the general scholastic atmosphere. It is an atmosphere that admits of no inspiration at all. It is an atmosphere from which living stimulating influences have been excluded from which stimulating and vigorous personalities are now being carefully eliminated, and in which dull, prosaic men prevail invincibly. The explanation of the inert commonness of "Kappa's" schoolboy lies not in his having learnt this or not learnt that, but in the fact that from seven to twenty he has been in the intellectual shadow of a number of good-hearted, sedulously respectable conscientiously manly, conforming, well-behaved men, who never, to the knowledge of their pupils and the public, at any rate, think strange thoughts do imaginative or romantic things, pay tribute to beauty, laugh carelessly, or countenance any irregularity in the world. All erratic and enterprising tendencies in him have been checked by them and brought at last to nothing; and so he emerges a mere residuum of decent minor dispositions. The dullness of the scholastic atmosphere the grey, intolerant mediocrity that is the natural or assumed quality of every upper-class schoolmaster, is the true cause of the spiritual etiolation of "Kappa's" young friend.

Now, it is a very grave thing, I know, to bring this charge against a great profession—to say, as I do say, that it is collectively and individually dull. But someone has to do this sooner or later; we have restrained ourselves and argued away from the question too long. There is, I allege, a great lack of vigorous and inspiring minds in our schools. Our upper-class schools are out of touch with the thought of the time, in a backwater of intellectual apathy. We have no original or heroic school-teachers. Let me ask the reader frankly what part our leading headmasters play in his intellectual world; if when some prominent one among them speaks or writes or talks, he expects anything more than platitudes and little things? Has he ever turned aside to learn what this headmaster or that thought of any question that interested him? Has he ever found freshness or power in a schoolmaster's discourse; or found a schoolmaster caring keenly for fine and beautiful things? Who does not know the schoolmaster's trite, safe admirations, his thin, evasive discussion, his sham enthusiasms for cricket, for fly-fishing, for perpendicular architecture, for boyish traits; his timid refuge in "good form," his deadly silences?

And if we do not find him a refreshing and inspiring person, and his mind a fountain of thought in which we bathe and are restored, is it likely our sons will? If the schoolmaster at large is grey and dull, shirking interesting topics and emphatic speech, what must he be like in the monotonous class-room? These may seem wanton charges to some, but I am not speaking without my book. Monthly I am brought into close contact with the pedagogic intelligence through the medium of three educational magazines. A certain morbid habit against which I struggle in vain makes me read everything I catch a schoolmaster writing. I am, indeed, one of the faithful band who read the Educational Supplement of the *Times*. In these papers schoolmasters write about their business, lectures upon the questions of their calling are reported at length, and a sort of invalid discussion moves with painful decorum through the correspondence column. The scholastic mind so displayed in action fascinates me. It is like watching a game of billiards with wooden cushes and beechwood balls.

Sec. 2

But let me take one special instance. In a periodical, now no longer living, called the *Independent Review*, there appeared some years ago a very curious and typical contribution by the Headmaster of Dulwich, which I may perhaps use as an illustration of the mental habits which seem inseparably associated with modern scholastic work. It is called "English Ideas on Education," and it begins— trite, imitative, undistinguished—thus:

"The most important question in a country is that of education, and the most important people in a country are those who educate its inhabitants. Others have most of the present in their hands: those who educate have all the future. With the present is bound up all the happiness only of the utterly selfish and the thoughtless among mankind; on the future rest all the thoughts of every parent and every wise man and patriot."

It is the opening of a boy's essay. And from first to last this remarkable composition is at or below that level. It is an entirely inconclusive paper, it is impossible to understand why it was written; it quotes nothing it says nothing about and was probably written in ignorance of "Kappa" or any other modern contributor to English ideas, and it occupied about six and a quarter of the large-type pages of this now vanished *Independent Review*. "English Ideas on Education"!—this very brevity is eloquent, the more so since the style is by no means succinct. It must be read to be believed. It is quite extraordinarily non-prehensile in quality and substance nothing is gripped and maintained and developed; it is like the passing of a lax hand over the surfaces of disarranged things. It is difficult to read, because one's mind slips over it and emerges too soon at the end, mildly puzzled though incurious still as to what it is all about. One perceives Mr. Gilkes through a fog dimly thinking that Greek has something vital to do with "a knowledge of language and man," that the classical master is in some mysterious way superior to the science man and more imaginative, and that science men ought not to be worried with the Greek that is too high for them; and he seems, too, to be under the odd illusion that "on all this" Englishmen "seem now to be nearly in agreement," and also on the opinion that games are a little overdone and that civic duties and the use of the rifle ought to be taught. Statements are made—the sort of statements that are suffered in an atmosphere where there is no swift, fierce opposition to be feared; they frill out into vague qualifications and butt gently against other partially contradictory statements. There is a classification of minds—the sort of classification dear to the Y.M.C.A. essayists, made for the purposes of the essay and unknown to psychology. There are, we are told, accurate unimaginative, ingenious minds capable of science and kindred vulgar things (such was Archimedes), and vague, imaginative minds, with the gift for language and for the treatment of passion and the higher indefinable things (such as Homer and Mr. Gilkes), and, somehow, this justifies those who are destined for "science" in dropping Greek. Certain "considerations," however, loom inconclusively upon this issue—rather like interested spectators of a street fight in a fog. For example, to learn a language is valuable "in proportion as the nation speaking it is great"—a most empty assertion; and "no languages are so good," for the purpose of improving style, "as the exact and beautiful languages of Rome and Greece."

Is it not time at least that this last, this favourite but threadbare article of the schoolmaster's creed was put away for good? Everyone who has given any attention to this question must be aware that the intellectual gesture is entirely different in highly inflected languages such as Greek and Latin and in so uninflected a language as English, that learning Greek to improve one's English style is like learning to swim in order to fence better, and that familiarity with Greek seems only too often to render a man incapable of clear, strong expression in English at all. Yet Mr. Gilkes can permit this old assertion, so dear to country rectors and the classical scholar, to appear within a column's distance of such style as this:

> "It is now understood that every subject is valuable, if it is properly taught; it will perform that which, as follows from the accounts given above of the aim of education, is the work most important in the case of boys—that is, it will draw out their faculties and make them useful in the world, alert, trained in industry, and able to understand, so far as their school lessons educated them, and make themselves master of any subject set before them."

This quotation is conclusive.

Sec. 3

I am haunted by a fear that the careless reader will think I am writing against upper-class schoolmasters. I am, it is undeniable, writing against their dullness, but it is, I hold, a dullness that is imposed upon them by the conditions under which they live. Indeed, I believe, could I put the thing directly to the profession—"Do you not yourselves feel needlessly limited and dull?"—should receive a majority of affirmative responses. We have, as a nation, a certain ideal of what a schoolmaster must be; to that he must by art or nature approximate, and there is no help for it but to alter our ideal. Nothing else of any wide value can be done until that is done.

In the first place, the received ideal omits a most necessary condition. We do not insist upon a headmaster or indeed any of our academic leaders and dignitaries, being a man of marked intellectual character, a man of intellectual distinction. It is assumed, rather lightly in many cases, that he has done "good work," as they say—the sort of good work that is usually no good at all, that increases nothing, changes nothing, stimulates no one, leads no whither. That, surely, must be altered. We must see to it that our leading schoolmasters at any rate must be men of insight and creative intelligence, men who could at a pinch write a good novel or produce illuminating criticism or take an original part in theological or philosophical discussion, or do any of these minor things. They must be authentic men, taking a line of their own and capable of intellectual passion. They should be able to make their mark outside the school, if only to show they carry a living soul into it. As things are, nothing is so fatal to a schoolmaster's career as to do that.

And closely related to this omission is our extreme insistence upon what we call high moral character, meaning, really, something very like an entire absence of moral character. We insist upon tact, conformity, and an unblemished record. Now, in these days, of warring opinion, these days of gigantic, strange issues that cannot possibly be expressed in the formulae of the smaller times that have gone before, tact is evasion, conformity formality, and silence an unblemished record, mere evidence of the damning burial of a talent of life. The sort of man into whose hands we give our sons' minds must never have experimented morally or thought at all freely or vigorously about, for example, God, Socialism, the Mosaic account of the Creation, social procedure, Republicanism, beauty, love, or, indeed, about anything likely to interest an intelligent adolescent. At the approach of all such things he must have acquired the habit of the modest cough, the infectious trick of the nice evasion. How can "Kappa" expect inspiration from the decorous resultants who satisfy these conditions? What brand can ever be lit at altars that have borne no fire? And you find the secondary schoolmaster who complies with these restrictions becoming the zealous and grateful agent of the tendencies that have made him what he is, converting into a practice those vague dreads of idiosyncrasy, of positive acts and new ideas, that dictated the choice of him and his rule of life. His moral teaching amounts to this: to inculcate truth-telling about small matters and evasion about large, and to cultivate a morbid obsession in the necessary dawn of sexual consciousness. So far from wanting to stimulate the imagination, he hates and dreads it. I find him perpetually haunted by a ridiculous fear that boys will "do something," and in his terror seeking whatever is dull and unstimulating and tiring in intellectual work, clipping their reading, censoring their periodicals, expurgating their classics, substituting the stupid grind of organised "games" for natural, imaginative play, persecuting loafers—and so achieving his end and turning out at last, clean-looking, passively well-behaved, apathetic, obliterated young men, with the nicest manners and no spark of initiative at all, quite safe not to "do anything" for ever.

I submit this may be a very good training for public servants, but it is not the way to make masters in the world. If we English believe we are indeed a masterful people, we must be prepared to expose our children to more and more various stimulations than we do; they must grow up free, bold, adventurous, initiated, even if they have to take more risks in the doing of that. An able and stimulating teacher is as rare as a fine artist, and is a thing worth having for your son, even at the price of shocking your wife by his lack of respect for that magnificent compromise, the Establishment, or you by his Socialism or by his Catholicism or Darwinism, or even by his erroneous choice of ties and collars. Boys who are to be free, masterly men must hear free men talking freely of religion, of philosophy, of conduct. They must have heard men of this opinion and that, putting what they believe before them with all the courage of conviction. They must have an idea of will prevailing over form. It is far more important that boys should learn from original, intellectually keen men than they should learn from perfectly respectable men, or perfectly orthodox men, or perfectly nice men. The vital thing to consider about your son's schoolmaster is whether he talked lifeless twaddle yesterday by way of a lesson, and not whether he loved unwisely or was born of poor parents, or was seen wearing a frock-coat in combination with a bowler, or confessed he doubted the Apostles' Creed, or called himself a Socialist, or any disgraceful thing like that, so many years ago. It is that sort of thing "Kappa" must invert if he wants a change in our public schools. You may arrange and rearrange curricula, abolish Greek, substitute "science"—it will not matter a rap. Even those model canoes of yours, "Kappa," will be wasted if you still insist upon model schoolmasters. So long as we require our schoolmasters to be politic, conforming, undisturbing men, setting up Polonius as an ideal for them, so long will their influence deaden the souls of our sons.

THE ENDOWMENT OF MOTHERHOOD

Some few years ago the Fabian Society, which has been so efficient in keeping English Socialism to the lines of "artfulness and the 'eighties," refused to have anything to do with the Endowment of Motherhood. Subsequently it repented and produced a characteristic pamphlet in which the idea was presented with a sort of minimising furtiveness as a mean little extension of outdoor relief. These Fabian Socialists, instead of being the daring advanced people they are supposed to be, are really in many things twenty years behind the times. There need be nothing shamefaced about the presentation of the Endowment of Motherhood. There is nothing shameful about it. It is a plain and simple idea for which the mind of the man in the street has now been very completely prepared. It has already crept into social legislation to the extent of thirty shillings.

I suppose if one fact has been hammered into us in the past two decades more than any other it is this: that the supply of children is falling off in the modern State; that births, and particularly good-quality births, are not abundant enough; that the birth-rate, and particularly the good-class birth-rate, falls steadily below the needs of our future.

If no one else has said a word about this important matter, ex-President Roosevelt would have sufficed to shout it to the ends of the earth. Every civilised community is drifting towards "race-suicide" as Rome drifted into "race-suicide" at the climax of her empire.

Well, it is absurd to go on building up a civilisation with a dwindling supply of babies in the cradles—and these not of the best possible sort—and so I suppose there is hardly an intelligent person in the English-speaking communities who has not thought of some possible remedy—from the naive scoldings of Mr.

Roosevelt and the more stolid of the periodicals to sane and intelligible legislative projects.

The reasons for the fall in the birth-rate are obvious enough. It is a necessary consequence of the individualistic competition of modern life. People talk of modern women "shirking" motherhood, but it would be a silly sort of universe in which a large proportion of women had any natural and instinctive desire to shirk motherhood, and, I believe, a huge proportion of modern women are as passionately predisposed towards motherhood as ever women were. But modern conditions conspire to put a heavy handicap upon parentage and an enormous premium upon the partial or complete evasion of offspring, and that is where the clue to the trouble lies. Our social arrangements discourage parentage very heavily, and the rational thing for a statesman to do in the matter is not to grow eloquent, but to do intelligent things to minimise that discouragement.

Consider the case of an energetic young man and an energetic young woman in our modern world. So long as they remain "unencumbered" they can subsist on a comparatively small income and find freedom and leisure to watch for and follow opportunities of self-advancement; they can travel, get knowledge and experience, make experiments, succeed. One might almost say the conditions of success and self-development in the modern world are to defer marriage as long as possible, and after that to defer parentage as long as possible. And even when there is a family there is the strongest temptation to limit it to three or four children at the outside. Parents who can give three children any opportunity in life prefer to do that than turn out, let us say, eight ill-trained children at a disadvantage, to become the servants and unsuccessful competitors of the offspring of the restrained. That fact bites us all; it does not require a search. It is all very well to rant about "race-suicide," but there are the clear, hard conditions of contemporary circumstances for all but the really rich, and so patent are they that I doubt if all the eloquence of Mr. Roosevelt and its myriad echoes has added a thousand babies to the eugenic wealth of the English-speaking world.

Modern married people, and particularly those in just that capable middle class from which children are most urgently desirable from the statesman's point of view, are going to have one or two children to please themselves but they are not going to have larger families under existing conditions, though all the ex-Presidents and all the pulpits in the world clamour together for them to do so.

If having and rearing children is a private affair, then no one has any right to revile small families; if it is a public service, then the parent is justified in looking to the State to recognise that service and offer some compensation for the worldly disadvantages it entails. He is justified in saying that while his unencumbered rival wins past him he is doing the State the most precious service in the world by rearing and educating a family, and that the State has become his debtor.

In other words, the modern State has got to pay for its children if it really wants them—and more particularly it has to pay for the children of good homes.

The alternative to that is racial replacement and social decay. That is the essential idea conveyed by this phrase, the Endowment of Motherhood.

Now, how is the paying to be done? That needs a more elaborate answer, of which I will give here only the roughest, crudest suggestion.

Probably it would be found best that the payment should be made to the mother, as the administrator of the family budget, that its amount should be made dependent upon the quality of the home in which the children are being reared, upon their health and physical development, and upon their educational success. Be it remembered, we do not want any children; we want good-quality children. The amount to be paid, I would particularly point out, should vary with the standing of the home. People of that excellent class which spends over a hundred a year on each child ought to get about that much from the State, and people of the class which spends five shillings a week per head on them would get about that, and so on. And if these payments were met by a special income tax there would be no social injustice whatever in such an unequality of payment. Each social stratum would pay according to its prosperity, and the only redistribution that would in effect occur would be that the childless people of each class would pay for the children of that class. The childless family and the small family would pay equally with the large family, incomes being equal, but they would receive in proportions varying with the health and general quality of their children. That, I think, gives the broad principles upon which the payments would be made.

Of course, if these subsidies resulted in too rapid a rise in the birth-rate, it would be practicable to diminish the inducement; and if, on the other hand, the birth-rate still fell, it would be easy to increase the inducement until it sufficed.

That concisely is the idea of the Endowment of Motherhood. I believe firmly that some such arrangement is absolutely necessary to the continuous development of the modern State. These proposals arise so obviously out of the needs of our time that I cannot understand any really intelligent opposition to them. I can, however, understand a partial and silly application of them. It is most important that our good-class families should be endowed, but the whole tendency of the timid and disingenuous progressivism of our time, which is all mixed up with ideas of charity and aggressive benevolence to the poor, would be to apply this—as that Fabian tract I mention does—only to the poor mother. To endow poor and bad-class motherhood and leave other people severely alone would be a proceeding so supremely idiotic, so harmful to our national quality, as to be highly probable in the present state of our public intelligence. It comes quite on a level with the policy of starving middle-class education that has left us with nearly the worst educated middle class in Western Europe.

The Endowment of Motherhood does not attract the bureaucratic type of reformer because it offers a minimum chance of meddlesome interference with people's lives. There would be no chance of "seeking out" anybody and applying benevolent but grim compulsions on the strength of it. In spite of its wide scope it would be much less of a public nuisance than that Wet Children's Charter, which exasperates me every time I pass a public-house on a rainy night. But, on the other hand, there would be an enormous stimulus to people to raise the quality of their homes, study infantile hygiene, seek out good schools for them—and do their duty as all good parents naturally want to do now—if only economic forces were not so pitilessly against them—thoroughly and well.

DOCTORS

In that extravagant world of which I dream, in which people will live in delightful cottages and ground rents will serve instead of rates, and everyone will have a chance of being happy—in that impossible world all doctors will be members of one great organisation for the public health, with all or most of their income guaranteed to them: I doubt if there will be any private doctors at all.

Heaven forbid I should seem to write a word against doctors as they are. Daily I marvel at the wonders the general practitioner achieves, having regard to the difficulties of his position.

But I cannot hide from myself, and I do not intend to hide from anyone else, my firm persuasion that the services the general practitioner is able to render us are not one-tenth so effectual as they might be if, instead of his being a private adventurer, he were a member of a sanely organised public machine. Consider what his training and equipment are, consider the peculiar difficulties of his work, and then consider for a moment what better conditions might be invented, and perhaps you will not think my estimate of one-tenth an excessive understatement in this matter.

Nearly the whole of our medical profession and most of our apparatus for teaching and training doctors subsist on strictly commercial lines by earning fees. This chief source of revenue is eked out by the wanton charity of old women, and conspicuous subscriptions by popularity hunters, and a small but growing contribution (in the salaries of medical officers of health and so forth) from the public funds. But the fact remains that for the great mass of the medical profession there is no living to be got except at a salary for hospital practice or by earning fees in receiving or attending upon private cases.

So long as a doctor is learning or adding to knowledge, he earns nothing, and the common, unintelligent man does not see why he should earn anything. So that a doctor who has no religious passion for poverty and self-devotion gets through the minimum of training and learning as quickly and as cheaply as possible, and does all he can to fill up the rest of his time in passing rapidly from case to case. The busier he keeps, the less his leisure for thought and learning, the richer he grows, and the more he is esteemed. His four or five years of hasty, crowded study are supposed to give him a complete and final knowledge of the treatment of every sort of disease, and he goes on year after year, often without co-operation, working mechanically in the common incidents of practice, births, cases of measles and whooping cough, and so forth, and blundering more or less in whatever else turns up.

There are no public specialists to whom he can conveniently refer the difficulties he constantly encounters; only in the case of rich patients is the specialist available; there are no properly organised information bureaus for him, and no means whatever of keeping him informed upon progress and discovery in medical science. He is not even required to set apart a month or so in every two or three years in order to return to lectures and hospitals and refresh his knowledge. Indeed, the income of the average general practitioner would not permit of such a thing, and almost the only means of contact between him and current thought lies in the one or other of our two great medical weeklies to which he happens to subscribe.

Now just as I have nothing but praise for the average general practitioner, so I have nothing but praise and admiration for those stalwart-looking publications. Without them I can imagine nothing but the most terrible intellectual atrophy among our medical men. But since they are private properties run for profit they have to pay, and half their bulk consists of the brilliantly written advertisements of new drugs and apparatus. They give much knowledge, they do much to ventilate perplexing questions, but a broadly conceived and properly endowed weekly circular could, I believe, do much more. At any rate, in my Utopia this duty of feeding up the general practitioners will not be left to private enterprise.

Behind the first line of my medical army will be a second line of able men constantly digesting new research for its practical needs—correcting, explaining, announcing; and, in addition, a force of public specialists to whom every difficulty in diagnosis will be at once referred. And there will be a properly organised system of reliefs that will allow the general practitioner and his right hand, the nurse, to come back to the refreshment of study before his knowledge and mind have got rusty. But then my Utopia is a Socialistic system. Under our present system of competitive scramble, under any system that reduces medical practice to mere fee-hunting nothing of this sort is possible.

Then in my Utopia, for every medical man who was mainly occupied in practice, I would have another who was mainly occupied in or about research. People hear so much about modern research that they do not realise how entirely inadequate it is in amount and equipment. Our general public is still too stupid to understand the need and value of sustained investigations in any branch of knowledge at all. In spite of all the lessons of the last century, it still fails to realise how discovery and invention enrich the community and how paying an investment is the public employment of clever people to think and experiment for the benefit of all. It still expects to get a Newton or a Joule for £800 a year, and requires him to conduct his researches in the margin of time left over when he has got through his annual eighty or ninety lectures. It imagines discoveries are a sort of inspiration that comes when professors are running to catch trains. It seems incapable of imagining how enormous are the untried possibilities of research. Of course, if you will only pay a handful of men salaries at which the cook of any large London hotel would turn up his nose, you cannot expect to have the master minds of the world at your service; and save for a few independent or devoted men, therefore, it is not reasonable to suppose that such a poor little dribble of medical research as is now going on is in the hands of persons of much more than average mental equipment. How can it be?

One hears a lot of the rigorous research into the problem of cancer that is now going on. Does the reader realise that all the men in the whole world who are giving any considerable proportion of their time to this cancer research would pack into a very small room, that they are working in little groups without any properly organised system of intercommunication, and that half of them are earning less than a quarter of the salary of a Bond Street shopwalker by those vastly important inquiries? Not one cancer case in twenty thousand is being properly described and reported. And yet, in comparison with other diseases, cancer is being particularly well attended to.

The general complacency with the progress in knowledge we have made and are making is ridiculously unjustifiable. Enormous things were no doubt done in the nineteenth century in many fields of knowledge, but all that was done was out of all proportion petty in comparison with what might have been done. I suppose the whole of the unprecedented progress in material knowledge of the nineteenth century was the work of two or three thousand men, who toiled against opposition, spite and endless disadvantages, without proper means of intercommunication and with wretched facilities for experiment. Such discoveries as were distinctively medical were the work of only a few hundred men. Now, suppose instead of that scattered band of un-co-ordinated workers a great army of hundreds of thousands of well-paid men; suppose, for instance, the community had kept as many scientific and medical investigators as it has bookmakers and racing touts and men about town—should we not know a thousand times as much as we do about disease and health and strength and power?

But these are Utopian questionings. The sane, practical man shakes his head, smiles pityingly at my dreamy impracticability, and passes them by.

AN AGE OF SPECIALISATION

There is something of the phonograph in all of us, but in the sort of eminent person who makes public speeches about education and reading, and who gives away prizes and opens educational institutions, there seems to be little else but gramophone.

These people always say the same things, and say them in the same note. And why should they do that if they are really individuals?

There is, I cannot but suspect, in the mysterious activities that underlie life, some trade in records for these distinguished gramophones, and it is a trade conducted upon cheap and wholesale lines. There must be in these demiurgic profundities a rapid manufacture of innumerable thousands of that particular speech about "scrappy reading," and that contrast of "modern" with "serious" literature, that babbles about in the provinces so incessantly. Gramophones thinly disguised as bishops, gramophones still more thinly disguised as eminent statesmen, gramophones K.C.B. and gramophones F.R.S. have brazened it at us time after time, and will continue to brazen it to our grandchildren when we are dead and all our poor protests forgotten. And almost equally popular in their shameless mouths is the speech that declares this present age to be an age of specialisation. We all know the profound droop of the eminent person's eyelids as he produces that discovery, the edifying deductions or the solemn warnings he unfolds from this proposition, and all the dignified, inconclusive rigmarole of that cylinder. And it is nonsense from beginning to end.

This is most distinctly *not* an age of specialisation. There has hardly been an age in the whole course of history less so than the present. A few moments of reflection will suffice to demonstrate that. This is beyond any precedent an age of change, change in the appliances of life, in the average length of life, in the general temper of life; and the two things are incompatible. It is only under fixed conditions that you can have men specialising.

They specialise extremely, for example, under such conditions as one had in Hindustan up to the coming of the present generation. There the metal worker or the cloth worker, the wheelwright or the druggist of yesterday did his work under almost exactly the same conditions as his predecessor did it five hundred years before. He had the same resources, the same tools, the same materials; he made the same objects for the same ends. Within the narrow limits thus set him he carried work to a fine perfection; his hand, his mental character were subdued to his medium. His dress and bearing even were distinctive; he was, in fact, a highly specialised man. He transmitted his difference to his sons. Caste was the logical expression in the social organisation of this state of high specialisation, and, indeed, what else is caste or any definite class distinctions but that? But the most obvious fact of the present time is the disappearance of caste and the fluctuating uncertainty of all class distinctions.

If one looks into the conditions of industrial employment specialisation will be found to linger just in proportion as a trade has remained unaffected by inventions and innovation. The building trade, for example, is a fairly conservative one. A brick wall is made to-day much as it was made two hundred years ago, and the bricklayer is in consequence a highly skilled and inadaptable specialist. No one who has not passed through a long and tedious training can lay bricks properly. And it needs a specialist to plough a field with horses or to drive a cab through the streets of London. Thatchers, old-fashioned cobblers, and hand workers are all specialised to a degree no new modern calling requires. With machinery skill disappears and unspecialised intelligence comes in. Any generally intelligent man can learn in a day or two to drive an electric tram, fix up an electric lighting installation, or guide a building machine or a steam plough. He must be, of course, much more generally intelligent than the average bricklayer, but he needs far less specialised skill. To repair machinery requires, of course, a special sort of knowledge, but not a special sort of training.

In no way is this disappearance of specialisation more marked than in military and naval affairs. In the great days of Greece and

Rome war was a special calling, requiring a special type of man. In the Middle Ages war had an elaborate technique, in which the footman played the part of an unskilled labourer, and even within a period of a hundred years it took a long period of training and discipline before the common discursive man could be converted into the steady soldier. Even to-day traditions work powerfully, through extravagance of uniform, and through survivals of that mechanical discipline that was so important in the days of hand-to-hand fighting, to keep the soldier something other than a man. For all the lessons of the Boer war we are still inclined to believe that the soldier has to be something severely parallel, carrying a rifle he fires under orders, obedient to the pitch of absolute abnegation of his private intelligence. We still think that our officers have, like some very elaborate and noble sort of performing animal, to be "trained." They learn to fight with certain specified "arms" and weapons, instead of developing intelligence enough to use anything that comes to hand.

But, indeed, when a really great European war does come and lets loose motor-cars, bicycles, wireless telegraphy, aeroplanes, new projectiles of every size and shape, and a multitude of ingenious persons upon the preposterously vast hosts of conscription, the military caste will be missing within three months of the beginning, and the inventive, versatile, intelligent man will have come to his own.

And what is true of a military caste is equally true of a special governing class such as our public schools maintain.

The misunderstanding that has given rise to this proposition that this is an age of specialisation, and through that no end of mischief in misdirected technical education and the like, is essentially a confusion between specialisation and the division of labour. No doubt this is an age when everything makes for wider and wider co-operations. Work that was once done by one highly specialised man—the making of a watch, for example—is now turned out wholesale by elaborate machinery, or effected in great quantities by the contributed efforts of a number of people. Each of these people may bring a highly developed intelligence to bear for a time upon the special problem in hand, but that is quite a different thing from specialising to do that thing.

This is typically shown in scientific research. The problem or the parts of problems upon which the inquiry of an individual man is concentrated are often much narrower than the problems that occupied Faraday or Dalton, and yet the hard and fast lines that once divided physicist from chemist, or botanist from pathologist have long since gone. Professor Farmer, the botanist, investigates cancer, and the ordinary educated man, familiar though he is with their general results, would find it hard to say which were the chemists and which the physicists among Professors Dewar and Ramsey Lord Rayleigh and Curie. The classification of sciences that was such a solemn business to our grandfathers is now merely a mental obstruction.

It is interesting to glance for a moment at the possible source of this mischievous confusion between specialisation and the division of labour. I have already glanced at the possibility of a diabolical world manufacturing gramophone records for our bishops and statesmen and suchlike leaders of thought, but if we dismiss that as a merely elegant trope, I must confess I think it is the influence of Herbert Spencer. His philosophy is pervaded by an insistence which is, I think, entirely without justification, that the universe, and every sort of thing in it, moves from the simple and homogeneous to the complex and heterogeneous. An unwary man obsessed with that idea would be very likely to assume without consideration that men were less specialised in a barbaric state of society than they are to-day. I think I have given reasons for believing that the reverse of this is nearer the truth.

IS THERE A PEOPLE?

Of all the great personifications that have dominated the mind of man, the greatest, the most marvellous, the most impossible and the most incredible, is surely the People, that impalpable monster to which the world has consecrated its political institutions for the last hundred years.

It is doubtful now whether this stupendous superstition has reached its grand climacteric, and there can be little or no dispute that it is destined to play a prominent part in the history of mankind for many years to come. There is a practical as well as a philosophical interest, therefore, in a note or so upon the attributes of this legendary being. I write "legendary," but thereby I display myself a sceptic. To a very large number of people the People is one of the profoundest realities in life. They believe—what exactly do they believe about the people?

When they speak of the People they certainly mean something more than the whole mass of individuals in a country lumped together. That is the people, a mere varied aggregation of persons, moved by no common motive, a complex interplay. The People, as the believer understands the word, is something more mysterious than that. The People is something that overrides and is added to the individualities that make up the people. It is, as it were, itself an individuality of a higher order—as indeed, its capital "P" displays. It has a will of its own which is not the will of any particular person in it, it has a power of purpose and judgment of a superior sort. It is supposed to be the underlying reality of all national life and the real seat of all public religious emotion. Unfortunately, it lacks powers of expression, and so there is need of rulers and interpreters. If they express it well in law and fact, in book and song, they prosper under its mysterious approval; if they do not, it revolts or forgets or does something else of an equally annihilatory sort. That, briefly, is the idea of the People. My modest thesis is that there exists nothing of the sort, that the world of men is entirely made up of the individuals that compose it, and that the collective action is just the algebraic sum of all individual actions.

How far the opposite opinion may go, one must talk to intelligent Americans or read the contemporary literature of the first French Revolution to understand. I find, for example, so typical a young American as the late Frank Norris roundly asserting that it is the People to whom we are to ascribe the triumphant emergence of the name of Shakespeare from the ruck of his contemporaries and the passage in which this assertion is made is fairly representative of the general expression of this sort of mysticism. "One must keep one's faith in the People—the Plain People, the Burgesses, the Grocers—else of all men the artists are most miserable and their teachings vain. Let us admit and concede that this belief is ever so sorely tried at times . . . But in the end, and at last, they will listen to the true note and discriminate between it and the false." And then he resorts to italics to emphasise: *"In the last analysis the People are always right."*

And it was that still more typical American, Abraham Lincoln, who declared his equal confidence in the political wisdom of this collective being. "You can fool all the people some of the time and some of the people all the time, but you cannot fool all the people all the time." The thing is in the very opening words of the American Constitution, and Theodore Parker calls it "the American idea" and pitches a still higher note: "A government of all the people, by all the people, for all the people; a government of all the principles of eternal justice, *the unchanging law of God."*

It is unavoidable that a collective wisdom distinct from any individual and personal one is intended in these passages. Mr. Norris, for example, never figured to himself a great wave of critical discrimination sweeping through the ranks of the various provision trades and a multitude of simple, plain burgesses preferring Shakespeare and setting Marlowe aside. Such a particularisation of his statement would have at once reduced it to absurdity. Nor does any American see the people particularised in that way. They believe in the People one and indivisible, a simple, mystical being, which pervades and dominates the community and determines its final collective consequences.

Now upon the belief that there is a People rests a large part of the political organisation of the modern world. The idea was one of the chief fruits of the speculations of the eighteenth century, and the American Constitution is its most perfect expression. One turns, therefore, inevitably to the American instance, not because it is the only one, but because there is the thing in its least complicated form. We have there an almost exactly logical realisation of this belief. The whole political machine is designed and expressed to register the People's will, literature is entirely rewarded and controlled by the effectual suffrages of the bookseller's counter, science (until private endowment intervened) was in the hands of the State Legislatures, and religion the concern of the voluntary congregations.

On the assumption that there is a People there could be no better state of affairs. You and I and everyone, except for a vote or a book, or a service now and then, can go about our business, you to your grocery and I to mine, and the direction of the general interests rests safe in the People's hands. Now that is by no means a caricature of the attitude of mind of many educated Americans. You find they have little or nothing to do with actual politics, and are inclined to regard the professional politician with a certain contempt; they trouble their heads hardly at all about literature, and they contemplate the general religious condition of the population with absolute unconcern. It is not that they are unpatriotic or morally trivial that they stand thus disengaged; it is that they have a fatalistic belief in this higher power. Whatever troubles and abuses may arise they have an absolute faith that "in the last analysis" the People will get it right.

And now suppose that I am right and that there is no People! Suppose that the crowd is really no more than a crowd, a vast miscellaneous confusion of persons which grows more miscellaneous every year. Suppose this conception of the People arose out of a sentimental idealisation, Rousseau fashion, of the ancient homogeneous peasant class—a class that is rapidly being swept out of existence by modern industrial developments— and that whatever slender basis of fact it had in the past is now altogether gone. What consequences may be expected?

It does not follow that because the object of your reverence is a dead word you will get no oracles from the shrine. If the sacred People remains impassive, inarticulate, non-existent, there are always the keepers of the shrine who will oblige. Professional politicians, venal and violent men, will take over the derelict political control, people who live by the book trade will alone have a care for letters, research and learning will be subordinated to political expediency, and a great development of noisily competitive religious enterprises will take the place of any common religious formula. There will commence a secular decline in the quality of public thought, emotion and activity. There will be no arrest or remedy for this state of affairs so long as that superstitious faith in the People as inevitably right "in the last analysis" remains. And if my supposition is correct, it should be possible to find in the United States, where faith in the people is indisputably dominant, some such evidence of the error of this faith. Is there?

I write as one that listens from afar. But there come reports of legislative and administrative corruption, of organised public blackmail, that do seem to carry out my thesis. One thinks of Edgar Allan Poe, who dreamt of founding a distinctive American literature, drugged and killed almost as it were symbolically, amid electioneering and nearly lied out of all posthumous respect by that scoundrel Griswold; one thinks of State Universities that are no more than mints for bogus degrees; one thinks of "Science" Christianity and Zion City. These things are quite insufficient for a Q.E.D., but I submit they favour my proposition.

Suppose there is no People at all, but only enormous, differentiating millions of men. All sorts of widely accepted generalisations will collapse if that foundation is withdrawn. I submit it as worth considering.

THE DISEASE OF PARLIAMENTS

Sec. 1

There is a growing discord between governments and governed in the world.

There has always been discord between governments and governed since States began; government has always been to some extent imposed, and obedience to some extent reluctant. We have come to regard it as a matter of course that under all absolutions and narrow oligarchies the community, so soon as it became educated and as its social elaboration developed a free class with private initiatives, so soon, indeed, as it attained to any power of thought and expression at all, would express discontent. But we English and Americans and Western Europeans generally had supposed that, so far as our own communities were concerned, this discontent was already anticipated and met by representative institutions. We had supposed that, with various safeguards and elaborations, our communities did, as a matter of fact, govern themselves. Our panacea for all discontents was the franchise. Social and national dissatisfaction could be given at the same time a voice and a remedy in the ballot box. Our liberal intelligences could and do still understand Russians wanting votes, Indians wanting votes, women wanting votes. The history of nineteenth-century Liberalism in the world might almost be summed up in the phrase "progressive enfranchisement." But these are the desires of a closing phase in political history. The new discords go deeper than that. The new situation which confronts our Liberal intelligence is the discontent of the enfranchised, the contempt and hostility of the voters for their elected delegates and governments.

This discontent, this resentment, this contempt even, and hostility to duly elected representatives is no mere accident of this democratic country or that; it is an almost world-wide movement. It is an almost universal disappointment with so-called popular government, and in many communities—in Great Britain particularly—it is manifesting itself by an unprecedented lawlessness in political matters, and in a strange and ominous contempt for the law. One sees it, for example, in the refusal of large sections of the medical profession to carry out insurance legislation, in the repudiation of Irish Home Rule by Ulster, and in the steady drift of great masses of industrial workers towards the conception of a universal strike. The case of the discontented workers in Great Britain and France is particularly remarkable. These people form effective voting majorities in many constituencies; they send alleged Socialist and Labour representatives into the legislative assembly; and, in addition, they have their trade unions with staffs of elected officials, elected ostensibly to state their case and promote their interests. Yet nothing is now more evident than that these officials, working-men representatives and the like, do not speak for their supporters, and are less and less able to control them. The Syndicalist movement, sabotage in France, and Larkinism in Great Britain, are, from the point of view of social stability, the most sinister demonstrations of the gathering anger of the labouring classes with representative institutions. These movements are not revolutionary movements, not movements for reconstruction such as were the democratic Socialist movements that closed the nineteenth century. They are angry and vindictive movements. They have behind them the most dangerous and terrible of purely human forces, the wrath, the blind destructive wrath, of a cheated crowd.

Now, so far as the insurrection of labour goes, American conditions differ from European, and the process of disillusionment will probably follow a different course. American labour is very largely immigrant labour still separated by barriers of language and tradition from the established thought of the nation. It will be long before labour in America speaks with the massed effectiveness of labour in France and England, where master and man are racially identical, and where there is no variety of "Dagoes" to break up the revolt. But in other directions the American disbelief in and impatience with "elected persons" is and has been far profounder than it is in Europe. The abstinence of men of property and position from overt politics, and the contempt that banishes political discussion from polite society, are among the first surprises of the visiting European to America, and now that, under an organised pressure of conscience, college-trained men and men of wealth are abandoning this strike of the educated and returning to political life, it is, one notes, with a prevailing disposition to correct democracy by personality, and to place affairs in the hands of autocratic mayors and presidents rather than to carry out democratic methods to the logical end. At times America seems hot for a Caesar. If no Caesar is established, then it will be the good fortune of the Republic rather than its democratic virtue which will have saved it.

And directly one comes to look into the quality and composition of the elected governing body of any modern democratic State, one begins to see the reason and nature of its widening estrangement from the community it represents. In no sense are these bodies really representative of the thought and purpose of the nation; the conception of its science, the fresh initiatives of its philosophy and literature, the forces that make the future through invention and experiment, exploration and trial and industrial development have no voice, or only an accidental and feeble voice, there. The typical elected person is a smart rather than substantial lawyer, full of cheap catchwords and elaborate tricks of procedure and electioneering, professing to serve the interests of the locality which is his constituency, but actually bound hand and foot to the specialised political association, his party, which imposed him upon that constituency. Arrived at the legislature, his next ambition is office, and to secure and retain office he engages in elaborate manoeuvres against the opposite party, upon issues which his limited and specialised intelligence indicates as electorally effective. But being limited and specialised, he is apt to drift completely out of touch with the interests and feelings of large masses of people in the community. In Great Britain, the United States and France alike there is a constant tendency on the part of the legislative body to drift into unreality, and to bore the country with the disputes that are designed to thrill it. In Great Britain, for example, at the present time the two political parties are both profoundly unpopular with the general intelligence, which is sincerely anxious, if only it could find a way, to get rid of both of them. Irish Home

Rule—an issue as dead as mutton, is opposed to Tariff Reform, which has never been alive. Much as the majority of people detest the preposterously clumsy attempts to amputate Ireland from the rule of the British Parliament which have been going on since the breakdown of Mr. Gladstone's political intelligence, their dread of foolish and scoundrelly fiscal adventurers is sufficiently strong to retain the Liberals in office. The recent exposures of the profound financial rottenness of the Liberal party have deepened the public resolve to permit no such enlarged possibilities of corruption as Tariff Reform would afford their at least equally dubitable opponents. And meanwhile, beneath those ridiculous alternatives, those sham issues, the real and very urgent affairs of the nation, the vast gathering discontent of the workers throughout the Empire, the racial conflicts in India and South Africa which will, if they are not arrested, end in our severance from India, the insane waste of national resources, the control of disease, the frightful need of some cessation of armament, drift neglected . . .

Now do these things indicate the ultimate failure and downfall of representative government? Was this idea which inspired so much of the finest and most generous thought of the eighteenth and nineteenth centuries a wrong idea, and must we go back to Caesarism or oligarchy or plutocracy or a theocracy, to Rome or Venice or Carthage, to the strong man or the ruler by divine right, for the political organisation of the future?

My answer to that question would be an emphatic No. My answer would be that the idea of representative government is the only possible idea for the government of a civilised community. But I would add that so far representative government has not had even the beginnings of a fair trial. So far we have not had representative government, but only a devastating caricature.

It is quite plain now that those who first organised the parliamentary institutions which now are the ruling institutions of the greater part of mankind fell a prey to certain now very obvious errors. They did not realise that there are hundreds of different ways in which voting may be done, and that every way will give a different result. They thought, and it is still thought by a great number of mentally indolent people, that if a country is divided up into approximately equivalent areas, each returning one or two representatives, if every citizen is given one vote, and if there is no legal limit to the presentation of candidates, that presently a cluster of the wisest, most trusted and best citizens will come together in the legislative assembly.

In reality the business is far more complicated than this. In reality a country will elect all sorts of different people according to the electoral method employed. It is a fact that anyone who chooses to experiment with a willing school or club may verify. Suppose, for example, that you take your country, give every voter one single vote, put up six and twenty candidates for a dozen vacancies, and give them no adequate time for organisation. The voters, you will find, will return certain favourites, A and B and C and D let us call them, by enormous majorities, and behind these at a considerable distance will come E, F, G, H, I, J, K, and L. Now give your candidates time to develop organisation. A lot of people who swelled A's huge vote will dislike J and K and L so much, and prefer M and N so much, that if they are assured that by proper organisation A's return can be made certain without their voting for him, they will vote for M and N. But they will do so only on that understanding. Similarly certain B-ites will want O and P if they can be got without sacrificing B. So that adequate party organisation in the community may return not the dozen a naive vote would give, but A, B, C, D, E, F, G, H, M, N, O, P. Now suppose that, instead of this arrangement, your community is divided into twelve constituencies and no candidate may contest more than one of them. And suppose each constituency has strong local preferences. A, B and C are widely popular; in every constituency they have supporters but in no constituency does any one of the three command a majority. They are great men, not local men. Q, who is an unknown man in most of the country, has, on the contrary, a strong sect of followers in the constituency for which A stands, and beats him by one vote; another local celebrity, E, disposes of B in the same way; C is attacked not only by S but T, whose peculiar views upon vaccination, let us say, appeal to just enough of C's supporters to let in S. Similar accidents happen in the other constituencies, and the country that would have unreservedly returned A, B, C, D, E, F, G, H, I, J, K and L on the first system, return instead O, P, Q, R, S, T, U, V, W, X, Y, Z. Numerous voters who would have voted for A if they had a chance vote instead for R, S, T, etc., numbers who would have voted for B, vote for Q, V, W, X, etc. But now suppose that A and B are opposed to one another, and that there is a strong A party and a strong B party highly organised in the country. B is really the second favourite over the country as a whole, but A is the first favourite. D, F, H, J, L, N, P, R, U, W, Y constitute the A candidates and in his name they conquer. B, C, E, G, I, K, M, O, Q, S, V are all thrown out in spite of the wide popularity of B and C. B and C, we have supposed, are the second and third favourites, and yet they go out in favour of Y, of whom nobody has heard before, some mere hangers-on of A's. Such a situation actually occurs in both Ulster and Home-Rule Ireland.

But now let us suppose another arrangement, and that is that the whole country is one constituency, and every voter has, if he chooses to exercise them, twelve votes, which, however, he must give, if he gives them all, to twelve separate people. Then quite certainly A, B, C, D will come in, but the tail will be different. M, N, O, P may come up next to them, and even Z, that eminent non-party man, may get in. But now organisation may produce new effects. The ordinary man, when he has twelve votes to give, likes to give them all, so that there will be a good deal of wild voting at the tails of the voting papers. Now if a small resolute band decide to plump for T or to vote only for A and T or B and T, T will probably jump up out of the rejected. This is the system which gives the specialist, the anti-vaccinator or what not, the maximum advantage. V, W, X and Y, being rather hopeless anyhow, will probably detach themselves from party and make some special appeal, say to the teetotal vote or the Mormon vote or the single tax vote, and so squeeze past O, P, Q, R, who have taken a more generalised line.

I trust the reader will bear with me through these alphabetical fluctuations. Many people, I know from colloquial experiences, do at about this stage fly into a passion. But if you will exercise self-control, then I think you will see my point that, according to the method of voting, almost any sort of result may be got out of an election except the production of a genuinely representative assembly.

And that is the a priori case for supposing, what our experience of contemporary life abundantly verifies, that the so-called representative assemblies of the world are not really representative at all. I will go farther and say that were it not for the entire inefficiency of our method of voting, not one-tenth of the present American and French Senators, the French Deputies, the American Congressmen, and the English Members of Parliament would hold their positions to-day. They would never have been heard of. They are not really the elected representatives of the people; they are the products of a ridiculous method of election; they are the illegitimate children of the party system and the ballot-box, who have ousted the legitimate heirs from their sovereignty. They are no more the expression of the general will than the Tsar or some President by *pronunciamento*. They are an accidental oligarchy of adventurers. Representative government has never yet existed in the world; there was an attempt to bring it into existence in the eighteenth century, and it succumbed to an infantile disorder at the very moment of its birth. What we have in the place of the leaders and representatives are politicians and "elected persons."

The world is passing rapidly from localised to generalised interests, but the method of election into which our fathers fell is the method of electing one or two representatives from strictly localised constituencies. Its immediate corruption was inevitable. If discussing and calculating the future had been, as it ought to be, a common, systematic occupation, the muddles of to-day might have been foretold a hundred years ago. From such a rough method of election the party system followed as a matter of course. In theory, of course, there may be any number of candidates for a constituency and a voter votes for the one he likes best; in practice there are only two or three candidates, and the voter votes for the one most likely to beat the candidate he likes least. It cannot be too strongly insisted that in contemporary elections we vote against; we do not vote for. If A, B and C are candidates, and you hate C and all his works and prefer A, but doubt if he will get as many votes as B, who is indifferent to you, the chances are you will vote for B. If C and B have the support of organised parties, you are still less likely to risk "wasting" your vote upon A. If your real confidence is in G, who is not a candidate for your constituency, and if B pledges himself to support G, while A retains the right of separate action, you may vote for B even if you distrust him personally. Additional candidates would turn any election of this type into a wild scramble. The system lies, in fact, wholly open to the control of political organisations, calls out, indeed, for the control of political organisations, and has in every country produced what is

197

so evidently demanded. The political organisations to-day rule us unchallenged. Save as they speak for us, the people are dumb.

Elections of the prevalent pattern, which were intended and are still supposed by simple-minded people to give every voter participation in government, do as a matter of fact effect nothing of the sort. They give him an exasperating fragment of choice between the agents of two party organisations, over neither of which he has any intelligible control. For twenty-five years I have been a voter, and in all that time I have only twice had an opportunity of voting for a man of distinction in whom I had the slightest confidence. Commonly my choice of a "representative" has been between a couple of barristers entirely unknown to me or the world at large. Rather more than half the men presented for my selection have not been English at all, but of alien descent. This, then, is the sum of the political liberty of the ordinary American or Englishman, that is the political emancipation which Englishwomen have shown themselves so pathetically eager to share. He may reject one of two undesirables, and the other becomes his "representative." Now this is not popular government at all; it is government by the profession of politicians, whose control becomes more and more irresponsible in just the measure that they are able to avoid real factions within their own body. Whatever the two party organisations have a mind to do together, whatever issue they chance to reserve from "party politics," is as much beyond the control of the free and independent voter as if he were a slave subject in ancient Peru.

Our governments in the more civilised parts of the world to-day are only in theory and sentiment democratic. In reality they are democracies so eviscerated by the disease of bad electoral methods that they are mere cloaks for the parasitic oligarchies that have grown up within their form and substance. The old spirit of freedom and the collective purpose which overthrew and subdued priestcrafts and kingcrafts, has done so, it seems, only to make way for these obscure political conspiracies. Instead of liberal institutions, mankind has invented a new sort of usurpation. And it is not unnatural that many of us should be in a phase of political despair.

These oligarchies of the party organisations have now been evolving for two centuries, and their inherent evils and dangers become more and more manifest. The first of these is the exclusion from government of the more active and intelligent sections of the community. It is not treated as remarkable, it is treated as a matter of course, that neither in Congress nor in the House of Commons is there any adequate representation of the real thought of the time, of its science, invention and enterprise, of its art and feeling, of its religion and purpose. When one speaks of Congressmen or Members of Parliament one thinks, to be plain about it, of intellectual riff-raff. When one hears of a pre-eminent man in the English-speaking community, even though that pre-eminence may be in political or social science, one is struck by a sense of incongruity if he happens to be also in the Legislature. When Lord Haldane disengages the Gifford lectures or Lord Morley writes a "Life of Gladstone" or ex-President Roosevelt is delivered of a magazine article, there is the same sort of excessive admiration as when a Royal Princess does a water-colour sketch or a dog walks on its hind legs.

Now this intellectual inferiority of the legislator is not only directly bad for the community by producing dull and stupid legislation, but it has a discouraging and dwarfing effect upon our intellectual life. Nothing so stimulates art, thought and science as realisation; nothing so cripples it as unreality. But to set oneself to know thoroughly and to think clearly about any human question is to unfit oneself for the forensic claptrap which is contemporary politics, is to put oneself out of the effective current of the nation's life. The intelligence of any community which does not make a collective use of that intelligence, starves and becomes hectic, tends inevitably to preciousness and futility on the one hand, and to insurgency, mischief and anarchism on the other.

From the point of view of social stability this estrangement of the national government and the national intelligence is far less serious than the estrangement between the governing body and the real feeling of the mass of the people. To many observers this latter estrangement seems to be drifting very rapidly towards a social explosion in the British Isles. The organised masses of labour find themselves baffled both by their parliamentary representatives and by their trade union officials. They are losing faith in their votes and falling back in anger upon insurrectionary ideals, upon the idea of a general strike, and upon the expedients of sabotage. They are doing this without any constructive proposals at all, for it is ridiculous to consider Syndicalism as a constructive proposal. They mean mischief because they are hopeless and bitterly disappointed. It is the same thing in France, and before many years are over it will be the same thing in America. That way lies chaos. In the next few years there may be social revolt and bloodshed in most of the great cities of Western Europe. That is the trend of current probability. Yet the politicians go on in an almost complete disregard of this gathering storm. Their jerrymandered electoral methods are like wool in their ears, and the rejection of Tweedledum for Tweedledee is taken as a "mandate" for Tweedledee's distinctive brand of political unrealities . . .

Is this an incurable state of things? Is this method of managing our affairs the only possible electoral method, and is there no remedy for its monstrous clumsiness and inefficiency but to "show a sense of humour," or, in other words, to grin and bear it? Or is it conceivable that there may be a better way to government than any we have yet tried, a method of government that would draw every class into conscious and willing co-operation with the State, and enable every activity of the community to play its proper part in the national life? That was the dream of those who gave the world representative government in the past. Was it an impossible dream?

Sec. 2

Is this disease of Parliaments an incurable disease, and have we, therefore, to get along as well as we can with it, just as a tainted and incurable invalid diets and is careful and gets along through life? Or is it possible that some entirely more representative and effective collective control of our common affairs can be devised?

The answer to that must determine our attitude to a great number of fundamental questions. If no better governing body is possible than the stupid, dilatory and forensic assemblies that rule in France, Britain and America to-day, then the civilised human community has reached its climax. That more comprehensive collective handling of the common interests to which science and intelligent Socialism point, that collective handling which is already urgently needed if the present uncontrolled waste of natural resources and the ultimate bankruptcy of mankind is to be avoided, is quite beyond the capacity of such assemblies; already there is too much in their clumsy and untrustworthy hands, and the only course open to us is an attempt at enlightened Individualism, an attempt to limit and restrict State activities in every possible way, and to make little private temporary islands of light and refinement amidst the general disorder and decay. All collectivist schemes, all rational Socialism, if only Socialists would realise it, all hope for humanity, indeed, are dependent ultimately upon the hypothetical possibility of a better system of government than any at present in existence.

Let us see first, then, if we can lay down any conditions which such a better governing body would satisfy. Afterwards it will be open to us to believe or disbelieve in its attainment. Imagination is the essence of creation. If we can imagine a better government we are half-way to making it.

Now, whatever other conditions such a body will satisfy, we may be sure that it will not be made up of members elected by single-member constituencies. A single-member constituency must necessarily contain a minority, and may even contain a majority of dissatisfied persons whose representation is, as it were, blotted out by the successful candidate. Three single-member constituencies which might all return members of the same colour, if they were lumped together to return three members would probably return two of one colour and one of another. There would still, however, be a suppressed minority averse to both these colours, or desiring different shades of those colours from those afforded them in the constituency. Other things being equal, it may be laid down that the larger the constituency and the more numerous its representatives, the greater the chance of all varieties of thought and opinion being represented.

But that is only a preliminary statement; it still leaves untouched all the considerations advanced in the former part of this discussion to show how easily the complications and difficulties of voting lead to a falsification of the popular will and understanding. But here we enter a region where a really scientific investigation has been made, and where established results are available. A method of election was worked out by Hare in the middle of the last century that really does seem to avoid or mitigate nearly every falsifying or debilitating possibility in elections; it was enthusiastically supported by J.S. Mill; it is now advocated by a special society—the Proportional

Representation Society—to which belong men of the most diverse type of distinction, united only by the common desire to see representative government a reality and not a disastrous sham. It is a method which does render impossible nearly every way of forcing candidates upon constituencies, and nearly every trick for rigging results that now distorts and cripples the political life of the modern world. It exacts only one condition, a difficult but not an impossible condition, and that is the honest scrutiny and counting of the votes.

The peculiar invention of the system is what is called the single transferable vote—that is to say, a vote which may be given in the first instance to one candidate, but which, in the event of his already having a sufficient quota of votes to return him, may be transferred to another. The voter marks clearly in the list of the candidates the order of his preference by placing 1, 2, 3, and so forth against the names. In the subsequent counting the voting papers are first classified according to the first votes. Let us suppose that popular person A is found to have received first votes enormously in excess of what is needed to return him. The second votes are then counted on his papers, and after the number of votes necessary to return him has been deducted, the surplus votes are divided in due proportion among the second choice names, and count for them. That is the essential idea of the whole thing. At a stroke all that anxiety about wasting votes and splitting votes, *which is the secret of all party political manipulation* vanishes. You may vote for A well knowing that if he is safe your vote will be good for C. You can make sure of A, and at the same time vote for C. You are in no need of a "ticket" to guide you, and you need have no fear that in supporting an independent candidate you will destroy the prospects of some tolerably sympathetic party man without any compensating advantage. The independent candidate does, in fact, become possible for the first time. The Hobson's choice of the party machine is abolished.

Let me be a little more precise about the particulars of this method, the only sound method, of voting in order to ensure an adequate representation of the community. Let us resort again to the constituency I imagined in my last paper, a constituency in which candidates represented by all the letters of the alphabet struggle for twelve places. And let us suppose that A, B, C and D are the leading favourites. Suppose that there are twelve thousand voters in the constituency, and that three thousand votes are cast for A—I am keeping the figures as simple as possible—then A has two thousand more than is needed to return him. *All* the second votes on his papers are counted, and it is found that 600, or a fifth of them, go to C; 500, or a sixth, go to E; 300, or a tenth, to G; 300 to J; 200, or a fifteenth, each to K and L, and a hundred each, or a thirtieth, to M, N, O, P, Q, R, S, T, W and Z. Then the surplus of 2,000 is divided in these proportions—that is a fifth of 2,000 goes to C, a sixth to E, and the rest to G, J, etc., in proportion. C, who already has 900 votes, gets another 400, and is now returned and has, moreover, 300 to spare; and the same division of the next votes upon C's paper occurs as has already been made with A's. But previously to this there has been a distribution of B's surplus votes, B having got 1,200 of first votes. And so on. After the distribution of the surplus votes of the elect at the top of the list, there is a distribution of the second votes upon the papers of those who have voted for the hopeless candidates at the bottom of the list. At last a point is reached when twelve candidates have a quota.

In this way the "wasting" of a vote, or the rejection of a candidate for any reason except that hardly anybody wants him, become practically impossible. This method of the single transferable vote with very large constituencies and many members does, in fact, give an entirely valid electoral result; each vote tells for all it is worth, and the freedom of the voter is only limited by the number of candidates who put up or are put up for election. This method, and this method alone, gives representative government; all others of the hundred and one possible methods admit of trickery, confusion and falsification. Proportional Representation is not a faddist proposal, not a perplexing ingenious complication of a simple business; it is the carefully worked out right way to do something that hitherto we have been doing in the wrong way. It is no more an eccentricity than is proper baking in the place of baking amidst dirt and with unlimited adulteration, or the running of trains to their destinations instead of running them without notice into casually selected sidings and branch lines. It is not the substitution of something for something else of the same nature; it is the substitution of right for wrong. It is the plain common sense of the greatest difficulty in contemporary affairs.

I know that a number of people do not, will not, admit this of Proportional Representation. Perhaps it is because of that hideous mouthful of words for a thing that would be far more properly named Sane Voting. This, which is the only correct way, these antagonists regard as a peculiar way. It has unfamiliar features, and that condemns it in their eyes. It takes at least ten minutes to understand, and that is too much for their plain, straightforward souls. "Complicated"—that word of fear! They are like the man who approved of an electric tram, but said that he thought it would go better without all that jiggery-pokery of wires up above. They are like the Western judge in the murder trial who said that if only they got a man hanged for this abominable crime, he wouldn't make a pedantic fuss about the question of *which* man. They are like the plain, straightforward promoter who became impatient with maps and planned a railway across Switzerland by drawing a straight line with a ruler across Jungfrau and Matterhorn and glacier and gorge. Or else they are like Mr. J. Ramsay Macdonald, M.P., who knows too well what would happen to him.

Now let us consider what would be the necessary consequences of the establishment of Proportional Representation in such a community as Great Britain—that is to say, the redistribution of the country into great constituencies such as London or Ulster or Wessex or South Wales, each returning a score or more of members, and the establishment of voting by the single transferable vote. The first, immediate, most desirable result would be the disappearance of the undistinguished party candidate; he would vanish altogether. He would be no more seen. Proportional Representation would not give him the ghost of a chance. The very young man of good family, the subsidised barrister, the respectable nobody, the rich supporter of the party would be ousted by known men. No candidate who had not already distinguished himself, and who did not stand for something in the public eye, would have a chance of election. There alone we have a sufficient reason for anticipating a very thorough change in the quality and character of the average legislator.

And next, no party organisation, no intimation from headquarters, no dirty tricks behind the scenes, no conspiracy of spite and scandal would have much chance of keeping out any man of real force and distinction who had impressed the public imagination. To be famous in science, to have led thought, to have explored or administered or dissented courageously from the schemes of official wire-pullers would no longer be a bar to a man's attainment of Parliament. It would be a help. Not only the level of parliamentary intelligence, but the level of personal independence would be raised far above its present position. And Parliament would become a gathering of prominent men instead of a means to prominence.

The two-party system which holds all the English-speaking countries to-day in its grip would certainly be broken up by Proportional Representation. Sane Voting in the end would kill the Liberal and Tory and Democratic and Republican party-machines. That secret rottenness of our public life, that hidden conclave which sells honours, fouls finance, muddles public affairs, fools the passionate desires of the people, and ruins honest men by obscure campaigns would become impossible. The advantage of party support would be a doubtful advantage, and in Parliament itself the party men would find themselves outclassed and possibly even outnumbered by the independent. It would be only a matter of a few years between the adoption of Sane Voting and the disappearance of the Cabinet from British public life. It would become possible for Parliament to get rid of a minister without getting rid of a ministry, and to express its disapproval of—let us say—some foolish project for rearranging the local government of Ireland without opening the door upon a vista of fantastical fiscal adventures. The party-supported Cabinet, which is now the real government of the so-called democratic countries, would cease to be so, and government would revert more and more to the legislative assembly. And not only would the latter body resume government, but it would also necessarily take into itself all those large and growing exponents of extra-parliamentary discontent that now darken the social future. The case of the armed "Unionist" rebel in Ulster, the case of the workman who engages in sabotage, the case for sympathetic strikes and the general strike, all these cases are identical in this, that they declare Parliament a fraud, that justice lies outside it and hopelessly outside it, and that to seek redress through Parliament is a waste of time and energy. Sane Voting would deprive all these destructive movements of the excuse and necessity for violence.

There is, I know, a disposition in some quarters to minimise the importance of Proportional Representation, as though it were a mere readjustment of voting methods. It is nothing of the sort; it is a prospective revolution. It will revolutionise government far more than a mere change from kingdom to republic or vice versa could possibly do; it will give a new and unprecedented sort of government to the world. The real leaders of the country will govern the country. For Great Britain, for example, instead of the secret, dubious and dubitable Cabinet, which is the real British government of to-day, poised on an unwieldy and crowded House of Commons, we should have open government by the representatives of, let us say, twenty great provinces, Ulster, Wales, London, for example, each returning from twelve to thirty members. It would be a steadier, stabler, more confident, and more trusted government than the world has ever seen before. Ministers, indeed, and even ministries might come and go, but that would not matter, as it does now, because there would be endless alternatives through which the assembly could express itself instead of the choice between two parties.

The arguments against Proportional Representation that have been advanced hitherto are trivial in comparison with its enormous advantages. Implicit in them all is the supposition that public opinion is at bottom a foolish thing, and that electoral methods are to pacify rather than express a people. It is possibly true that notorious windbags, conspicuously advertised adventurers, and the heroes of temporary sensations may run a considerable chance upon the lists. My own estimate of the popular wisdom is against the idea that any vividly prominent figure must needs get in; I think the public is capable of appreciating, let us say, the charm and interest of Mr. Sandow or Mr. Jack Johnson or Mr. Harry Lauder or Mr. Evan Roberts without wanting to send these gentlemen into Parliament. And I think that the increased power that the Press would have through its facilities in making reputations may also be exaggerated. Reputations are mysterious things and not so easily forced, and even if it were possible for a section of the Press to limelight a dozen or so figures up to the legislature, they would still have, I think, to be interesting, sympathetic and individualised figures; and at the end they would be only half a dozen among four hundred men of a repute more naturally achieved. A third objection is that this reform would give us group politics and unstable government. It might very possibly give us unstable ministries, but unstable ministries may mean stable government, and such stable ministries as that which governs England at the present time may, by clinging obstinately to office, mean the wildest fluctuations of policy. Mr. Ramsay Macdonald has drawn a picture of the too-representative Parliament of Proportional Representation, split up into groups each pledged to specific measures and making the most extraordinary treaties and sacrifices of the public interest in order to secure the passing of these definite bills. But Mr. Ramsay Macdonald is exclusively a parliamentary man; he knows contemporary parliamentary "shop" as a clerk knows his "guv'nor," and he thinks in the terms of his habitual life; he sees representatives only as politicians financed from party headquarters; it is natural that he should fail to see that the quality and condition of the sanely elected Member of Parliament will be quite different from these scheming climbers into positions of trust with whom he deals to-day. It is the party system based on insane voting that makes governments indivisible wholes and gives the group and the cave their terrors and their effectiveness. Mr. Ramsay Macdonald is as typical a product of existing electoral methods as one could well have, and his peculiarly keen sense of the power of intrigue in legislation is as good evidence as one could wish for of the need for drastic change.

Of course, Sane Voting is not a short cut to the millennium, it is no way of changing human nature, and in the new type of assembly, as in the old, spite, vanity, indolence, self-interest, and downright dishonesty will play their part. But to object to a reform on that account is not a particularly effective objection. These things will play their part, but it will be a much smaller part in the new than in the old. It is like objecting to some projected and long-needed railway because it does not propose to carry its passengers by immediate express to heaven.

THE AMERICAN POPULATION

The social conditions and social future of America constitute a system of problems quite distinct and separate from the social problems of any other part of the world. The nearest approach to parallel conditions, and that on a far smaller and narrower scale, is found in the British colonies and in the newly settled parts of Siberia. For while in nearly every other part of the world the population of to-day is more or less completely descended from the prehistoric population of the same region, and has developed its social order in a slow growth extending over many centuries, the American population is essentially a transplanted population, a still fluid and imperfect fusion of great fragments torn at this point or that from the gradually evolved societies of Europe. The European social systems grow and flower upon their roots, in soil which has made them and to which they are adapted. The American social accumulation is a various collection of cuttings thrust into a new soil and respiring a new air, so different that the question is still open to doubt, and indeed there are those who do doubt, how far these cuttings are actually striking root and living and growing, whether indeed they are destined to more than a temporary life in the new hemisphere. I propose to discuss and weigh certain arguments for and against the belief that these ninety million people who constitute the United States of America are destined to develop into a great distinctive nation with a character and culture of its own.

Humanly speaking, the United States of America (and the same is true of Canada and all the more prosperous, populous and progressive regions of South America) is a vast sea of newly arrived and unstably rooted people. Of the seventy-six million inhabitants recorded by the 1900 census, ten and a half million were born and brought up in one or other of the European social systems, and the parents of another twenty-six millions were foreigners. Another nine million are of African negro descent. Fourteen million of the sixty-five million native-born are living not in the state of their birth, but in other states to which they have migrated. Of the thirty and a half million whites whose parents on both sides were native Americans, a high proportion probably had one if not more grand-parents foreign-born. Nearly five and a half million out of thirty-three and a half million whites in 1870 were foreign-born, and another five and a quarter million the children of foreign-born parents. The children of the latter five and a quarter million count, of course, in the 1900 census as native-born of native parents. Immigration varies enormously with the activity of business, but in 1906 it rose for the first time above a million.

These figures may be difficult to grasp. The facts may be seen in a more concrete form by the visitor to Ellis Island, the receiving station for the immigrants into New York Harbour. One goes to this place by tugs from the United States barge office in Battery Park, and in order to see the thing properly one needs a letter of introduction to the commissioner in charge. Then one is taken through vast barracks littered with people of every European race, every type of low-class European costume, and every degree of dirtiness, to a central hall in which the gist of the examining goes on. The floor of this hall is divided up into a sort of maze of winding passages between lattice work, and along these passages, day after day, incessantly, the immigrants go, wild-eyed Gipsies, Armenians, Greeks, Italians, Ruthenians, Cossacks, German peasants, Scandinavians, a few Irish still, impoverished English, occasional Dutch; they halt for a moment at little desks to exhibit papers, at other little desks to show their money and prove they are not paupers, to have their eyes scanned by this doctor and their general bearing by that. Their thumb-marks are taken, their names and heights and weights and so forth are recorded for the card index; and so, slowly, they pass along towards America, and at last reach a little wicket, the gate of the New World. Through this metal wicket drips the immigration stream—all day long, every two or three seconds, an immigrant with a valise or a bundle, passes the little desk and goes on past the well-managed money-changing place, past the carefully organised separating ways that go to this railway or that, past the guiding, protecting officials—into a new world. The great majority are young men and young women between seventeen and thirty, good, youthful, hopeful peasant stock. They stand in a long string, waiting to go through that wicket, with bundles, with little tin boxes, with cheap portmanteaus with odd packages, in pairs, in families, alone, women with children, men with strings of dependents, young couples. All day that string of human beads waits there, jerks forward, waits again; all day and every day, constantly replenished, constantly dropping the end beads through the wicket, till the units mount to hundreds and the hundreds to thousands . . . In such a prosperous year as 1906 more immigrants passed through that wicket into America than children were born in the whole of France.

This figure of a perpetual stream of new stranger citizens will serve to mark the primary distinction between the American social problem and that of any European or Asiatic community.

The vast bulk of the population of the United States has, in fact, only got there from Europe in the course of the last hundred years, and mainly since the accession of Queen Victoria to the throne of Great Britain. That is the first fact that the student of the American social future must realise. Only an extremely small proportion of its blood goes back now to those who fought for freedom in the days of George Washington. The American community is not an expanded colonial society that has become autonomous. It is a great and deepening pool of population accumulating upon the area these predecessors freed, and since fed copiously by affluents from every European community. Fresh ingredients are still being added in enormous quantity, in quantity so great as to materially change the racial quality in a score of years. It is particularly noteworthy that each accession of new blood seems to sterilise its predecessors. Had there been no immigration at all into the United States, but had the rate of increase that prevailed in 1810-20 prevailed to 1900, the population, which would then have been a purely native American one, would have amounted to a hundred million—that is to say, to approximately nine million in excess of the present total population. The new waves are for a time amazingly fecund, and then comes a rapid fall in the birth-rate. The proportion of colonial and early republican blood in the population is, therefore, probably far smaller even than the figures I have quoted would suggest.

These accesses of new population have come in a series of waves, very much as if successive reservoirs of surplus population in the Old World had been tapped, drained and exhausted. First came the Irish and Germans, then Central Europeans of various types, then Poland and Western Russia began to pour out their teeming peoples, and more particularly their Jews, Bohemia, the Slavonic states, Italy and Hungary followed and the latest arrivals include great numbers of Levantines, Armenians and other peoples from Asia Minor and the Balkan Peninsula. The Hungarian immigrants have still a birth-rate of forty-six per thousand, the highest birth-rate in the world.

A considerable proportion of the Mediterranean arrivals, it has to be noted, and more especially the Italians, do not come to settle. They work for a season or a few years, and then return to Italy. The rest come to stay.

A vast proportion of these accessions to the American population since 1840 has, with the exception of the East European Jews, consisted of peasantry, mainly or totally illiterate, accustomed to a low standard of life and heavy bodily toil. For most of them the transfer to a new country meant severance from the religious communion in which they had been bred and from the servilities or subordinations to which they were accustomed They brought little or no positive social tradition to the synthesis to which they brought their blood and muscle.

The earlier German, English and Scandinavian incomers were drawn from a somewhat higher social level, and were much more closely akin in habits and faith to the earlier founders of the Republic.

Our inquiry is this: What social structure is this pool of mixed humanity developing or likely to develop?

Sec. 2

If we compare any European nation with the American, we perceive at once certain broad differences. The former, in comparison with the latter, is evolved and organised; the latter, in comparison with the former, is aggregated and chaotic. In nearly every European country there is a social system often quite elaborately classed and defined; each class with a sense of function, with an idea of what is due to it and what is expected of it. Nearly everywhere you find a governing class, aristocratic in spirit, sometimes no doubt highly modified by recent economic and industrial changes, with more or less of the tradition of a feudal nobility, then a definite great mercantile class, then a large self-respecting middle class of professional men, minor merchants, and so forth, then a new industrial class of employees in the manufacturing and urban districts, and a peasant population rooted to the land. There are, of course, many local modifications of this form: in France the nobility is mostly expropriated; in England, since the days of John Bull, the peasant has lost his common rights and his holding, and become an "agricultural labourer" to a newer class of more extensive farmer. But these are differences in detail; the fact of the organisation, and the still more important fact of the traditional feeling of organisation, remain true of all these older communities.

And in nearly every European country, though it may be somewhat despoiled here and shorn of exclusive predominance there, or represented by a dislocated "reformed" member, is the Church, custodian of a great moral tradition, closely associated with the national universities and the organisation of national thought. The typical European town has its castle or great house, its cathedral or church, its middle-class and lower-class quarters. Five miles off one can see that the American town is on an entirely different plan. In his remarkable "American Scene," Mr. Henry James calls attention to the fact that the Church as one sees it and feels it universally in Europe is altogether absent, and he adds a comment as suggestive as it is vague. Speaking of the appearance of the Churches, so far as they do appear amidst American urban scenery, he says:

> "Looking for the most part no more established or seated than a stopped omnibus, they are reduced to the inveterate bourgeois level (that of private, accommodated pretensions merely), and fatally despoiled of the fine old ecclesiastical arrogance, ... The field of American life is as bare of the Church as a billiard-table of a centre-piece; a

truth that the myriad little structures 'attended' on Sundays and on the 'off' evenings of their 'sociables' proclaim as with the audible sound of the roaring of a million mice . . .

"And however one indicates one's impression of the clearance, the clearance itself, in its completeness, with the innumerable odd connected circumstances that bring it home, represents, in the history of manners and morals, a deviation in the mere measurement of which hereafter may well reside a certain critical thrill. I say hereafter because it is a question of one of those many measurements that would as yet, in the United States, be premature. Of all the solemn conclusions one feels as 'barred,' the list is quite headed in the States, I think, by this particular abeyance of judgment. When an ancient treasure of precious vessels, overscored with glowing gems and wrought artistically into wondrous shapes, has, by a prodigious process, been converted through a vast community into the small change, the simple circulating medium of dollars and 'nickels,' we can only say that the consequent permeation will be of values of a new order. Of *what* order we must wait to see."

America has no Church. Neither has it a peasantry nor an aristocracy, and until well on in the Victorian epoch it had no disproportionately rich people.

In America, except in the regions where the negro abounds, there is no lower stratum. There is no "soil people" to this community at all; your bottom-most man is a mobile freeman who can read, and who has ideas above digging and pigs and poultry-keeping, except incidentally for his own ends. No one owns to subordination As a consequence, any position which involves the acknowledgment of an innate inferiority is difficult to fill; there is, from the European point of view, an extraordinary dearth of servants, and this endures in spite of a great peasant immigration. The servile tradition will not root here now; it dies forthwith. An enormous importation of European serfs and peasants goes on, but as they touch this soil their backs begin to stiffen with a new assertion.

And at the other end of the scale, also, one misses an element. There is no territorial aristocracy, no aristocracy at all, no throne, no legitimate and acknowledged representative of that upper social structure of leisure, power and State responsibility which in the old European theory of Society was supposed to give significance to the whole. The American community, one cannot too clearly insist, does not correspond to an entire European community at all, but only to the middle masses of it, to the trading and manufacturing class between the dimensions of the magnate and the clerk and skilled artisan. It is the central part of the European organism without either the dreaming head or the subjugated feet. Even the highly feudal slave-holding "county family" traditions of Virginia and the South pass now out of memory. So that in a very real sense the past of the American nation is in Europe, and the settled order of the past is left behind there. This community was, as it were, taken off its roots, clipped of its branches, and brought hither. It began neither serf nor lord, but burgher and farmer; it followed the normal development of the middle class under Progress everywhere and became capitalistic. The huge later immigration has converged upon the great industrial centres and added merely a vast non-servile element of employees to the scheme.

America has been and still very largely is a one-class country. It is a great sea of human beings detached from their traditions of origin. The social difference from Europe appears everywhere, and nowhere more strikingly than in the railway carriages. In England the compartments in these are either "first class," originally designed for the aristocracy, or "second class," for the middle class, or "third class," for the populace. In America there is only one class, one universal simple democratic car. In the Southern States, however, a proportion of these simple democratic cars are inscribed with the word "White," whereby nine million people are excluded. But to this original even-handed treatment there was speedily added a more sumptuous type of car, the parlour car, accessible to extra dollars; and then came special types of train, all made up of parlour cars and observation cars and the like. In England nearly every train remains still first, second and third, or first and third. And now, quite outdistancing the differentiation of England, America produces private cars and private trains, such as Europe reserves only for crowned heads.

The evidence of the American railways, then, suggests very strongly what a hundred other signs confirm, that the huge classless sea of American population is not destined to remain classless, is already developing separations and distinctions and structures of its own. And monstrous architectural portents in Boston and Salt Lake City encourage one to suppose that even that churchless aspect, which so stirred the speculative element in Mr. Henry James, is only the opening formless phase of a community destined to produce not only classes but intellectual and moral forms of the most remarkable kind.

Sec. 3

It is well to note how these ninety millions of people whose social future we are discussing are distributed. This huge development of human appliances and resources is here going on in a community that is still, for all the dense crowds of New York, the teeming congestion of East Side, extraordinarily scattered. America, one recalls, is still an unoccupied country across which the latest developments of civilisation are rushing. We are dealing here with a continuous area of land which is, leaving Alaska out of account altogether, equal to Great Britain, France, the German Empire, the Austro-Hungarian Empire, Italy, Belgium, Japan, Holland, Spain and Portugal, Sweden and Norway, Turkey in Europe, Egypt and the whole Empire of India, and the population spread out over this vast space is still less than the joint population of the first two countries named and not a quarter that of India.

Moreover, it is not spread at all evenly. Much of it is in undistributed clots. It is not upon the soil; barely half of it is in holdings and homes and authentic communities. It is a population of an extremely modern type. Urban concentration has already gone far with it; fifteen millions of it are crowded into and about twenty great cities, another eighteen millions make up five hundred towns. Between these centres of population run railways indeed, telegraph wires, telephone connections, tracks of various sorts, but to the European eye these are mere scratchings on a virgin surface. An empty wilderness manifests itself through this thin network of human conveniences, appears in the meshes even at the railroad side.

Essentially, America is still an unsettled land, with only a few incidental good roads in favoured places, with no universal police, with no wayside inns where a civilised man may rest, with still only the crudest of rural postal deliveries, with long stretches of swamp and forest and desert by the track side, still unassailed by industry. This much one sees clearly enough eastward of Chicago. Westward it becomes more and more the fact. In Idaho, at last, comes the untouched and perhaps invincible desert, plain and continuous through the long hours of travel. Huge areas do not contain one human being to the square mile, still vaster portions fall short of two . . .

It is upon Pennsylvania and New York State and the belt of great towns that stretches out past Chicago to Milwaukee and Madison that the nation centres and seems destined to centre. One needs but examine a tinted population map to realise that. The other concentrations are provincial and subordinate; they have the same relation to the main axis that Glasgow or Cardiff have to London in the British scheme.

Sec. 4

When I speak of this vast multitude, these ninety millions of the United States of America as being for the most part peasants de-peasant-ised and common people cut off from their own social traditions, I do not intend to convey that the American community is as a whole traditionless. There is in America a very distinctive tradition indeed, which animates the entire nation, gives a unique idiom to its press and all its public utterances, and is manifestly the starting point from which the adjustments of the future must be made.

The mere sight of the stars and stripes serves to recall it; "Yankee" in the mouth of a European gives something of its quality. One thinks at once of a careless abandonment of any pretension, of tireless energy and daring enterprise, of immense self-reliance, of a disrespect for the past so complete that a mummy is in itself a comical object, and the blowing out of an ill-guarded sacred flame, a delightful jest. One thinks of the enterprise of the sky-scraper and the humour of "A Yankee at the Court of King Arthur," and of "Innocents Abroad." Its dominant notes are democracy, freedom, and confidence. It is religious-spirited without superstition consciously Christian in the vein of a nearly Unitarian

Christianity, fervent but broadened, broadened as a halfpenny is broadened by being run over by an express train, substantially the same, that is to say, but with a marked loss of outline and detail. It is a tradition of romantic concession to good and inoffensive women and a high development of that personal morality which puts sexual continence and alcoholic temperance before any public virtue. It is equally a tradition of sporadic emotional public-spiritedness, entirely of the quality of gallantry, of handsome and surprising gifts to the people, disinterested occupation of office and the like. It is emotionally patriotic, hypotheticating fighting and dying for one's country as a supreme good while inculcating also that working and living for oneself is quite within the sphere of virtuous action. It adores the flag but suspects the State. One sees more national flags and fewer national servants in America than in any country in the world. Its conception of manners is one of free plain-spoken men revering women and shielding them from most of the realities of life, scornful of aristocracies and monarchies, while asserting simply, directly, boldly and frequently an equal claim to consideration with all other men. If there is any traditional national costume, it is shirt-sleeves. And it cherishes the rights of property above any other right whatsoever.

Such are the details that come clustering into one's mind in response to the phrase, the American tradition.

From the War of Independence onward until our own times that tradition, that very definite ideal, has kept pretty steadily the same. It is the image of a man and not the image of a State. Its living spirit has been the spirit of freedom at any cost, unconditional and irresponsible. It is the spirit of men who have thrown off a yoke, who are jealously resolved to be unhampered masters of their "own," to whom nothing else is of anything but secondary importance. That was the spirit of the English small gentry and mercantile class, the comfortable property owners, the Parliamentarians, in Stuart times. Indeed even earlier, it is very largely the spirit of More's "Utopia." It was that spirit sent Oliver Cromwell himself packing for America, though a heedless and ill-advised and unforeseeing King would not let him go. It was the spirit that made taxation for public purposes the supreme wrong and provoked each country, first the mother country and then in its turn the daughter country, to armed rebellion. It has been the spirit of the British Whig and the British Nonconformist almost up to the present day. In the Reform Club of London, framed and glazed over against Magna Charta, is the American Declaration of Independence, kindred trophies they are of the same essentially English spirit of stubborn insubordination. But the American side of it has gone on unchecked by the complementary aspect of the English character which British Toryism expresses.

The War of Independence raised that Whig suspicion of and hostility to government and the freedom of private property and the repudiation of any but voluntary emotional and supererogatory co-operation in the national purpose to the level of a religion, and the American Constitution with but one element of elasticity in the Supreme Court decisions, established these principles impregnably in the political structure. It organised disorganisation. Personal freedom, defiance of authority, and the stars and stripes have always gone together in men's minds; and subsequent waves of immigration, the Irish fleeing famine, for which they held the English responsible, and the Eastern European Jews escaping relentless persecutions, brought a persuasion of immense public wrongs, as a necessary concomitant of systematic government, to refresh without changing this defiant thirst for freedom at any cost.

In my book, "The Future in America," I have tried to make an estimate of the working quality of this American tradition of unconditional freedom for the adult male citizen. I have shown that from the point of view of anyone who regards civilisation as an organisation of human interdependence and believes that the stability of society can be secured only by a conscious and disciplined co-ordination of effort, it is a tradition extraordinarily and dangerously deficient in what I have called a *"sense of the State."* And by a "sense of the State" I mean not merely a vague and sentimental and showy public-spiritedness—of that the States have enough and to spare—but a real sustaining conception of the collective interest embodied in the State as an object of simple duty and as a determining factor in the life of each individual. It involves a sense of function and a sense of "place," a sense of a general responsibility and of a general well-being overriding the individual's well-being, which are exactly the senses the American tradition attacks and destroys.

For the better part of a century the American tradition, quite as much by reason of what it disregards as of what it suggests, has meant a great release of human energy, a vigorous if rough and untidy exploitation of the vast resources that the European invention of railways and telegraphic communication put within reach of the American people. It has stimulated men to a greater individual activity, perhaps, than the world has ever seen before. Men have been wasted by misdirection no doubt, but there has been less waste by inaction and lassitude than was the case in any previous society. Great bulks of things and great quantities of things have been produced, huge areas brought under cultivation, vast cities reared in the wilderness.

But this tradition has failed to produce the beginnings or promise of any new phase of civilised organisation, the growths have remained largely invertebrate and chaotic, and, concurrently with its gift of splendid and monstrous growth, it has also developed portentous political and economic evils. No doubt the increment of human energy has been considerable, but it has been much less than appears at first sight. Much of the human energy that America has displayed in the last century is not a development of new energy but a diversion. It has been accompanied by a fall in the birth-rate that even the immigration torrent has not altogether replaced. Its insistence on the individual, its disregard of the collective organisation, its treatment of women and children as each man's private concern, has had its natural outcome. Men's imaginations have been turned entirely upon individual and immediate successes and upon concrete triumphs; they have had no regard or only an ineffectual sentimental regard for the race. Every man was looking after himself, and there was no one to look after the future. Had the promise of 1815 been fulfilled, there would now be in the United States of America one hundred million descendants of the homogeneous and free-spirited native population of that time. There is not, as a matter of fact, more than thirty-five million. There is probably, as I have pointed out, much less. Against the assets of cities, railways, mines and industrial wealth won, the American tradition has to set the price of five-and-seventy million native citizens who have never found time to get born, and whose place is now more or less filled by alien substitutes. Biologically speaking, this is not a triumph for the American tradition. It is, however, very clearly an outcome of the intense individualism of that tradition. Under the sway of that it has burnt its future in the furnace to keep up steam.

The next and necessary evil consequent upon this exaltation of the individual and private property over the State, over the race that is and over public property, has been a contempt for public service. It has identified public spirit with spasmodic acts of public beneficence. The American political ideal became a Cincinnatus whom nobody sent for and who therefore never left his plough. There has ensued a corrupt and undignified political life, speaking claptrap, dark with violence, illiterate and void of statesmanship or science, forbidding any healthy social development through public organisation at home, and every year that the increasing facilities of communication draw the alien nations closer, deepening the risks of needless and disastrous wars abroad.

And in the third place it is to be remarked that the American tradition has defeated its dearest aims of a universal freedom and a practical equality. The economic process of the last half-century, so far as America is concerned has completely justified the generalisations of Marx. There has been a steady concentration of wealth and of the reality as distinguished from the forms of power in the hands of a small energetic minority, and a steady approximation of the condition of the mass of the citizens to that of the so-called proletariat of the European communities. The tradition of individual freedom and equality is, in fact, in process of destroying the realities of freedom and equality out of which it rose. Instead of the six hundred thousand families of the year 1790, all at about the same level of property and, excepting the peculiar condition of seven hundred thousand blacks, with scarcely anyone in the position of a hireling, we have now as the most striking, though by no means the most important, fact in American social life a frothy confusion of millionaires' families, just as wasteful, foolish and vicious as irresponsible human beings with unlimited resources have always shown themselves to be. And, concurrently with the appearance of these concentrations of great wealth, we have appearing also poverty, poverty of a degree that was quite unknown in the United States for the first century of their career as an independent nation. In the last few decades slums as frightful as any in Europe have appeared with terrible rapidity, and there has been a development of the viler side of industrialism, of sweating and base employment of the most ominous kind.

In Mr. Robert Hunter's "Poverty" one reads of "not less than eighty thousand children, most of whom are little girls, at present employed in the textile mills of this country. In the South there are now six times as many children at work as there were twenty years ago. Child labour is increasing yearly in that section of the country. Each year more little ones are brought in from the fields and hills to live in the degrading and demoralising atmosphere of the mill towns . . ."

Children are deliberately imported by the Italians. I gathered from Commissioner Watchorn at Ellis Island that the proportion of little nephews and nieces, friends' sons and so forth brought in by them is peculiarly high, and I heard him try and condemn a doubtful case. It was a particularly unattractive Italian in charge of a dull-eyed little boy of no ascertainable relationship . . .

In the worst days of cotton-milling in England the conditions were hardly worse than those now existing in the South. Children, the tiniest and frailest, of five and six years of age, rise in the morning and, like old men and women, go to the mills to do their day's labour; and, when they return home, "wearily fling themselves on their beds, too tired to take off their clothes." Many children work all night—"in the maddening racket of the machinery, in an atmosphere insanitary and clouded with humidity and lint."

"It will be long," adds Mr. Hunter in his description, "before I forget the face of a little boy of six years, with his hands stretched forward to rearrange a bit of machinery, his pallid face and spare form already showing the physical effects of labour. This child, six years of age, was working twelve hours a day."

From Mr. Spargo's "Bitter Cry of the Children" I learn this much of the joys of certain among the youth of Pennsylvania:

"For ten or eleven hours a day children of ten and eleven stoop over the chute and pick out the slate and other impurities from the coal as it moves past them. The air is black with coal dust, and the roar of the crushers, screens and rushing mill-race of coal is deafening. Sometimes one of the children falls into the machinery and is terribly mangled, or slips into the chute and is smothered to death. Many children are killed in this way. Many others, after a time, contract coal-miners asthma and consumption, which gradually undermine their health. Breathing continually day after day the clouds of coal dust, their lungs become black and choked with small particles of anthracite . ."

In Massachusetts, at Fall River, the Hon. J.F. Carey tells how little naked boys, free Americans, work for Mr. Borden, the New York millionaire, packing cloth into bleaching vats, in a bath of chemicals that bleaches their little bodies like the bodies of lepers . . .

Altogether it would seem that at least one million and a half children are growing up in the United States of America stunted and practically uneducated because of unregulated industrialism. These children, ill-fed, ill-trained mentally benighted, since they are alive and active, since they are an active and positive and not a negative evil, are even more ominous in the American outlook than those five and sixty million of good race and sound upbringing who will now never be born.

Sec. 5

It must be repeated that the American tradition is really the tradition of one particular ingredient in this great admixture and stirring up of peoples. This ingredient is the Colonial British, whose seventeenth century Puritanism and eighteenth century mercantile radicalism and rationalism manifestly furnished all the stuff out of which the American tradition is made. It is this stuff planted in virgin soil and inflated to an immense and buoyant optimism by colossal and unanticipated material prosperity and success. From that British middle-class tradition comes the individualist protestant spirit, the keen self-reliance and personal responsibility, the irresponsible expenditure, the indiscipline and mystical faith in things being managed properly if they are only let alone. "State-blindness" is the natural and almost inevitable quality of a middle-class tradition, a class that has been forced neither to rule nor obey, which has been concentrated and successfully concentrated on private gain.

This middle-class British section of the American population was, and is to this day, the only really articulate ingredient in its mental composition. And so it has had a monopoly in providing the American forms of thought. The other sections of peoples that have been annexed by or have come into this national synthesis are *silent* so far as any contribution to the national stock of ideas and ideals is concerned. There are, for example, those great elements, the Spanish Catholics, the French Catholic population of Louisiana, the Irish Catholics, the French-Canadians who are now ousting the sterile New Englander from New England, the Germans, the Italians the Hungarians. Comparatively they say nothing. From all the ten million of coloured people come just two or three platform voices, Booker Washington, Dubois, Mrs. Church Terrell, mere protests at specific wrongs. The clever, restless Eastern European Jews, too, have still to find a voice. Professor Münsterberg has written with a certain bitterness of the inaudibility of the German element in the American population. They allow themselves, he remonstrates, to count for nothing. They did not seem to exist, he points out, even in politics until prohibitionist fury threatened their beer. Then, indeed, the American German emerged from silence and obscurity, but only to rescue his mug and retire again with it into enigmatical silence.

If there is any exception to this predominance of the tradition of the English-speaking, originally middle-class, English-thinking northerner in the American mind, it is to be found in the spread of social democracy outward from the festering tenement houses of Chicago into the mining and agrarian regions of the middle west. It is a fierce form of socialist teaching that speaks throughout these regions, far more closely akin to the revolutionary Socialism of the continent of Europe than to the constructive and evolutionary Socialism of Great Britain. Its typical organ is *The Appeal to Reason*, which circulates more than a quarter of a million copies weekly from Kansas City. It is a Socialism reeking with class feeling and class hatred and altogether anarchistic in spirit; a new and highly indigestible contribution to the American moral and intellectual synthesis. It is remarkable chiefly as the one shrill exception in a world of plastic acceptance.

Now it is impossible to believe that this vast silence of these imported and ingested factors that the American nation has taken to itself is as acquiescent as it seems. No doubt they are largely taking over the traditional forms of American thought and expression quietly and without protest, and wearing them; but they will wear them as a man wears a misfit, shaping and adapting it every day more and more to his natural form, here straining a seam and there taking in a looseness. A force of modification must be at work. It must be at work in spite of the fact that, with the exception of social democracy, it does not anywhere show as a protest or a fresh beginning or a challenge to the prevailing forms.

How far it has actually been at work is, perhaps, to be judged best by an observant stroller, surveying the crowds of a Sunday evening in New York, or read in the sheets of such a mirror of popular taste as the Sunday edition of the *New York American* or the *New York Herald*. In the former just what I mean by the silent modification of the old tradition is quite typically shown. Its leading articles are written by Mr. Arthur Brisbane, the son of one of the Brook Farm Utopians, that gathering in which Hawthorne and Henry James senior, and Margaret Fuller participated, and in which the whole brilliant world of Boston's past, the world of Emerson, Longfellow, Thoreau, was interested. Mr. Brisbane is a very distinguished man, quite over and above the fact that he is paid the greatest salary of any journalist in the world. He writes with a wit and directness that no other living man can rival, and he holds up constantly what is substantially the American ideal of the past century to readers who evidently need strengthening in it. It is, of course, the figure of a man and not of a State; it is a man, clean, clean shaved and almost obtrusively strong-jawed, honest, muscular, alert, pushful, chivalrous, self-reliant, non-political except when he breaks into shrewd and penetrating voting—"you can fool all the people some of the time," etc.—and independent—independent—in a world which is therefore certain to give way to him.

His doubts, his questionings, his aspirations, are dealt with by Mr. Brisbane with a simple direct fatherliness with all the beneficent persuasiveness of a revivalist preacher. Millions read these leaders and feel a momentary benefit, en route for the more actual portions of the paper. He asks: "Why are all men gamblers?" He discusses our Longing for Immortal Imperfection, and "Did we once live on the moon?" He recommends the substitution of whisky and soda for neat whisky, drawing an illustration from the comparative effect of the diluted and of the undiluted liquid as an eye-wash ("Try whisky on your friend's eyeball!" is the heading), sleep ("The man who loses sleep will make a failure of his life, or at least diminish greatly his chances of success"), and the education of the feminine intelligence ("The cow that kicks her weaned calf is all heart"). He makes identically the same confident appeal to the moral motive which was for so long the salvation of the Puritan individualism from which the American tradition derives. "That hand," he writes, "which supports the head of the new-born baby, the mother's hand, supports the civilisation of the world."

But that sort of thing is not saving the old native strain in the population. It moves people, no doubt, but inadequately. And here is a passage that is quite the quintessence of Americanism, of all its deep moral feeling and sentimental untruthfulness. I wonder if any man but an American or a British nonconformist in a state of rhetorical excitement ever believed that Shakespeare wrote his plays or Michael Angelo painted in a mood of humanitarian exaltation, *"for the good of all men."*

> "What *shall* we strive for? *Money?*
>
> "Get a thousand millions. Your day will come, and in due course the graveyard rat will gnaw as calmly at your bump of acquisitiveness as at the mean coat of the pauper.
>
> "Then shall we strive for *power?*
>
> "The names of the first great kings of the world are forgotten, and the names of all those whose power we envy will drift to forgetfulness soon. What does the most powerful man in the world amount to standing at the brink of Niagara, with his solar plexus trembling? What is his power compared with the force of the wind or the energy of one small wave sweeping along the shore?
>
> "The power which man can build up within himself, for himself, is nothing. Only the dull reasoning of gratified egotism can make it seem worth while.
>
> "Then what is worth while? Let us look at some of the men who have come and gone, and whose lives inspire us. Take a few at random:
>
> "Columbus, Michael Angelo, Wilberforce, Shakespeare, Galileo, Fulton, Watt, Hargreaves—these will do.
>
> "Let us ask ourselves this question: 'Was there any *one thing* that distinguished *all* their lives, that united all these men, active in fields so different?'

"Yes. Every man among them, and every man whose life history is worth the telling, did something for *the good of other men*.

"Get money if you can. Get power if you can; Then, if you want to be more than the ten thousand million unknown mingled in the dust beneath you, see what good you can do with your money and your power.

"If you are one of the many millions who have not and can't get money or power, see what good you can do without either:

"You can help carry a load for an old man. You can encourage and help a poor devil trying to reform. You can set a good example to children. You can stick to the men with whom you work, fighting honestly for their welfare.

"Time was when the ablest man would rather kill ten men than feed a thousand children. That time has gone. We do not care much about feeding the children, but we care less about killing the men. To that extent we have improved already.

"The day will come when we shall prefer helping our neighbour to robbing him—legally—of a million dollars.

"Do what good you can *now*, while it is unusual, and have the satisfaction of being a pioneer and an eccentric."

It is the voice of the American tradition strained to the utmost to make itself audible to the new world, and cracking into italics and breaking into capitals with the strain. The rest of that enormous bale of paper is eloquent of a public void of moral ambitions, lost to any sense of comprehensive things, deaf to ideas, impervious to generalisations, a public which has carried the conception of freedom to its logical extreme of entire individual detachment. These tell-tale columns deal all with personality and the drama of personal life. They witness to no interest but the interest in intense individual experiences. The engagements, the love affairs, the scandals of conspicuous people are given in pitiless detail in articles adorned with vigorous portraits and sensational pictorial comments. Even the eavesdroppers who write this stuff strike the personal note, and their heavily muscular portraits frown beside the initial letter. Murders and crimes are worked up to the keenest pitch of realisation, and any new indelicacy in fashionable costume, any new medical device or cure, any new dance or athleticism, any new breach in the moral code, any novelty in sea bathing or the woman's seat on horseback, or the like, is given copious and moving illustration, stirring headlines, and eloquent reprobation. There is a coloured supplement of knock-about fun, written chiefly in the quaint dialect of the New York slums. It is a language from which "th" has vanished, and it presents a world in which the kicking by a mule of an endless succession of victims is an inexhaustible joy to young and old. "Dat ole Maud!" There is a smaller bale dealing with sport. In the advertisement columns one finds nothing of books, nothing of art; but great choice of bust developers, hair restorers, nervous tonics, clothing sales, self-contained flats, and business opportunities . . .

Individuality has, in fact, got home to itself, and, as people say, taken off its frills. All but one; Mr. Arthur Brisbane's eloquence one may consider as the last stitch of the old costume—mere decoration. Excitement remains the residual object in life. The *New York American* represents a clientele to be counted by the hundred thousand, manifestly with no other solicitudes, just burning to live and living to burn.

Sec. 6

The modifications of the American tradition that will occur through its adoption by these silent foreign ingredients in the racial synthesis are not likely to add to it or elaborate it in any way. They tend merely to simplify it to bare irresponsible non-moral individualism. It is with the detail and qualification of a tradition as with the inflexions of a language; when another people takes it over the refinements disappear. But there are other forces of modification at work upon the American tradition of an altogether more hopeful kind. It has entered upon a constructive phase. Were it not so, then the American social outlook would, indeed, be hopeless.

The effectual modifying force at work is not the strangeness nor the temperamental maladjustment of the new elements of population, but the conscious realisation of the inadequacy of the tradition on the part of the more intelligent sections of the American population. That blind national conceit that would hear no criticism and admit no deficiency has disappeared. In the last decade such a change has come over the American mind as sometimes comes over a vigorous and wilful child. Suddenly it seems to have grown up, to have begun to weigh its powers and consider its possible deficiencies. There was a time when American confidence and self-satisfaction seemed impregnable; at the slightest qualm of doubt America took to violent rhetoric as a drunkard resorts to drink. Now the indictment I have drawn up harshly, bluntly and unflatteringly in Sec. 4 would receive the endorsement of American after American. The falling birth-rate of all the best elements in the State, the cankering effect of political corruption, the crumbling of independence and equality before the progressive aggregation of wealth—he has to face them, he cannot deny them. There has arisen a new literature, the literature of national self-examination, that seems destined to modify the American tradition profoundly. To me it seems to involve the hope and possibility of a conscious collective organisation of social life.

If ever there was an epoch-marking book it was surely Henry Demarest Lloyd's "Wealth against Commonwealth." It marks an epoch not so much by what it says as by what it silently abandons. It was published in 1894, and it stated in the very clearest terms the incompatibility of the almost limitless freedom of property set up by the constitution, with the practical freedom and general happiness of the mass of men. It must be admitted that Lloyd never followed up the implications of this repudiation. He made his statements in the language of the tradition he assailed, and foreshadowed the replacement of chaos by order in quite chaotic and mystical appeals. Here, for instance, is a typical passage from "Man, the Social Creator".

> "Property is now a stumbling-block to the people, just as government has been. Property will not be abolished, but, like government, it will be democratised.
>
> "The philosophy of self-interest as the social solution was a good living and working synthesis in the days when civilisation was advancing its frontiers twenty miles a day across the American continent, and every man for himself was the best social mobilisation possible.

"But to-day it is a belated ghost that has overstayed the cock-crow. These were frontier morals. But this same, everyone for himself, becomes most immoral when the frontier is abolished and the pioneer becomes the fellow-citizen and these frontier morals are most uneconomic when labour can be divided and the product multiplied. Most uneconomic, for they make closure the rule of industry, leading not to wealth, but to that awful waste of wealth which is made visible to every eye in our unemployed—not hands alone, but land, machinery, and, most of all, hearts. Those who still practise these frontier morals are like criminals, who, according to the new science of penology, are simply reappearances of old types. Their acquisitiveness once divine like Mercury's, is now out of place except in jail. Because out of place, they are a danger. A sorry day it is likely to be for those who are found in the way when the new people rise to rush into each other's arms, to get together, to stay together and to live together. The labour movement halts because so many of its rank and file—and all its leaders—do not see clearly the golden thread of love on which have been strung together all the past glories of human association, and which is to serve for the link of the new Association of Friends who Labour, whose motto is 'All for All.'"

The establishment of the intricate co-operative commonwealth by a rush of eighty million flushed and shiny-eyed enthusiasts, in fact, is Lloyd's proposal. He will not face, and few Americans to this day will face, the cold need of a great science of social adjustment and a disciplined and rightly ordered machinery to turn such enthusiasms to effect. They seem incurably wedded to gush. However, he did express clearly enough the opening phase of American disillusionment with the wild go-as-you-please that had been the conception of life in America through a vehement, wasteful, expanding century. And he was the precursor of what is now a bulky and extremely influential literature of national criticism. A number of writers, literary investigators one may call them, or sociological men of letters, or magazine publicists—they are a little difficult to place—has taken up the inquiry into the condition of civic administration, into economic organisation into national politics and racial interaction, with a frank fearlessness and an absence of windy eloquence that has been to many Europeans a surprising revelation of the reserve forces of the American mind, President Roosevelt, that magnificent reverberator of ideas, that gleam of wilful humanity, that fantastic first interruption to the succession of machine-made politicians at the White House, has echoed clearly to this movement and made it an integral part of the general intellectual movement of America.

It is to these first intimations of the need of a "sense of the State" in America that I would particularly direct the reader's attention in this discussion. They are the beginnings of what is quite conceivably a great and complex reconstructive effort. I admit they are but beginnings. They may quite possibly wither and perish presently; they may much more probably be seized upon by adventurers and converted into a new cant almost as empty and fruitless as the old. The fact remains that, through this busy and immensely noisy confusion of nearly a hundred millions of people, these little voices go intimating more and more clearly the intention to undertake public affairs in a new spirit and upon new principles, to strengthen the State and the law against individual enterprise, to have done with those national superstitions under which hypocrisy and disloyalty and private plunder have sheltered and prospered for so long.

Just as far as these reform efforts succeed and develop is the organisation of the United States of America into a great, self-conscious, civilised nation, unparalleled in the world's history, possible; just as far as they fail is failure written over the American future. The real interest of America for the next century to the student of civilisation will be the development of these attempts, now in their infancy, to create and realise out of this racial hotchpotch, this human chaos, an idea, of the collective commonwealth as the datum of reference for every individual life.

Sec. 7

I have hinted in the last section that there is a possibility that the new wave of constructive ideas in American thought may speedily develop a cant of its own. But even then, a constructive cant is better than a destructive one. Even the conscious hypocrite has to do something to justify his pretences, and the mere disappearance from current thought of the persuasion that organisation is a mistake and discipline needless, clears the ground of one huge obstacle even if it guarantees nothing about the consequent building.

But, apart from this, are there more solid and effectual forces behind this new movement of ideas that makes for organisation in American medley at the present time?

The speculative writer casting about for such elements lights upon four sets of possibilities which call for discussion. First, one has to ask: How far is the American plutocracy likely to be merely a wasteful and chaotic class, and how far is it likely to become consciously aristocratic and constructive? Secondly, and in relation to this, what possibilities of pride and leading are there in the great university foundations of America? Will they presently begin to tell as a restraining and directing force upon public thought? Thirdly, will the growing American Socialist movement, which at present is just as anarchistic and undisciplined in spirit as everything else in America, presently perceive the constructive implications of its general propositions and become statesmanlike and constructive? And, fourthly, what are the latent possibilities of the American women? Will women as they become more and more aware of themselves as a class and of the problem of their sex become a force upon the anarchistic side, a force favouring race-suicide, or upon the constructive side which plans and builds and bears the future?

The only possible answer to each one of these questions at present is guessing and an estimate. But the only way in which a conception of the American social future may be reached lies through their discussion.

Let us begin by considering what constructive forces may exist in this new plutocracy which already so largely sways American economic and political development. The first impression is one of extravagant and aimless expenditure, of a class irresponsible and wasteful beyond all precedent. One gets a Zolaesque picture of that aspect in Mr. Upton Sinclair's "Metropolis," or the fashionable intelligence of the popular New York Sunday editions, and one finds a good deal of confirmatory evidence in many incidental aspects of the smart American life of Paris and the Riviera. The evidence in the notorious Thaw trial, after one has discounted its theatrical elements, was still a very convincing demonstration of a rotten and extravagant, because aimless and functionless, class of rich people. But one has to be careful in this matter if one is to do justice to the facts. If a thing is made up of two elements, and one is noisy and glaringly coloured, and the other is quiet and colourless, the first impression created will be that the thing is identical with the element that is noisy and glaringly coloured. One is much less likely to hear of the broad plans and the quality of the wise, strong and constructive individuals in a class than of their foolish wives, their spendthrift sons, their mistresses, and their moments of irritation and folly.

In the making of very rich men there is always a factor of good fortune and a factor of design and will. One meets rich men at times who seem to be merely lucky gamblers, who strike one as just the thousandth man in a myriad of wild plungers, who are, in fact, chance nobodies washed up by an eddy. Others, again, strike one as exceptionally lucky half-knaves. But there are others of a growth more deliberate and of an altogether higher personal quality. One takes such men as Mr. J.D. Rockefeller or Mr. Pierpont Morgan— the scale of their fortunes makes them public property—and it is clear that we are dealing with persons on quite a different level of intellectual power from the British Colonel Norths, for example, or the South African Joels. In my "Future in America" I have taken the former largely at Miss Tarbell's estimate, and treated him as a case of acquisitiveness raised in Baptist surroundings. But I doubt very much if that exhausts the man as he is to-day. Given a man brought up to saving and "getting on" as if to a religion, a man very acquisitive and very patient and restrained, and indubitably with great organising power, and he grows rich beyond the dreams of avarice. And having done so, there he is. What is he going to do? Every step he takes up the ascent to riches gives him new perspectives and new points of view.

It may have appealed to the young Rockefeller, clerk in a Chicago house, that to be rich was itself a supreme end; in the first flush of the discovery that he was immensely rich, he may have thanked Heaven as if for a supreme good, and spoken to a Sunday school gathering as if he knew himself for the most favoured of men. But all that happened twenty years ago or more. One does not keep on in that sort of satisfaction; one settles down to the new facts. And such men as Mr. Rockefeller and Mr. Pierpont Morgan do not live in a made and protected world with their minds trained, tamed and fed and shielded from outside impressions as royalties do. The thought of the world has washed about them; they have read and listened to the discussion of themselves for some decades; they have had sleepless nights of self-examination. To succeed in acquiring enormous wealth does not solve the problem of life; indeed, it reopens it in a new form. "What shall I do with myself?" simply recurs again. You may have decided to devote yourself to getting on, getting wealthy. Well, you have got it. Now, again, comes the question: "What shall I do?"

Mr. Pierpont Morgan, I am told, collected works of art. I can understand that satisfying a rich gentleman of leisure, but not a man who has felt the sensation of holding great big things in his great big hands. Saul, going out to seek his father's asses, found a kingdom—and became very spiritedly a king, and it seems to me that these big industrial and financial organisers, whatever in their youth they proposed to do or be, must many of them come to realise that their organising power is up against no less a thing than a nation's future. Napoleon, it is curious to remember once wanted to run a lodging-house, and a man may start to corner oil and end the father of a civilisation.

Now, I am disposed to suspect at times that an inkling of such a realisation may have come to some of these very rich men. I am inclined to put it among the possibilities of our time that it may presently become clearly and definitely the inspiring idea of many of those who find themselves predominantly rich. I do not see why these active rich should not develop statesmanship, and I can quite imagine them developing very considerable statesmanship. Because these men were able to realise their organising power in the absence of economic organisation, it does not follow that they will be fanatical for a continuing looseness and freedom of property. The phase of economic liberty ends itself, as Marx long ago pointed out. The American business world becomes more and more a managed world with fewer and fewer wild possibilities of succeeding. Of all people the big millionaires should realise this most acutely, and, in fact, there are many signs that they do. It seems to me that the educational zeal of Mr. Andrew Carnegie and the university and scientific endowments of Mr. Rockefeller are not merely showy benefactions; they express a definite feeling of the present need of constructive organisation in the social scheme. The time has come to build. There is, I think, good reason for expecting that statesmanship of the millionaires to become more organised and scientific and comprehensive in the coming years. It is plausible at least to maintain that the personal quality of the American plutocracy has risen in the last three decades, has risen from the quality of a mere irresponsible wealthy person towards that of a real aristocrat with a "sense of the State." That one may reckon the first hopeful possibility in the American outlook.

And intimately connected with this development of an attitude of public responsibility in the very rich is the decay on the one hand of the preposterous idea once prevalent in America that politics is an unsuitable interest for a "gentleman," and on the other of the democratic jealousy of any but poor politicians. In New York they talk very much of "gentlemen," and by "gentlemen" they seem to mean rich men "in society" with a college education. Nowadays, "gentlemen" seem more and more disposed towards politics, and less and less towards a life of business or detached refinement. President Roosevelt, for example, was one of the pioneers in this new development, this restoration of virility to the gentlemanly ideal. His career marks the appearance of a new and better type of man in American politics, the close of the rule of the idealised nobody.

The prophecy has been made at times that the United States might develop a Caesarism, and certainly the position of president might easily become that of an imperator. No doubt in the event of an acute failure of the national system such a catastrophe might occur, but the more hopeful and probable line of development is one in which a conscious and powerful, if informal, aristocracy will play a large part. It may, indeed, never have any of the outward forms of an aristocracy or any definite public recognition. The Americans are as chary of the coronet and the known aristocratic titles as the Romans were of the word King. Octavius, for that reason, never called himself king nor Italy a kingdom. He was just the Caesar of the Republic, and the Empire had been established for many years before the Romans fully realised that they had returned to monarchy.

The American universities are closely connected in their development with the appearance and growing class-consciousness of this aristocracy of wealth. The fathers of the country certainly did postulate a need of universities, and in every state Congress set aside public lands to furnish a university with material resources. Every State possesses a university, though in many instances these institutions are in the last degree of feebleness. In the days of sincere democracy the starvation of government and the dislike of all manifest inequalities involved the starvation of higher education. Moreover, the entirely artificial nature of the State boundaries, representing no necessary cleavages and traversed haphazard by the lines of communication, made some of these State foundations unnecessary and others inadequate to a convergent demand. From the very beginning, side by side with the State universities, were the universities founded by benefactors; and with the evolution of new centres of population, new and extremely generous plutocratic endowments appeared. The dominant universities of America to-day, the treasure houses of intellectual prestige, are almost all of them of plutocratic origin, and even in the State universities, if new resources are wanted to found new chairs, to supply funds for research or publication or what not, it is to the more State-conscious wealthy and not to the State legislature that the appeal is made almost as a matter of course. The common voter, the small individualist has less constructive imagination—is more individualistic, that is, than the big individualist.

This great network of universities that is now spread over the States, interchanging teachers, literature and ideas, and educating not only the professions but a growing proportion of business leaders and wealthy people, must necessarily take an important part in the reconstruction of the American tradition that is now in progress. It is giving a large and increasing amount of attention to the subjects that bear most directly upon the peculiar practical problems of statecraft in America, to psychology, sociology and political science. It is influencing the press more and more directly by supplying a rising proportion of journalists and creating an atmosphere of criticism and suggestion. It is keeping itself on the one hand in touch with the popular literature of public criticism in those new and curious organs of public thought, the ten-cent magazines; and on the other it is making a constantly more solid basis of common understanding upon which the newer generation of plutocrats may meet. That older sentimental patriotism must be giving place under its influence to a more definite and effectual conception of a collective purpose. It is to the moral and intellectual influence of sustained scientific study in the universities, and a growing increase of the college-trained element in the population that we must look if we are to look anywhere for the new progressive methods, for the substitution of persistent, planned and calculated social development for the former conditions of systematic neglect and corruption in public affairs varied by epileptic seizures of "Reform."

Sec. 9

A third influence that may also contribute very materially to the reconstruction of the American tradition is the Socialist movement. It is true that so far American Socialism has very largely taken an Anarchistic form, has been, in fact, little more than a revolutionary movement of the wages-earning class against the property owner. It has already been pointed out that it derives not from contemporary English Socialism but from the Marxist social democracy of the continent of Europe, and has not even so much of the constructive spirit as has been developed by the English Socialists of the Fabian and Labour Party group or by the newer German evolutionary Socialists. Nevertheless, whenever Socialism is intelligently met by discussion or whenever it draws near to practicable realisation, it becomes, by virtue of its inherent implications, a constructive force, and there is no reason to suppose that it will not be intelligently met on the whole and in the long run in America. The alternative to a developing Socialism among the labouring masses in America is that revolutionary Anarchism from which it is slowly but definitely marking itself off. In America we have to remember that we are dealing with a huge population of people who are for the most part, and more and more evidently destined under the present system of free industrial competition, to be either very small traders, small farmers on the verge of debt, or wages-earners for all their lives. They are going to lead limited lives and worried lives—and they know it. Nearly everyone can read and discuss now, the process of concentrating property and the steady fixation of conditions that were once fluid and adventurous goes on in the daylight visibly to everyone. And it has to be borne in mind also that these people are so far under the sway of the American tradition that each thinks himself as good as any man and as much entitled to the fullness of life. Whatever social tradition their fathers had, whatever ideas of a place to be filled humbly and seriously and duties to be done, have been left behind in Europe. No Church dominates the scenery of this new land, and offers in authoritative and convincing tones consolations hereafter for lives obscurely but faithfully lived. Whatever else happens in this national future, upon one point the patriotic American may feel assured, and that is of an immense general discontent in the working class and of a powerful movement in search of a general betterment. The practical forms and effects of that movement will depend almost entirely upon the average standard of life among the workers and their general education. Sweated and ill-organised foreigners, such as one finds in New Jersey living under conditions of great misery, will be fierce, impatient and altogether dangerous. They will be acutely exasperated by every picture of plutocratic luxury in their newspaper, they will readily resort to destructive violence. The western miner, the western agriculturist, worried beyond endurance between the money-lender and railway combinations will be almost equally prone to savage methods of expression. *The Appeal to Reason*, for example, to which I have made earlier reference in this chapter, is furious to wreck the present capitalistic system, but it is far too angry and impatient for that satisfaction to produce any clear suggestion of what shall replace it.

To call this discontent of the seething underside of the American system Socialism is a misnomer. Were there no Socialism there would be just as much of this discontent, just the same insurgent force and desire for violence, taking some other title and far more destructive methods. This discontent is a part of the same planless confusion that gives on the other side the wanton irresponsible extravagances of the smart people of New York. But Socialism alone, of all the forms of expression adopted by the losers in the economic struggle, contains constructive possibilities and leads its adherents towards that ideal of an organised State, planned and developed, from which these terrible social stresses may be eliminated, which is also the ideal to which sociology and the thoughts of every constructive-minded and foreseeing man in any position of life tend to-day. In the Socialist hypothesis of collective ownership and administration as the social basis, there is the germ of a "sense of the State" that may ultimately develop into comprehensive conceptions of social order, conceptions upon which enlightened millionaires and unenlightened workers may meet at last in generous and patriotic co-operation.

The chances of the American future, then, seem to range between two possibilities just as a more or less constructive Socialism does or does not get hold of and inspire the working mass of the population. In the worst event—given an emotional and empty hostility to property as such, masquerading as Socialism—one has the prospect of a bitter and aimless class war between the expropriated many and the property-holding few, a war not of general insurrection but of localised outbreaks, strikes and brutal suppressions, a war rising to bloody conflicts and sinking to coarsely corrupt political contests, in which one side may prevail in one locality and one in another, and which may even develop into a chronic civil war in the less-settled parts of the country or an irresistible movement for secession between west and east. That is assuming the greatest imaginable vehemence and short-sighted selfishness and the least imaginable intelligence on the part of both workers and the plutocrat-swayed government. But if the more powerful and educated sections of the American community realise in time the immense moral possibilities of the Socialist movement, if they will trouble to understand its good side instead of emphasising its bad, if they will keep in touch with it and help in the development of a constructive content to its propositions, then it seems to me that popular Socialism may count as a third great factor in the making of the civilised American State.

In any case, it does not seem to me probable that there can be any national revolutionary movement or any complete arrest in the development of an aristocratic phase in American history. The area of the country is too great and the means of communication between the workers in different parts inadequate for a concerted rising or even for effective political action in mass. In the worst event—and it is only in the worst event that a great insurrectionary movement becomes probable—the newspapers, magazines, telephones and telegraphs, all the apparatus of discussion and popular appeal, the railways, arsenals, guns, flying machines, and all the material of warfare, will be in the hands of the property owners, and the average of betrayal among the leaders of a class, not racially homogeneous, embittered, suspicious united only by their discomforts and not by any constructive intentions, will necessarily be high. So that, though the intensifying trouble between labour and capital may mean immense social disorganisation and lawlessness, though it may even supply the popular support in new attempts at secession, I do not see in it the possibility and force for that new start which the revolutionary Socialists anticipate; I see it merely as one of several forces making, on the whole and particularly in view of the possible mediatory action of the universities, for construction and reconciliation.

Sec. 10

What changes are likely to occur in the more intimate social life of the people of the United States? Two influences are at work that may modify this profoundly. One is that spread of knowledge and that accompanying change in moral attitude which is more and more sterilising the once prolific American home, and the second is the rising standard of feminine education. There has arisen in this age a new consciousness in women. They are entering into the collective thought to a degree unprecedented in the world's history, and with portents at once disquieting and confused.

In Sec. 5 I enumerated what I called the silent factors in the American synthesis, the immigrant European aliens, the Catholics, the coloured blood, and so forth. I would now observe that, in the making of the American tradition, the women also have been to a large extent, and quite remarkably, a silent factor. That tradition is not only fundamentally middle-class and English, but it is also fundamentally masculine. The citizen is the man. The woman belongs to him. He votes for her, works for her, does all the severer thinking for her. She is in the home behind the shop or in the dairy at the farmhouse with her daughters. She gets the meal while the men talk. The American imagination and American feeling centre largely upon the family and upon "mother." American ideals are homely. The social unit is the home, and it is another and a different set of influences and considerations that are never thought of at all when the home sentiment is under discussion, that, indeed, it would be indelicate to mention at such a time, which are making that social unit the home of one child or of no children at all.

That ideal of a man-owned, mother-revering home has been the prevalent American ideal from the landing of the *Mayflower* right down to the leader writing of Mr. Arthur Brisbane. And it is clear that a very considerable section among one's educated women contemporaries do not mean to stand this ideal any longer. They do not want to be owned and cherished, and they do not want to be revered. How far they represent their sex in this matter it is very hard to say. In England in the professional and most intellectually active classes it is scarcely an exaggeration to say that *all* the most able women below five-and-thirty are workers for the suffrage and the ideal of equal and independent citizenship, and active critics of the conventions under which women live to-day. It is at least plausible to suppose that a day is approaching when the alternatives between celibacy or a life of economic dependence and physical subordination to a man who has chosen her, and upon whose kindness her happiness depends, or prostitution, will no longer be a satisfactory outlook for the great majority of women, and when, with a newly aroused political consciousness, they will be prepared to exert themselves as a class to modify this situation. It may be that this is incorrect, and that in devotion to an accepted male and his children most women do still and will continue to find their greatest satisfaction in life. But it is the writer's impression that so simple and single-hearted a devotion is rare, and that, released from tradition—and education, reading and discussion do mean release from tradition—women are as eager for initiative, freedom and experience as men. In that case they will persist in the present agitation for political rights, and these secured, go on to demand a very considerable reconstruction of our present social order.

It is interesting to point the direction in which this desire for independence will probably take them. They will discover that the dependence of women at the present time is not so much a law-made as an economic dependence due to the economic disadvantages their sex imposes upon them. Maternity and the concomitants of maternity are the circumstances in their lives, exhausting energy and earning nothing, that place them at a discount. From the stage when property ceased to be chiefly the creation of feminine agricultural toil (the so-called primitive matriarchate) to our present stage, women have had to depend upon a man's willingness to keep them, in order to realise the organic purpose of their being. Whether conventionally equal or not, whether voters or not, that necessity for dependence will still remain under our system of private property and free independent competition. There is only one evident way by which women as a class can escape from that dependence each upon an individual man and from all the practical inferiority this dependence entails, and that is by so altering their status as to make maternity and the upbringing of children a charge not upon the husband of the mother but upon the community. The public Endowment of Maternity is the only route by which the mass of women can reach that personal freedom and independent citizenship so many of them desire.

Now, this idea of the Endowment of Maternity—or as it is frequently phrased, the Endowment of the Home—is at present put forward by the modern Socialists as an integral part of their proposals, and it is interesting to note that there is this convergent possibility which may bring the feminist movement at last altogether into line with constructive Socialism. Obviously, before anything in the direction of family endowment becomes practicable, public bodies and the State organisation will need to display far more integrity and efficiency than they do in America at the present time. Still, that is the trend of things in all contemporary civilised communities, and it is a trend that will find a powerful reinforcement in men's solicitudes as the increasing failure of the unsupported private family to produce offspring adequate to the needs of social development becomes more and more conspicuous. The impassioned appeals of President Roosevelt have already brought home the race-suicide of the native-born to every American intelligence, but mere rhetoric will not in itself suffice to make people, insecurely employed and struggling to maintain a comfortable standard of life against great economic pressure, prolific. Presented as a call to a particularly onerous and quite unpaid social duty the appeal for unrestricted parentage fails. Husband and wife alike dread an excessive burthen. Travel, leisure, freedom, comfort, property and increased ability for business competition are the rewards of abstinence from parentage, and even the disapproval of President Roosevelt and the pride of offspring are insufficient counterweights to these inducements. Large families disappear from the States, and more and more couples are childless. Those who have children restrict their number in order to afford those they have some reasonable advantage in life. This, in the presence of the necessary knowledge, is as practically inevitable a consequence of individualist competition and the old American tradition as the appearance of slums and a class of millionaires.

These facts go to the very root of the American problem. I have already pointed out that, in spite of a colossal immigration, the population of the United States was at the end of the nineteenth century over twenty millions short of what it should have been through its own native increase had the birth-rate of the opening of the century been maintained. For a hundred years America has been "fed" by Europe. That feeding process will not go on indefinitely. The immigration came in waves as if reservoir after reservoir was tapped and exhausted. Nowadays England, Scotland, Ireland, France and Scandinavia send hardly any more; they have no more to send. Germany and Switzerland send only a few. The South European and Austrian supply is not as abundant as it was. There may come a time when Europe and Western Asia will have no more surplus population to send, when even Eastern Asia will have passed into a less fecund phase, and when America will have to look to its own natural increase for the continued development of its resources.

If the present isolated family of private competition is still the social unit, it seems improbable that there will be any greater natural increase than there is in France.

Will the growing idea of a closer social organisation have developed by that time to the possibility of some collective effort in this matter? Or will that only come about after the population of the world has passed through a phase of absolute recession? The peculiar constitution of the United States gives a remarkable freedom of experiment in these matters to each individual state, and local developments do not need to wait upon a national change of opinion; but, on the other hand, the superficial impression of an English visitor is that any such profound interference with domestic autonomy runs counter to all that Americans seem to hold dear at the present time. These are, however, new ideas and new considerations that have still to be brought adequately before the national consciousness, and it is quite impossible to calculate how a population living under changing conditions and with a rising standard of education and a developing feminine consciousness may not think and feel and behave in a generation's time. At present for all political and collective action America is a democracy of untutored individualist men who will neither tolerate such interference between themselves and the women they choose to marry as the Endowment of Motherhood implies, nor view the "kids" who will at times occur even in the best-regulated families as anything but rather embarrassing, rather amusing by-products of the individual affections.

I find in the London *New Age* for August 15th, 1908, a description by Mr. Jerome K. Jerome of "John Smith," the average British voter. John Smith might serve in some respects for the common man of all the modern civilisations. Among other things that John Smith thinks and wants, he wants:

> "a little house and garden in the country all to himself. His idea is somewhere near half an acre of ground. He would like a piano in the best room; it has always been his dream to have a piano. The youngest girl, he is convinced, is musical. As a man who has knocked about the world and has thought, he quite appreciates the argument that by co-operation the material side of life can be greatly improved. He quite sees that by combining a dozen families together in one large house better practical results can be obtained. It is as easy to direct the cooking for a hundred as for half a dozen. There would be less waste of food, of coals, of lighting. To put aside one piano for one girl is absurd. He sees all this, but it does not alter one little bit his passionate craving for that small house and garden all to himself. He is built that way. He is typical of a good many other men and women built on the same pattern. What are you going to do with them? Change them—their instincts, their very nature, rooted in the centuries? Or, as an alternative, vary Socialism to fit John Smith? Which is likely to prove the shorter operation?"

That, however, is by the way. Here is the point at issue:

"He has heard that Socialism proposes to acknowledge woman's service to the State by paying her a weekly wage according to the number of children that she bears and rears. I don't propose to repeat his objections to the idea; they could hardly be called objections. There is an ugly look comes into his eyes; something quite undefinable, prehistoric, almost dangerous, looks out of them . . . In talking to him on this subject you do not seem to be talking to a man. It is as if you had come face to face with something behind civilisation, behind humanity, something deeper down still among the dim beginnings of creation . . ."

Now, no doubt Mr. Jerome is writing with emphasis here. But there is sufficient truth in the passage for it to stand here as a rough symbol of another factor in this question. John Smithism, that manly and individualist element in the citizen, stands over against and resists all the forces of organisation that would subjugate it to a collective purpose. It is careless of coming national cessation and depopulation, careless of the insurgent spirit beneath the acquiescences of Mrs. Smith, careless of its own inevitable defeat in the economic struggle, careless because it can understand none of these things; it is obstinately muddle-headed, asserting what it conceives to be itself against the universe and all other John Smiths whatsoever. It is a factor with all other factors. The creative, acquisitive, aggressive spirit of those bigger John Smiths who succeed as against the myriads of John Smiths who fail, the wider horizons and more efficient methods of the educated man, the awakening class-consciousness of women, the inevitable futility of John Smithism, the sturdy independence that makes John Smith resent even disciplined co-operation with Tom Brown to achieve a common end, his essential incapacity, indeed, for collective action; all these things are against the ultimate triumph, and make for the ultimate civilisation even of John Smith.

It may be doubted if the increasing collective organisation of society to which the United States of America, in common with all the rest of the world, seem to be tending will be to any very large extent a national organisation. The constitution is an immense and complicated barrier to effectual centralisation. There are many reasons for supposing the national government will always remain a little ineffectual and detached from the full flow of American life, and this notwithstanding the very great powers with which the President is endowed.

One of these reasons is certainly the peculiar accident that has placed the seat of government upon the Potomac. To the thoughtful visitor to the United States this hiding away of the central government in a minute district remote from all the great centres of thought, population and business activity becomes more remarkable more perplexing, more suggestive of an incurable weakness in the national government as he grasps more firmly the peculiarities of the American situation.

I do not see how the central government of that great American nation of which I dream can possibly be at Washington, and I do not see how the present central government can possibly be transferred to any other centre. But to go to Washington, to see and talk to Washington, is to receive an extraordinary impression of the utter isolation and hopelessness of Washington. The National Government has an air of being marooned there. Or as though it had crept into a corner to do something in the dark. One goes from the abounding movement and vitality of the northern cities to this sunny and enervating place through the negligently cultivated country of Virginia, and one discovers the slovenly, unfinished promise of a city, broad avenues lined by negro shanties and patches of cultivation, great public buildings and an immense post office, a lifeless museum, an inert university, a splendid desert library, a street of souvenir shops, a certain industry of "seeing Washington," an idiotic colossal obelisk. It seems an ideal nest for the tariff manipulator, a festering corner of delegates and agents and secondary people. In the White House, in the time of President Roosevelt, the present writer found a transitory glow of intellectual activity, the spittoons and glass screens that once made it like a

London gin palace had been removed, and the former orgies of handshaking reduced to a minimum. It was, one felt, an accidental phase. The assassination of McKinley was an interruption of the normal Washington process. To this place, out of the way of everywhere, come the senators and congressmen, mostly leaving their families behind them in their states of origin, and hither, too, are drawn a multitude of journalists and political agents and clerks, a crowd of underbred, mediocre men. For most of them there is neither social nor intellectual life. The thought of America is far away, centred now in New York; the business and economic development centres upon New York; apart from the President, it is in New York that one meets the people who matter, and the New York atmosphere that grows and develops ideas and purposes. New York is the natural capital of the United States, and would need to be the capital of any highly organised national system. Government from the district of Columbia is in itself the repudiation of any highly organised national system.

But government from this ineffectual, inert place is only the most striking outcome of that inflexible constitution the wrangling delegates of 1787-8 did at last produce out of a conflict of State jealousies. They did their best to render centralisation or any coalescence of States impossible and private property impregnable, and so far their work has proved extraordinarily effective. Only a great access of intellectual and moral vigour in the nation can ever set it aside. And while the more and more sterile millions of the United States grapple with the legal and traditional difficulties that promise at last to arrest their development altogether, the rest of the world will be moving on to new phases. An awakened Asia will be reorganising its social and political conceptions in the light of modern knowledge and modern ideas, and South America will be working out its destinies, perhaps in the form of a powerful confederation of states. All Europe will be schooling its John Smiths to finer discipline and broader ideas. It is quite possible that the American John Smiths may have little to brag about in the way of national predominance by A.D. 2000. It is quite possible that the United States may be sitting meekly at the feet of at present unanticipated teachers.

THE POSSIBLE COLLAPSE OF CIVILISATION

(New Year, 1909.)

The Editor of the *New York World* has asked me to guess the general trend of events in the next thirty years or so with especial reference to the outlook for the State and City of New York. I like and rarely refuse such cheerful invitations to prophesy. I have already made a sort of forecast (in my "Anticipations") of what may happen if the social and economic process goes on fairly smoothly for all that time, and shown a New York relieved from its present congestion by the development of the means of communication, and growing and spreading in wide and splendid suburbs towards Boston and Philadelphia. I made that forecast before ever I passed Sandy Hook, but my recent visit only enhanced my sense of growth and "go" in things American. Still, we are nowadays all too apt to think that growth is inevitable and progress in the nature of things; the Wonderful Century, as Dr. Alfred Russel Wallace called the nineteenth, has made us perhaps over-confident and forgetful of the ruins of great cities and confident prides of the past that litter the world, and here I will write about the other alternative, of the progressive process "hitting something," and smashing.

There are two chief things in modern life that impress me as dangerous and incalculable. The first of these is the modern currency and financial system, and the second is the chance we take of destructive war. Let me dwell first of all on the mysterious possibilities of the former, and then point out one or two uneasy developments of the latter.

Now, there is nothing scientific about our currency and finance at all. It is a thing that has grown up and elaborated itself out of very simple beginnings in the course of a century or so. Three hundred years ago the edifice had hardly begun to rise from the ground, most property was real, most people lived directly on the land, most business was on a cash basis, oversea trade was a proportionately small affair, labour was locally fixed. Most of the world was at the level at which much of China remains to-day—able to get along without even coinage. It was a rudimentary world from the point of view of the modern financier and industrial organiser. Well, on that rude, secure basis there has now been piled the most chancy and insecurely experimental system of conventions and assumptions about money and credit it is possible to imagine. There has grown up a vast system of lending and borrowing, a world-wide extension of joint-stock enterprises that involve at last the most fantastic relationships. I find myself, for example, owning (partially, at least) a bank in New Zealand, a railway in Cuba, another in Canada, several in Brazil, an electric power plant in the City of Westminster, and so on, and I use these stocks and shares as a sort of interest-bearing money. If I want money to spend, I sell a railway share much as one might change a hundred-pound banknote; if I have more cash than I need immediately I buy a few shares. I perceive that the value of these shares oscillates, sometimes rather gravely, and that the value of the alleged money on the cheques I get also oscillates as compared with the things I want to buy; that, indeed, the whole system (which has only existed for a couple of centuries or so, and which keeps on getting higher and giddier) is perpetually swaying and quivering and bending and sagging; but it is only when such a great crisis occurs as that of 1907 that it enters my mind that possibly there is no limit to these oscillations, that possibly the whole vast accidental edifice will presently come smashing down.

Why shouldn't it?

I defy any economist or financial expert to prove that it cannot. That it hasn't done so in the little time for which it has existed is no reply at all. It is like arguing that a man cannot die because he has never been known to do so. Previous men have died, previous civilisations have collapsed, if not of acute, then of chronic financial disorders.

The experience of 1907 indicated very clearly how a collapse might occur. A panic, like an avalanche, is a thing much easier to start than stop. Previous panics have been arrested by good luck; this last one in America, for example, found Europe strong and prosperous and helpful. In every panic period there is a huge dislocation of business enterprises, vast multitudes of men are thrown out of employment, there is grave social and political disorder; but in the end, so far, things have an air of having recovered. But now, suppose the panic wave a little more universal—and panic waves tend to be more extensive than they used to be. Suppose that when securities fall all round, and gold appreciates in New York, and frightened people begin to sell investments and hoard gold, the same thing happens in other parts of the world. Increase the scale of the trouble only two or three times, and would our system recover? Imagine great masses of men coming out of employment, and angry and savage, in all our great towns; imagine the railways working with reduced staffs on reduced salaries or blocked by strikers; imagine provision dealers stopping consignments to retailers, and retailers hesitating to give credit. A phase would arrive when the police and militia keeping order in the streets would find themselves on short rations and without their weekly pay.

What we moderns, with our little three hundred years or so of security, do not recognise is that things that go up and down may, given a certain combination of chances, go down steadily, down and down.

What would you do, dear reader—what should I do—if a slump went on continually?

And that brings me to the second great danger to our modern civilisation, and that is War. We have over-developed war. While we have left our peace organisation to the niggling, slow, self-seeking methods of private enterprise; while we have left the breeding of our peoples to chance, their minds to the halfpenny press and their wealth to the drug manufacturer, we have pushed forward the art of war on severely scientific and Socialist lines; we have put all the collective resources of the community and an enormous proportion of its intelligence and invention ungrudgingly into the improvement and manufacture of the apparatus of destruction. Great Britain, for example, is content with the railways and fireplaces and types of housing she had fifty years ago; she still uses telephones and the electric light in the most tentative spirit; but every ironclad she had five-and-twenty years ago is old iron now and abandoned. Everything crawls forward but the science of war; that rushes on. Of what will happen if presently the guns begin to go off I have no shadow of doubt. Every year has seen the disproportionate increase until now. Every modern European state is more or less like a cranky, ill-built steamboat in which some idiot has mounted and loaded a monstrous gun with no apparatus to damp its recoil. Whether that gun hits or misses when it is fired, of one thing we may be absolutely certain—it will send the steamboat to the bottom of the sea.

Modern warfare is an insanity, not a sane business proposition. Its preparation eats more and more into the resources which should be furnishing a developing civilisation; its possibilities of destruction are incalculable. A new epoch has opened with the coming of the navigable balloon and the flying machine. To begin with, these things open new gulfs for expenditure; in the end they mean possibilities of destruction beyond all precedent. Such things as the *Zeppelin* and the *Ville de Paris* are only the first pigmy essays of the aeronaut. It is clear that to be effective, capable of carrying guns and comparatively insensitive to perforation by shot and shell, these things will have to be very much larger and as costly, perhaps, as a first-class cruiser. Imagine such monsters of the air, and wild financial panic below!

Here, then, are two associated possibilities with which to modify our expectation of an America advancing steadily on the road to an organised civilisation, of New York rebuilding herself in marble, spreading like a garden city over New Jersey and Long Island and New York State, becoming a new and greater Venice, queen of the earth.

Perhaps, after all, the twentieth century isn't going to be so prosperous as the nineteenth. Perhaps, instead of going resistlessly onward, we are going to have a set-back. Perhaps we are going to be put back to learn over again under simpler conditions some of those necessary fundamental lessons our race has learnt as yet insufficiently well—honesty and brotherhood, social collectivism, and the need of some common peace-preserving council for the whole world.

THE IDEAL CITIZEN

Our conceptions of what a good citizen should be are all at sixes and sevens. No two people will be found to agree in every particular of such an ideal, and the extreme divergences upon what is necessary, what is permissible, what is unforgivable in him, will span nearly the whole range of human possibility and conduct. As a consequence, we bring up our children in a mist of vague intimations, in a confusion of warring voices, perplexed as to what they must do, uncertain as to what they may do, doomed to lives of compromise and fluctuating and inoperative opinion. Ideals and suggestions come and go before their eyes like figures in a fog. The commonest pattern, perhaps—the commonest pattern certainly in Sunday schools and edifying books, and on all those places and occasions when morality is sought as an end—is a clean and able-bodied person, truthful to the extent that he does not tell lies, temperate so far as abstinence is concerned, honest without pedantry, and active in his own affairs, steadfastly law-abiding and respectful to custom and usage, though aloof from the tumult of politics, brave but not adventurous, punctual in some form of religious exercise, devoted to his wife and children, and kind without extravagance to all men. Everyone feels that this is not enough, everyone feels that something more is wanted and something different; most people are a little interested in what that difference can be, and it is a business that much of what is more than trivial in our art, our literature and our drama must do to fill in bit by bit and shade by shade the subtle, the permanent detail of the answer.

It does very greatly help in this question to bear in mind the conflict of our origins. Every age is an age of transition, of minglings, of the breaking up of old, narrow cultures, and the breaking down of barriers, of spiritual and often of actual interbreeding.

Not only is the physical but the moral and intellectual ancestry of everyone more mixed than ever it was before. We blend in our blood, everyone of us, and we blend in our ideas and purposes, craftsmen, warriors, savages, peasants, and a score of races, and an endless multitude of social expedients and rules. Go back but a hundred generations in the lineage of the most delicate girl you know, and you will find a dozen murderers. You will find liars and cheats, lascivious sinners, women who have sold themselves, slaves, imbeciles, devotees, saints, men of fantastic courage, discreet and watchful persons, usurers, savages, criminals and kings, and every one of this miscellany, not simply fathering or mothering on the way to her, but teaching urgently and with every grade of intensity, views and habits for which they stand. Something of it all has come to her, albeit much may seem forgotten. In every human birth, with a new little variation, a fresh slight novelty of arrangement the old issues rise again. Our ideas, even more than our blood, flow from multitudinous sources.

Certain groups of ideas come to us distinctively associated with certain marked ways of life. Many, and for a majority of us, it may be, most of our ancestors were serfs or slaves. And men and women who have had, generation after generation, to adapt themselves to slavery and the rule of a master, develop an idea of goodness very different from that of princes. From our slave ancestry, says Lester Ward, we learnt to work, and certainly it is from slavery we derive the conception that industry, even though it be purposeless industry, is a virtue in itself. The good slave, too, has a morality of restraints; he abstains from the food he handles and hungers for, and he denies himself pride and initiative of every sort. He is honest in not taking, but he is unscrupulous about adequate service. He makes no virtue of frankness, but much of kindly helpfulness and charity to the weak. He has no sense of duty in planning or economising. He is polite and soft-spoken, and disposed to irony rather than denunciation, ready to admire cuteness and condone deception. Not so the rebel. That tradition is working in us also. It has been the lot of vast masses of population in every age to be living in successful or unsuccessful resistance to mastery, to be dreading oppression or to be just escaped from it. Resentment becomes a virtue then, and any peace with the oppressor a crime. It is from rebel origins so many of us get the idea that disrespectfulness is something of a duty and obstinacy a fine thing. And under the force of this tradition we idealise the rugged and unmanageable, we find something heroic in rough clothes and hands, in bad manners, insensitive behaviour, and unsociableness. And a community of settlers, again, in a rough country, fighting for a bare existence, makes a virtue of vehemence, of a hasty rapidity of execution. Hurried and driven men glorify "push" and impatience, and despise finish and fine discriminations as weak and demoralising things. These three, the Serf, the Rebel, and the Squatter, are three out of a thousand types and aspects that have gone to our making. In the American composition they are dominant. But all those thousand different standards and traditions are our material, each with something fine, and each with something evil. They have all provided the atmosphere of upbringing for men in the past. Out of them and out of unprecedented occasions, we in this newer age, in which there are no slaves, in which every man is a citizen, in which the conveniences of a great and growing civilisation makes the frantic avidity of the squatter a nuisance, have to set ourselves to frame the standard of our children's children, to abandon what the slave or the squatter or the rebel found necessary and that we find unnecessary, to fit fresh requirements to our new needs. So we have to develop our figure of the fine man, our desirable citizen in that great and noble civilised state we who have a "sense of the state" would build out of the confusions of our world.

To describe that ideal modern citizen now is at best to make a guess and a suggestion of what must be built in reality by the efforts of a thousand minds. But he will be a very different creature from that indifferent, well-behaved business man who passes for a good citizen to-day. He will be neither under the slave tradition nor a rebel nor a vehement elemental man. Essentially he will be aristocratic, aristocratic not in the sense that he has slaves or class inferiors, because probably he will have nothing of the sort, but aristocratic in the sense that he will feel the State belongs to him and he to the State. He will probably be a public servant; at any rate, he will be a man doing some work in the complicated machinery of the modern community for a salary and not for speculative gain. Typically, he will be a professional man. I do not think the ideal modern citizen can be a person living chiefly by buying for as little as he can give and selling for as much as he can get; indeed, most of what we idolise to-day as business enterprise I think he will regard with considerable contempt. But, then, I am a Socialist, and look forward to the time when the economic machinery of the community will be a field not for private enrichment but for public service.

He will be good to his wife and children as he will be good to his friend, but he will be no partisan for wife and family against the common welfare. His solicitude will be for the welfare of all the children of the community; he will have got beyond blind instinct; he will have the intelligence to understand that almost any child in the world may have as large a share as his own offspring in the parentage of his great-great-grandchildren His wife he will treat as his equal; he will not be "kind" to her, but fair and frank and loving, as one equal should be with another; he will no more have the impertinence to pet and pamper her, to keep painful and laborious things out of her knowledge to "shield" her from the responsibility of political and social work, than he will to make a Chinese toy of her and bind her feet. He and she will love that they may enlarge and not limit one another.

Consciously and deliberately the ideal citizen will seek beauty in himself and in his way of living. He will be temperate rather than harshly abstinent, and he will keep himself fit and in training as an elementary duty. He will not be a fat or emaciated person. Fat, panting men, and thin, enfeebled ones cannot possibly be considered good citizens any more than dirty or verminous people. He will be just as fine and seemly in his person as he can be, not from vanity and self-assertion but to be pleasing and agreeable to his fellows. The ugly dress and ugly bearing of the "good man" of to-day will be as incomprehensible to him as the filth of a palaeolithic savage is to us. He will not speak of his "frame," and hang clothes like sacks over it; he will know and feel that he and the people about him have wonderful, delightful and beautiful bodies.

And—I speak of the ideal common citizen—he will be a student and a philosopher. To understand will be one of his necessary duties. His mind, like his body, will be fit and well clothed. He will not be too busy to read and think, though he may be too busy to rush about to get ignorantly and blatantly rich. It follows that, since he will have a mind exercised finely and flexible and alert, he will not be a secretive man. Secretiveness and secret planning are vulgarity; men and women need to be educated, and he will be educated out of these vices. He will be intensely truthful, not simply in the vulgar sense of not misstating facts when pressed, but truthful in the manner of the scientific man or the artist, and as scornful of concealment as they; truthful, that is to say, as the expression of a ruling desire to have things made plain and clear, because that so they are most beautiful and life is at its finest . . .

And all that I have written of him is equally true and applies word for word, with only such changes of gender as are needed, to the woman citizen also.

SOME POSSIBLE DISCOVERIES

The present time is harvest home for the prophets. The happy speculator in future sits on the piled-up wain, singing "I told you so," with the submarine and the flying machine and the Marconigram and the North Pole successfully achieved. In the tumult of realisations it perhaps escapes attention that the prophetic output of new hopes is by no means keeping pace with the crop of consummations. The present trend of scientific development is not nearly so obvious as it was a score of years ago; its promises lack the elementary breadth of that simpler time. Once you have flown, you have flown. Once you have steamed about under water, you have steamed about under water. There seem no more big things of that kind available—so that I almost regret the precipitance of Commander Peary and Captain Amundsen. No one expects to go beyond that atmosphere for some centuries at least; all the elements are now invaded. Conceivably man may presently contrive some sort of earthworm apparatus, so that he could go through the rocks prospecting very much as an earthworm goes through the soil, excavating in front and dumping behind, but, to put it moderately, there are considerable difficulties. And I doubt the imaginative effect. On the whole, I think material science has got samples now of all its crops at this level, and that what lies before it in the coming years is chiefly to work them out in detail and realise them on the larger scale. No doubt science will still yield all sorts of big surprising effects, but nothing, I think, to equal the dramatic novelty, the demonstration of man having got to something altogether new and strange, of Montgolfier, or the Wright Brothers, of Columbus, or the Polar conquest. There remains, of course, the tapping of atomic energy, but I give two hundred years yet before that . . .

So far, then, as mechanical science goes I am inclined to think the coming period will be, from the point of view of the common man, almost without sensational interest. There will be an immense amount of enrichment and filling-in, but of the sort that does not get prominently into the daily papers. At every point there will be economies and simplifications of method, discoveries of new artificial substances with new capabilities, and of new methods of utilising power. There will be a progressive change in the apparatus and quality of human life—the sort of alteration of the percentages that causes no intellectual shock. Electric heating, for example, will become practicable in our houses, and then cheaper, and at last so cheap and good that nobody will burn coal any more. Little electric contrivances will dispense with menial service in more and more directions. The builder will introduce new, more convenient, healthier and prettier substances, and the young architect will become increasingly the intelligent student of novelty. The steam engine, the coal yard, and the tail chimney, and indeed all chimneys, will vanish quietly from our urban landscape. The speeding up and cheapening of travel, and the increase in its swiftness and comfort will go on steadily—widening experience. A more systematic and understanding social science will be estimating the probable growth and movement of population, and planning town and country on lines that would seem to-day almost inconceivably wise and generous. All this means a quiet broadening and aeration and beautifying of life. Utopian requirements, so far as the material side of things goes, will be executed and delivered with at last the utmost promptness . . .

It is in quite other directions that the scientific achievements to astonish our children will probably be achieved. Progress never appears to be uniform in human affairs. There are intricate correlations between department and department. One field must mark time until another can come up to it with results sufficiently arranged and conclusions sufficiently simplified for application Medicine waits on organic chemistry, geology on mineralogy, and both on the chemistry of high pressures and temperature. And subtle variations in method and the prevailing mental temperament of the type of writer engaged, produce remarkable differences in the quality and quantity of the stated result. Moreover, there are in the history of every scientific province periods of seed-time, when there is great activity without immediate apparent fruition, and periods, as, for example, the last two decades of electrical application, of prolific realisation. It is highly probable that the physiologist and the organic chemist are working towards co-operations that may make the physician's sphere the new scientific wonderland.

At present dietary and regimen are the happy hunting ground of the quack and that sort of volunteer specialist, half-expert, half-impostor, who flourishes in the absence of worked out and definite knowledge. The general mass of the medical profession, equipped with a little experience and a muddled training, and preposterously impeded by the private adventure conditions under which it lives, goes about pretending to the possession of precise knowledge which simply does not exist in the world. Medical research is under-endowed and stupidly endowed, not for systematic scientific inquiry so much as for the unscientific seeking of remedies for specific evils—for cancer, consumption, and the like. Yet masked, misrepresented limited and hampered, the work of establishing a sound science of vital processes in health and disease is probably going on now, similar to the clarification of physics and chemistry that went on in the later part of the eighteenth and the early years of the nineteenth centuries. It is not unreasonable to suppose that medicine may presently arrive at far-reaching generalised convictions, and proceed to take over this great hinterland of human interests which legitimately belongs to it.

But medicine is not the only field to which we may reasonably look for a sudden development of wonders. Compared with the sciences of matter, psychology and social science have as yet given the world remarkably little cause for amazement. Not only is our medicine feeble and fragmentary, but our educational science is the poorest miscellany of aphorisms and dodges. Indeed, directly one goes beyond the range of measurement and weighing and classification, one finds a sort of unprogressive floundering going on, which throws the strongest doubts upon the practical applicability of the current logical and metaphysical conceptions in those fields. We have emerged only partially from the age of the schoolmen In these directions we have not emerged at all. It is quite possible that in university lecture rooms and forbidding volumes of metaphysical discussion a new emancipation of the human intellect and will is even now going on. Presently men may be attacking the problems of the self-control of human life and of human destiny in new phrases and an altogether novel spirit.

Guesses at the undiscovered must necessarily be vague, but my anticipations fall into two groups, and first I am disposed to expect a great systematic increment in individual human power. We probably have no suspicion as yet of what may be done with the human body and mind by way of enhancing its effectiveness I remember talking to the late Sir Michael Foster upon the possibilities of modern surgery, and how he confessed that he did not dare for his reputation's sake tell ordinary people the things he believed would some day become matter-of-fact operations. In that respect I think he spoke for very many of his colleagues. It is already possible to remove almost any portion of the human body, including, if needful, large sections of the brain; it is possible to graft living flesh on living flesh, make new connections, mould, displace, and rearrange. It is also not impossible to provoke local hypertrophy, and not only by knife and physical treatment but by the subtler methods of hypnotism, profound changes can be wrought in the essential structure of a human being. If only our knowledge of function and value were at all adequate, we could correct and develop ourselves in the most extraordinary way. Our knowledge is not adequate, but it may not always remain inadequate.

We have already had some very astonishing suggestions in this direction from Doctor Metchnikoff. He regards the human stomach and large intestine as not only vestigial and superfluous in the human economy, but as positively dangerous on account of the harbour they afford for those bacteria that accelerate the decay of age. He proposes that these viscera should be removed. To a layman like myself this is an altogether astounding and horrifying idea, but Doctor Metchnikoff is a man of the very greatest scientific reputation, and it does not give him any qualm of horror or absurdity to advance it. I am quite sure that if a gentleman called upon me "done up" in the way I am dimly suggesting, with most of the contents of his abdomen excavated, his lungs and heart probably enlarged and improved, parts of his brain removed to eliminate harmful tendencies and make room for the expansion of the remainder, his mind and sensibilities increased, and his liability to fatigue and the need of sleep abolished, I should conceal with the utmost difficulty my inexpressible disgust and terror. But, then, if M. Blériot, with his flying machine, ear-flaps and goggles, had soared down in the year 54 B.C., let us say, upon my woad-adorned ancestors—every family man in Britain was my ancestor in those days—at Dover, they would have had entirely similar emotions. And at present I am not discussing what is beautiful in humanity, but what is possible—and what, being possible, is likely to be attempted.

It does not follow that because men will some day have this enormous power over themselves, physically and mentally, that they will necessarily make themselves horrible—even by our present standards quite a lot of us would be all the slenderer and more active and graceful for "Metchnikoffing"—nor does surgery exhaust the available methods. We are still in the barbaric age, so far as our use of food and drugs is concerned. We stuff all sorts of substances into our unfortunate interiors and blunder upon the most various consequences. Few people of three score and ten but have spent in the aggregate the best part of a year in a state of indigestion, stupid, angry or painful indigestion as the case may be. No one would be so careless and ignorant about the fuel he burnt in his motor-car as most of us are about the fuel we burn in our bodies. And there are all sort of stimulating and exhilarating things, digesting things, fatigue-suppressing things, exercise economising things, we dare not use because we are afraid of our ignorance of their precise working. There seems no reason to suppose that human life, properly understood and controlled, could not be a constant succession of delightful and for the most part active bodily and mental phases. It is sheer ignorance and bad management that keep the majority of people in that disagreeable system of states which we indicate by saying we are "a bit off colour" or a little "out of training." It may seem madly Utopian now to suggest that practically everyone in the community might be clean, beautiful, incessantly active, "fit," and long-lived, with the marks of all the surgery they have undergone quite healed and hidden, but not more madly Utopian than it would have seemed to King Alfred the Great if one had said that practically everyone in this country, down to the very swineherds, should be able to read and write.

Metchnikoff has speculated upon the possibility of delaying old age, and I do not see why his method should not be applied to the diurnal need of sleep. No vital process seems to be absolutely fated in itself; it is a thing conditioned and capable of modification. If Metchnikoff is right—and to a certain extent he must be right—the decay of age is due to changing organic processes that may be checked and delayed and modified by suitable food and regimen. He holds out hope of a new phase in the human cycle, after the phase of struggle and passion, a phase of serene intellectual activity, old age with all its experience and none of its infirmities. Still more are fatigue and the need for repose dependent upon chemical changes in the body. It would seem we are unable to maintain exertion, partly through the exhaustion of our tissues, but far more by the loading of our blood with fatigue products—a recuperative interlude must ensue. But there is no reason to suppose that the usual food of to-day is the most rapidly assimilable nurture possible, that a rapidly digestible or injectable substance is not conceivable that would vastly accelerate repair, nor that the elimination and neutralisation of fatigue products might not also be enormously hastened. There is no inherent impossibility in the idea not only of various glands being induced to function in a modified manner, but even in the insertion upon the circulation of interceptors and artificial glandular structures. No doubt that may strike even an adventurous surgeon as chimerical, but consider what people, even authoritative people, were saying of flying and electric traction twenty years ago. At present a man probably does not get more than three or four hours of maximum mental and physical efficiency in the day. Few men can keep at their best in either physical or intellectual work for so long as that. The rest of the time goes in feeding, digesting, sleeping, sitting about, relaxation of various kinds. It is quite possible that science may set itself presently to extend systematically that proportion of efficient time. The area of maximum efficiency may invade the periods now demanded by digestion, sleep, exercise, so that at last nearly the whole of a man's twenty-four hours will be concentrated on his primary interests instead of dispersed among these secondary necessary matters.

Please understand I do not consider this concentration of activity and these vast "artificialisations" of the human body as attractive or desirable things. At the first proposal much of this tampering with the natural stuff of life will strike anyone, I think, as ugly and horrible, just as seeing a little child, green-white and still under an anaesthetic, gripped my heart much more dreadfully than the sight of the same child actively bawling with pain. But the business of this paper is to discuss things that may happen, and not to evolve dreams of loveliness. Perhaps things of this kind will be manageable without dreadfulness. Perhaps man will come to such wisdom that neither the knife nor the drugs nor any of the powers which science thrusts into his hand will slay the beauty of life for him. Suppose we assume that he is not such a fool as to let that happen, and that ultimately he will emerge triumphant with all these powers utilised and controlled.

It is not only that an amplifying science may give mankind happier bodies and far more active and eventful lives, but that psychology and educational and social science, reinforcing literature and working through literature and art, may dare to establish serenities in his soul. For surely no one who has lived, no one who has watched sin and crime and punishment, but must have come to realise the enormous amount of misbehaviour that is mere ignorance and want of mental scope. For my own part I have never believed in the devil. And it may be a greater undertaking but no more impossible to make ways to goodwill and a good heart in men than it is to tunnel mountains and dyke back the sea. The way that led from the darkness of the cave to the electric light is the way that will lead to light in the souls of men, that is to say, the way of free and fearless thinking, free and fearless experiment, organised exchange of thoughts and results, and patience and persistence and a sort of intellectual civility.

And with the development of philosophical and scientific method that will go on with this great increase in man's control over himself, another issue that is now a mere pious aspiration above abysses of ignorance and difficulty, will come to be a manageable matter. It has been the perpetual wonder of philosophers from Plato onward that men have bred their dogs and horses and left any man or woman, however vile, free to bear offspring in the next generation of men. Still that goes on. Beautiful and wonderful people die childless and bury their treasure in the grave, and we rest content with a system of matrimony that seems designed to perpetuate mediocrity. A day will come when men will be in possession of knowledge and opportunity that will enable them to master this position, and then certainly will it be assured that every generation shall be born better than was the one before it. And with that the history of humanity will enter upon a new phase, a phase which will be to our lives as daylight is to the dreaming of a child as yet unborn.

THE HUMAN ADVENTURE

Alone among all the living things this globe has borne, man reckons with destiny. All other living things obey the forces that created them; and when the mood of the power changes, submit themselves passively to extinction Man only looks upon those forces in the face, anticipates the exhaustion of Nature's kindliness, seeks weapons to defend himself. Last of the children of Saturn, he escapes their general doom. He dispossesses his begetter of all possibility of replacement, and grasps the sceptre of the world. Before man the great and prevalent creatures followed one another processionally to extinction; the early monsters of the ancient seas, the clumsy amphibians struggling breathless to the land, the reptiles, the theriomorpha and the dinosaurs, the bat-winged reptiles of the Mesozoic forests, the colossal grotesque first mammals, the giant sloths, the mastodons and mammoths; it is as if some idle dreamer moulded them and broke them and cast them aside, until at last comes man and seizes the creative wrist that would wipe him out of being again.

There is nothing else in all the world that so turns against the powers that have made it, unless it be man's follower fire. But fire is witless; a little stream, a changing breeze can stop it. Man circumvents. If fire were human it would build boats across the rivers and outmanoeuvre the wind. It would lie in wait in sheltered places, smouldering, husbanding its fuel until the grass was yellow and the forests sere. But fire is a mere creature of man's; our world before his coming knew nothing of it in any of its habitable places, never saw it except in the lightning flash or remotely on some volcanic coronet. Man brought it into the commerce of life, a shining, resentful slave, to hound off the startled beasts from his sleeping-place and serve him like a dog.

Suppose that some enduring intelligence watched through the ages the successions of life upon this planet, marked the spreading first of this species and then that, the conflicts, the adaptations, the predominances, the dyings away, and conceive how it would have witnessed this strange dramatic emergence of a rare great ape to manhood. To such a mind the creature would have seemed at first no more than one of several varieties of clambering frugivorous mammals, a little distinguished by a disposition to help his clumsy walking with a stake and reinforce his fist with a stone. The foreground of the picture would have been filled by the rhinoceros and mammoth, the great herds of ruminants, the sabre-toothed lion and the big bears. Then presently the observer would have noted a peculiar increasing handiness about the obscurer type, an unwonted intelligence growing behind its eyes. He would have perceived a disposition in this creature no beast had shown before, a disposition to make itself independent of the conditions of climate and the chances of the seasons. Did shelter fail among the trees and rocks, this curious new thing began to make itself harbours of its own; was food irregular, it multiplied food. It began to spread out from its original circumstances, fitting itself to novel needs, leaving the forests, invading the plains, following the watercourses upward and downward, presently carrying the smoke of its fires like a banner of conquest into wintry desolations and the high places of the earth.

The first onset of man must have been comparatively slow, the first advances needed long ages. By small degrees it gathered pace. The stride from the scattered savagery of the earlier stone period to the first cities, historically a vast interval, would have seemed to that still watcher, measuring by the standards of astronomy and the rise and decline of races and genera and orders, a, step almost abrupt. It took, perhaps, a thousand generations or so to make it. In that interval man passed from an animal-like obedience to the climate and the weather and his own instincts, from living in small family parties of a score or so over restricted areas of indulgent country, to permanent settlements, to the life of tribal and national communities and the beginnings of cities. He had spread in that fragment of time over great areas of the earth's surface, and now he was adapting himself to the Arctic circle on the one hand and to the life of the tropics on the other; he had invented the plough and the ship, and subjugated most of the domestic animals; he was beginning to think of the origin of the world and the mysteries of being. Writing had added its enduring records to oral tradition, and he was already making roads. Another five or six hundred generations at most bring him to ourselves. We sweep into the field of that looker-on, the momentary incarnations of this sempiternal being, Man. And after us there comes—

A curtain falls.

The time in which we, whose minds meet here in this writing, were born and live and die, would be to that imagined observer a mere instant's phase in the swarming liberation of our kind from ancient imperatives. It would seem to him a phase of unprecedented swift change and expansion and achievement. In this last handful of years, electricity has ceased to be a curious toy, and now carries half mankind upon their daily journeys, it lights our cities till they outshine the moon and stars, and reduces to our service a score of hitherto unsuspected metals; we clamber to the pole of our globe, scale every mountain, soar into the air, learn how to overcome the malaria that barred our white races from the tropics, and how to draw the sting from a hundred such agents of death. Our old cities are being rebuilt in towering marble; great new cities rise to vie with them. Never, it would seem, has man been so various and busy and persistent, and there is no intimation of any check to the expansion of his energies.

And all this continually accelerated advance has come through the quickening and increase of man's intelligence and its reinforcement through speech and writing. All this has come in spite of fierce instincts that make him the most combatant and destructive of animals, and in spite of the revenge Nature has attempted time after time for his rebellion against her routines, in the form of strange diseases and nearly universal pestilences. All this has come as a necessary consequence of the first obscure gleaming of deliberate thought and reason through the veil of his animal being. To begin with, he did not know what he was doing. He sought his more immediate satisfaction and safety and security. He still apprehends imperfectly the change that comes upon him. The illusion of separation that makes animal life, that is to say, passionate competing and breeding and dying, possible, the blinkers Nature has put upon us that we may clash against and sharpen one another, still darken our eyes. We live not life as yet, but in millions of separated lives, still unaware except in rare moods of illumination that we are more than those fellow beasts of ours who drop off from the tree of life and perish alone. It is only in the last three or four thousand years, and through weak and tentative methods of expression, through clumsy cosmogonies and theologies, and with incalculable confusion and discoloration, that the human mind has felt its way towards its undying being in the race. Man still goes to war against himself, prepares fleets and armies and fortresses, like a sleep-walker who wounds himself, like some infatuated barbarian who hacks his own limbs with a knife.

But he awakens. The nightmares of empire and racial conflict and war, the grotesques of trade jealousy and tariffs, the primordial dream-stuff of lewdness and jealousy and cruelty, pale before the daylight which filters between his eyelids. In a little while we individuals will know ourselves surely for corpuscles in his being, for thoughts that come together out of strange wanderings into the coherence of a waking mind. A few score generations ago all living things were in our ancestry. A few score generations ahead, and all mankind will be in sober fact descendants from our blood. In physical as in mental fact we separate persons, with all our difference and individuality, are but fragments, set apart for a little while in order that we may return to the general life again with fresh experiences and fresh acquirements, as bees return with pollen and nourishment to the fellowship of the hive.

And this Man, this wonderful child of old earth, who is ourselves in the measure of our hearts and minds, does but begin his adventure now. Through all time henceforth he does but begin his adventure. This planet and its subjugation is but the dawn of his existence. In a little while he will reach out to the other planets, and take that greater fire, the sun, into his service. He will bring his solvent intelligence to bear upon the riddles of his individual interaction, transmute jealousy and every passion, control his own increase, select and breed for his embodiment a continually finer and stronger and wiser race. What none of us can think or will, save in a disconnected partiality, he will think and will collectively. Already some of us feel our merger with that greater life. There come moments when the thing shines out upon our thoughts. Sometimes in the dark sleepless solitudes of night, one ceases to be so-and-so, one ceases to bear a proper name, forgets one's quarrels and vanities, forgives and understands one's enemies and oneself, as one forgives and understands the quarrels of little children, knowing oneself indeed to be a being greater than one's personal accidents, knowing oneself for Man on his planet, flying swiftly to unmeasured destinies through the starry stillnesses of space.

BIBLIOBAZAAR

The essential book market!

Did you know that you can get any of our titles in large print?

Did you know that we have an ever-growing collection of books in many languages?

Order online:
www.bibliobazaar.com

Find all of your favorite classic books!

Stay up to date with the latest government reports!

At BiblioBazaar, we aim to make knowledge more accessible by making thousands of titles available to you- *quickly and affordably.*

Contact us:
BiblioBazaar
PO Box 21206
Charleston, SC 29413

Printed in Great Britain
by Amazon